Praise for Jess Faraday

Turnbull House

"With characters who are layered with charm and complexity, settings that play out visually like a full color series of daguerreotypes on the mind, a mystery that reveals how far apart Ira and Goddard have grown since Ira walked out two years before, and a fluid prose that draws the reader into the lives of the characters and the time of the story, *Turnbull House* is as flawless a historical novel as I've ever read."—*The Novel Approach*

"*Turnbull House* was special. So addicting. I needed to read more. The characters were distinct, sexy, and believable."—*Books A to Z*

The Left Hand of Justice

The Left Hand of Justice "is an exciting book with drama, romance, and mystery. The characters were interesting and strong. Once you get into the story, it is hard to put the book down."—*Curve* magazine

The Affair of the Porcelain Dog

"*The Affair of the Porcelain Dog* is an excellent mystery. The characters are complex and in general not what they seem on first sight. Many unexpected twists and turns keep the novel intriguing right up to the end. The historical setting of late Victorian London is portrayed accurately. It is recommended for mystery collections at public libraries, especially those in gay- and lesbian-friendly areas, and college and university collections." —Gay, Lesbian, Bisexual, and Transgender Round Table of the American Library Association

"Jess Faraday takes you into a very bleak, dangerous, and inhuman realm. A world without mercy. But despite all this, she's able to deliver a beautiful and romantic story…This clever multi-layered mystery skillfully combined with some very strong characters will definitely keep you in suspense until the very end."—*Booked Up Reviews*

"The author builds a credible plot through the actions of diverse, fully-nuanced characters, which keeps the reader interested…Excellent first novel by a promising new author, which I give five stars out of five." —Bob Lind, *Echo Magazine*

"Sherlock Holmes Meets Oscar Wilde. Faraday has written a brilliant Victorian mystery…The careful plot is arranged like a set of nesting boxes. With Faraday's smashing writing and research, Victorian London comes alive through the eyes of a 19th century outlier."—*The Bright List*

By the Author

The Affair of the Porcelain Dog

The Left Hand of Justice

Turnbull House

Fool's Gold

Visit us at www.boldstrokesbooks.com

FOOL'S GOLD

by

Jess Faraday

A Division of Bold Strokes Books

2015

FOOL'S GOLD

ISBN 13: 978-1-62639-340-0

This Trade Paperback Original Is Published By
Bold Strokes Books, Inc.
P.O. Box 249
Valley Falls, NY 12185

First Edition: April 2015

Credits
Editor: Shelley Thrasher
Production Design: Stacia Seaman
Cover Design by Gabrielle Pendergrast

For my uncle, Jim Bradley, who loved trains.

CHAPTER ONE

June 1895

My friend Bess Lazarus once said that some people come into our lives to teach us a lesson. I'm quite certain she wasn't talking about Cain Goddard when she said it—Bess being a cornerstone of her church, and Cain Goddard being, aside from my most memorable former lover, one of London's most feared crime lords. But the idea fit nonetheless. Goddard had come and gone from my life too many times in the past seven years, causing too much havoc each time, for any of it to be a coincidence. And though I wasn't quite ready to start seeing a Divine Hand behind it all, when I truly thought about it, I knew there had to be a reason, even if it was just my own stubborn nature, that I hadn't been able to dismiss him completely from my mind.

"Somebody's thinking deep thoughts," Lawrence said, stretching lazily in the patch of sunlight streaming through the bedroom window onto his naked form. A compact twenty-five-year-old with muscles rippling under creamy skin dusted with golden hair, he knew he was appealing but wasn't smug about it. I rolled over and kissed his perfect pointed chin.

"Nothing worth worrying about."

"Nothing is, I find."

"And that's why I enjoy your company so much."

"Deep thoughts give you wrinkles." He traced the creases at the edge of my right eye with his square finger. "Though I must say, they suit you."

"You just like older men."

Smiling sleepily, he shrugged his wide shoulders. His main accomplishments at Cambridge had been leading the rugby club to glory and sleeping his way through his college. He led his adult life in much the same way. "What can I say? Men my age are empty-headed, flighty, and only after one thing."

"Which is why I like you," I said.

He stared at me for a split second in mock affront, then clouted me with his pillow.

I'd met Lawrence several years earlier, at the American Bar. My life had been a screaming mess at the time, but I'd remembered his open smile and the kind twinkle in his eyes. I'd gone back every now and then to look for him, and one of those times I'd found him. He was as easy a companion as his smile had suggested he would be. Enthusiastic and undemanding. Exactly the balm my bruised spirit had needed after Cain Goddard had turned my life upside down—again. We looped in and out of each other's orbits a couple times a month—always companionable, never deep enough to argue over anything. He probably maintained a handful of similar companions, and I didn't mind. What we had was pleasant, ephemeral, and limited.

Lawrence would never, for example, see my flat.

We always met at his—that is, the set of rooms his parents maintained for him in Chelsea. Lawrence came from money and would have been horrified at my single room on Aldersgate Street. My room horrified me at times. But we never discussed my lodgings, or the fact that I supported myself as a secretary-typist, or spent my free time educating street children in Spitalfields. Our days and nights passed like spun sugar and the smoke from fine tobacco. Theatres, restaurants, the occasional party—always ending up between the starched, lavender-scented sheets of his overstuffed bed. If I were to disappear, he wouldn't miss me for long before the next handsome face caught his eye. And I liked it that way.

"What are your plans for the day, then?" he asked, his gentle way of indicating that our time was coming to an end.

"I'm not sure," I replied. "Perhaps I'll go for a walk in the park."

It wasn't a grand lie, but my answer hadn't been completely honest. The reason I'd been thinking about Goddard was folded twice and tucked into the breast pocket of my waistcoat. After a little less than three years of silence, Goddard had summoned me back to the home we'd once shared on York Street. At one point, the invitation would have filled me with dread-tinged excitement. After all this time, though, all that remained was mild curiosity. Goddard's ill-gotten riches held no more temptation for me. Neither did the idea of his company, though I'd loved him once. Yes, it was an excellent morning for a walk, and

I would indeed take the route through Hyde Park—because it was the most direct path to the house on York Street, but more importantly because it pleased me to do so.

The weather was delightful. Undiluted sun bathed the chic streets of Chelsea, filtering through the trees and caressing the manicured grass as I entered the park from the south. The air was still—warm and moist, like a kiss—but not yet hot enough to make me want to toss my jacket into the Serpentine. It had been under the great weeping beech tree near the grand entrance—could it really be six years ago?—that Goddard had bared his feelings and asked me to stay on at York Street permanently. And I...I had hesitated. A fortunate thing, for it had become clear, not long after, the price at which my life of luxury was being purchased. If that hadn't forced me to realize I'd outgrown being kept by Cain Goddard, then our catastrophic reunion a few years later would have.

For an instant I was back in that alley off Fleet Street, the noise of passing revelers echoing in my ears while Goddard vented his anger on my flesh. The assault had been a sharp reminder of Goddard's darker side. For while I'd once known him privately as a kind and generous benefactor, I'd lost sight of the fact that he was also the dreaded Duke of Dorset Street, with discipline to maintain and a reputation to uphold. I'd broken discipline by prying into his business affairs. Worse, I'd injured his pride on a very personal level. His retaliation had been, of course, completely out of proportion. But in the framework in which Goddard operated, it had been both logical and fitting.

He'd made some extraordinary gestures of apology since then. I'd consented to meet him twice. But even after nearly three years, in his warm, reasonable tones I heard only the tight echoes of anger. The gentle brush of his fingers was, to me, as a steely, bruising grip. His eyes were the worst, though, for the unbearable mixture of arrogance and shame was as fresh and real as it had been when I'd stood over him at the end of that terrible night, my fist throbbing as his split lower lip swelled and purpled in the moonlight.

Goddard knew I'd never forgive him, never trust him again. It had been ever so long since he'd last contacted me, and I certainly hadn't reached out to him. It was curiosity that was causing me to respond to his summons now, that was all. And to my credit, I was deliberately an hour late. Even so, suddenly drenched in sweat and clenching my fists until my knuckles went white, I nearly turned back.

The air brushed my cheek with another kiss. It was fruitless to keep reminding myself of these things. Too much had passed, both good and bad, between Goddard and myself, for there to be any profit in weighing the panic coursing through my veins against the sentimental tightening in my chest. Every time Goddard's world and mine overlapped, it was always to remind me of our fundamental incompatibility. Best to have done with it, once and for all. Turning, I headed north and exited the park through the marble columns of the grand entrance.

Cain Goddard lived near the intersection of York Street and the Baker Street made famous in those stories in *The Strand*. To the east of that lay Regent's Park, then City University. From there, my own home was a sharp drop south. Goddard's house was three stories of brick, polished glass, painted wood, and scrubbed steps. He maintained three servants, all women, and to a person discreet, hardworking, and exorbitantly paid. Though he'd given up the academic ambitions that had been scuppered by a scandal involving one of his students, he hadn't abandoned his passion for knowledge. It was a sure bet that those three women were the best-educated servants on York Street.

I reached the corner at Gloucester Place, waited for a lorry to rumble past, and then crossed the road. York Street was sedate that morning, while up ahead, Baker Street, perpendicular, bustled with activity. A movement in the front window of Goddard's house—a twitch of the lace curtain, the flash of a face in the glass—caused my pulse to race. I'd not have expected Goddard to be waiting in the vestibule like an excited child, but rather sitting in the morning room with his *Literary Quarterly*, waiting for his housekeeper to deliver me to him. I walked faster in spite of myself.

It's hard to say what stopped me just short of the front stairs. The street fell suddenly quiet, as if all of London were holding its breath. Behind the lace curtain, I could make out Goddard's profile in silhouette. He had turned away from the window and was examining his watch. The silence was so complete at that moment, I swear I could hear the gold timepiece ticking in his hand.

And then the building exploded, outward and up, showering the street and lamps and houses with burning chunks of brick and glass.

CHAPTER TWO

F ire!" I shouted. Blinded and burning, I scrambled to my feet. "For God's sake, someone fetch the fire brigade!"

Windows screeched open. Doors slammed. Well-shod feet slapped the pavement all around me. Everything sounded faraway and muffled, as if my ears were stuffed with cotton wool. My face felt on fire, and I had shards of glass like needles in my scalp and hands. My hat. Where was my hat?

The municipal fire alarm wailed. At least forty such alarms were positioned around London, and Regent's Park had more than its share. People streamed out of doors and alleys, and the pavement was suddenly clotted with neighbors and Baker Street idlers drawn by the promise of excitement.

"Blimey, Mr. Ira, sir!" Two arms pulled me out of the way as a chunk of smoldering debris crashed to the ground where I'd been standing. As my vision began to clear, I made out the thin form of Goddard's housekeeper, Eileen. Her brown hair was swept back into a serious bun, and her pinched features were grave. "What's happened, sir? Did you see? Good Lord, Mr. Ira, your face!"

"The house...Dr. Goddard..." I stammered as she picked bits of glass from the side of my neck. Something warm and wet slithered down my left cheek. Absently I wiped at it with my sleeve.

"Lord, is he inside?" she demanded, looking up from her work.

I nodded. "What about your cook? The downstairs maid?"

She gestured behind her, toward two young women—a plump, ginger-haired lass and a scrawny brunette—who were clutching each other in fright. "We're all here. Me, Annie, and Daisy. It's our day off. We were on our way to the zoo when we heard the noise."

"He gave you a whole day off?" My ears were still ringing. I couldn't have heard right. Two afternoons a month was what Goddard allowed, and never all three servants at once.

"Can you credit it?" She glanced toward the burning wreckage that had been her home...and had once been mine.

A discomfiting thought began to take shape in my mind but scattered as four draught horses thundered up York Street, pulling a pumper wagon behind them. The ladies and I moved to the side as the crowd parted. There wasn't much in the way of flame, at least from where I was standing, but the air was heavy and hot with smoke.

"Oh, Mr. Ira, your *face*," she wailed again.

"Is it really that bad?"

She squinted at me appraisingly. Then she licked a thumb and drew it down my cheek.

"Ouch!"

She cracked a smile. "Ain't as bad as I thought. It's going to hurt plenty, though. And you really should wash when you get home."

A pair of canvas-swaddled firemen jumped down from the wagon and pushed past me. Nudging Eileen out of the way, I grabbed one man's thick sleeve as he passed.

"There's a man in there. On the ground floor."

"We'll do what we can, sir." His voice was muffled by the hood that hid his head. His words were puffs of condensation against the dark glass faceplate.

"I'm sure he's alive. Can't you go any faster?"

"I said we'll do our best." He pushed me gently but firmly to the side. I ran after them and was nearly up the stairs when a section of the front wall collapsed at my toes.

"Sir, you can't be 'ere." A pair of hands grasped me roughly this time and pulled me down the steps.

"But—"

"Keep 'im away!" the first fireman snapped.

"Mr. Adler? What are you doing here?"

I whirled to face the familiar voice, the comforting but unyielding hands grasping me by the shoulders.

"Mr. Watkins!" I cried. Henry Watkins was Goddard's second-in-command. A good man. This wasn't the first time he'd kept me from chasing Goddard into a burning building. Beneath his tidy bowler and ginger whiskers, Watkins looked grave. What was he doing there?

"Come away, now, Mr. Adler. Ain't nuffin' you can do here 'cept get yourself hurt. And I guarantee Dr. Goddard wouldn't want that."

Wouldn't he?

What kind of a thought was that? And yet my initial apprehension was fast coalescing into an idea that turned my blood to ice. Goddard had sent the servants away for the entire day. He'd instructed me to come at ten o'clock. If I'd been on time, I'd be lying under a pile of burning rubble with him. Had that been his intent? It was insane, and yet...

"Let me go," I said, twisting away from Goddard's man. Watkins was strong enough to have kept his grip, but he turned me loose without a fight.

"They found someone!" a man cried.

Sparing Watkins a brief glance, I ran toward where two firemen were emerging from the wreckage, dragging a third man by the arms. It was Goddard all right. I could tell from his suit, though his face had been mutilated in the blast, and every inch of exposed skin was burnt black. As the firemen set him down, his gold watch—the one I'd given him years ago on his birthday—spilled out of his ruined waistcoat.

"Be careful!" I cried, my suspicions fading to insignificance in the presence of Goddard's very real injuries. "What do you think you're doing, dragging him like that? This man needs a hospital!"

One of the firemen looked at me for a moment, his expression unreadable through the tinted faceplate. Through the darkened glass, I thought I could make out heavy, slab-like cheeks and a nose that had been broken too many times.

"Sorry, sir," the man said, his gravelly East End voice at once familiar and strange. "'E don't need no 'orspital. Not no more. Wot 'e need is a coffin maker."

I squinted at the badge pinned to his protective jacket. The metal was fire-blackened to the point where the engraved name and number were almost indecipherable. *Stimson*, I thought. And was it 949? Or 494? Or were some of those eights? Then his words registered.

"A coffin maker?"

My chest contracted painfully. I fought the hot, cinder-laden air for breath. Whether Goddard had set the blast and whether he'd intended to take me with him was unimportant. Whatever conflicts remained between us were immaterial. He was dead, now, and I'd never see him again.

"Mr. Adler," Watkins said, suddenly at my shoulder. He spoke softly and rapidly. "Mrs. Murphy and her young ladies shouldn't be seein' this up close, like. Help me get them somewheres safe."

He set a hand on my shoulder but didn't force the issue. A few seconds passed, and then Watkins knelt down, unhooked Goddard's watch from the chain, and set it in my hands. The crystal was cracked, the metal burnt black, but it was still ticking. I staggered back while more firemen rushed up the stairs with a canvas litter and a sheet. As they loaded Goddard onto the stretcher, none too gently, Watkins said again, "Mr. Adler, the ladies is waitin'."

We ended up in the back room of a middling teahouse on Baker Street. Watkins looked out of place there amid the lace and flowers, though the ladies seemed comfortable, which was the important thing. Eileen and her girls looked surprisingly well for having lost both their home and their positions. I, on the other hand, was very close to being sick.

Watkins nudged my arm with his elbow, nodding toward the cup going cold in front of me. "Hot, sweet tea for a shock. Me mum always swore by it."

Normally I abhor sugar in my tea, but I forced a bit down. It did make me feel better. Eileen had dabbed at my cuts and abrasions with a moist serviette. They still stung, but at least they were clean. The ladies sipped politely as Watkins poured himself a second cup. No one had touched the biscuits.

"Well," Eileen ventured. "That's that, then."

The resignation in her voice—much too much of it for someone just turned twenty—pulled me out of my misery. She exhaled heavily, tucking a strand of mousy hair back into its now-disheveled bun. She suddenly looked very slight and fragile in her once-crisp housekeeper's dress. Where would she go now? What would she do?

"Do you have a place to stay, Eileen?" I asked. "And your girls?" My mind raced. Where could I put them? Surely not in my single room.

Eileen's thin fingers twisted the black fabric of her skirt. "I got an auntie in Brixton I can stay wiv'. Annie and Daisy, too, for a bit. Pity we can't get no reference." Her careful, precise speech, cultivated through years under Goddard's tutelage, was fast slipping back into her native East End dialect.

"I'll check with the solicitor, miss," Watkins said. "I'm sure Dr. Goddard made some sort of provision, like. You remember how he always had fings planned."

"I'll write you a reference, Eileen," I said. After all, she'd worked for me, too, while I'd lived at York Street. I handed her my card.

"Thanks, Mr. Ira."

The door of the private room opened then, and an apologetic waitress informed us that the cab Watkins had ordered for the ladies had arrived. Watkins and I walked them to the curb and bid them farewell. As the carriage pulled away, he set a hand on my shoulder.

"Now that the ladies is seen to, there's business to discuss." He ushered me back into the private room of the teahouse and shut the door behind us.

I sat, and he lowered himself onto the chair across from me. I hadn't been in Goddard's inner circle for many years, but Watkins had been instrumental in the business Goddard and I had conducted since then. I doubted he knew about Goddard's and my intimate history, but instinct seemed to have informed him that I'd been a close personal acquaintance.

"I'll send a message to the coffin maker." He ticked off the points on one hand as if he'd memorized them. "An' another one to Mr. Wiley at the Necropolis Company. Dr. Goddard wanted cremation wiv' a second-class nonconformist burial. No service. All paid in advance." He gave me an apologetic glance. "I'm sorry, Mr. Adler, there weren't no mention of a rail ticket for you."

I nodded. Goddard would ride that last train—to the sprawling necropolis outside of London—with essential personnel only. No ceremony, as little expense as possible. Ashes to ashes.

"But you're going with him?" I asked. "He won't be...alone." Why this thought should bother me when I hadn't seen the man in years, or wanted to, I couldn't say, but I suddenly found the thought of it unbearable.

"That's right, sir."

"Good." I paused. "You seem to know a lot about Goddard's plans for this particular contingency."

"It were me job to know," he said with a shrug.

"It were?" I asked. "I mean, it was?" Of course it was. And Goddard's number two would be moving up, now. "Oh...yes...I suppose congratulations are in order."

I didn't know if that was the right thing to say to someone who had just ascended to the head of a criminal organization, but Watkins seemed to appreciate the sentiment. I doubted he was rapacious enough to expand the empire Goddard had started, but he would maintain it well. He would be especially good, I realized, at settling any remaining conflicts between Goddard's organization and its rivals before those conflicts erupted into war.

Which opened up another explanation for the explosion. Goddard wasn't the only shark infesting the murky waters of London's underworld. Though he found it a waste of resources to initiate conflict, I'd personally seen Goddard stab some very dangerous people in the back when it seemed expedient to do so. Such people were not in the habit of turning the other cheek.

"Any idea who might have done this?" I asked.

Watkins's expression sharpened. He gave one curt nod. "I got me ideas. But you know I can't say nuffin' 'bout that. Dr. Goddard—"

"Would have wanted me kept out of it entirely."

"For your own safety."

His tone betrayed no deception. If Goddard had planned, for whatever reason, to blow us both to eternity, he hadn't let Watkins in on it. And a dramatic murder-suicide was hardly Goddard's style. Yet I couldn't shake my suspicions regarding the timing of the explosion, or the fact that Goddard had sent the servants away for the day. If he hadn't intended to deliver us both to a fiery death, what had he, after a disastrous parting and two and a half years of silence, actually intended?

"There's the matter of the will," Watkins said. "I ain't read the document, but Dr. Goddard's solicitor were under instructions to contact you. Name of Caruthers."

Now that was curious. I had no idea what to make of it.

"I'll...expect him," I said. "Well, I suppose that's that, then, as Eileen would say." I rose, reaching into my pocket for some coins, but Watkins shook his head.

"Already taken care of, Mr. Adler."

"Thank you." They say there's no honor among thieves, but Watkins was as solid a man as I'd ever known. That he'd worked for the Duke of Dorset Street was no matter. He carried out his duties faithfully, with good judgment and alacrity. Had things gone differently between Goddard and myself, we might have been friends. As we shook hands, I said, "And good luck, Mr. Watkins. I always knew you'd get on."

CHAPTER THREE

I tried to go back a few times to Turnbull House, the youth shelter I'd built with Tim and Bess Lazarus. But the way everyone walked on glass around me just made me more aware of the unreasonable degree to which Goddard's death was affecting me. Perhaps I was mourning what might have been, had events not conspired to push me out of Goddard's nest. More likely I was feeling the death of illusion. For unless I'd maintained a wall of deliberate ignorance, I could not have remained at York Street indefinitely, knowing the human cost of my silk sheets and Egyptian tobacco. And I didn't know if I would ever completely forgive his inexcusable assault in that alley off Fleet Street. Goddard's death should have meant nothing by this point. A few lines at the back of a newspaper. At one time the news might have even made me happy.

Yet the finality of his absence sat heavy on my shoulders. It wasn't merely that he was gone from my life—he had been for years—but now it would always be so.

My desk at home was piling up with paying work, but I found it impossible to concentrate. A good fuck might have cleared my head. Then again, it might have shattered me completely. The gossamer spun-sugar threads that connected Lawrence and myself would never have weathered the strain. I ended up spending the next few days walking the sun-dappled streets, and the evenings staggering around the smoke-filled cider house around the corner, slopping sour beer onto the sawdust floors until they threw me out.

It was inevitable, perhaps, that my peregrinations should lead me back to the burnt-out shell of the house on York Street. That, and my own curiosity. I was no stranger to explosions, having investigated, not long ago, a sugar refinery that had been gutted when a makeshift laboratory blew up in the basement. I was no expert, either—for that,

I'd have had to defer to my friend Andrew St. Andrews, who had explored the refinery with me and advised me of the story told by the ash and residues. But I was in no mood for company during that first week after Goddard's death. Nor for a proper investigation, if it came down to it. No, I just wanted to see the place again, to make sure I hadn't, perversely, imagined it all.

Nearly a week had passed since the explosion. The city had cleared the rubble from the pavement and erected a token fence around the property, with a warning sign or two. However, it looked as if it would fall to the new owners of the property—should Watkins manage to unload it—to tear down the building. The neighbors couldn't have been pleased. Still, at least the vagrants and vandals had left the place alone. I could see part of the inlaid entryway table buried under a pile of books and rubble. There was no food debris, no telltale whiff of urine. One of the perks of living in a neighborhood like Goddard's, I supposed, though it was more likely due to the mountain of a man standing guard just inside the ruined entryway. I didn't recognize him, but he looked like someone Watkins might have chosen for the task— tall, hard-bodied, gruff-featured, and wearing a wicked knife at his belt. When I stopped on the pavement before Goddard's house, he met my eye but didn't acknowledge my nod.

The sun hadn't yet set, but it was on its way down. I stood at the base of the front steps, trying to ignore the guard's hard stare. The explosion had torn the front door off its hinges and blown the entryway and the front half of the morning room to Kingdom Come. The damage extended to the base of the staircase leading to the upper floors. However, the stairs at the top appeared unscathed. Much of the facade had come down on the right side, and if I stood on tiptoes, I could look all the way down where the servants' stairs had been, into a basically undamaged kitchen. The left side of the house appeared almost entirely intact. Goddard's private office was back there. If Watkins had any sense, he'd have cleared it out the minute the firemen had disappeared.

Had Goddard's crimes caught up with him? Watkins had certainly thought so. For a moment, I considered hiring St. Andrews to look into the matter. Of course I probably couldn't afford him now. He'd been making quite a name for himself as a consulting detective, and any past favors I'd done him were long since repaid. I looked up to the window, beyond which lay the bed that Goddard and I had once shared. Even with the remains of the house staring me in the face, it still seemed unreal. As I stepped up onto the bottom front stair, a chunk of plaster broke free of the ceiling and shattered on the charred floorboards. The guard stepped out into full view, his expression challenging me to take one step closer. Taking my cue, I stepped down, turned, and began the long walk home.

When I arrived back at my room, I lay down on my bed and stayed there until some days later, when a letter arrived from Mr. Caruthers.

The will was to be read the following Tuesday at eleven. When the day came, I sobered up, put on my best, and went down to the solicitor's office in St. James's. There wasn't much to say, and that was good. The solicitor's words slipped past me like dream fragments. I tried to concentrate, but the words seemed to disintegrate before I could attach any meaning to them. Eileen and the other two received their references, I think, and a bit of cash—as did Turnbull House. Another lump was set aside for some sort of fighting-arts club. At the conclusion of the meeting, Mr. Caruthers handed me an envelope, which I tucked into my pocket. At this point, eyes burning, and fighting the lump in my throat, I fled.

The envelope stayed in my jacket pocket for the next week, at which point Dr. Tim Lazarus, my closest friend and my partner in the Turnbull House venture, took his life in his hands and came to visit.

"I say, Adler." He tucked his picklocks back into his pocket and walked into the room, dramatically fanning the air in front of his face. "A bit whiffy in here, don't you think?"

I shrugged. I couldn't remember the last time I'd had a scrub. I'd been wearing the same clothes for days, and I didn't care.

"At least open the window," he said.

Lazarus was, as always, dressed crisply and well, though not well enough to intimidate the patients in his East End clinic, or the street children he looked after at Turnbull House. He smelled of soap and shaving powder, and his salt-and-pepper hair had been trimmed that very morning. He sported a new and rather daring set of sideburns. Feeling a flicker of self-consciousness, I ran a hand over my own black briar patch of a beard.

When I didn't abandon my little nest of sheets on the edge of the bed, he crossed to the window himself. I groaned as he pushed the curtain aside, but even as I pulled the bedclothes around my head and rolled toward the wall, I secretly appreciated the rush of fresh air. His lively footsteps came back across the room to my bed, and he poked me gently with the toe of one sharp boot.

"Now, get up and wash."

I glared at him over my shoulder.

"Don't look at me that way. I'm a doctor."

I did as I was told. Sometimes that's the best a person can do. And the truth was, even I recognized it was time to pull myself out of my cocoon of self-pity. I just hadn't known how. Slowly I peeled off the covers and sat up.

My flat looked different in the light of day. Same tired desk and chair, same tattered commode-screen, same traffic-worn rug underneath it all. But while I'm generally tidy, I'd let the place descend into squalor. Dirty clothes on the floor. Dirty dishes beside them. I didn't have enough possessions to clutter up the place, but what I did have I'd allowed to congeal into an appalling mess. Good God, had I no pride at all?

I stood and shambled toward the washstand. Lazarus had already filled the pitcher and the enamel basin. I poked a tentative finger at the water.

"Not just hands and face. Take your shirt off, too."

"You'd like that," I muttered. But, after splashing off my face, I dutifully ran a wet cloth under my arms and over my torso. Surprisingly, my mood began to lift with the grime. I leaned over the basin and used my shaving cup to pour water over my head. My scalp tingled as I scrubbed with my fingers. By the time I toweled my hair dry and brushed my teeth, I was feeling almost optimistic.

"Better?" he asked, snatching away my old shirt before I could put it back on. He nodded toward the clean one he'd taken from my wardrobe.

"Infinitely."

"Good."

He smiled. On the cusp of forty, Dr. Tim Lazarus was the person who had known me the longest. Efficient, quick-thinking, and eminently logical—at least when he wasn't overwhelming himself with the virtuous burdens of charity work and family life—Tim was my best friend, and I was lucky to have him.

"Now, you've wallowed in your loss long enough. It's time to decide what you're going to do."

"Do?"

"All of London, it seems, has been storming Turnbull House in an attempt to procure your typing services. Apparently you haven't been responding to queries sent to your home." He nodded pointedly at the unopened post piled near the wall where it had been slipped beneath the front door. "And while our messenger service thanks you for the sixpence each message brings in, I can't help but think your ignoring your clients is venturing into the realm of self-destructiveness. As your friend and physician, I'm telling you it's time to make some decisions."

I dropped back down onto my bed and ran a hand over my face. He was right. He was almost always right.

"I've tried to work, Tim. My desk is overflowing. But every time I look at it, it makes my eyes cross. I can't concentrate. I get so frustrated I want to throw it all onto the fire."

Lazarus sat down on the bed beside me. "Believe it or not, I understand. Tell me, do you actually need the work?"

"What?"

"If you were to toss it all in the bin, would you be in danger of losing the rent?"

"I don't think so." There'd been quite a bit of work in the past few months, come to think of it. I'd learned to live frugally and had even managed to put a bit aside. "But some of it was paid in advance."

"Then you do have to finish that. As for the rest, I shall inform your clients that due to a sudden illness, you're unable to take on any new projects. Agreed?"

I watched him walk to my desk, sweep the great cloud of papers into a pile, and tamp the pile into a neat stack. This he brought back and set on the floor at my feet.

"Now, I'm going to hold up each of these papers in turn. All you have to do is say 'yes' if you've already received payment for it. Can you do that?"

"I'm not an invalid, Tim," I said, though the gratitude I felt at this simple kindness was profound. As the unwieldy mass of paper was gradually reduced to two neat stacks, I felt the tension drain from my shoulders and neck. The final pile of obligatory work appeared quite manageable. "That's all?" I asked. "I could polish that off in a day."

"Then do it," Tim said. "And when you've finished, have a shave, then come see me at Turnbull House. I have a proposition for you." He stood.

"Thank you," I said as he made his way to the door, though the words didn't seem even remotely sufficient.

He turned. "Think nothing of it." He paused. "You've been a good friend to me, Ira. Better than I deserve. I'm glad I could return the favor.

By the way, Dr. Goddard left a generous bequest to Turnbull House. I'm almost ashamed of all those things I said about the man over the years."

"Oh yes, of course. I meant to give you the papers from the solicitor." I stood to get to my coat, where Mr. Caruthers's envelope still waited in the pocket.

Lazarus frowned. "But the papers arrived several days ago, along with the cheque."

"Then what did the solicitor give me?"

Lazarus shrugged. "Some sort of disposition, I would imagine. You mean to say you didn't look?"

"I figured it was about the Turnbull House bequest."

"Ira!"

I nearly tripped over myself trying to get to the coat. My mind raced, wondering what Goddard could possibly have left to me. When I fished the envelope out of the pocket, the reminder was suddenly more than I could bear. I thrust it at Lazarus. He frowned.

"Please," I said.

Shrugging, he did as I asked. I watched his eyes travel over the text as he read and reread the letter. Finally he looked up.

"Well?" I demanded.

"Well." He folded the letter and held it out to me. His fingers were shaking. "It seems, Mr. Adler, you are now an extremely wealthy man."

Chapter Four

A well-paid butler earns fifty-two pounds per annum plus room and board. A clerk can pull in around ninety. The leasehold for the two-story Turnbull House building was purchased for four hundred eleven quid and change.

The quarter million waiting for me in a strongbox in St. James's was enough to render both Lazarus and me incapable of speech for a full five minutes.

It was poetic justice, I supposed, that I'd have to go through Rupert Sudworth to get it. One final ironic touch. Or, more likely, Goddard hadn't taken into account the inconvenience to me of dealing with Sudworth in the event of his own unexpected death.

"Luncheon on me?" I asked.

Lazarus smiled grimly. "For the rest of your life."

I shaved, slicked back my hair, and we went to the Criterion. For me, the place was resonant with memories: the Mecca for men who preferred men's company—which is why Goddard would never take me there; the last time I saw my late friend Nate Turnbull, for whom we named our youth shelter; the site of many pleasant evenings with Wilde and his friends; my first meal following a short stint in police custody; the place I first set eyes on Lawrence.

For Lazarus, luncheon there was a once-in-a-lifetime experience of unspeakable luxury, and I was happy to provide it.

"More champagne?" I asked, tipping the bottle toward him. He demurred.

"Can't very well go back to the shelter tipsy. Perhaps if I were a man of leisure." He smirked.

"I didn't ask for this."

"I know, Adler." He paused for a moment, then gestured for

me to refill his glass. He raised it. "To Cain Goddard, a man…of contradictions."

I tapped my glass against his, and we polished off the remainder of the bottle. The table was covered with plates bearing the remains of an obscene number of obscenely expensive dishes. I leaned discreetly back against my chair, tempted to unbutton my waistcoat. Lazarus stifled a belch. After a tense moment of silence, I cleared my throat.

"You said you had some sort of proposition," I said.

"Oh, yes. Fancy a trip to California?"

"Excuse me?"

He smirked again, pleased, no doubt, that such a stolid man as himself was still capable of surprising someone whose life must have seemed a continuous parade of mind-altering sex, fancy meals, and explosions.

"Bess, as you know, comes from across the pond—a little town called Pyrite, in Central California. A distant relative passed away recently and left her family a gold claim. The mine was exhausted in the fifties. At least that's what everyone believed. But someone's been pressuring Bess's mother to sell. She's recently widowed, if you remember."

I did remember. The months after Bess received the news of her father's passing a year earlier had been difficult for everyone. It had really hammered home how dependent we all had become upon Bess's indefatigable energy and relentless optimism.

"There's a younger sister as well," Tim said. "But aside from that, they have no other people in the area, and the would-be buyer is becoming aggressive. Bess thought we'd go to lend her some support, and I thought you might like to leave London for a bit. There's also the matter of Claire."

Claire was Tim and Bess's precocious almost-four-year-old daughter. Having inherited her father's intellect and her mother's charisma, she was well on her way to becoming the most appealing little martinet the world had ever known. She was the only person in the world for whom I'd happily drop to all fours and bark like a dog, for example. At least without money being exchanged. I adored her. And yet…

"You want me to go as your nanny?" I asked.

Lazarus shrugged. "Do you have anything better to do at present?"

I thought for a moment. With the money Goddard had left me, I was free to do as I pleased. But with the reality of his death still a raw spot on my soul, I wasn't sure anything would ever please me again. Perhaps a change of scenery would do me good. And if I was spending all my time trying to keep Claire out of mischief—as Herculean a task as it sounds—I wouldn't have time to dwell on my own misery.

"When are you leaving?" I asked.

"Day after tomorrow."

"So I have quite a bit of time to think about it, then."

"I figured I'd put the idea to you the next time you showed up at Turnbull House. Not my fault you stayed away so long. But at least we've already taken care of your tickets. Quite expensive, by the way, and not eligible for refund."

"So there's no pressure, either," I said.

Lazarus grinned.

Well, really, what did I have to keep me in London? Turnbull House was doing fine without me. There were plenty more talented— and motivated—secretaries than I. And Lawrence? I'd miss Lawrence. But there was nothing between us that would suffer irreparable damage by my absence for a month or two. Or even longer.

I raised my glass again. "I'll do it."

"I'm glad to hear it."

"But I want something in return."

Lazarus quirked an eyebrow.

"Go with me to deal with Rupert Sudworth."

"Who the devil is Rupert Sudworth?"

"Exactly."

Sudworth was a financier and had been instrumental in a number of Goddard's schemes. He was successful, charming, and also, I believe, a psychopath. I'd known a number of young men who had come to a bad end after being drawn into his web. Nothing that could be proved, of course, but I wasn't the only one who felt the temperature drop when Rupert Sudworth entered the room. Sudworth's particular expertise was making dirty money look clean. Apparently this included the money Goddard had left me. I'd brushed elbows with Sudworth some years ago and was not looking forward to doing it again.

"Seems a small price to pay," Lazarus said, seeming pleasantly surprised. "Shall we take care of it this afternoon?"

"It's your funeral," I said darkly.

❖

The wood-paneled halls of Sudworth's building on King Street were whisper-quiet. Lazarus and I cringed at the heavy sound of our ordinary boots on the polished floors, as an impeccably dressed young man led us down a dimly lit corridor to Sudworth's office. The lackey knocked once, carefully opened the door, and then disappeared into the shadows. My discomfort with the trappings of extreme wealth stemmed from instinct. I didn't belong there, and never would. Lazarus, too, harbored a horror of the corridors of power, though his derived from experience. Glancing at him, I could see that he was feeling the walls pressing in just as I was. It was as if we were so small and inconsequential that those silent corridors could have swallowed us up, and no one would remember we'd ever existed.

Sudworth was sitting at his desk. It surprised me that we'd interrupted his working. I didn't know where he found the time between making rentboys vanish and rigging the stock exchange. Sudworth was a handsome man in his late thirties—dark hair and eyes, with pointed, imperious features. When he saw me, his wide mouth spread into a smile, though his eyes were so cold and hard I doubted a smile had ever touched them. "Mr. Adler, what a pleasure. I've been expecting you. Please, come in."

Lazarus entered on my heels, glancing around nervously at the framed oil paintings on the walls, the exquisite furniture, and the thick, wool carpet beneath Sudworth's freshly polished rosewood desk. With a wince, I realized he was probably reliving his last journey into the white stone bowels of St. James's. After nearly a decade of hiding under an assumed name, Lazarus had found himself face-to-face with an old enemy—a former commanding officer, whose criminal activities during their service in Afghanistan, Lazarus had threatened to expose. The officer had kidnapped Lazarus and taken him to a mahogany-paneled, Persian-carpeted room much like this one. When I found him, the officer's men had beaten Lazarus beyond recognition and were about to deliver him to a slow and grisly death. Lazarus looked at me, confirming my suspicions.

Sorry, I mouthed.

"And who have you brought with you?" Sudworth asked.

"This is my colleague, Dr. Lazarus."

Sudworth's smile broadened. "Your *colleague*. How splendid. Please, sit, both of you. Would you care for a drink?"

Lazarus reddened slightly at the implication in Sudworth's voice.

He tugged discreetly at his cravat, then perched at the edge of one of the leather upholstered chairs before the desk.

"No, thank you," I said, taking the other chair.

I'd known Sudworth by reputation for some time. In my former line of work, word spread quickly about exceptional clients—exceptionally generous, exceptionally bizarre, or, in Sudworth's case, exceptionally cruel. I hadn't actually set eyes on the man until that night in 1891, when I'd helped a friend extricate himself from Sudworth's clutches. It was at that time I'd learned that Sudworth and Goddard were friends. Not surprising, perhaps, that a crooked financier and London's best-dressed crime lord should find more than a little common ground.

What did surprise me was the lack of apparent consequence, for my friend, for me, or for Goddard, who had distracted Sudworth while I convinced my friend to leave his fancy dinner and flee. I'd calculated the risk of the move based on two factors—first, that Marcus had only just met Sudworth, and Sudworth probably hadn't yet invested enough time or money in Marcus to consider his escape a loss worth pursuing. Second, I'd hoped against hope that Sudworth, from his seat across the crowded restaurant, hadn't seen me urging Marcus to leave, or, if he had, that he wouldn't recognize me if he saw me again. That had been three and a half years ago, and even now I couldn't be sure.

"Such a pity about Dr. Goddard," Sudworth said, his mouth a grim line of studied regret. "You must miss him terribly."

Lazarus and I exchanged a look. Goddard had never been one to gossip about his personal life, though I wouldn't put it past Sudworth to fish for information he might later use to advantage.

"Actually, we haven't been in contact for several years," I said.

"Is that so? Well, considering the sum he left you, your last meeting must have been memorable."

I cleared my throat. I'd never forget the last time Goddard and I had carried out any meaningful interaction, but the experience had been nothing like what Sudworth was implying. "Believe me, Mr. Sudworth, the bequest was as much a surprise to me as Goddard's passing."

"Yes. I understand the water heater exploded. Terrible, dangerous things."

Something sharp-edged and cold passed between Sudworth and me at that moment. It was hard to explain. Sudworth was lying. I couldn't put my finger on how I knew, but I did. What's more, he seemed to know that I knew. He seemed to be waiting for me to contradict him.

Lazarus, as if sensing the tension, shifted uncomfortably in his seat. Suddenly, I couldn't conclude our business fast enough.

"You're obviously busy," I said. "I shouldn't keep you any longer. Here's the letter from Mr. Caruthers." I produced the letter from Goddard's solicitor, belatedly smoothing out the creases, and pushed it across the table to Sudworth.

He read it through and laid it on the blotter. The moment had passed. He was smiling pleasantly, now. "Everything appears to be in order. Would you prefer cash or a cheque?"

"A cheque," Lazarus answered before I could say anything. He turned to me. "Surely you don't want to be carrying that amount of cash around the city with you."

Sudworth frowned. "Don't you have a bank account, Mr. Adler? I'd be more than happy to set one up for you."

No, I did not have a bank account. I'd never had anything to put in one. It might have been wise to take Sudworth up on his offer, but the realization of his possible role in Goddard's death had me panicking inside. If I had to spend another moment in his presence, I might just jump out of my skin.

"Thank you, but I've already made arrangements. A cheque would be best."

"Excellent." Sudworth stood. "Excuse me for a moment while I draw it up."

The minute the financier disappeared through the door, I was out of my seat like a shot.

"What the devil was that about?" Lazarus demanded.

"He knows something about what happened to Goddard."

"What makes you think that?"

"The comment about the water heater. Goddard's house had one water heater, and it was in the second-floor bath. If you'd seen the damage, you'd know there was no way the explosion originated on the second floor."

Lazarus's eyes widened. "Ira, are you sure?"

"Sure that Sudworth is lying? Yes. Sure that he's the devil himself? Mostly. Sure that he had something to do with the explosion? Who the hell knows, but it certainly seems that way."

"Was there ever an investigation? Maybe he read about the water heater in the papers. They often get their facts wrong."

The door opened again and I quickly sat back down in my chair.

Sudworth glanced curiously from me to Lazarus. Then he returned to his seat behind the desk and laid down the cheque for my inspection. While I looked at it, trying not to hyperventilate—*Pay to the order of Ira Adler: Two hundred fifty thousand pounds*—he produced a thin stack of papers and a pen.

"Sign where indicated, and it's all yours."

It seemed to take forever to read, sign, and initial the pages, but eventually I was able to lay the pen down. Sudworth reached a hand over the table to seal the meeting. I had to wait until my fingers stopped trembling.

"It was a pleasure doing business with you, Mr. Adler. I wish you success. If you have any questions, please don't hesitate to contact me."

I nodded, tucking the cheque into the inside pocket of my waistcoat. My mind was a swirling mess of conflicting thoughts and emotions. Had I imagined the current of menace that had passed between us while we discussed the explosion? Had he really failed to recognize me from that fateful night at the Wellington, where I'd convinced Marcus to run? It didn't matter, now, I thought, as Lazarus led me by the elbow down the hall. If Sudworth had wanted to detain us, he would have. And now that we were walking out the front door, I'd never have to deal with him again.

Outside, the air was fresh. The sun pressed through the thin layer of clouds and warmed the cold, white marble of the buildings that ran up and down either side of the street.

"You understand, now, why I wanted you to go with me," I said to Lazarus as we hurried down the front steps and made our way to the sidewalk. How grateful I was to be out of that building and away from the festering pile of evil that was Rupert Sudworth! "Even without that whole business about the water heater, he still would have put your hackles up. He was a friend of Goddard's, you know."

"That doesn't surprise me a bit," Lazarus said tightly.

Lazarus walked faster, as if to distance himself physically from Sudworth's lair—as well, perhaps, as to burn off the residual panic that must have been coursing through his system. He averted his eyes as we passed the East India Officers Club on the other side of the square. Lazarus could not possibly have forgotten his ordeal there. More than six years had passed, but one doesn't survive what he did without some kind of lasting damage. Lazarus was such a tireless, law-abiding do-gooder, it was easy to forget he hadn't been born that way—that his desire to save every last person, body and soul, stemmed from having been witness to—and sometimes victim of—some of the greatest evils perpetrated by man.

I let him walk ahead of me for a bit. I didn't begrudge him his solitude when he needed it. When he reached the corner, he turned and waited.

"I do hope," he said, leaning in and dropping his voice as I came up beside him, "that you've finally learned your lesson about rich and dangerous men."

CHAPTER FIVE

Of course I'd learned my lesson. Otherwise I'd have been back at York Street the moment Goddard had crooked his little finger. At one point in my life, I did like the dangerous ones. There had been a time when Sudworth would have been just my cup of tea. It was a matter of maturity that I'd disciplined myself to stay away from his type. It would be nice if I could find a satisfying replacement, though. I patted the cheque through the breast of my coat.

"You're not going to carry that around with you all day, are you?" Lazarus asked.

"I thought I'd ask Mr. Humphrey to deposit it somewhere or... something." Mr. Humphrey was the financial manager for Turnbull House. Tim and I had hired him after the shelter's messenger service became so successful we couldn't keep up with the accounting. If anyone would know what to do with that kind of money, he would.

Tim nodded. "That's a good idea. Let's do it right now. Look, the bus is coming."

A red, horse-drawn omnibus was making its way down the street. From the sign on the front of the vehicle, it would drop us very near Mr. Humphrey's office. Tim started walking toward the stop on the next block.

"Wait," I said.

Tim stopped, glanced over his shoulder, irritated.

"There's something I need you to see, first."

He rolled his eyes but started back toward me. It was a mark of our friendship that he didn't question me, not even when I began to lead him in the opposite direction—north, up Duke Street, toward Regent's Park. We arrived at the ruins of Goddard's home about forty minutes later. It looked exactly the same as it had when I'd last been there: a scorched hole blasted through the right side of the facade, through which we could see the destroyed vestibule, the gaping cavity where the servants' stairs had been, and the pristine corridor and office on the left. How fortunate for Goddard's books and furniture that the June weather had been so uncharacteristically fine.

"Look, Tim, and tell me there's any possibility at all that this damage was caused by an upstairs water heater."

The afternoon sun pushed against the clouds, giving the wreckage an eerie glow. A curl of wallpaper flapped in the warm, particulate-laden breeze. Tim leaned in closer to examine the effect of the blast on the stairs—the bottom had sustained some wood damage, but as one ascended, the damage became less until it was nothing at all. He turned to me.

"You're right." He shrugged. "But that doesn't mean the papers didn't make a mistake. It doesn't mean Mr. Sudworth had anything to do with it."

"Doesn't mean he didn't."

"Very well, as long as we're playing this game, why don't we try to figure out where the explosion *did* originate?"

At that moment the guard stepped out from behind the ruins of the house and pinned us with a hard stare. Lazarus glanced nervously at me.

"Never mind him," I said. "Just stay off the stairs."

We stood behind the fence for quite a while, examining the building from different angles. The guard kept us in his flinty gaze, occasionally touching the top of his knife handle but, as I'd predicted, made no other move. I'm no detective, but I did manage to read a few things from the scene.

"From the destruction of the front right side of the facade, I'd say the blast was centered in the vestibule, near the doorway of the morning room. The front half of the morning room was blown away, but the back portion is intact. As is the entire left side of the house." I frowned. "Couldn't have been a very strong explosion, though, if it didn't do more damage than this."

"I agree," Lazarus said. "Did Goddard keep any machinery in the vestibule?"

"Aside from the grandfather clock? No. And you can see for yourself that the kitchen stove is in one piece. And the morning-room fireplace as well."

Lazarus nodded. "The clock would have been a good place to hide a device."

"Yes, it would have." I turned to him. "So you agree the explosion was deliberate."

"Oh, yes. But did Sudworth set it?"

"Not himself. He'd have hired someone. There's also another possibility."

I told him how Goddard had given all of his servants an unprecedented full day off, all together. I mentioned that I'd been an hour late, and that when I'd arrived, Goddard had been checking his watch.

"What does that suggest to you?" I asked.

"That he was wondering exactly how late you intended to be," Lazarus said.

"Possibly. But if he'd planted a time-delay bomb, he might also have been thinking it was time to clip the wires and find some other way to do the job."

Lazarus narrowed his eyes. His expression was disbelieving, but I could tell that he didn't find the idea completely implausible.

"Simultaneous murder and suicide? Forgive my skepticism, Adler. You have your charms, but somehow I can't see you inspiring that level of passion in someone you've been rejecting for nearly six years."

"Perhaps not," I said. "But you have to admit it's a reasonable conclusion, given the evidence."

"*A* reasonable conclusion. One of many."

"Touché."

"I wonder if the fire brigade is investigating this. They have a station in this area, don't they?"

"In Regent's Park? I should think so. But why would they talk to us?"

"That's a good question," Lazarus said. "If they thought it was a criminal matter, they'd have turned it over to the police."

"Why would the police tell us anything?"

Lazarus slapped the back of his hand against his palm. "They wouldn't," he said decisively. "But they'd line up to speak to the Holmes of St. John's Wood. How fortunate that he lives just around the corner. Come on."

Andrew St. Andrews, Consulting Detective, lived at 222 Baker Street, which was not a coincidence. He idolized Sherlock Holmes and even went so far as to don the cape and hat, weather permitting. He did not emulate Holmes's monkish lifestyle, however. St. Andrews was a man of wealth and extravagant tastes. And he'd redecorated since my last visit. The vestibule now sparkled with bronze and gold flourishes fit for the Sun King. Not to my taste, but elegant nonetheless.

"Mr. Adler!" St. Andrews exclaimed as his man Fenwick took our coats and hats. "Please allow me to express my condolences." He pressed my hand between both of his. "It's been a long time since either of us has been on speaking terms with Dr. Goddard, but I can tell that we both feel his passing most keenly." He turned to Lazarus and clasped his hand as well. "Tim, it's so good to see you, my friend. It's been too long. I do hope Bess and Claire are well. Please, gentlemen, do come in."

St. Andrews was in many ways my opposite. Where I was of average height, he towered. My build was on the thin side, while he was rangy and growing a paunch. My hair and eyes were dark, and I favored a beard. He, by contrast was clean shaven, with a head of messy, light-brown curls. But he was a kind man, generous and good-humored. Much, much more so than I. And we had both loved Cain Goddard once. We had both, in our turn, been loved by him. So as different as we were in almost every other way, in this moment, in this way, we were as one.

"Thank you, Mr. St. Andrews," I said as he preceded us into the parlor. More gilt and lacquer, but very tastefully done.

"Please. We've been through so much together. Call me Andrew, and I shall call you Ira."

"Of course."

It seemed silly to have to say it aloud. We'd known one another for nearly seven years, during the course of which he'd saved my life once and sprung me from jail twice. For my part, I'd introduced him to his hero, Arthur Conan Doyle. I'd also provided him with two employees and some business advice, both of which had helped to turn a misguided hobby into a thriving business in private investigation. Our interactions always precipitated life-changing events, and yet our paths crossed so infrequently that we were in the strange position of knowing each other very closely without ever having formally transitioned to Christian names.

"Ah, Cain," St. Andrews said, while Lazarus and I took our seats on a breathtakingly expensive lacquered sofa. He went to a small, glass-fronted liquor cabinet and produced a crystal decanter and three glasses. "Whiskey?"

"A bit early, don't you think?" Lazarus asked.

"Yes, please," I replied.

St. Andrews poured out two glasses and handed one to me. "Such a waste," he said, raising his drink. "Such a brilliant mind."

I tapped his glass with my own and threw back a belt of very old, very expensive liquor.

Goddard and St. Andrews had met long ago, during happier times. Goddard had taught literature at Cambridge, and St. Andrews had been his student. The scandal that had resulted from the discovery of their affair had somehow escaped the attention of the police, but it had ruined both men's academic careers forever. Goddard had never forgiven St. Andrews. Not that it mattered now.

"I had always hoped he'd see the error of his ways. Or retire once he'd amassed a large enough fortune." St. Andrews sighed heavily as he sank down onto a chair that appeared to have been specially built to hold his large frame. "Not that he'd ever have given me the satisfaction of knowing."

"At least it was quick," I said. "He probably never knew what happened."

"We believe the explosion was deliberately set," Lazarus stated.

St. Andrews frowned. "Of course it was."

"Why do you say that?" I asked.

"Given his associations and his line of work, the question was never whether, but when. That, and in no way could the water heater have exploded like that chap wrote in *The Times*. I couldn't resist poking around the place a bit," he admitted. "It being just around the corner."

"It was in *The Times*?" I asked.

The Times was the newspaper for people like St. Andrews and Rupert Sudworth—the rich and well connected. Could it be that Sudworth was merely repeating what he'd read? That he'd had nothing at all to do with the explosion? It would have made things so much easier to believe that. And yet, I couldn't deny that strange tension that had passed between Sudworth and myself when he'd mentioned it.

"It was in a number of papers," St. Andrews said. "I kept the articles if you want to see them."

"I would, very much, thank you."

St. Andrews stood and retrieved a file folder from the top drawer of the writing desk in the corner. He stopped briefly to refill his glass, then brought the folder to me. I opened it on the sofa between Lazarus and myself, gesturing for Lazarus to help himself.

"The first article appeared in *The Times,* on the bottom of page three, the day after the blast." St. Andrews spoke as I glanced over the piece in question. "Dr. Goddard wasn't a public figure—quite the opposite. But an incident like that in this neighborhood—a neighborhood with more than its share of *Times* readers—doesn't happen every day. There are only the two articles, though—the first, which describes the blast, and the one the day after, which explains the water-heater theory."

"Which is false," I said.

"Clearly. The article in *The Daily News*, you'll see, is the same information in different words. It was the series of pieces in *The Daily Telegraph* that caught my eye. The penny press tends to be a lot less squeamish about these things, and a lot less interested in protecting the delicate sensibilities of its readership."

I smirked. The bulk of the readership of *The Telegraph* could be found swilling gin in Whitechapel on a Saturday night. My fingers quickly found the coarse paper, which I held by the edges to keep the cheap ink from rubbing off on my fingertips. Unlike its posh counterpart, *The Telegraph* seemed to be giving continuous coverage of the explosion from a variety of perspectives. The penny press thrived on drama and mayhem.

"The first article, you'll see, delivers the water-heater theory. But subsequent articles by different authors present some alternatives."

"This one's from today," Lazarus said, holding up a smudged slip of newsprint. "A plot involving a shadowy consortium of Royals and certain international business interests. What nonsense."

"Not that unreasonable, considering Goddard himself sat at the head of a shadowy business consortium," St. Andrews said.

"I don't know."

"There was that business on Fitzroy Street. Royals were involved in that," I said.

Lazarus shook his head. "After all this time? That's really a stretch. And look. This article points to a conspiracy of florists, who thought Goddard meant to use the results of his botanical experiments to put them out of business."

I took the article from his fingers and glanced over it. Ridiculous, of course. Bold lettering marking the article below caught my eye— ATTACK IN ST. JOHN'S WOOD! Someone had attacked a woman with a knife near the Baker Street entrance to Regent's Park—not very far from Goddard's front door. The neighborhood wasn't what it once was, it appeared. I'd have been interested to read more, but St. Andrews had clipped the article through the middle. I handed the paper back to Tim.

"Goddard wasn't a florist," I said.

"No," St. Andrews interjected. "But he did publish a very interesting monograph about medicinal hybrids. He holds letters of patent for at least ten different varieties, you know."

"No, I didn't know. Blimey." Goddard had been spending a lot of time noodling in his greenhouse. I should have sensed he wasn't just making prettier roses.

"This author speculates that a séance conjured up something that may still be at large. Oh, for Heaven's sake!" Lazarus tossed the article into the folder and wiped his fingers on his trousers.

"Now that is preposterous," St. Andrews said. "Dr. Goddard was an atheist."

"So the penny rags will consider anything, as long as it sells papers, and the respectable papers won't print anything except that rubbish about the water heater." I closed the folder in disgust. "Where does that leave us?"

St. Andrews stroked his freshly shaved chin. "The water-heater story is obviously someone's official word. Either police or fire brigade. I have contacts with the police, but if the fire brigade reported it as a water-heater explosion, there won't be a criminal investigation."

"We're not firemen, and we saw through that story right away," I said.

"Which means that someone influential fed the story to someone high up in the fire brigade," said Lazarus. "And whatever anyone who had actually been there had seen, this was the explanation they were to give."

St. Andrews nodded. "Which leaves us with the question of who planted the story—someone who wanted Goddard out of the way, or someone working for Goddard himself?"

"Wait, what?" Lazarus said.

"We have to consider every reasonable possibility," St. Andrews said. "That includes assassination by someone outside Goddard's organization, by someone within it, and yes, it does include suicide."

"I told you so," I said to Lazarus.

In response to St. Andrews's questioning look, I relayed my suspicions. St. Andrews listened carefully. When I was finished, he said, "It's a possibility, I suppose. Though with that as a motive, I'd place the probability somewhere between that of the séance and the florists' conspiracy."

"So now what?" I asked.

"Now, I propose we split up," St. Andrews said. "Ira, since you were actually present at the time of the explosion, why don't you try to speak to some of the firemen who were there? See what they think happened, maybe see if they'll talk about who started the water-heater story. I'll see what the police have to say about it. And, Tim, if it wouldn't be too much trouble, perhaps you, being a fixture on the East End, could track down one or two of these reporters whose stories aren't complete balderdash and see if they have anything concrete to offer. We can meet back here tomorrow evening and compare notes."

Lazarus said, "I'm afraid we won't have time. We're leaving for America the day after tomorrow."

"Oh?" St. Andrews asked.

"A family matter. Ira's coming as well. Sort of a holiday."

"Oh," St. Andrews said. He looked as confused as I felt. Why had Lazarus dropped this in St. Andrews's lap if he'd no intention of following through with the investigation?

"I'll speak to the firemen," I said.

Lazarus whipped his head toward me. "*You* don't have time, either. You have to put your documents in order, buy new clothes, acquire *luggage*, for God's sake—"

"I can do all those things tomorrow. And still have time to interview a fireman or two."

"Ira!"

"Gentlemen, friends, please." St. Andrews's calm voice cut through what was well on its way to becoming a heated argument. "I was only hoping to offer you the opportunity to be involved in the investigation, should you desire. My Irregulars and I," he said, referring to the two employees I'd sent him nearly four years before, "are perfectly capable of gathering evidence and conducting interviews. If you let me know where you'll be staying in America, I'll be happy to apprise you of further developments."

"Thank you," Lazarus said, his tone entirely too self-satisfied. St. Andrews handed him a pen and paper, and I watched Lazarus scribble out an address.

"I'll speak to the firemen," I repeated, looking a dare at Lazarus. He glowered at me but remained silent.

"Only if you have time, Ira," St. Andrews said. "I wouldn't want to interfere with such a momentous journey."

St. Andrews stood, and Lazarus and I followed him to the door.

"I'll speak to someone tonight," I repeated, "and send word to you tomorrow. Thank you, Andrew, for everything."

His Christian name felt strange on my tongue, but it made St. Andrews smile. He shook my hand. "I shall look forward to your findings. Good afternoon, gentlemen."

"You're not serious about this, are you?" Lazarus asked as we walked briskly down the street. The sun was hanging low in the sky, tinting the dirty cloud layer orange. "You're not actually going to start investigating that man's death?"

I turned. "Yes. Yes, I am."

"Ira, we're leaving for—"

"You don't have to tell me again. I know what I promised you, and I'll do it. But I have to do this first. Don't you understand?"

"No," he said.

I shook my head. "It doesn't matter. It won't take me more than an hour or two to talk to some firemen. Tomorrow I'll make my preparations for the trip. There's plenty of time."

Tim stared. That vein on his forehead was starting to pulse. "That's not the point," he said.

"What is the point?"

He took a breath, as if preparing to launch into some complicated explanation. Then, glancing at me, he shook his head and let it out. "The officially recognized cause of the explosion was a faulty water heater. Why can't you accept that?"

"Why...what? For the same reason you know it's not true. You saw for yourself, Tim. If you want to go back to the house, we can go up the stairs and I can show you the blasted water heater. I guarantee it will be in pristine condition. I don't understand. A few minutes ago, you were nodding and agreeing—"

"I wasn't."

"But it was your idea to go see St. Andrews!"

"Hoping he would either try to talk you out of pursuing this or, if worse came to worse, that he'd take the case on himself. Which he has. Ira, you don't have time to meddle in this. You need to get your travel documents in order, buy—"

"I know! You've told me several times already!" I took a deep breath and began again in a more reasonable tone. "Why don't you want me to pursue this?"

"Do I really have to spell it out?"

"Yes. At this point, I believe you do."

His brown eyes bored into me. When he spoke, there was a tension in his voice I hadn't heard in a long time. "It's over, Ira. This nonsense with Goddard. This…this…obsession of yours. It's unhealthy. It's always been unhealthy. And now you're free of him. Not just free, but free and richer than Andrew St. Andrews. You can be anything. You can do anything. You can be with anyone you wish. What about that nice young man you've been spending time with?"

"Lawrence? What does he have to do with this?"

But Lazarus wasn't finished. "And what about the rest of us, Ira? What about the people who have been here all along?"

"You mean you?" I asked, more confused than ever.

"Me, Bess, Claire, Pearl, Lawrence—the people who have been here with you in good times and bad. The people who have managed to harbor some sort of affection for you without causing you to end up in jail, or be beaten by thugs, or shot at, or nearly burnt to death in a sugarhouse, or almost drowned in the Thames, or blown halfway to smithereens in the middle of St. John's Wood, or…or…or…What about us, Ira? We need you, now. Cain Goddard is dead. Murdered? Probably. But if so, he brought it on himself. Nothing you do can change that, and nothing you discover will make you any better off for it. In fact, if you go kicking the wrong hornet's nest, you may end up dead yourself. And then where would we be? All your true friends? Forget him, Ira. We need you, and, quite frankly, you owe us. What do you say to that?"

I blinked. Stepped back a step. Of all the things to which Lazarus might have cultivated offense, I'd never imagined…I mean, I hadn't seen Goddard in years. Hadn't wanted to. And though thoughts of him sometimes came unbidden, I hadn't contemplated our past in any depth until his last summons.

Was I really using his murder as an excuse to push away my friends? Lazarus clearly thought so. I watched outrage overtake his features as he misinterpreted my stunned silence for wavering.

"I see," he said coldly.

"No, Tim, wait."

He nodded, setting his jaw, which was trembling with anger. "You send word when you have your priorities straight. But don't take too long. Day after tomorrow, we're leaving on the eleven o'clock to Liverpool."

CHAPTER SIX

The longer I lived, the more it seemed that certain patterns in my life were repeating themselves. In my early twenties, I'd been aimless, earning my living on my knees—or on my back, or pressed up against the wall of an alley. You understand my meaning. Lazarus had treated me a few times at his clinic. A few times after that, he'd become my client. It had meant more to him than that, but he'd been too inexperienced with sex to know what to say, and I'd been too inexperienced with the emotional side of intimacy to see what was happening. When Goddard offered to pay for my exclusive companionship, I'd seen it as a business decision. To Lazarus it had been a betrayal.

That had been ever so long ago—so long that neither of us gave it a second conscious thought. But sometimes the undertones were so obvious it must have seemed like a slap across the face to Lazarus. Like that day. It didn't matter that Goddard was dead, that Lazarus was married, and that I'd not be with either of them physically ever again. Deep in Lazarus's heart, he must have felt that I was fobbing him off again—he, who had been through so much with me—to chase that bastard Goddard.

Looking at it that way, I couldn't blame him for being angry.

It was too bad he'd already stepped onto an omnibus and I couldn't tell him as much.

But why had Goddard's death affected me to this degree? I had loved him once, it's true. But so many times, love isn't enough. And our love was so long in the past that it shouldn't have counted for much. Still, the times that circumstances brought us together had changed my life irrevocably. Our interactions since that time, both good and ill, had set my life on its present trajectory. Goddard had educated me, given me a trade, and taught me how to speak, dress, and act as a member of the educated middle class. With one hand, he'd interfered and manipulated, while with the other he'd showered me with unspeakable generosity. Then with one unforgivable act, he forever shattered the fragile reconciliation we had been building.

Why had he summoned me back to York Street years after perpetrating that final, violent act of severance? This was the question, I realized, I couldn't let drop. Had he intended to kill us both—to send us together to a hell in which neither of us believed? Had he wanted to take his ultimate revenge? Or had there been a more altruistic motive? Perhaps he'd wanted to free me, somehow—to exit this life in one glorious blaze and leave me with more money than I knew what to do with, in some final, twisted act of apology. I'd probably never know for sure. And even if I did learn the truth, it would most likely not profit me any.

Lazarus was right. I was chasing my tail and, worse, neglecting the ones who needed me in order to chase it. And yet even knowing this, I wasn't ready to let the matter go. I'd square things with Lazarus tomorrow. Tomorrow I'd get my documents in order and buy a set of luggage.

But tonight, I was going to find a fireman.

❖

After a quick trip to Mr. Humphrey's office, where I exchanged the cheque for a receipt and a respectable sum of money for a few months of travel, I looped back on the bus to the fire-brigade station near Horseferry Road. Numerous fire stations were scattered across the city, but this was the one closest to Goddard's home. I assumed it would have been the one to respond to the fire. Evening was coming. The shadows were growing long, and the haze that sat over the city day and night was turning from sickly orange to gray. As I walked through the front door, a number of well-muscled men passed me going out. It must have been a change of shift.

"Good evening, sir. How can I help you?" asked the desk officer as I approached. He was a stout man in his fifties, with the build of someone who had performed physical work for a long time and the softness of someone who had spent his recent years behind a desk.

"I'm looking for information about the York Street explosion last week."

"Ah, yes." The man adjusted his spectacles. He met my eyes. "Water-heater explosion. You see, when the water gets hot enough, it generates steam. The steam expands very quickly, which can lead to an explosion. If the tank is corroded, or—"

"Yes, I read about it in *The Times*. Was that the conclusion of the firemen responding to the incident?" In response to his level stare, I explained, "It's just that *The Telegraph* had some different ideas about what might have happened. I was wondering if anyone was investigating any other theories."

The man frowned, stroking his thick mustache. "May I ask what your interest is, sir?"

Believe it or not, I had actually taken the time to work through an answer to this very question—one that was close enough to the truth that it could be verified.

"The man who died in the explosion was a close friend of mine. I suppose I just wanted to be certain of the facts of his death."

The fireman's demeanor changed from suspicion to understanding. "Of course, sir. The official report states that a faulty water heater caused the explosion. But if you'd like to speak unofficially, the men sometimes like to gather at the pub on Great Peter Street after their shift. You might find someone there who was at the scene."

"Like Fireman Stimson?" I asked, remembering the badge worn by the fireman who had pulled Goddard from the wreckage.

The desk officer's bushy eyebrows drew together. "Stimson? Don't know where you heard that name, sir. Only Stimson I know's Fireman Fourth Class Robert Stimson, who died in the Alhambra Theatre fire some years ago."

I racked my memory to see whether I might have remembered the name wrong. But in my mind's eye, I could see the name engraved clearly on the blackened metal badge. I shook my head.

"I must have been mistaken then. Thank you for your help."

The pub on Great Peter Street was a tight, dark hole in the wall with tarnished brass fittings and a strolling chanteuse whose salad days were well behind her. I ordered a pint of bitter and stood with my back to the sticky wooden bar. It was early evening by that point. Through the window, I watched a lamplighter use a hook to open the glass box atop the lamppost across the street, then use a second tool to light the flame. A warm light spread out from the streetlamp, bathing the nearby pavement in a warm glow.

The chanteuse floated across the stained floorboards in my direction. Catching my eye, she smiled lasciviously—a disconcerting expression on such a grandmotherly face—and warbled over the discordant jangle of the piano. Looking away, I sipped my bitter and examined the clientele.

It was a normal-sized crowd for early evening on a weekday. Laborers, mostly, from their loud voices and tired clothing. Mostly between the ages of twenty-five and fifty, and, with the exception of the chanteuse, all men. I wouldn't have recognized the firemen sitting at the corner back table had they not brushed past me coming out of the fire station. But there they were, and here was I.

Summoning the barman, I said, "Please send a round to the firemen there in the back. Tell them I'm grateful for a job well done."

I slipped the man the appropriate coins and watched him deliver a tray of beers to the table, along with my explanation. A cheer rose from the little group, and the men turned in my direction and raised their glasses. One gestured for me to join them. Bringing my own pint, I took the proffered chair.

"Now, then, mate," said one of the men—in his mid-twenties, with a thick blond mustache and matching sideburns. "To what does we owe such an act of kindness?"

"Just wanted to thank you for your quick response to that explosion on York Street last week," I said.

"You one of the neighbors?"

I almost laughed at the thought. On the other hand, it wasn't an unreasonable conclusion based on my clothing, speech, and what must have seemed like prissiness when I wiped a few drops of spilled beer from my chair before sitting on it.

"The man who died in the explosion was a friend of mine," I said. "I was coming to see him when it happened."

"Ah, yeah," another man said. Younger, clean shaven, with dark hair. "I seen you." He turned to his friends. "You're that one tried to run inside." The men laughed.

Embarrassed, I said, "Yes, that was me."

"Well, sorry for your loss, mate, but glad to see you up and about buyin' pints. Burns is the name." The dark-haired man extended his hand across the table.

Clasping it, I said, "A fitting name for a fireman. Ira Adler, at your service."

There were four men at the table. Burns, in his early twenties, appeared to be the youngest, though none looked to have reached forty. Fireman Stimson, who had pronounced Goddard dead in his laconic, East End way, was not among them.

"And this is Morris," he said, gesturing to the blond man. "Franklin, and Collier."

"Were you all at the fire on York Street?" I asked. "Forgive me. You all look the same in your hoods and jackets."

They laughed. Burns said, "Me, Morris, and Collier was there. Franklin was on his day off."

"But there were more than three firemen that day," I said.

"Them others was from Soho Station."

"I see. Is that Fireman Stimson's station?"

Burns frowned. Collier stroked his chin.

"You mean Robbie Stimson?" Franklin asked.

"I don't know his first name," I said. "His badge read STIMSON."

"Robbie Stimson's been dead for years," Franklin said.

"You must've read it wrong, sir," Collier said, laying a meaty, callused hand on my shoulder and squeezing it with a purpose that gave me pause. He was a fatherly sort, with graying hair, mustache, and sideburns. "There ain't no Stimson at Westminster nor at Soho Station neither."

I looked from one face to the other. "I'm quite certain that was the name on the badge. Big man, face like a clay slab, broken nose?"

Burns blew out a long breath. Franklin and Collier shrugged.

Morris glanced away so quickly I almost missed it.

"Anyway," I said, plastering on an earnest expression. "Amazing the water heater could do such damage. It was the water heater, right? That's what I read in *The Times*."

"Yeah, it were the water heater all right," Burns said, relaxing. "Them things can be dangerous if not properly maintained."

"It's strange, though," I said. "I thought the only water heater in that house was on the second floor."

Silence fell over the table: as thick and heavy as cotton wool. Collier looked down at his scuffed boots. Morris cleared his throat.

"Excuse me, lads," Morris said. "Nature calls."

He pushed away from the table, swilling back the last of his pint. I watched him find his way to the rear exit. He knew something. They all did. And, with the prescience born of experience, I knew that Morris either intended to tell me what he knew or to offer me half a shilling for services I'd not performed for almost a decade.

I'd give him a few moments before making my own exit.

"Every explosion's different, that's what I always say," Franklin said tentatively.

"Yeah," Collier added. "Sometimes you'd swear it were somefin' completely different what caused it—somefin' what weren't even in that part of the house. Sometimes it might look that way."

"Especially to the untrained eye," Burns added apologetically.

"I'm sure you're right," I said. "And it couldn't possibly make any difference now." I stood, drinking back the last few drops of my bitter. "Thank you again, gentlemen, for everything you did and continue to do."

I tipped my hat in their direction, then made my way to the front door.

I walked nonchalantly past the front window of the pub, then quickly made my way around the corner to the alley. Morris was waiting, as I knew he would be. Buckling—not unbuckling—his belt, he looked up and gestured for me to join him between two piles of refuse. The air in the alley stank of garbage, tobacco, and piss.

"You wanted—"

He cut off my words with a lightning-quick fist to the face. How fortunate that there was a pile of waste to catch my fall. As I sat there on my arse in a sea of moldering pub leavings, a sudden, warm gush of blood ran down my chin.

Morris stepped back, rubbing his knuckles. "It were the water heater, understand?"

I scrambled to my feet, shielding my nose with my hands, then took out a handkerchief to stanch the blood. There was an ugly grating sound as I nudged the pieces of cartilage back into place. I tried not to scream. My entire head throbbed in rhythm with my racing heart, as I blinked away spots.

"It were the water heater," Morris said again. "That's all you need to know."

He turned, seemingly unconcerned about any retaliation from my part, and swaggered back toward the rear of the pub. My lips formed the word *Wait!* But caution prevailed. I watched him duck back inside, then picked up my hat. Tipping my head back, hat under my arm, the handkerchief still pressed to my face, I walked quickly in the opposite direction toward the street. As I stumbled out onto Monck Street, I caught sight of a red-jacketed Turnbull messenger.

"You! Boy!" I called, still holding my head back. The motion sent a trickle of blood down my throat, and I gagged.

The messenger turned. He wasn't one of the residents, but I remembered when Tim had hired him. The messenger service was expanding so quickly we'd been forced to take on additional help from outside the shelter. This young man—Clyde, that was his name—was light of build, light-haired, with a snub nose. He was thirteen. As he trotted over, I penned a quick note to St. Andrews.

There's been a break in the case, so to speak. Meet me tomorrow morning at the teashop near my building on Aldersgate Street.

"Sir?" the boy asked, narrowing his eyes at my no-doubt hideous appearance.

When I spoke, my voice was cracked, nasal, and muffled by the handkerchief. I slipped him the note and two tanners. "Take this to Mr. St. Andrews at 222 Baker Street, and keep the change."

The boy's eyes grew wide. He cracked a grin at the sight of the coins. Then, drawing a serious expression, he nodded. "Yes sir. Right away, sir."

I watched him skip off happily, note in one hand, coins in the other. Then I turned and started toward home.

CHAPTER SEVEN

Is that the 'break' in the case you were referring to?" St. Andrews asked, nodding toward my deformed face. I detected mischief in his tone, but his expression was kind. It was well into midmorning, and despite the elaborate breakfast spread he'd no doubt enjoyed at home, St. Andrews had already wolfed down his weak tea and half the plate of sandwiches and pastries. He was waiting politely for me to consume my half, though his eyes kept darting longingly toward the food.

"I thought you'd appreciate the pun," I said. "And finish the sandwiches if you like. It hurts too much to eat right now."

"Oh, ta!" While he dug in with his characteristic enthusiasm, I traced a finger over the plaster holding my nose together. I'd always thought a broken nose looked rugged. On other people. Damn it.

"That's a good splint," St. Andrews said. "Did Tim Lazarus do that?"

I shook my head. "Lazarus would have broken my neck to match the nose, if he'd heard how it happened. There was a clinic nearby. I went there."

St. Andrews wiped his mouth with a serviette that was frayed and softened from use, and nodded knowingly. Despite the down-at-heel atmosphere and questionable food, the teahouse was crowded that morning. His expression turning thoughtful, St. Andrews glanced at the other patrons, then leaned in close, lowering his voice.

"So, if I understand correctly, we have one fireman back from the dead, though no one saw him but you, and three more who are quite alive, who know something about the explosion and are willing to commit violence in order to keep it secret." He grinned. "This does sound promising."

I grunted and broke off half a stale scone. Spreading it with a bit of clotted cream—surprisingly fresh and tasty-looking—I took a cautious bite. Ouch. I set it down on my plate and glared at it.

"I hate to admit it, but Lazarus is right. I really don't have time to pursue this further."

"Say no more. Andrew St. Andrews is on the case."

"Just don't send any of your Irregulars to interview firemen," I said, thinking of the two young women I'd placed in his employ.

St. Andrews shook his head vigorously. "Never."

The proprietress came by—a stocky woman in a stained apron, who looked as disheveled and careworn as the rest of the place. "Anyfin' more for you gentlemen?"

I glanced at the empty sandwich plate and drained teapot. "No, thank you. I believe we're finished."

Without further ceremony, she set the bill on the table. St. Andrews reached for his money. Waving away the offer, I set a couple of coins on the table, which the proprietress pocketed before reaching for the teapot.

"Ta again, Ira," St. Andrews said, standing. We gathered our coats and hats from the hooks near the door. "Now, one doesn't travel to America every day. Is there any way I can expedite your preparations?"

"As a matter of fact," I said, "there is."

I'd never traveled abroad before. I'd never even been outside of London. But St. Andrews had, and he not only knew what I'd need in terms of documents but also which palms to grease, should there be a problem in obtaining them. It was surprising, in the end, how little actual proof of identity was required. Had I been traveling to the Continent, I'd have needed nothing at all.

"But you're going to America," St. Andrews wisely said. "You'll likely need at least your birth record and possibly a letter from your employer."

"I'll be traveling with my employer," I said.

"Then that's sorted. Let's take care of the other."

Since I had no idea where or under what circumstances I'd come into the world—and the number of records offices in London was truly daunting—we started at the workhouse on Baker's Row, where I'd lived from age three. For better or for worse, it was still running—and greatly expanded from what I remembered. And miracle of miracles, they maintained meticulous records. Thank you, Mum, for leaving me there, and not with some shady baby farmer.

Rose Adler was her name, by the way, in case you were curious—at least according to the file the old clerk slid across the desk to me with one claw-like hand, while snatching up my coin with the other. Rose died in 1870, on the floor of a Limehouse opium den. Buried in a mass pauper's grave in St. Bride's. Survived by one child, Ira, father unknown. I was born on October 14, it turned out—not in December, as I'd always believed. At least I'd known the year—1864. How embarrassing it would have been to have mistaken *that*. The fourteenth of October is the feast day of St. Callistus, in case anyone cares. I didn't. Rose Adler was Jewish, a fact that would bring a smile to the face of Mrs. Levi, who owned my favorite bakery and was determined to see me happily settled with a nice girl.

When we were finished, I found a red-jacketed Turnbull House runner—London seemed to be crawling with them, these days—and sent a message to Tim. It was gratifying to see the shelter's messenger service prospering. We had started it as a way to help the shelter meet expenses when donations were slow. At the time, it had seemed like a risk to charge sixpence to send a message, when any urchin would do it for a penny. But people had found the price quite reasonable when a well-known and highly respectable institution like Turnbull House backed the service.

The uniforms had been Goddard's idea.

I glanced at my watch. I had toyed with the idea of taking the Necropolis train to Surrey to pay my respects to Goddard's remains. There was no time, though, never mind that I could easily afford it now. No, now it was time to address the vexed question of trousers.

For a brief, two-year window in my life I'd enjoyed an unlimited clothing budget. When I'd lived with Goddard at York Street, I'd spent an appalling amount of money on tailors and various sartorial consultants. I'd left most of those clothes behind when I'd moved on, though. And although I was making decent money as a secretary, I'd been reluctant to piss it away on bright waistcoats and eccentric cravats that would be out of fashion by the time I arrived home. I owned a few well-made, interchangeable pieces, mostly secondhand, all of them of conservative, classic design. My shoes were comfortable and in good repair. But I'd no idea what they wore in America. And, quite frankly, now that I had both the means and the excuse to refresh my wardrobe, I couldn't wait to indulge myself a bit.

It went without saying that no tailor could reasonably be expected to outfit me for God knew how long in a foreign country on a single day's notice. Thus it was that St. Andrews and I found ourselves at Whiteley's in Bayswater. If one was to be forced to buy ready-to-wear clothing, we reasoned, at least one could do so with a view of Kensington Gardens.

"Third floor, gentlemen's apparel," St. Andrews announced as we emerged into a vast maze of glass-fronted counters, the stock temptingly arrayed within. Whiteley's boasted seventeen departments and employed over six thousand people. Somehow I managed to keep from gaping as St. Andrews led me to a long counter, behind which a series of shelves held a dizzying number of ready-made shirts in silk and linen folded for immediate sale.

A young, impeccably coiffed man in a chic black suit looked up as we approached. A shadow passed across his face as he took in my plastered nose and purpled, swollen features. But the moment he saw St. Andrews at my side, the shadow passed and sunshine reigned once more.

"Good morning, Mr. St. Andrews," the man said with the relish of one welcoming back a generous and faithful customer.

"Good morning, Mr. Cuttle. My friend, Mr. Adler, is traveling to America, for about a month, I believe. He will need clothing appropriate to the adventure."

"Certainly, sir. Will it be on your account?"

St. Andrews chuckled and glanced at me sheepishly. "No. I'm here for moral support only. But tell me, do you know what's fashionable in California right now?"

By the time we left the third floor, poor Mr. Cuttle was pushing an enormous trolley, upon which were stacked no fewer than seventy boxes containing shirts, trousers, jackets, waistcoats, cravats, and even a few of those strange, thin ties that Mr. Cuttle said all the American gentlemen were wearing. There was a new bowler, though I didn't need one, and an odd but very striking hat with a flat top and a wide brim, apparently for deflecting the relentless American sunshine. New shoes, new boots, and underclothes. A few bottles of cologne and enough toiletries to stock a chemist's shop. As we approached possibly the largest lift known to mankind, I had to stop and lean against the wall to catch my breath.

"Sorry," I said. "It's all a lot to take in."

"Understandable," St. Andrews said kindly.

"I'm serious, Andrew." His name still felt strange on my lips. "I don't know how we'll manage to get all this back to my flat—or even if it'll all fit inside."

St. Andrews studied me for a moment, then laughed and summoned our esteemed shop assistant with a joyous clap.

"My dear Mr. Cuttle, all this commercial activity has proven quite tiring. Would you be so good as to pack this all into the appropriate number of steamer trunks, throw in a couple of lovely new suitcases, and deliver the lot to the address Mr. Adler will presently supply?"

Mr. Cuttle responded with a wide smile of such unctuousness that left no doubt that he'd been waiting his entire life to do just that. "Of course, sir. Shall I call you a cab as well?"

No question about it, I thought as I arranged for my purchases to be delivered to Aldersgate Street, and the bill to be sent to Mr. Humphrey, there was a lot to be said for excessive wealth. I would become accustomed to it, in time. However, I doubted I'd ever maneuver with the same facility as one who had grown up with it.

"What would I have done without your help, Andrew?" I asked as we stepped outside into a warm, sunny afternoon. Mr. Cuttle, my generous tip bulging in the pocket of his waistcoat, waved from the door, as if we were beloved relatives departing on a ship. "You must allow me to repay you, somehow."

St. Andrews cocked his head. "Bring me back a good story. Something with cowboys in it." His expression grew dreamy. "I do so like cowboys."

I laughed. "Consider it done. In the meantime, may I stand you dinner? I was thinking about taking Lawrence to the Savoy. Would you care to join us?"

The mischief returned to St. Andrews's face, and he chuckled again. "Oh, Lawrence Grey, is it? I know Lawrence. No, Ira, I wouldn't dream of intruding on your good-byes. Enjoy your dinner. And enjoy Lawrence," he said wickedly. "But bring me back a cowboy story. Or even a cowboy, if you can manage it."

Chapter Eight

The cab dropped me back at Aldersgate Street at one thirty. My trunks arrived an hour or so later, with a complement of sturdy young men to carry them up the stairs. If the men were surprised to be delivering such a wealth of goods to such a rude destination, at least they were polite enough not to say it. I tipped them handsomely and then, locking the door behind them, promptly collapsed onto my bed. I'd sent a message to Lawrence after St. Andrews and I had parted ways, summoning him to dinner at the Savoy at nine. That left me several hours for a well-deserved nap.

I arrived at the Savoy freshly bathed and shaven, and half an hour early. The maître d'hôtel hesitated when I approached—caught, no doubt, between the appalling spectacle of my battered face and the more appealing implications of my new, unabashedly expensive black suit, silk shirt, and bright-gold waistcoat.

"You're a bit early, sir," he said in an apologetic tone. "I'm afraid your table isn't ready yet. Perhaps you'd care to have a drink at the bar while we prepare it for you."

"Perhaps I would," I said magnanimously. "And I'd appreciate it, if you would be so kind as to send a bottle of your best champagne to the table once my guest and I have been seated."

"Of course, sir."

Moments later, I was standing at a polished wooden bar, a tumbler of eighteen-year-old Islay malt in my hand, scanning a dining room filled with the Great and the Good of London. What a strange, twisting journey from the workhouse on Baker's Row to here! And off to America in the morning. Who ever would have thought it?

I certainly wouldn't have. Not before I'd fallen in with Cain Goddard, at any rate. A wistful feeling came over me then. For better or for worse, I missed him.

I still don't know what happened that day, I said, silently, to him. *I'm not sure I ever will. I owe you so much more than to hop on a train and leave the question for St. Andrews—of all people!—to ponder. But I tried, and it's the best I can do. At least for now. I'm sorry.*

I drained the glass, set it down on the bar, and turned to find Lawrence at my side.

"More deep thoughts," he said, appreciatively rubbing the fine fabric of my jacket between his finger and thumb.

"More wrinkles, I suppose."

"Don't worry. The broken nose distracts from them." His words were teasing, but his tone was concerned. "Dear, dear, I'd no idea you were such a bruiser. You must tell me what happened."

Before I could respond, the maître d'hôtel arrived to take us to our table.

The Savoy was on fire with lively conversation and the pop and fizz of champagne. Mahogany walls surrounded us, carved and inlaid, and set off by crisp white linen tablecloths and red leather chairs. Enormous French doors opened onto a marble-paved courtyard, where Lawrence and I would later take our after-meal coffee by the central fountain, while watching the night traffic traverse the Thames.

"Your invitation was a pleasant surprise," he said, as he tucked himself into his seat at our table.

The table was small but well situated, with a view of the dining room to one side and the courtyard to the other. At that point, though, the only view that interested me was the vision directly in front of me. He'd had a haircut that day and was wearing the bright-green cravat and waistcoat he'd had on the first time I'd laid eyes on him at the Criterion.

"I was beginning to wonder if you'd bored of me," he said.

I laughed. "Never. My life has been rather complicated lately. I'm sorry it's kept me away."

He waved off the apology with a smile. "It happens, alas. Still… the Savoy. You must have something important to tell me."

"I do, as a matter of fact. And it's my treat tonight."

"Oh," he said, his tone filled with pleasure but his eyes growing wary.

Whenever we dined out, each of us always paid his own way. I'd chosen the Savoy because, even given his generous allowance, it was a little out of Lawrence's reach. Which meant that, under normal circumstances, it was well and truly out of mine—a fact he must have sensed at some level, even if we'd never discussed my situation.

"I came into some money recently," I said. "I wanted to share my good fortune."

He grinned and clapped his hands. "Well, in that case, I shall have to order champagne." At that moment, the waiter arrived with a bottle of Perrier Jouet and two flutes. "Oh!" He laughed. "I see you already have!"

"You've been very good to me, Lawrence," I said, as the waiter popped the cork and filled our glasses. "I'm not sure if you knew this, but when we met, my life was unsettled in many ways. Your friendship has helped me to…settle. It's meant a lot." I raised my glass.

He raised his glass, too, though his expression was tinged with rue. "You're dismissing me."

"I'm going to America," I replied.

"O-ho!" He tapped his glass against mine and we drained them. "Well, in that case, I must wish you bon voyage. Or, perhaps more appropriately," and here he imitated the flat, nasal American accent, "Have a nice trip. So you're dismissing me and then you're going *to* America." By God, he was delightful when he pouted. "So? When are you leaving? How long will you be gone? What's his name?"

I laughed and refilled our glasses. "Leaving tomorrow, gone for a month, maybe two. And *her* name is Claire."

He spluttered into his champagne. "*Claire?*" Then he frowned. "That sounds familiar. Should I know her?"

"I may have mentioned her. She's my friend's daughter. They're going to visit family in California and invited me to go along all expenses paid, if I agreed to look after Claire. Frankly, I think they have the better end of that deal."

"Mmm. Better you than me." He winked.

Tension crept into the silence between us, as we both tried to figure out what to say after that. I gazed out across the crowded dining room, looking for the waiter, while Lawrence examined the bottom of his empty flute. He poured himself another glass. When he spoke, his tone was light, but he wouldn't look at me.

"So I won't be seeing you again," he said.

"Don't be silly. I'll be back in a month. It'll be like I never left."

He looked up through his long lashes. His lips curled in a smile, but his eyes said he knew better. At that moment, the waiter appeared. I gestured for Lawrence to go first. Then I put in my order. When I looked back at him, the expression was gone, replaced by the lighthearted facetiousness that had attracted me to him in the first place.

I've had few more enjoyable dinners than that one, both as far as the food was concerned—well worth every farthing—and the company as well. Our conversation flowed with the champagne—and the procession of wines and liquors that followed—as always skating around the deeper questions. After the last plate was cleared, we retrieved our coats and hats, and emerged into the cool London evening. The Great Clock tolled one in deep, sonorous tones that shook the air around us.

"I suppose you have to go home to pack now," Lawrence said as his driver pulled a smart-looking hansom up to the curb.

"Actually, Whiteley's took care of the packing." The thought made me smile. "I've never been to America. I had to have new clothes and suitcases, didn't I?"

Lawrence laughed. "That sounds more like me than you." He cocked his head and looked at me curiously. "There's a lot I don't know about you, Mr. Adler."

"There's a lot we don't know about each other, Mr. Grey. Though it's a bit late to be thinking about these things now."

I opened the front gate of the hansom and gestured for him to alight. Stepping up, he moved to the far side of the bench in an unspoken invitation. I hesitated for a split second, then climbed in beside him and closed the gate in front of our knees. He knocked on the roof, and the hansom began to roll.

By the time we arrived back at his rooms, our various champagnes, wines, cognacs, and whiskeys had caught us up. We stumbled up the front stairs, giggling and hanging on to one another like a pair of overprivileged Piccadilly fops—which wasn't far off the mark, I supposed. His noisy attack on the door with his key—all in the name of sparing the butler a rude awakening—reduced us practically to hysterics. Finally inside, he locked the door behind him.

"Shh." He made a show of listening for the footsteps or voices of awakened servants. He looked back at me, eyes sparkling with mischief and alcohol. "Safe…for now."

He stripped off his coat and hung it on the hook near my head. I did the same, then pulled his floppy tie loose and yanked at his silk shirt until a couple of the tiny bone buttons clattered to the floor. I took a moment to let my fingers appreciate the solid, rugby-hardened muscles of his chest and stomach, and the spray of coarse hair that covered them, before he pinned me against the front door, his muscular arms holding me fast.

Then he dove in for a kiss and crushed my poor, broken nose with his enthusiasm.

"Oh, dear!" he cried, admirably holding back a giggle as I yelped in pain and clutched at the plaster. "I'm so sorry, Ira. Can you forgive me?"

He blinked fetchingly through the dim light the streetlamp was pouring through the glass panel at the top of the front door. My nose throbbed in time with my racing heart, but of course I would forgive him. I'd forgive him anything.

"Try again," I said. "But lower this time." I pushed his muscular shoulders gently downward until he knelt obligingly at my feet. Lawrence was nothing if not obliging.

His deft fingers made quick work of my belt buckle and trouser buttons. As he peeled back the fabric, a slow grin spread across his face. He took me in his mouth, and the world melted away in a dark wave of hot, wet velvet.

"No more than a month, promise me," he whispered when he pulled back for a breath. "I should die if you stayed away longer than that."

"Don't be silly." I took his chin in my hand, intending to chide him for exaggerating. Then I turned his face upward and realized he was not. What's more, if I were to be completely honest, I'd have had to admit to a similar sentiment stirring within my own breast. How had this come to pass, when we'd both taken conscious measures to prevent it? "Don't be silly," I said again, raking my fingers through his thick hair. "Of course I won't be any longer. Probably not even that long."

CHAPTER NINE

I woke as dawn was breaking and Lawrence's little housemaid was stirring in her attic room. From the sound of it, she was pulling on her stockings and would soon be down to light the fires. Though she no doubt loved Lawrence to distraction—as everyone who knew him did—she was his parents' employee, not his. I'd no idea whether they knew, or cared, about his sexual eccentricities, and no desire to be the one to bring the matter to their attention. The trials of Oscar Wilde had half of London looking for sodomites under their beds, and the other half sharpening their pitchforks. My poor former employer had been locked away at Pentonville not even a month earlier, and the press and public were desperate for another lamb to satisfy their bloodlust. Lawrence was discreet, but was discretion enough? His family's money could shield him from the law, provided he didn't make a spectacle of himself. But it could also buy a world of trouble for my young friend, should his parents decide to make him disappear into a private sanatorium or some other place where his behavior would cease to be an embarrassment.

I was fortunate in that way, I supposed. Even before Goddard's bequest had ensured my financial independence, I'd only answered to myself.

I scrawled a quick note, laid it on my pillow, quickly kissed his forehead, and gathered up my clothes. Peeking out the door and finding the hallway clear, I darted into the spare bedroom, threw back the bedclothes, and gave the pillow a punch. Then I dressed and made my way downstairs. As I was shrugging on my coat, the maid came down the stairs.

"Oh!" She squinted, and I realized that between the early morning gloom and my broken nose, she must not have recognized me. I was about to identify myself, when she suddenly blurted, "Mr. Adler, sir!"

She'd seen me before, of course. Lawrence's friends were a fun-loving group and often stayed in the spare bedroom, or on the sofa in the morning room, when their carousing lasted into the night.

"Good morning, Iris," I said. I touched the plaster covering my nose and winced. "Sorry to alarm you. I must look a fright."

She shrugged. "I seen worse. You want some breakfast on a tray before you go?"

"No, no. I'm meant to be somewhere early, and when I arrive, I can't look like I spent the night on the floor of a pub."

"I suppose not, sir," she said with a wry smile.

I put my new bowler on my head and gave it a tap. She crossed to the door and opened it for me.

"Please give my apologies to Lawrence and tell him I hope his head doesn't feel too god-awful," I said.

"Certainly, sir."

"And do look after yourself, Iris."

Dawn was chilly and gray, even in Chelsea. It was a miracle I found a cab that early. I could have walked, I supposed, but my head had started to pound, and my poor, battered nose throbbed to its rhythm. I was no teetotaler, but my body's capacity to absorb alcohol without effect seemed to diminish with every passing year. I hadn't slept more than three hours, and by the time I arrived at Victoria Station, I'd be feeling wretched indeed. I just hoped Claire would be on her best behavior.

The cab brought me to Aldersgate Street about twenty minutes later. Stepping down, I fished the appropriate coins from my pocket, promising the driver to make it well worth his while to return at nine to take me, and my luggage, to Victoria Station. Sinking down onto my bed, I tried to sleep, but I couldn't still my thoughts.

Goddard was dead. I was finally coming to terms with the idea. It would have helped if I'd been able to figure out who or why. But at least I'd given St. Andrews something to work with. The fact that I was leaving for America in a few short hours—now that gave me pause. The idea had seemed so abstract when Lazarus had proposed it. But the intervening days had passed quickly, and now the enormity of my promise was upon me. And then there was Lawrence. We enjoyed each other's company but had deliberately pushed away the idea of anything deeper. He was young and flighty, and I...well, I'd been looking for something unchallenging and fun. We had a pleasant arrangement, and it stood to reason that we'd both miss it. I hadn't counted on his developing more than a passing sentimental attachment. I *really* hadn't bargained for developing more than that myself.

Would the idea have come up at all if I hadn't announced I was leaving? I doubted it. I doubted it very much. Both Lawrence and I had our own reasons for maintaining a certain shallowness of acquaintance. And yet somehow, despite our best efforts, it had become more than that. And in a few short hours I'd be on a train.

And there was no chance, I thought, glancing at Goddard's damaged but still recalcitrantly ticking pocket watch, of getting some sleep before the driver returned at nine.

I rolled out of bed and stumbled over to the washstand. Stripping down to my underthings, I filled the washbowl and ran a wet cloth over my face, chest, and under my arms. Then I gave my beard some attention. My hair grew dark, fast, and thick. This had proved convenient during a period of experimentation, where I'd tried all sorts of new styles, with varying degrees of success. But who knew what would be fashionable in America? And who knew what sort of creams and soaps would be available to keep my choice in a reputable condition? Did cowboys even shave? There was nothing for it, really. I lathered up and cleared it all away. Then I slapped on a bit of cologne and helped myself to the new clothes that Mr. Cuttle and his assistants had packed into my new trunks.

There's something about brand-new clothing—not just the fact that I'd not purchased any since leaving York Street. The scratch of crisp, new linen drawn across the skin, the smell and crack of leather shoes heretofore unsullied by any man's feet—these things were fundamental sensate pleasures I'd denied myself for too long. I transferred my watch chain from my waistcoat pocket. Pausing, I glanced at the one Watkins had given me the day of the explosion—the one I'd given Goddard for his birthday all those years ago. Detaching my own trusty watch, I set it down on my bedside table and replaced it with the cracked, charred reminder of York Street.

When the driver returned at nine, both I, and my luggage, were ready.

❖

I'd caught a second wind by the time we reached Victoria Station. Many people considered the station to be a symbol of Britain's greatness, her dominance over the rest of the world, and now I understood why—high, glass ceilings arched overhead, supported by painted Corinthian columns and lacy ironwork buttresses, while down below, train tracks stretched out in all directions until they disappeared from view. The station was already crowded with people in their travel finery. Mine was not the only peacock-blue waistcoat nor the only new bowler. I was happy to see more than a few women who had adopted rational dress for their journey. The thought of sitting for several hours in a tight corset made me twitch. Others were daring the new, fitted skirts and jackets in striking colors. Excitement hummed in the air, building on the echoes of voices and footsteps off the glass and iron. For the moment, anyway, it was more than enough to take my mind off my throbbing head and nose.

I found the vast board showing departures and arriving trains, then, with two porters in tow, made my way to the platform from which my own train would be leaving. I tipped the porters, then took out my pocket watch. It was a little after ten. Where were Lazarus and his brood? I'd have expected them to be there already, waiting impatiently. Crossing my arms, I leaned against one of my trunks and felt for my cigarette case. No sooner had I found it than a sharp little voice cut through the din.

"Ira! Ira! Ira!"

Claire Amelia Campbell Lazarus had broken away from her parents and was racing toward me. She was a dark-blue blur of motion—having taught her parents early that light-colored clothing was incompatible with tree-climbing and puddle-stomping—and she slammed into my legs like a miniature steam train.

"Good morning, Mr. Adler," Bess called from behind her, futilely attempting to model politeness while she walked as quickly as was decorous in a vain effort to catch up. She and her daughter were dressed in very similar dark-blue cloaks over dresses of sturdy fabric and comfortable design, with sensible, well-made shoes beneath. Their single extravagance was a pair of matching midnight-colored velvet hats. Bess was attempting to sound cross, but her dark curls were bouncing, her cheeks were flushed with excitement, and her bright brown eyes danced with a smile.

"Morning, Ira," Claire mumbled into my neck as I crouched to pick her up. Her informality didn't bother me nearly as much as it did her parents. She was like her mother—she did as she pleased. I was just happy she'd stopped calling me Doggie.

"Good morning, Raisin Bun."

She pulled back, wrinkling her round little face in a frown. "Why do you keep calling me that?"

"Because you're as plump and sweet as one, and that's all your mother would eat just before you were born. Why, here's a raisin, now!" I pretended to pick one out of her chocolate-colored ringlets. But instead of dissolving in giggles like she normally would have, she pushed my hand away and squinted at my face.

"What's happened to your nose?" I stifled a cry as she tapped the plaster experimentally. "Papa always says if you don't stop sticking it where it doesn't belong, someone's going to punch it flat. Is that what happened?"

I laughed. "Papa always says that, does he? Well, he wasn't far off this time, I'm afraid."

Her eyes widened, and I stopped. The past five years at Turnbull House had taught me to temper my more colorful expressions. However, I was still learning how much honesty was too much for a little one. Breaking one's nose in a fight was nothing for the rough-and-tumble Turnbull House gang. But though Tim and Bess didn't hide their daughter from the ugliness of the world, I was quite sure they weren't raising her to be a brawling street tough.

"Well, actually," I corrected myself, "I found myself in an argument with a door. It was a most obstinate door," I explained as she started to laugh. "And it started the argument, not me. But in the end, it was faster and stronger than me. The police had to use a crowbar to pry it off. Rotten door went home without a scratch."

At that point, thankfully, Tim and Bess arrived to see nothing more than Uncle Ira reducing their cherub to gales of laughter. Bess breathed a sigh of relief, and Tim smiled.

"Glad to see you're here in plenty of time," Lazarus said to me. He was looking dapper in his best brown suit, his boots freshly polished, and holding what looked to be a new leather suitcase. A porter followed him, dragging a single steamer trunk. "Good God, what's happened to your nose?"

"You really don't want to know."

"Oh, but I do."

"He stuck it where it didn't belong." Claire hooted. "And then the police had to use a crowbar to pull his face out of the door!"

"Sounds about right," Lazarus said, peering closer. "That's a good plaster. Who did it?"

"Some quack at a charity clinic. They're all pretty much the same, you know."

My friend the former charity-clinic physician ignored the good-natured jab. "I could have patched it for you. Why didn't you come to me?"

"Because then I'd have had to tell you what really happened."

"Leave him alone, Tim," Bess said. "Let's get our luggage sorted and get on the train. Where are the tickets?"

Tim fixed me with a look that said we'd revisit this issue sooner rather than later. "Tickets are here." He held up a fat envelope, then, looking at my trunks, frowned and said, "Ira, just how long are you planning to stay in California?"

I looked from his trunk—the one that, apparently, contained provisions for his entire family—then glanced sheepishly at my own two, with three suitcases piled on top.

"Mr. Cuttle packed them."

"Who?"

"At Whiteley's. St. Andrews took me shopping, and..."

Stifling a smirk, Lazarus shook his head. "Oh, never mind." He issued some instructions to his own porter, who promptly whistled up some help. "I assume you'll tip generously," he told me as the men began to lug away our baggage.

"I always do."

Our train pulled into the station then: a sleek, shiny metal monster that chuffed up the tracks toward us, then hissed to a stop. The doors opened, and passengers began to stagger out the doors. Claire was starting to wiggle, so I set her down but held her hand firmly. The platform was crawling with people and filled with all sorts of unseen dangers into which my charge would be only too happy to run headlong.

"Ira!" another voice called.

I turned to see Lawrence striding through the crowd. He was resplendent in a dove-gray frock coat with a crimson waistcoat and matching floppy bow tie. An exquisite gray hat covered his blond curls, and though his blue eyes were slightly bloodshot from the night's excesses, they sparkled merrily.

"I found your note," he said, stopping just short of me. Given our drunken declarations, I hadn't felt right simply leaving. I'd invited him to see us off, if he cared to. Apparently he did. Spying Claire, he knelt down and offered his hand. "You must be the Lady Claire. My name is Lawrence. I'm only a lowly earl's son, but I'm ever so pleased to meet you."

Claire, suddenly shy, giggled and allowed him to press her chubby hand between his.

"I'm glad you came," I said as he rose.

For a moment we stood there, caught between the things we desperately wanted to say and the fact that there was no way to say them while surrounded by people. Claire, sensing the tension, began to fuss. I let go her hand, and she dashed off in the direction of her parents.

"I'm going to miss you, you know," Lawrence said, finally.

We stepped out of the crush of people, toward a peaceful spot near the wall. I could still taste the salt of his good-bye on my tongue, hear his gasped oaths as we...

Smiling, I said, "No, you won't." His expression registered hurt, and I was reminded how very young he was, and how very unaccustomed to true loss. I adjusted the corners of his high collar. They were always getting stuck beneath his ties. "You'll find someone else to fill the hole in your social schedule. Probably before you even leave the station."

His smile turned pained. "But I shall miss *you*. And, truth be told, I'm quite jealous of your adventure. I've always wanted to see New York."

"The only parts of New York I'll be seeing are the docks and the train station."

"Still."

"Just one month," I said, resisting the urge to brush my fingers over his newly shaved cheek. "And I'll write when I get there. No, I'll send a telegram. It'll be faster."

"I'd like that."

An awkward few seconds passed. Lawrence shuffled his feet, and I tugged at the scratchy collar of the new shirt I'd purchased for the trip. As much money as I'd spent on it, you'd think it might be a bit more comfortable. I hadn't really expected Lawrence would come to see me off. I'd tried very hard to convince myself his new sentimentality would fade away when the alcohol left his system. And I really hadn't expected my own sentiments to last through the morning. It would figure that the first time my personal life took a pleasant turn, I'd have one foot on a train.

"Why are you laughing?" Lawrence asked, a gentle smile playing at the edges of his lips.

"Because I'm going to miss you, as well. Quite a bit, actually."

His smile broadened. I really wanted to kiss him right then. But with Wilde's name on the sharp tongue of every gossip in London, neither of us needed the sort of trouble that would bring. Instead, I took out an envelope I'd prepared and handed it to him.

"This is my solicitor's card, and instructions for the disposal of my belongings, should I be trampled in a cattle stampede or run over by tumbleweeds."

He gave a sharp little gasp. Again I was struck by how little of the world he actually knew, for such a jaded young man.

"Please be careful, Ira. Don't get into a gunfight, or eaten by a bear, or—"

"Don't worry." I laughed. "One month, no more. I'll bring you back your own ten-gallon hat, if you haven't forgotten my name by then."

He looked so forlorn at that, and I realized how cruel my words must have sounded in light of his newly discovered attachment. Perhaps it was my way of distancing myself from the sting of separation. Whatever the reason, it was unnecessarily harsh.

"I didn't mean that," I said. My throat had gone unexpectedly tight. "You've meant a lot to me, Lawrence. More than you can imagine. And I'll be ever so happy to see you again when I return."

He nodded. Bit his lower lip. "I...I am quite fond of you, you know."

"And I of you."

Any subsequent displays of gross sentimentality were scuttled by the arrival of a panicked Bess.

"Ira, where's Claire?"

I frowned. "Isn't she with you?"

"With *me*? Ira, we hired *you* to look after her!"

My heart began to pound as I scanned the thick clots of people gathering around the doors of the train. Men in open-cut coats and top hats. Women in colorful dresses. A scattering of children—just not the one with whose safety I'd been charged. How could I have lost her before we'd even boarded the train?

"Claire!" I shouted, my voice rising.

"I'll look over there," Lawrence said, and rushed toward the waiting room.

I nodded. "Claire!" I called again. I pushed through the crowd, caught a flash of dark blue out of the corner of my eye, and whirled. No—that was some woman's cloak. "Claire!"

Suddenly, I saw her. She was near the entrance to the main hall, holding court with a well-dressed man, her dark curls bobbing beneath her little velvet hat as she related some story. To this day I couldn't say what it was about the man that raised my hackles. He was outfitted like a gentleman. His smile seemed friendly enough. If pressed, I might have said there was something predatory in his posture. He was bending to speak to her, much like Lawrence had. But Lawrence had knelt. This man was crouched such that if she were to bolt, he could spring after her with little effort.

Suddenly she turned to me. "Ira!"

She dashed toward me. The man did spring after her but, seeing me bearing down on them, stopped, a nervous laugh coming from behind his pointed beard.

"There's Daddy," the man said through clenched teeth. "We were just waiting for him, weren't we, love?"

Claire threw her arms around my legs. I wrapped a protective arm around her shoulders. "Who's your friend, Claire?" I asked shakily. My pulse was racing. I felt light-headed and suddenly very, unreasonably angry with this man.

The man stopped short, well out of my reach, and tipped his silk top hat. He was about my age, give a year or two. Like Lawrence, he was blond and dripping with money. Unlike Lawrence, however, he gave off an unmistakable stench of menace.

"We were just having a chat, that's all," the man said, brushing a bit of imaginary lint from the sleeve of his black coat.

"About what?" I demanded.

The man met my eyes. What I saw there chilled me. But not as much as his subsequent smile. "About how it never profits a man to go sniffing around things that are none of his concern. Good day, Mr. Adler."

With a smirk the man turned and disappeared into the crowd.

"Who was that?" Claire asked.

"I don't know, but Raisin Bun, promise me you'll never go off by yourself like that again."

"I promise."

Apparently forgetting her promise the moment the words left her mouth, she danced three steps to the left before I caught her collar in my hand. Footsteps slapped up behind me, and a hand came down on my shoulder. I whirled.

"Good God in Heaven, Lawrence!" I cried, my heart still pounding.

I'd expected to find his easy smile, the amusement of a prank between friends. But when I turned, his expression was serious.

"Did you know that man?" he asked, his voice filled with horror.

"Never seen him before. Who is he?"

"I don't know his name, but he works with Rupert Sudworth."

Oh, God. *Oh, God!* Now I knew I hadn't been imagining Sudworth's smug hints back at his office in St. James's. I hadn't any tangible evidence, but it couldn't be clearer, now, that Sudworth had had a hand in Goddard's death. *He* had planted the water-heater story with the fire brigade. After breaking my nose, Fireman Morris had probably reported back to him, and he'd sent his well-dressed little friend to restate the warning.

Between this and Wilde's arrest, I was suddenly very happy to be leaving London for a bit.

Then an even more disturbing thought struck me. "Lawrence, do I want to know how you would recognize one of Sudworth's lackeys?"

His expression told me he found the idea as disconcerting as I had. "I was visiting my father at the Houses of Parliament last spring." Lawrence's father, he'd mentioned once, was a member of the House of Lords. "We passed Sudworth and his associate in the corridor, and my father introduced us." He gave a little shudder. "Sudworth was pleasant, but I noted something *unsavory* about him. No, more than merely unsavory, it was..." He looked at me, then, and in his clear eyes, I saw once again the cosseted child of privilege who worried about me being eaten by a bear in America. "Believe me, Ira, that's as close as I'd ever want to come to either of them. Please don't tell me *you*..."

"Not in this lifetime or any other," I replied shortly. "Right. Come here, Raisin Bun."

Keeping one foot over both of Claire's, I balanced a scrap of paper on the crown of her hat and took out a pen. When I finished the note, I folded it and handed it to Lawrence. "Do you know Andrew St. Andrews?" I asked.

He gave a nervous laugh. "Does anyone *not* know him?"

"Take this directly to his Baker Street rooms. Make certain you're not followed, and don't breathe a word of this to anyone. And do look after yourself, Lawrence." This time I couldn't help laying a discreet hand on his elbow. "If you should come to harm because of my actions, I don't think I could bear it."

CHAPTER TEN

I'm happy to report that our train arrived in Liverpool without further incident. This is because I told Bess I'd found Claire talking to a grandmotherly woman with a poodle, rather than to a silk hat-wearing minion of Rupert sodding Sudworth. They say confession is good for the soul, but I'd prefer to discuss that with my maker after a long, happy life, rather than after being pushed under a locomotive at the tender age of thirty by Elizabeth Campbell Lazarus. Understandably, Bess spent the entire journey sitting in my seat next to Claire, while I sat across from them with Tim. When the train pulled into Liverpool Central Station, we took our bags and exited the cabin.

"It was a very kind gesture to move us up to first class," Lazarus said. "I don't think I've ever enjoyed such a comfortable ride."

"Does it make up, somewhat, for my disastrous performance as your nanny?"

"I think it'd be best for everyone if we were simply traveling companions from now on. Besides, you no longer need the employment. Still," he said, looking wistfully back at the wood-paneled cabin, the well-padded, freshly upholstered seats, and the glass decorated with frosted flourishes. "This was very, very decent of you." Sighing, he pulled the inlaid door shut and used his sleeve to rub away a fingerprint.

"Don't let him get used to it, Ira," Bess said, weaving Claire's hand firmly through her arm. "He may never go back to Turnbull House."

"Turnbull House would carry on just as well without us," Tim said, a bit sadly.

"What rubbish," muttered Bess. "The place would crumble without you, and you know it."

Tim and Bess had left the shelter in the care of nurse Pearl Brandt, who ran Tim's Stepney Street clinic, and a Miss Fields, who would be teaching the residents in Bess's absence. In addition, Jack Flip, a

Turnbull House graduate who had gone on to bigger and better things, had promised to stop by now and then. Of course the shelter would function without Tim for a few weeks, I but wondered how he would function without the weight of the responsibilities to which he'd become so accustomed.

"I'm hungry," Claire said.

Bess glanced at the watch pinned to the breast of her jacket. "It is close to teatime."

"Then I suggest we send our baggage along to the hotel and find a tearoom fit for Lady Claire," I said, taking the little girl's other hand. She had been remarkably patient and well behaved on the train, and she hadn't said a word to her parents about Sudworth's man. "Come along, Lazarus family. Uncle Ira is buying."

Food and a sound night's sleep can work miracles upon a person's mental state. By the time we found our way to the Port of Liverpool the next morning, our petty irritations had faded in our minds, and we were, the four of us, filled with high spirits. Seagulls wheeled above us on the cool, fishy breeze, and though the motion of the water beneath the dock made me dizzy, I felt a rush of excitement at the prospect of our journey.

"There she is," Tim said, gesturing to a vast, gleaming steamship. "The SS *Teutonic*."

"She's magnificent," Bess said.

"She'd better be, if we're going to be stuck aboard for an entire week," I replied.

The *Teutonic* had once made the passage to New York in five days, though our journey would probably take closer to seven. She was impressive, though, I had to admit—almost six hundred feet long from bow to stern, with three masts and two great smokestacks painted bright yellow, which contrasted with her sleek, black body. That morning her flags were flying, the gangplank was down, and well-dressed passengers were already beginning to make their way aboard.

"Just wait until you see the inside," Tim said. "There are restaurants, swimming pools, a smoking lounge—even a library! Pity the best parts will be closed to third-class passengers, but we'll at least be able to catch a glimpse in passing."

I stopped. "Third class? You mean *steerage*?"

I tried to imagine little Claire bumping about a huge dormitory filled with rough men and foul-mouthed women; meals served up in buckets; stagnant and pestilence-riddled air breathed in and out of the same thousand sets of lungs for five to seven days.

"Our family will have its own cabin, Ira. This is a White Star ship, after all. Though I should very much have liked to see that library."

"Steerage!" I cried again. Then I shook my head. "No."

"What do you mean, no? Ira—"

His protest caught in his throat as Claire chose that moment to shout "Bird!" and tear off after a seagull. As Bess dashed after her, I snatched the tickets from Tim's hand and strode off in the direction of the ship.

"Won't be but a moment," I called over my shoulder. Lazarus could do what he wanted, but no way would I allow Bess and Claire to spend seven days crammed like sardines in the bowels of a ship—not while I had the means to do something about it. And not while I was still mortified about what had almost happened to Claire while I was meant to be watching her.

"Come back here, Adler!" Lazarus cried, but he was looking toward Bess. I ignored him.

"Can I help you, sir?"

I stopped at the pleasant voice and the equally pleasant countenance that had suddenly appeared between myself and the *Teutonic*. A bright-eyed young man in his mid-twenties, with creamy skin, a spray of freckles across his upturned nose, and a head full of cropped, sand-colored waves, he, even more fortuitously, wore the dapper dark-blue and white uniform of a White Star employee. I was suddenly struck by the urge to ask him to turn around so I could see how the trousers were cut from behind.

"I was looking for the ticketing office," I replied, shaking my head clear of the pleasant images dancing there. "By some mistake, my party has found itself booked into steerage."

He took the documents from my hand and looked me up and down, taking in my fine linen coat and silk shirt; thin, bright-blue, American-style tie and matching waistcoat. His gaze lingered at my crotch for just an instant—but it was an instant that would have earned him a beating from a different man. It spoke volumes about his ability to judge character—or at least about his experience. He flicked his eyes back to mine, a shadow of amusement playing about his lips.

"Third class? Oh, that won't do. Not at all, Doctor."

He had read the name on the first ticket and taken me for Lazarus. God forbid. But it could only help my cause to be mistaken for an upstanding member of society. I didn't correct him. He handed the documents back.

"Can anything be done about it at this late hour?" I asked, casually reaching into my trouser pocket and producing a few coins.

He cocked an eyebrow. "Oh, I'm sure we can think of something." He caught his lower lip in his teeth. "But why don't you keep your money in case you wish to share a bottle of wine with someone you meet on board, say below the starboard side staircase on the promenade deck around ten this evening?"

He met my eyes again, and I found myself biting back a laugh. His interest was flattering, and not unwelcome. Briefly I thought of Lawrence and felt a hot flash of guilt. Just a few hours before, we'd both confessed to a depth of feeling that could easily have led to something more—something neither of us had, to that point, imagined but that we both, I think, would have liked to explore. On the other hand, neither Lawrence nor I had made any promises. As fond of me as he'd claimed to be, he'd not revealed any intention to abandon his other playmates, nor entreated me to stay true. I'd only been half joking when I'd predicted he'd find a new admirer before leaving Victoria Station.

And I'd be gone only a month. We would have plenty of time to explore deeper sentiments, should those sentiments survive this short separation.

"In the meantime," my dapper friend continued, seemingly unaware of my dilemma, "the ticketing office is just over there. You'll find that plenty of second-class staterooms are available. Every bit as nice as first class, but half the price, and you won't have to spend seven days surrounded by overfed aristocrats and swindling businessmen." A cheeky grin softened his sharp words.

"Thank you." It would be a good compromise, I thought, between my desire for comfort and Tim's all-encompassing social conscience. "I shall do that."

My new friend was about to utter some witticism, I could tell, when a commotion broke out near the gangplank. Through the crowd that was gathering, I caught sight of an empty wheelchair, a set of suitcases scattered around it, and someone struggling on the ground.

"Oh, dear," my young man said. He shrugged one well-formed shoulder and sighed. "I'd best see if I can help. One's work, it seems, is never done."

"Ten o' clock, then?" I called as he turned to leave, affording me a glimpse of a magnificent posterior set off by well-cut white trousers. Smiling back over his shoulder, he gave a little toss of his head, then walked purposefully toward the bother at the foot of the gangplank.

Whistling a little tune, I set off to change our reservations.

❖

Our second-class suite turned out to be more than adequate, both for Tim's moral sensibilities and for my desire to assuage my guilt. The staterooms were located on the upper deck toward the stern—plenty of windows, wide corridors, and access to the fresh sea air. There was a fine dining saloon nearby, and we had access to both the library and an elegant smoking room on the promenade deck. Our suite consisted of separate bedrooms for the Lazaruses and myself, connected by a common area. The lavatory and baths were conveniently but not uncomfortably near.

"Oh, Tim, have you ever seen anything so lovely?" Bess flung herself down onto a generous double bed in one of the rooms. She ran her fingers over the crimson velvet spread, as if she'd never experienced such luxury. While porters brought our trunks into the common area, Claire grinned at her reflection in the wood-paneled walls.

"I say." I addressed one of the porters. "When do you expect we'll be departing?"

The man dropped his end of the trunk he was carrying, tipped it to a stand, and gave it a pat. Pushing his cap back onto his balding pate, he ran a crisply uniformed forearm across his brow. It was the same uniform worn by the young man with whom I'd later be sharing the bottle of Bordeaux I'd purchased, but with slightly different piping on the sleeves.

"Oh, it'll be a little while, yet, sir. The captain don't want to leave until he hears from the ship's doctor."

"The doctor? Is the captain unwell?" Lazarus asked, appearing in the doorway of his room. He'd removed his jacket and was rolling up the sleeves of his shirt.

"One of the passengers had a fall. White Star don't want him filing no complaint, so they're holding up the ship until the doctor sees him."

"Was that the man with the wheelchair near the gangplank? I think I saw that happen," I said.

The porter nodded. "Colonel Wright, sir. He tried to walk up onto the ship, but his legs gave way. I say if he needs a wheelchair, he shouldn't be walking up no gangplank no ways, but I figure White Star wants to be sure they're in the clear."

"A colonel, you say?" Tim asked. "Do you know where he served?" Tim had been a surgeon in the Second Afghan War—a fact he'd hidden for a long time, though in recent years, he'd rather enjoyed making the acquaintance of other veterans.

The porter looked thoughtful. "Couldn't tell you, sir. But his name's Wright. Colonel Jeremiah Wright."

Tim frowned. "Never heard of him. How old would you say he is?"

The porter shrugged and straightened his cap. "Couldn't say for sure, but he looks sixty, sixty-five. Now, were there anything else before I go?"

Lazarus shook his head. The porters left, and he turned to me.

"Sixty to sixty-five. That's about the right age to have been a higher officer in Afghanistan. There weren't that many about. One would think I'd at least have heard his name. Hmm." He shrugged. "Ah, well, I suppose there are worse reasons for delay and worse places to be stuck waiting."

"Like steerage," I said.

A few hours later we were at sea, and the English coastline was a mere suggestion behind us on the horizon. Bess had decided to take some sun, and Lazarus was stretched out on his bed, up to his ears in Kipling. Though I had, through my own incompetence, relieved myself of my official nanny duties, I was as bored as Claire was, and almost as close to causing some sort of disturbance to amuse myself.

Standing, I cleared my throat. "I understand there's a well-appointed playroom on the promenade deck. Lady Claire, would you care to investigate with me?"

"Playroom! Playroom!"

She sprang up from the floor, where she'd been methodically removing objects from her mother's handbag and arranging them along the edge of the carpet.

"Yes, please, Mr. Adler," Tim intoned from his berth. "And put your mother's things back in her bag before you go."

I watched as Claire carefully replaced Bess's items and fastened the bag shut. Then, duly chastened, she took my hand.

We made our way down the stairs to the spacious promenade deck: an eighth of a mile of shaded, unobstructed walking surface, punctuated by smoking rooms, shops, the famous ship's library, and all manner of amusements for first- and second-class passengers. The afternoon was bright, with a crisp, clean breeze that I was sorry to leave behind at the door of the children's room. As Claire and I stepped inside, my resignation turned to horror.

The playroom was indeed well stocked with rocking horses, balls, sets of draughts and chess, dollies—even a tricycle. It was also jammed to the rafters with squealing, sticky-fingered children trailing cake crumbs and snot. As Claire launched herself into the fray, I shrank into a corner, reflexively swiping at my cuffs and trouser legs while genteel clusters of nannies alternately gaped at the unexpected intrusion of this unruly male and tittered behind their hands.

"The first time is a shock, is it not?" remarked a young woman to my right. I was quite certain she hadn't been there when I'd entered. She must have come in just after I did.

Dressed in a governess's plain, sturdy clothing, she was blond and fine-featured, like Claire's porcelain-faced dolly. She wore a frayed, knitted shawl wrapped around her shoulders and neck. It seemed a bit much for the weather, but there had been a breeze on deck, and many of the women I'd known seemed to feel cold more keenly than I did. This young lady's precise, deliberate way of speaking—and the fact that she'd spoken first—hinted at a background closer to my own than to that suggested by her clipped, upper-middle-class pronunciation. Which is why I didn't latch onto the opportunity for adult conversation as if it were a life preserver. As hard as she must have worked to attain her current position, I was loath to jeopardize her livelihood by giving the appearance of impropriety.

"The secret is to never show your fear," she said. "They can smell it, like dogs."

As if sensing some impending disaster, the young woman suddenly—and rather like a dog herself—whipped her head toward a toddler with a wooden locomotive in his hand, who was approaching an unsuspecting child from behind.

"Cuthbert!" Her tone made me pull up straight. "You will not hit that child with that train!" The child didn't turn toward her voice nor acknowledge her words. But after a tottering step or two farther, he seemed to forget what he was doing and wandered off in another direction. The nanny turned back to me with a smile. "After a while it becomes second nature. That's not your daughter, clearly."

I glanced toward Claire, who had somehow, in the short time since we'd entered, gathered a crowd of children around her and was instructing them to build some grand edifice from alphabet blocks.

"My friends' daughter," I replied, abandoning my attempt to protect the governess from the consequences of her boldness. If she wasn't bothered, I wouldn't be. "We're traveling together. Thought I'd give them a rest for an hour or two. She's quite a handful."

"I can see that." She turned to face me directly. "Excuse my forwardness. It's just been me and him since we left London, and I'm losing my mind. My name is Lila Wood."

I gave a little bow. "Pleased to meet you, Miss Wood. My name is—"

"That's quite a set of bruises," she said. "And a plaster, too, no less. Did someone bash *you* with a toy train?"

I laughed. I couldn't help it.

"I'm sorry. I swear I don't know how to speak to adults anymore," she went on, though she didn't sound sorry at all.

"It's all right," I said. "You remind me of my friend Bess—that little one's mother." I nodded toward Claire. "She, too, is a handful."

Miss Wood arched her artfully shaped eyebrows. "Do you like complicated women?" She let out a little giggle. "Oh, dear, that really was uncivilized of me. You must think me quite rude."

"Actually, I find it refreshing," I stammered, though my ears suddenly felt hot. This young lady was not my type, to say the least, but her brash flirtation and unexpected charm left me temporarily flummoxed. "That is to say, I've never had much use for the vague back-and-forth that people seem to find so necessary before saying what they really mean. I rather respect a person who speaks plainly."

"Exactly!" Miss Wood leaned in confidentially. "That's one reason I'm happy to be accompanying the family to America. I hear they're a frightfully direct people, Americans. Have you ever been?"

"Me? I've never been outside of London."

"Me either!" She clapped her hands together delightedly. "Oh, my, we seem to have quite a bit in common. We're going to be such good friends, I can tell." She grinned wickedly and laid a hand on my elbow.

"Ah." I drew back physically as well as conversationally.

Her boldness, I could see now, was more than high spirits. She was looking for male company, either because she was keen for a shipboard adventure or, more likely, because she was looking to supplement her income. Either way, what unutterable daring in so public a place, with her little charge not ten feet away. And how lost on me—more than she could ever know—were her efforts.

"Shall we step outside for a moment?" she asked, appearing to take my silence for assent. "The children will be quite all right, I'm sure, with twenty nannies looking on."

I followed her, thinking to quietly dismiss her advances in private. As I shut the door behind us, the fresh sea air hit me like a cool wave.

"My dear Miss Wood," I said with a chuckle.

"A ship is such a romantic setting, don't you think?"

"For some, perhaps, but—"

She took my elbow and blinked up at me with wide, blue eyes. "It brings together people who might never have otherwise met—and, who, once the journey has ended, are unlikely to ever meet again, if you understand my meaning."

"My dear Miss Wood, I really must—"

"Oh!" cried another voice. My heart leaped to my throat as a certain sandy-haired young man in ship's uniform rounded the corner. "Good afternoon, Doctor. Missus. Hope you're enjoying your journey so far."

"Yes…" I stammered. "Quite."

With a wink, my young man tipped his hat and continued along the promenade, the fabric of his exquisitely cut trousers swishing together as he strode down the polished floorboards.

"Doctor," cooed Miss Wood appraisingly.

"I really must go." I untangled my arm from hers and smoothed down the arm of my coat. "I've enjoyed talking to you, Miss Wood, but it would be a mistake for us to meet again."

"If you say so," she said, not at all dissuaded.

"I do."

My head spinning, I began to walk away. Then she called.

"Doctor? Doctor!" Good God, she meant me! I turned. She gestured toward the nursery door. "Aren't you forgetting someone?"

CHAPTER ELEVEN

The second-class dining saloon far exceeded my expectations—Tim's, as well, from the way he gaped at the high ceilings tinted ivory and gold, the gold-touched wood paneling, and the brasswork polished to a gleam. He let out a long breath when we finally took our places in plush chairs fixed to the floor before one of the long, wooden tables arranged in rows across the large hall.

As for me, I was too busy looking over my shoulder for Miss Wood. There was no sign of her, to my relief. Perhaps she and her charge had taken an early supper.

"What ever is the matter, Ira?" Bess asked, fiddling with her silverware. "You're as jumpy as a jackrabbit."

"A what?"

"I'll have the consommé," she said to the waiter, handing him her menu card. "Followed by the roast beef with cauliflower and potatoes, and the brandy snaps for dessert."

"Yes, ma'am."

She turned back to me. "I suppose we're all a bit nervous about the trip. But hasn't everything been just splendid so far?"

"The playroom was certainly impressive," I replied. Then, turning to the waiter, "Olives on toast, potage à la reine, roast duck, and rice. No dessert for me tonight."

"Very good, sir. And for you, sir?" The waiter turned to Lazarus.

"My daughter will also have the consommé with, ah, the mutton cutlets and rice. Ice cream for dessert. As for me…" Tim, who had been toying with the idea of vegetarianism for the last few months, heaved a great sigh. "Well, the same for me, I suppose."

The waiter nodded, collected his menu card, and disappeared into the rapidly filling saloon.

"Don't worry, Tim," I said. "One day they'll have filet au lettuce and turnip cutlets on every menu."

"I wouldn't expect you to understand, Adler," he said primly. Then, smiling, he leaned back in his chair and raised his wineglass. "Small irritations aside, I can't imagine a more pleasant way to travel. I hope the voyage hasn't been too hard for you first-timers. As for me, I must say that I find second class aboard the *Teutonic* to be far superior to Her Majesty's accommodations for soldiers bound for Afghanistan."

"Hear, hear," Bess said.

"And while we have Ira to thank, again, for our sumptuous surroundings, we shouldn't forget that it's Bess's mother who is giving us the excuse to make the trip in the first place."

"Granny!" squealed Claire.

"Yes," said Tim, raising his glass. "To Granny and her gold mine."

"Depleted gold mine," Bess added. "Though apparently that's not enough to dissuade Samuel Curtis."

Her expression turned sour at the mention of the man who had been pressuring her mother to sell the claim that had been bequeathed to her.

"If the claim is as worthless as you say, why doesn't your mother want to sell?" I asked.

She took a thoughtful sip from her water glass. "I really couldn't tell you. Of course I wouldn't sell Samuel Curtis a teaspoon of vinegar if his throat were on fire. There's something about him that just makes a person *want* to thwart him. You can judge for yourself. I'm sure you'll meet him soon enough."

"So you know the man?" I asked.

"I met him when I went back to California for my father's funeral. My parents had retired there because they wanted to give Irene the chance to lead a normal life—already having failed their older daughter by dragging her all over Asia bandaging lepers until she was too old and intractable to find a husband."

"You found me," Tim said. "And I like you intractable. I certainly couldn't keep the Turnbull House group in line by myself."

"But you have to admit, I was very fortunate to meet you. I was nearly thirty when we were married. Not that I was pinning my hopes on marriage, but most men—"

"I'm not most men," Tim said with mock affront.

Bess sent her husband a look so sweet, I felt it in my teeth. "No, darling, you're certainly not. At any rate, I don't think Samuel Curtis was quite what my parents had in mind for Irene—especially not when he asked my father's permission to begin courting her the day after her sixteenth birthday."

"That's not so uncommon," Tim said.

"It wasn't uncommon in the areas where my parents did their missionary work, either, so they had a lot of time to observe what that meant on a practical level. They wanted Irene to have the opportunity to marry if she wished, but they didn't want her to tie herself down to some man my father's age and start having babies when she wasn't much more than a baby herself. Whatever she did with her life, they wanted her to be mature enough to make a considered decision."

"Very sensible," I said.

"I thought so."

I continued. "Do you think their refusal had anything to do with Curtis later going after your mother's gold claim?"

Bess looked thoughtful. "I don't think so. Curtis is an extremely wealthy man. Cattle. And not bad looking. He found another girl right away—Dottie. She was a year ahead of Irene in school. They're married now. It's for the best, really. After following our parents all over the world, it was difficult for Irene to adjust to life in a town of a few hundred people. And she's such a lively girl. I think we all expected she'd be off to some far-flung place doing missionary work of her own one day. She'd be miserable stuck in Pyrite for the rest of her life—even if it was on the biggest ranch in Central California."

The food arrived then, and for a while everything was quiet while we tucked into probably the finest meal the Lazarus family had enjoyed in quite a while.

What strange and varied paths we all followed through life. Bess had been born—somewhere near Ningpo, I think—to missionary parents. Irene followed about a decade later. When Bess was in her late twenties, the family was stopping in London on their way back to the States. They met Pearl Brandt—Tim's nurse at the Bethnal Green clinic—at a church service. When it was time to continue on to America, Bess felt called to stay in London and work with the poor on the East End. Pearl helped her establish herself and, a year or two later, introduced her to Tim.

Who at that point had just broken his heart over a fickle little rotter named Adler.

"Leave Curtis to me," Tim was saying when I emerged from my thoughts. "I'd wager I'm more than a match for some bloated American plutocrat."

"I'm not too bad in a fight, if it comes to it," I said.

"I doubt it will come to blows," Bess said with a smile. "Not physically, anyway. But are you saying you fancy another bout so soon after having your nose broken?"

My hand went reflexively to my plaster. Which reminded me, of course, that I was meeting my young man later that evening. Egad.

"When can I remove this?" I asked.

"Worried about your handsome face?" Lazarus asked.

"Maybe."

"If it's not hurting anymore, we can take it off after dinner."

"Really?"

Lazarus smirked. "Why? Have somewhere to be?"

I looked at Bess and Claire. Then I raised my glass. "To Granny!"

❖

Ten o'clock couldn't come fast enough. As promised, Lazarus had removed the plaster from my nose the moment we returned to the stateroom. The clinic doctor hadn't done a bad job, I thought as I inspected my face in a wood-framed mirror. The bruises were still shocking—like a purple mask across the middle part of my face. As for the nose itself, only a small rise near the bridge evidenced the damage. Not in a bad way, though. In fact, from a certain angle it was rather dashing.

"You look rugged," Bess said playfully. "It suits you."

"It's not bad at all, is it?" Giving my reflection one final glance, I straightened the sleeves of one of the new jackets I'd bought with St. Andrews and slapped on a bit of cologne. Out of the corner of my eye, I caught Bess smiling as she watched my preparations. My preferences were no secret to her and Tim, who were as close to family as I had. I'm not sure how she reconciled her religious convictions with this knowledge, but, strangely, I couldn't help thinking that on some level, she was happy for me.

"I'm going for a walk," I said, tucking my bottle of Bordeaux beneath my arm. As an afterthought, I took the thoughtfully provided corkscrew and two water glasses from their place on the sideboard.

"Mind you're quiet when you return," said Tim. "If you wake

Claire, you'll be putting her back to bed."

Few people were walking the promenade at ten o'clock. Those who were, were too engaged in their own business to stick their noses into mine. The air was chilly, and above the ship, a clear, moonless sky spread out like black velvet riddled with thousands of pinpricks of light.

"It's quite a sight, isn't it, Doctor?" a soft voice asked as I wandered past. My new friend stepped out from below the staircase to stand beside me. Lamplight gleamed on his round face, erasing the freckles and giving his skin a smooth, marble sheen. "I lived in London my whole life and never saw anything like it. My first trip out, I knew I could never go back to a place where I couldn't see the stars. I've made a study of the constellations. There's Hydra the Water Snake, for instance." He pointed as I set the glasses down on one of the metal slat stairs. "That's the largest one. And Leo the Lion is right there, standing on his head."

As he nattered on, I uncorked the wine. The dark ruby red looked black in the light of the single lamp. Quiet wrapped us like a thick blanket, interrupted only by his soft, even voice and the *shoosh* of the water rushing across the steel sides of the ship. I poured the first glass and set it in his hand. Then I poured my own. We raised our wine in a silent salute and drank.

"Where's home now?" I asked.

He smiled—lamplight on straight, even teeth—and gestured toward the spacious expanse of the sea. "All around us. It's hard work, but I couldn't imagine doing anything else."

"Must be lonely sometimes."

His full lips twisted wryly. "Actually, I've never had so much company in my life, and it changes every seven days. But that's not what you want to hear."

"No, it's not."

I took the glass from his hand, set it down, and tugged at his cuff, pulling him after me into the shadows beneath the staircase. There, invisible in the darkness, he pushed me up against the wall, gently, but with surprising strength, and pinned me there with a kiss. His lips were soft, his tongue expert. His mouth tasted like my Bordeaux. The heat rising off his skin brought the evening chill into sharp focus.

"You've lost your plaster," he said, brushing his fingers over my newly exposed nose.

"It was time."

"Doctor knows best." The fingers explored the new hump near the bridge. "Such a ruffian," he purred. "How did it happen?"

"Rather personal question, considering I don't even know your name," I murmured as he nibbled the sensitive skin beneath my ear.

He took my hand and thrust it down the front of his trousers. "Call me Nicholas."

And he was. Knickerless, that is. A brave choice while wearing such tight trousers. He gave a little sigh when I closed my hand around his cock. He was already hard, and from the dimensions my fingers perceived, I was glad I'd saved my appetite.

The softest metallic creak broke the quiet—too far away to be the stairs above us, thankfully, but it was clear we were no longer alone.

"Shh," I said.

I watched as two figures emerged from around the corner near the bow—a young man pushing a wheelchair and a much-older man sitting upon it. They were facing away from us. Even if they hadn't been, though, the proximity of the lamp would have made it impossible to distinguish their features. Distance obscured their words, but from the old man's gestures, it looked as if he, too, was pointing out the constellations to his companion.

"Colonel Wright and his attendant," whispered Nicholas.

"So the ship's doctor considers him fit to travel after his fall?"

"Apparently."

"I heard he served in Afghanistan. Do you know where? One of my traveling companions was at the Sherpur Cantonment and was curious."

"I've no idea." Placing my hand firmly back in his crotch, Nicholas turned my chin toward him. "Shall I introduce you so you can ask him yourself?" The edge in his tone told me what my answer had better be.

I turned my head and nipped the tip of his thumb. "Why, when the most engaging company is right here with me?"

"That's more like it."

I grasped his arse and pulled his hips to mine. Feeling my arousal, he sighed happily and melted into me. I marveled again at the size of the cock pressing into my hip and wondered just how much we could get away with under the stairs without calling attention to ourselves.

"I want to taste every inch of you," I murmured, running my tongue around the edge of his ear.

"Then I suggest we go back to my cabin, Doctor. I doubt either the Colonel or your pretty blond wife would appreciate the disturbance."

CHAPTER TWELVE

It was our fourth day at sea before I saw Colonel Wright again. It was just after lunch, and Lazarus had gone to investigate the swimming pool. Bess had stationed herself on one of the lounge chairs with a book, and Claire and I had taken our luncheon scraps to the upper deck to feed the seagulls. We'd just tossed the scraps over the rail—eliciting squeals of joy from both the seagulls and Claire as the birds caught their treats midair—when we spied the Colonel's attendant pushing an empty wheelchair onto the promenade deck below.

The young man was tall and well built. Dressed in a fine blue-and-white striped seersucker jacket, straw boater, and linen trousers, he looked more like the heir to some lucrative plantation in India than an old man's paid companion. If the Colonel was paying him well enough to work in such finery, the pair was likely traveling first class.

"What's that chair for?" Claire asked.

"Shh." It was a clear day, with blue skies, fluffy white clouds, and a strong breeze. The wind carried Claire's words away quickly enough that I wasn't worried about offending the man below. However, it was never too early to begin to teach an outgoing child discretion.

A moment later the Colonel tottered out, balancing—painfully, it appeared—with a brass-headed cane. He carried himself in a cautious, stooped posture. His clothing, like the attendant's, was crisp and expensive—linen in somber dark colors. On his head he wore a hat with an unusually large crown—or at least it appeared that way from above. I watched as the attendant stopped and waited patiently for the old man to catch up.

It was a touching scene. The Colonel was clearly discontented to be wheeled about unless absolutely necessary. The dutiful young man brought the chair nonetheless, for when the Colonel's strength inevitably failed. Which appeared to be at that moment.

I watched as the Colonel put a hand on the chair to steady himself, then reluctantly lowered himself onto it. Remembering how he'd attempted to walk up the gangplank unassisted on the first day of the voyage—and had made such a spectacle of himself falling—I felt for him. And for his attendant. Despite the patience and good humor with which he doted on the Colonel—attention that suggested his investment in the position went beyond money and fine clothing—it must have been difficult at times to wait on such a proud man, a physical man from his bearing, and one who had doubtless once been accustomed to command.

"What's the chair for?" Claire asked again. Loudly.

"Shh." I cautioned her again. Then, more softly I said, "Sometimes people's legs don't work as well as they should. A chair helps them to move around."

"Oh," she said, seemingly satisfied. Then she cupped her hands around her mouth and shouted down to them. "What's happened to his legs?"

The young man's head whipped back toward our voices. I wanted to disappear into the floorboards. Certainly one allows children a certain latitude, but to insult a man crippled in defense of country and King! I was opening my mouth to stammer an apology, when the attendant's ice-blue eyes met mine. Good God!

"Marcus blooming Harrington!" I gasped.

"Who's Marcus blooming Harrington?"

"An old friend of mine."

Marcus and I had met many years ago under circumstances which, given my relatively conventional life at present, seem almost ridiculous now. And yet at the time they'd been inevitable. I'd been creeping around a male brothel looking for a friend who had gone missing. Marcus had been the brothel's star performer. Then the police arrived. Andrew St. Andrews had come to my rescue—as well he should have; the raid had been part of a botched investigation on his part. Marcus, who'd had no such patron, had gone down for gross indecency and languished in Pentonville for two years. Following his release, he'd stayed with me for a brief time before taking a job with a bookseller. He'd fallen in with Rupert Sudworth for a bit, but I'd helped him escape before Sudworth had sunk his claws too far in. I'd not seen Marcus since then. Not because we'd parted badly, but because life had simply taken us in different directions. And now, apparently, it had seen fit to cross our paths once more.

As for the Colonel, he wasn't any relative of Marcus's that I knew of. Marcus had been raised by his sister—two orphans in a squalid cellar room on Drury Lane. Given this fact and the obvious tenderness between the two men, it wasn't hard to guess the nature of their relationship. Marcus always did have a soft spot for rich men. Who didn't? I hoped this one was treating him well. My friend looked healthy and happy. And from the old man's condition—as much patient as patron—I guessed he probably couldn't be doing Marcus any physical harm.

It was difficult to pair the aimless, overgrown street urchin I'd known with this young man who navigated his duties with an appearance of competence and professionalism. On the other hand, though Marcus was no intellectual, his desperate background had given him a certain shrewdness of character and the ability to work hard when necessary. If he'd decided that this was the direction he wanted for his life, he'd be as capable as anyone of turning his boat that way.

From all appearances, it seemed to have done him good.

I opened my mouth to call to him, but before I could, he quickly turned around and wheeled the Colonel back inside.

"Come back, Marcus blooming Harrington!" Claire cried. But Marcus didn't seem inclined to listen.

"Come on," I said, scooping Claire up in my arms—a solid, squirming bundle of flesh and dark-blue cloth.

"Where do you know him from?" she asked as I ran toward the stairs. Between her keen perspicacity, her dark curls, and her flashing eyes, she reminded me more of Bess every day.

"Just a friend. From long, long ago."

"He didn't look happy to see you."

"No," I said. "And I intend to find out why."

The iron staircase clanged and shook under my footsteps. It was a short hop from there to the promenade. The first-class staterooms were through a set of double doors, past the main lobby with its glass-fronted shops and private parlors, and down a series of wood-paneled corridors leading to the bow. I followed Marcus through the double doors but lost him in a crowd of bejeweled first-class women with their parasols and feathered hats, and their equally decorative top-hat-wearing escorts.

"Shit," I muttered.

I thought to tuck Claire under my arm and keep running, but there were so many people—and so many already giving us the once-over—I didn't want to cause a panic. Also, Claire was a plump little thing and was already beginning to feel like a bag of wet sand. Setting her gently on the ground, I took her hand.

"Walk quickly," I told her. "But not so quickly as to make people think you've stolen something."

She looked at me with a gleam in her eye that had made me think, on more than one occasion, that she was going to be trouble when she was older.

We passed through the lobby and followed the corridor past numerous stateroom doors, a grand staircase gleaming with polished, inlaid wood and brass, and around a corner, to where our hallway intersected another. There were doors everywhere. Given the identical doors, the caramel-colored wood paneling, and the carpets in the same color, I had the strange sensation I might never find my way back. Somewhere in front of us, a door clicked shut, and Marcus stepped out into the corridor.

"Ira," he said with false cheerfulness. "What an unexpected pleasure."

His voice was deeper than I remembered, and smooth. Someone had helped him round out his nasal vowels and polish his rough consonants to a middle-class shine.

"I agree, Marcus. Why did you run? Where's your friend? Employer, is it?"

"I wasn't running. Colonel Wright had tired himself out. I was taking him back to the stateroom to rest. And I'm Mr. Spark, now."

"Mr. Bright Spark?" I was joking.

His mouth became a serious line. "Mr. Benjamin Spark, if you please. It's the only name the Colonel knows me by, and I'd prefer it stay that way."

"Ah, the Colonel. The reason our departure was delayed for more than an hour."

"Colonel Wright is a war hero," Marcus said, raising his chin. "Though he doesn't like to talk about it."

"And you're his companion?" I asked.

"That's right. Companion, valet, whatever he needs."

Marcus bounced up and down on the balls of his feet, still blocking the way to the door. Then, with an air of decision, he started back toward the lobby. I followed, along with Claire, who took Marcus's hand and grinned up at him.

"Is this your daughter?" he asked, his expression confused and more than a little terrified.

"This is Tim Lazarus's daughter, Claire. Do you remember Dr. Lazarus and his wife from Turnbull House?"

His smile faltered. He remembered but clearly didn't want to be reminded of the person he'd been—a hustler and one-time cocaine fiend just out of chokey—when he and Lazarus had first met.

"Pleased to meet you, miss," he said to Claire, clumsily extracting his hand from hers.

"Pleased to meet you, too, Marcus Blooming."

"Dr. And Mrs. Lazarus are traveling to California to settle some business with her family," I said. "Claire and I are just here to ride the big boat. And you?"

"Yes. Us, too. Business and family, business and family." He gave a nervous little smile.

"Is New York your final destination?"

"Yes, yes it is," he said a little too quickly.

Liar, I thought. But I didn't press him. Having gone to the trouble of changing his name, he clearly wanted to keep his past at arm's length. Still, it was obvious he wanted to be rid of me as quickly as possible, and that stung. We emerged into the crowded lobby, where some sort of musical ensemble was setting up in one corner, and it appeared, thankfully, to be a more interesting spectacle than our uncomfortable conversation. Nonetheless, Marcus looked around self-consciously, and I felt unaccountably guilty.

"Forgive me, Mr. Spark," I said. "I didn't mean to intrude. I was simply happy to see an old friend—and to see you getting on so well in the world. Claire and I should be getting back to our bird-spotting, now. Perhaps we'll see each other again before we land in New York."

I hadn't intended the last bit to be anything more than a conversational gesture—a way for us to smoothly part ways. But Marcus seemed to take it as some sort of threat.

"Don't ruin this for me, Ira," he said through clenched teeth.

"What? I...I would never...I just..."

He leaned in close. Sound nutrition had put meat on his bones, and he'd been engaging in some sort of exercise. The skinny young man I'd once known was now well muscled, and threat flashed in his eyes. My heart pounded when he actually made a fist. Then, glancing around and noticing that well-coiffed heads were turning to see what the fuss was about, he forced out his index finger in a threat more suited to the first-class lobby of the SS *Teutonic*.

"I worked hard to get this position." He wagged his finger in my face, his voice tense. "I work hard to keep it. Don't ruin it for me."

I frowned. Did Marcus worry that I'd scuttle his prospects by telling Colonel Wright how he and I had met? From what I'd seen of their interactions, I'd guess the Colonel already knew something of Marcus's talents. From what I'd seen, Marcus and the Colonel likely did a lot more behind closed doors than smoke cigars and play cards.

Perhaps he thought I was after his job. Did he really believe I wanted to be a valet-and-more to a half-crippled old man? Did he somehow think that Colonel Wright would prefer my company to his? Was the Colonel so flighty that he would dismiss his companion aboard ship and take up with a new one just like that?

Still, it was none of my business. I meant neither of them any mischief.

"All right," I said, taking a step back, hands held up in surrender. "I'm very happy with my current situation, Mr. Spark. And I'm glad you've found yourself such a favorable position. I wish you the best with it. I was just trying to be friendly. But if you prefer, we can forget we ever ran into each other. If you stay in first class and I stay in second, I doubt our paths will cross again."

Relief crossed his features. Exhaling heavily, Marcus stepped back, straightening the lapels of his pressed seersucker jacket.

"I think that's for the best." He gave a sad, embarrassed little smile. "I'm sorry, Ira. It really is good to see you. But under the circumstances, I don't think we should meet again."

CHAPTER THIRTEEN

I didn't spare Marcus a lot of thought over the next day or so. We were never close friends to begin with, though one might think he'd have been more kindly disposed toward someone who had once done so much for him. But no one can control what another person thinks of him, no matter how badly he wants to. Besides, on the fifth night of the journey I found myself with more pressing issues to deal with.

Specifically, the generously proportioned cock pressing into my hip.

"My turn, now," I whispered, my own climax still surging through my body. My skin buzzed with it. My ears rang. Smiling in the dark, metal box of his cabin, I slid down the slick, hot expanse of Nicholas's chest, over the pressed linen of his trousers, and knelt at his feet.

"I can't see the buttons," I whispered.

He laughed his breathy, voiceless laugh—it was after midnight, and though one might assume the other senior officers who rated the cabins on either side were asleep, the thin walls magnified every little sound. He guided my shaking fingers to his fly, which was already pulled taut by his straining cock.

"Is this better, Doctor?"

I opened my mouth to correct him. It seemed silly to let him keep thinking I was something I was not. On the other hand, no mischief had come of my deception, and, with only two days left aboard, it wasn't likely to. And it wasn't as if I knew what *his* exact position was— though it was clear he had some sort of specialized skill. The bulk of the ship's staff slept in communal dormitories below decks.

"Infinitely," I breathed.

I quickly unbuttoned his trousers and freed him. The trousers slid silently to the floor. I grasped his cock in one hand, feeling his pulse pound beneath the smooth skin. I skimmed my thumb over the tip and caught a drop of moisture that had gathered there. He shivered.

"I don't know if I'd rather eat this or fuck it," I mused.

Again that throaty laugh. "I suggest you decide quickly."

We both jumped at the sound of footsteps in the corridor. When someone knocked on Nicholas's door, the sound vibrated through the metal walls. I shot to my feet.

"Into the closet!" he whispered.

He didn't need to ask nicely. Squeezing past him in the narrow, dark passage between the padded ledge of his bed and the close, metal wall, I dove into the little recess—which was large enough to hold exactly two uniforms and one half of a grown man—and pulled the door shut behind me. It didn't quite close, though I'd smashed myself as far back against the wall as I could. I heard a muffled *swoosh* and imagined Nicholas pulling the blanket from his bed and wrapping himself in it. I only hoped the stifling metal box in which I was now trapped wasn't magnifying the sound of my breathing or of my pounding heart.

Nicholas cleared his throat and answered the door. I tried hard to listen to what was being said, but they were keeping their voices low, and I couldn't make out a single word. Eventually the interloper left, and I heard Nicholas close and latch his door.

"I have to go," he whispered when I emerged.

"What? Why?"

"The captain needs me. There's been an incident." He'd turned the lamp on low and was hastily putting his clothes back on. "Wait until you're certain no one's about, then wait five minutes more. After that, go back to your cabin and stay there."

"What's happening?" I asked.

He paused his preparations and laid a hand on my cheek. "A bit of bother, but nothing for you to be concerned about. Go back to your wife and get some sleep."

"She's not my—"

He silenced me with a deep kiss that scattered my thoughts and destroyed my objections. Pulling back, he smiled.

"We'll meet again soon, Doctor. I wouldn't dream of letting you leave the ship without finishing what we started."

He turned and put his hand on the doorknob.

"It's just that—" I said.

"Yes?"

"I don't even know what you do on this ship." A stupid remark. A desperate bid to keep him there with me a moment longer. He saw through it immediately but didn't hold it against me. He smiled again.

"I'm the chief security officer."

❖

From the bed of a crime lord to the arms of a cop! Panic coursed through my veins as I darted through the bare hallways where the crew was housed. I was a child again, running through the East End Streets just ahead of a baton-waving bobby. I was a young man in a black Maria headed for the jail under Bow Street. It was a mere few years ago, and I was locked in a cell at New Scotland Yard, wondering whether I wasn't actually better off there than out on the streets where a vengeful Cain Goddard was plotting my death.

I paused in the doorway between the crew's stripped-down steel warren and the thickly carpeted, wood-paneled world of cabin-class passengers. My fingers shook. I forced back a few deep breaths. This was silly. I hadn't committed a crime—at least not one in which the chief security officer hadn't himself enthusiastically participated. I'd no reason to fear the law. And yet old reactions change slowly.

I drew another long breath. Straightening my cravat, I stepped into the hall.

As one who has done his share of housebreaking, and an even greater share of sneaking in and out of other men's beds, it wasn't difficult to find my way back to my stateroom unnoticed. I heard movements and voices near the stern, so I made my way toward the bow. The upper deck was silent—all the respectable, middle-class passengers being fast asleep behind their polished wooden doors. The lush golden carpet swallowed my footsteps, and for one terrifying moment, I felt as if I were the only one aboard the ship.

That is, until I rounded the corner.

"I don't know who you are, or how you found our stateroom, but Dr. Lazarus is not available for consultation. Not at this hour." Bess was standing in the doorway, wrapped in her thick, quilted robe. A cap concealed her dark hair. Her face was alight with protective outrage.

"But—"

"Dr. Lazarus has earned his vacation. If it's an emergency, summon the ship's physician."

She was speaking to a woman—a young, blond woman, I noticed with growing unease—who was clad in the dark, sensible clothes of a governess. As I approached, the woman turned.

"I believe the man can speak for himself," she said triumphantly.

"What's all this, then?" I asked.

"This young woman wants—"

"A word with you, Doctor," Miss Wood said.

"Doctor?" Bess demanded.

"Er..."

"It's Cuthbert," Miss Wood said, her tone suddenly heavy with worry. "He has a terrible, racking cough and can't seem to catch his breath."

"Sound like the croup," Bess said. "The ship's doctor should be able to—"

"Sounds like the croup to me," I echoed in an authoritative tone. "Come, Miss Wood." I stepped away and gestured for the governess to follow. I'd no intention, of course, of carrying out an examination of her train-wielding brat. What I wanted was to end this argument before it became a spectacle.

"Don't you need your bag?" Miss Wood asked.

"My what?"

"Your...your doctor's bag. With your stethoscope and little pills?"

"Oh, yes, I suppose I do." Bess's eyes went wide and she began to sputter. I looked imploringly at her. *Please*, I mouthed. Then I turned to Miss Wood. "One moment."

The second I was within reach, Bess grabbed my arm. "I don't know what you're playing at, Ira," she growled. "But—"

"I'm trying to get this woman out of your hair, and Tim's, as quickly and quietly as possible. Don't worry. I'll take her straight to the ship's physician."

"Why does she keep calling you 'Doctor'?"

"It's a long story, but I swear I'll set her straight once we're out of the corridor. Have you noticed how the sound carries?" Her expression turned dubious. "Just hand me a bag. Any bag. It really doesn't matter which one."

She gave me a stony look but disappeared back into the stateroom. A moment later she emerged with the canvas satchel she used to carry amusements for Claire. "Here's your bag, *Doctor*."

"Thank you," I said, kissing her cheek. "Now go back to sleep. I'll handle this."

Miss Wood was walking toward the end of the corridor. When I caught up with her, she took my elbow.

"Oh, thank you, Doctor! Thank you! I'm ever so grateful!"

She led me around the corner, down another hallway, and up the stairs to the promenade deck, prattling unctuously the entire way. We exited onto the deck, at which point, she took my wrist in a surprisingly effective lock and forced me beneath a staircase.

"Miss Wood, what on Earth?"

For the second time that night, my words were forced back by a judiciously applied tongue. I tried to push her off, but she clung like a limpet and dove back in.

"What about Cuthbert?" I gasped when she pulled back to take a breath.

"Sod Cuthbert. There's nothing wrong with the little monster. I just wanted to get you alone." Her voice was throaty now, heavy with lust. The Liverpool twang she'd been hiding so well was creeping in around the edges. Her hands were everywhere.

"Miss Wood, I really don't think—"

"Shut up and kiss me," she growled, mashing her face into mine— quite a feat considering she had to stand on her toes to do it. Good God, how many hands did the woman *have*?

I felt an uncomfortable flush of rage. If she'd been a man, or even a stoutly built woman, I'm certain I'd have struck her. But she was birdlike and stood more than a head shorter than I. Intellectually, I realized she could do me little harm. It wasn't as if I hadn't faced greater dangers. But one of those dangers had been a very similar assault by one Cain Goddard. An assault my body would never forget, nor my mind forgive.

"Get off!" I shouted, and I pushed again. Too hard, this time. I knew it even before she fell. Tangled in the strap of Bess's satchel, she hung for a moment, suspended in the harsh light of the lamp. Then the strap snapped, and Miss Wood staggered backward and fell onto the deck in a heap of skirts and shawl.

"Miss Wood?"

As the red cleared from my vision, worry crept in. If I'd injured her, she could tell the authorities anything. They'd be happy to assume that I'd been the one to force my affections. Nicholas might believe me, but he wouldn't be able to tell anyone why.

She sat up slowly, straightening her hat. A drop of blood hung beneath one nostril, gleaming in the lamplight. With an unladylike sniff, she wiped it away with the back of her hand. She looked up at me with new respect in her eyes, her mouth forming a sharp, crafty smile.

"Well," she said. All middle-class pretense had drained from her voice, and I was left with the distinct impression of a hard-bitten doxy with a knife in her handbag and a razor in her boot. An impression only augmented by the long, jagged scar that stretched across the smooth skin beneath her chin.

"Are you all right?" The scar was long healed, but the image it conjured was shocking. Someone, at some point, had *cut her throat*. I put out a hand to help her up, then reconsidered. Her joint lock had been the work of an expert. "I didn't intend to hurt you," I said. "It's just... My God..."

Her hand went to her throat, and she scowled. Snatching up her shawl, she wrapped it around her neck once more, then stood and brushed off her skirt. When she spoke again, her voice was filled with false bravado, but beneath it, it trembled a bit. "I guess I...I was right about what kind of man you are, Doctor."

"What do you mean by that?" Under British law, the kind of man I was could get two years at hard labor for nothing at all, if the accusation was phrased the right way.

Her smile became victorious.

"This isn't finished, Doctor. We'll be in contact."

With a defiant toss of her head, she turned, sweeping her shawl over her shoulder. I stood speechless and watched her disappear around the corner.

CHAPTER FOURTEEN

N icholas!" I hissed. I smacked at his door with the flat of my hand. There were only a few hours left before dawn, and I really didn't want to wake his neighbors, but I had to speak to him before she did. A moment later, the door cracked open, and my gorgeous security officer peeked out of the dark through bleary eyes.

"Oh, Doctor." Yawning, he ran a hand through his thick, light-brown waves. "I was rather hoping you'd come back tomorrow."

"I know. I'm sorry. I have to speak with you."

Stifling a sigh, he wrapped his blanket tighter around his shoulders and stepped back from the door. He was bare chested beneath the blanket and wore red-and-white striped pajama bottoms. It was strangely endearing. I followed him inside, closing the door behind me.

"I'm not Dr. Lazarus," I said as he coaxed a dim light from his lamp. The little flame bobbed and weaved behind the glass bulb, casting moving shadows onto the metal walls. He'd opened his porthole, but the room still smelled faintly of sex. "My name is Ira Adler. The doctor and his wife are traveling with me. It was his ticket—"

"Wait, wait." Nicholas set the lamp down and turned. "You're who, now?"

"Back in Liverpool you looked at the tickets I was holding. Dr. Lazarus had purchased them, and his name was on them. You assumed I was him, and I didn't correct you—"

"Why not?"

I was embarrassed to say that I'd rather enjoyed having Nicholas mistake me for someone more important. Someone with an education and a respectable profession. Someone a handsome sailor might admire.

"I didn't think it would matter, since we wouldn't see each other again after we reached New York," I said instead.

"I see."

"Anyway, the point is, if someone comes to you with accusations against Dr. Lazarus, they're really aimed at me."

"Accusations?"

His tone was all business, now, despite the pajamas. He sat on the edge of the bed and gestured for me to do the same. I drew a long breath and told him everything. He listened intently, chin in hand. I caught a glimpse of what had to be a formidable brain—analyzing, parsing, and judging every word that came out of my mouth. After I finished, he sat there for a moment, nodding. His expression was thoughtful—not particularly friendly, but not antagonistic, either.

"For obvious reasons, I'm inclined to believe you didn't force yourself on her," he said. "At least not sexually. But obvious reasons would only take you from frying pan to fire, if that's the story she chooses to spread." Exhaling heavily, he pulled up his legs and crossed them in front of him on the mattress. "Her behavior was most suspicious, though, and not just because young ladies rarely go about aggressively molesting men. Are you missing anything? Billfold? Watch?"

The thought had occurred to me, of course. This wasn't the first time an ambitious woman had used the same technique to pick my pocket. But a second check wouldn't hurt. I quickly patted down my jacket and trousers, finding my stateroom key, Goddard's gold watch, and the coins I'd been carrying all day.

"No. Everything's accounted for."

"What about your bag?"

I held up the flimsy fabric satchel. "Empty. It usually holds Claire's toys. Claire is Dr. Lazarus's daughter."

He frowned. "Why were you carrying an empty bag?"

I laughed. "I wasn't on my way to burgle anyone, if that's what you're implying."

Nicholas, not joking, raised his eyebrows. Good God, he was actually considering it! I felt a flash of outrage at the thought.

"Miss Wood came to my room," I sputtered. "Claiming that her charge was ill. She wasn't taking no for an answer, and she was being quite loud about it. I wanted to take her away before she woke the neighbors."

"And a doctor always carries his bag," Nicholas said.

"Exactly!" Only then did I recognize the dry disbelief in his tone. "I was taking her straight to the ship's physician when she accosted me."

Nicholas said nothing but continued to dissect me with his gaze. Did he seriously suspect *me* of something, now?

"What is it? I can hear the tumblers clicking."

"That's a rather specific metaphor. Do you have experience picking locks?"

I had, of course. But this clearly wasn't the time to boast about that particular set of skills.

"I beg your pardon!"

"Well, you've already demonstrated you're not averse to deception, *Doctor*."

"Yes, well, sorry about that, but it doesn't make me a cracksman."

"A cracksman?" Triumph glittered in his eyes. I saw him bite back a little smile. The unexpected intrusion of East London into my carefully cultivated middle-class speech must have confirmed some brewing suspicion. "That's not a term I'd expect to hear from someone of your background."

"My background has nothing to do with this!" Really, I was beginning to wonder whether Miss Wood had somehow brought her story to him before I arrived.

"*Have* you cracked a safe, then?" His hand had somehow found mine, and he was examining my fingertips with unnerving intentness. I jerked my hand away.

"No! And if you remember, we were talking about false accusations of assault, not burglary."

He sighed again, and his sinewy shoulders slumped.

"Ah, but we are talking about burglary, I'm afraid." He chuckled. "Another crime it would be difficult to pin on you, seeing as your cock was in my mouth at the time it happened. The incident that kept you from returning the favor," he explained. "It concerns your friend Colonel Wright."

"*My* friend?"

"Well, his attendant, at any rate, Mr. Spark. I saw you speaking at length on the promenade deck the other day. I figured you must know one another."

"No!" I scrambled to think what Nicholas must have seen. An argument, or at least a slightly heated exchange. "Claire had said something about the Colonel's wheelchair. Mr. Spark didn't find it amusing. We were apologizing."

"I see." There was a slight hardening of his tone, of the set of his jaw. He didn't believe it, even though much of what I'd said was true.

"What was stolen, if I might ask?"

He frowned, continuing to skewer me with that policeman's eye of his. Eventually, I suppose, he decided there was no harm in answering that particular question.

"Documents, and a substantial amount of money."

"They kept that in their stateroom?"

"No, they kept it in the ship's safe for most of the journey. Mr. Spark removed it in preparation for disembarkation. The Colonel's condition requires that they take extra time for tasks to which you and I don't give a second thought. Mr. Spark wanted to have everything in order before they left."

I'll bet he did, I thought. Marcus had been a thief when I'd known him. He'd stolen from me, after I'd given him a roof, a job, and a place at my table. At the same time, he'd seemed so proud of his new position—and so protective of it. I couldn't actually bring myself to believe he would steal the Colonel's valuables and abandon him. If their relationship was as I suspected, the Colonel would likely have made some sort of provision for Marcus in his will. At the very least, it was an idiotic time to perpetrate the theft, with almost two days to go until New York.

"What sort of documents?" I asked.

Nicholas cocked his head. "I can't tell you that. But I do hope that the stolen property doesn't represent the sum of the Colonel's resources, or when he gets to California, he may find himself quite destitute."

California! I knew Marcus had been lying when he'd said they were stopping in New York. It seemed prudent to keep it to myself that I, too, was California-bound. Egad. I hoped that didn't mean Marcus and I would be running into each other out on the range, or wherever it was that Californians tended to congregate.

According to Nicholas, Marcus had been with the Colonel at dinner when the theft occurred, which was why Nicholas was still looking for other suspects. But might Marcus have slipped off for a few moments under the pretense of a cigarette or nature's call? It wouldn't surprise me to learn he'd taken the money, but I wasn't sure about the documents. When I'd known him five years earlier, he'd barely been able to sound out the alphabet. He'd probably learned to read and write a bit since then, but he wasn't exactly the scholarly type. Even if he'd been able to fight his way through the text of a legal document, I doubted he'd have been able to make heads or tails of its significance.

"You seem to be giving the matter inordinately deep thought, Mr. Adler."

I snorted. "Deep thoughts give you wrinkles." Lawrence's words. I swallowed around the sudden tightness in my throat. "It seems an interesting case, that's all."

"*Case?*" He cocked an eyebrow appraisingly. "For the first time in a long while, I find myself wishing there were more than seven days between Liverpool and New York. I imagine you have some cracking stories to tell. Out of curiosity, how *did* you break your nose?"

"Bar fight," I said, bristling in response to the barely veiled suspicion returning to his voice.

"I wonder how the other man fared."

"I really should be going."

I slid off the bed. Nicholas stood as I moved for the door. I half expected him to try to restrain me. "Please don't leave," he said instead.

I turned, hand on the doorknob. "Because you've finally found a crime to charge me with?"

"No. I'm sorry," he said, suddenly contrite. Color tinged his boyish face—his freckled cheeks and snub nose. He ran a hand through his sleep-mussed hair. The canny detective had receded for the moment, and I glimpsed the awkward, eager young man who had so charmed me back in Liverpool. "My enthusiasm for the job does tend to put people off at times," he explained. "It's just…you have to admit you're not what you…that is, there's more to you than you let on, and that fascinates me. I'm not accusing you of anything."

"Yet."

"Yet," he conceded. "But let's not part this way. I know. We'll have a look at the passenger roster. You can tell me more about your Miss Wood, in case she decides to make trouble."

"You're not going to clap me in shackles the moment my back is turned?"

His mouth quirked. "Not unless you ask me to."

I laughed, relieved to be moved down a few places on his list of suspects. "Not fucking likely," I muttered.

I averted my eyes while he slipped into a shirt, trousers, and shoes. As pleasing as his form was, it seemed wrong, somehow, to ogle the man while he was acting in an official capacity. After he dressed, I followed him through a labyrinth of narrow steel corridors and doorways clearly made for smaller men. Eventually we climbed a hidden flight of stairs and emerged before a sequence of official-looking doors. Nicholas stopped before the one marked N. FLYNN, CHIEF OF SECURITY, and produced a key.

"Come inside," he said, motioning for me to enter.

His office was only slightly larger than his cabin, but it was a model of tidiness and efficiency. Shelves built into one wall housed books, manuals, and ledgers organized by size. The wooden desk against the far wall was clear, save for a blotter—perfectly centered, of course—a wooden box that held pens and a bottle of ink, and another box with loose paper. On the wall above the desk hung a large, round clock and a wall sconce. Between them was a window, which now provided a view of Nicholas's beloved constellations.

"This is the current passenger list." Nicholas's voice brought me out of my thoughts. He laid a binder on the desk and opened it to the first page of the manifest. Licking a finger, he began to page through it. "You said you met Miss Wood in the children's room, which is available to both first- and second-class passengers."

"She's traveling with the Pearce family," I said, looking over his shoulder. He inched aside to give me a better view. I could feel his warmth through his shirt, smell traces of my own cologne.

"Hmm…Pearce…"

"The boy's name is Cuthbert."

"What was the woman's name again?"

"Wood. Lila Wood. She's blond, maybe twenty-two, twenty-three. A little stick of a thing about this high," I held my hand just below my shoulder. "She has a taste for drab clothing, and oh, yes, a very distinctive scar, as if someone had tried to cut her throat. She usually covers it with a scarf."

At some point during my description, Nicholas had gone very, very still. Tension thrummed in the air, and I wouldn't have been surprised to see him begin to quiver like a hunting dog who'd caught a scent. He turned to me very slowly.

"I saw you speaking to a woman of that description near the children's room on the first day. I assumed she was your wife. You let me think she was—for five days."

"Nicholas…"

He held up a hand. "I mentioned her at least twice. You didn't even blink."

"She's not my wife. I swear to you I never met her before this."

"And the only reason you didn't correct me is because our..." He gestured between us with his hand. "Meant so little you didn't think it mattered?"

"For God's sake, Nicholas! You're the one who said he was so happy to change company every seven days. Don't try to stitch me up because you're having regrets!"

He stopped. Blinked. Then smiled a little sadly. "Yes, I did say that, didn't I? Well."

Sighing, he turned back to the roster. My eyes followed his finger down the pages listing the second-class passengers.

"Ah, yes, here she is. Strange." He frowned, running his finger down the page one more time. "Miss Lila Wood...She appears to be traveling with someone named Pearce. However, there's no child. Very curious indeed. I shall have to speak to her straight away."

A great yawn swallowed up the last few words, and in that instant, I saw not a sharp-eyed detective keen to implicate me, but a tired, rather lonely young man who was looking down the barrel of a crime quite a bit more complex than he'd originally thought. I saw his shoulders sag a fraction—perhaps as the prospect of sleep grew more distant. A pillow-flattened section of his hair was sticking straight up from his head. I wanted to comb it back with my fingers.

"I hope you'll come find me once the matter is settled," I said.

A smile twitching at the edges of his lips, he regarded me shyly out of the corner of his eye. I gave his shoulder a playful nudge. He turned suddenly and leaned into me, pinning me against the neat bookshelves with a kiss I felt all the way to my toes.

"I know there's more happening than you're telling me," he murmured into my ear between nibbles. His chest was warm against mine. His hands, unexpectedly iron-strong, circled my wrists and held them to the canvas-bound volumes behind me. "I'm choosing to trust you for now. But if it turns out you had anything to do with this evening's theft, I'll see you rot in prison."

CHAPTER FIFTEEN

B elieve it or not, it wasn't the direst threat a lover had ever issued. And because I was innocent, at least as regarded the theft, I took N. Flynn, Chief of Security, over his desk with enthusiasm and a clear conscience. The sun was peeking over the horizon when I finally crept down to my own deck and let myself back into my stateroom. Discarding the satchel onto the common-room floor, and my clothes onto the foot of my bed, I shut my bedroom door and slipped beneath the brocaded duvet just as pink light began to push at the window shade.

Not a moment later, it seemed, I woke to the sound of a little voice chanting "Shit! Shit! Shit!"

I sat straight up in my bed when I realized it was Claire. Pushing off the heavy duvet, I slid my feet into my velvet slippers and glanced at Goddard's watch on the bedside table. Half past two, and the mid-afternoon sun was flooding through the little round window on the back wall. Good God, I'd slept away the better part of the day.

"Shit! Shit! Shit! Shit!" Claire sang.

"Claire!" I cried. There was a pause in the obscene patter. "Don't let your mother—"

"His Majesty has awakened," said Bess in the common room that separated her bedroom from my own. "Allow me to extend my humble gratitude for teaching my daughter her new favorite word."

Shit, I thought. Then I called, "Sorry, Bess."

I scrambled into a fresh set of clothes, then hurriedly folded the ones from the previous day and shoved them into one of the suitcases. We'd be docking in New York at some point that evening or the next morning, and I wanted to be able to disembark at my leisure. I dabbed on a bit of cologne, smoothed down my hair and tie, and emerged into the common area, only to find chaos.

"What happened here?" I asked.

Toys were strewn everywhere. Papers lay across the red Persian carpet and all over the desk, covered with the little drawings Tim sometimes did to amuse his daughter. The crushed remains of a biscuit were ground into the carpet near the foot of a chair, across which Lazarus sprawled—shirttail pulled out, tie askew, edges of waistcoat unrestrained and flapping. He looked as if he'd just emerged from the business end of a cyclone. Bess bustled about in her daughter's wake, picking up and straightening just as Claire found something else to dismantle. The air was thick and tinged with a vague barnyard smell. Tim and Bess subscribed to a modern child-rearing philosophy taught by a Dr. Browning, which, as far as I could tell, indulged obnoxious behavior while imposing rather draconian limitations on sugary treats.

"There's been a theft on board," Tim said wearily. "Everyone's been confined to quarters. They brought luncheon on a tray. Yours is over there." He gestured toward a plate on the desk—lukewarm slices of meat, a piece of dry bread, and some wilted greens. Delicious.

"Oh," I said, trying not to sound ungrateful.

Tim rose with a groan, swept the satchel up from the floor, and, with the air of a clockwork toy badly in need of winding, began to collect his daughter's playthings. Her favorite doll. A wooden horse. Some sort of truly revolting-looking blankety-thing. I don't know why I'd assumed we'd be spared a visit from security, or any attendant inconveniences, but I supposed I had. Ah, well.

"From what I can ascertain, they've finished with first class and are working their way through second. No, they haven't paid us a visit yet," Tim said, answering the question I hadn't asked. "I understand you had a late night. Attending a sick child, was it, Doctor?"

I winced. "It's a long story."

He shrugged. "We've nothing but time."

I gave an abbreviated account of my short, unfortunate association with Miss Lila Wood, or whatever her name actually was. I tried to dwell more on Miss Wood's perfidy than on the fact that I'd allowed her—not to mention the ship's chief of security—to assume I was a physician for nearly a week. Neither Bess nor her husband, however, was about to let that omission pass unremarked.

"So in addition to having the security staff rifle through my possessions, I can expect to be brought up on assault charges as well?" Tim asked. He sounded resigned but not surprised.

"No. No, I went straight to the ship's security officer and explained everything."

"I'm sure he was thrilled to see you at his door in the small hours."

"Yes, he wasn't expecting me back until tonight," I said under my breath. "But I took pains to clear your name, Tim, and to provide him with mine, so you needn't worry about my carelessness coming back to bite you."

"Well, for that I must thank you."

Bess interrupted us. "The good news is, we should be arriving in New York early tomorrow morning."

"Hopefully they'll have found Colonel Wright's documents by then," I said.

Bess and Tim simultaneously turned to look at me.

"Is that what was stolen? Do you know something about it?" Bess demanded.

At the same time, Tim shook his head. "Colonel Wright, again! That man seems determined to interfere with our journey, whether he knows it or not."

"He's in a push-chair," Claire said. She was circling around her father's chair in some sort of pagan-inspired dance. When she paused near his knee, he caught her wrists in his hands and pulled her onto his lap. "His legs don't work."

"We may be seeing more of him," I added. "He's on his way to California as well."

"How do you know that?" Tim asked as Claire poked at his eyes through his reading spectacles. I ignored him.

"California's a very large place, Ira," Bess said.

"Is it?"

"The land area is almost twice that of all of Britain."

"My God," I said. "And just how far away is it from New York?"

"About a week by train."

The mind boggled. And the heart sank. I'd told Lawrence I'd be no more than a month, but I'd grossly underestimated both the size of the country and how long it would take to cross it. We'd be a month in transit alone.

"Do you have somewhere else to be?" Tim asked.

"No, but I'll need to send a telegram as soon as we arrive in New York."

A knock on the door interrupted this merry conversation. When I opened it, Nicholas stood there with two crisply dressed men in white uniforms. Nicholas himself looked far from crisp. His lack of sleep was apparent in the bags under his eyes, and he looked as if he'd been holding back a yawn all morning. Even so, he was dashing in his gold-trimmed, dark-blue jacket. I had to school my face to avoid betraying the fact that we were actually quite intimately acquainted. For his part, he regarded me with such cool professionalism that I almost wondered if I hadn't been balls-deep in someone else just a few hours before.

"Good day, sir. I'm Mr. Flynn, Chief of Ship's Security." He indicated the two men standing behind him. "These are Mr. Farnsworth and Mr. Holden." He flicked a glance at the roster in his hand. "Would you be Dr. Lazarus?"

"Not for all the tea in China," I said. Then, straightening, I cleared my throat. "I'm Mr. Adler. Dr. and Mrs. Lazarus are inside. Please come in."

I stepped aside to let them pass. As they entered, Tim stood, sliding Claire gently to the floor.

"I'm Dr. Lazarus, and this is Mrs. Lazarus and our daughter, Claire." Tim switched the toy-filled satchel to his left shoulder, then offered his right hand. Nicholas gave it a firm shake and made a short bow toward Bess.

"Mr. Flynn, Chief of Security. These are my associates, Mr. Farnsworth and Mr. Holden. No doubt you've already heard that we've had a theft aboard ship." While his men began to poke through the papers and other detritus, Nicholas continued. "White Star apologizes for the inconvenience, and I, personally, apologize for the disruption of your journey. Once you and your belongings have been searched, you'll be free to leave your cabin. Until then, your patience and cooperation are greatly appreciated."

"Certainly," Tim said.

Nicholas supervised as his men carefully tore the room apart, piece by piece. Gradually, he made his way over to the corner where I was standing.

"Yours is the last second-class cabin, and still no sign of your young woman."

"She's not *my*—" I said.

"I interviewed Miss Wood—the real Miss Wood, legitimately traveling second class. She's nothing like the woman I saw you with."

"My attacker is in steerage, then, no doubt."

"In all likelihood. A woman with a scar like you described wouldn't stand out so much there. Though she certainly would in the children's room. I should think she'd have attracted a lot of attention."

"She was wearing a shawl. I remember thinking its position was a bit unusual, but there was a breeze on deck, so I figured she was cold."

Thinking back, I remembered how the little boy, who couldn't have been much more than two, hadn't acknowledged Miss Wood's rebuke—or even the governess herself. But Claire had been just as oblivious at that age. And Cuthbert—or whoever the boy had actually been—hadn't, in the end, hit the other child with the train.

"No. Which adds another layer of suspicion. What was she doing in the playroom without a child?"

"Not the most likely place to troll for male company," I added.

"You're certain you'd never seen her before that day?"

"Absolutely."

"Hmm. Then we do have a mystery on our hands."

His tone seemed earnest. I was relieved he seemed to be giving his suspicions a rest as far as my role in the theft was concerned. He still didn't quite trust me—no cop worth his salt would, considering my earlier deceptions and the discrepancies in my history that he'd deftly ferreted out. Something told me if I betrayed the tentative confidence he'd placed in me, he'd pursue me with terrifying vigor.

Nicholas's men, having simultaneously finished the searches of their respective halves of the common room, moved on to the bedrooms. Nicholas watched my reaction carefully as one of the men entered my space. My response must have seemed sufficiently innocent, because once the man had shut the door behind him, Nicholas leaned in and lowered his voice.

"I'd really like to see you again before the ship docks in the morning. Unfortunately, the search will likely last into the evening, not to mention the subsequent paperwork. By the time this is finished, I'll be wanting supper and bed more than anything else."

"I understand," I said.

Just then Mr. Farnsworth emerged from my bedroom. "Sir, a word."

"Excuse me, Mr. Adler." Nicholas and his man stepped into my bedroom and conferred for a moment. When he emerged, the warmth was gone from his voice. "Mr. Adler, may I speak to you outside?"

"I-I suppose."

"What's going on?" Lazarus asked as Nicholas ushered me into the hallway.

"I'll only be a moment," I reassured him, though I didn't feel a bit reassured myself.

Nicholas quietly shut the door behind us. The corridor was silent and still—all the other second-class passengers having been released from their house arrest. The change in my friend's demeanor was making me nervous, which I'm certain would have made me look guilty, had I been I guilty of anything. I tried to look nonchalant as I leaned up against the wood paneling.

"What is it, Nicholas?"

He glowered at me for a moment, then pulled out a pen and a small notebook. "Where do you do your banking, Mr. Adler?" His words were innocuous enough, but his tone was pulled tight, as if he was angry. As if he'd found my transgression at last and was taking it personally.

"I…have a chap," I said.

"Name?"

"Mr. Allen Humphrey."

Nicholas scratched the name into his little book.

"And he's associated with which bank?"

"I…I'm not certain. Martins, I believe. Tim…er…Dr. Lazarus would know."

He blew out a long breath, shaking his head. When he spoke again, his gaze was flinty and his jaw was set hard.

"Have you any dealings—any at all—with Rupert Sudworth or Midlands Bank?"

"Never!" I said vehemently. Not anymore, at least. And collecting a cheque from the man could hardly be considered *dealings*.

"I see." His tone grew cold. He looked like he'd have been happy to throw me against a wall or two, if it wouldn't have caused a commotion.

"What…"

He rapped on the door. His man Farnsworth opened it.

"I need to speak to Mr. Adler in greater detail," Nicholas said to him. "His party shall remain in their cabin while I do so, and you shall guard the door. Should they need anything, you shall send Mr. Holden to fetch it."

"Yes, sir," the man said.

"As for you," Nicholas said, turning to me, anger—and deep, deep disappointment—in his eyes, "I trust you'll accompany me to my office without forcing me to march you through first class in shackles."

Chapter Sixteen

When we reached the corridor where Nicholas's office was located, he didn't open his door, but the one next to it. The unmarked room was bare, with metal walls, a window, and a chair that was bolted to the floor. An interrogation room—or a jail cell. Either way, the sight of it sent a jolt of panic through me.

"Inside, please," Nicholas said, though it wasn't a request.

My entire body tightened with alarm, I twisted against his hard grip. But he was quicker and more muscular than I and deftly maneuvered us across the threshold, shutting the door behind us.

"No! Wait!" I cried.

"Yes. You're going to wait here until this is all sorted. More than likely, you'll be leaving in police custody."

"What?"

"You heard me." His eyes were as sharp as his voice. "You've made quite a fool of me, Mr. Adler. I don't appreciate that."

"I really wish you'd tell me—"

"Don't make me shackle you to the chair."

Cold sweat gathered between my shoulder blades and ran down my back. My pulse raced. I could feel it in my ears. I've a horror of enclosed spaces. Being shackled inside one might well drive me over the edge. I lunged toward the door, but he put himself between it and me. Then, jaw clenched tight, he drove me backward and shoved me down violently onto the chair.

"I'm serious," he said, holding me against it with one hand. His other hand had already formed a fist. He was breathing quickly and something dangerous flickered in his eyes.

"All right," I said. I tried to banish thoughts of metal walls, the heavy door, or how long it would take to run out of air in this shrinking chamber. As my posture relaxed, a bit of the murder left his expression. "Just...do you have to lock the door?"

Pulling his hand away, he gave a short, sharp laugh. But something in my expression must have reached him, for his jawline softened slightly. He said, "I can open the window. There's nothing above or below, and you certainly can't fit through it."

Swallowing hard, I nodded.

"I'll need to search you first. Stand up."

He went through my clothes thoroughly and efficiently, looking— for what?—and finding nothing. Apparently satisfied, he bade me sit again.

And then the bastard really did shackle my arm to the chair.

"Only for a moment," he said when I started to protest.

The metal was cold and felt tighter than I knew it actually was, but I forced myself to take deep breaths as he crossed to the window. My shoulders relaxed a fraction as he wrenched open the portal. When he returned to unlock the shackle, I nearly whimpered.

"Mr. Farnsworth found something rather damning in your coat pocket," he said as he jiggled the key in the lock of the manacle. I tried not to panic when it stuck. "We'll speak more of it in a little while, but first I need to put my facts in order. More to the point, I must bring my temper under control."

"Nicholas, I really didn't—"

"Don't say it." The lock sprang open and I rubbed my wrist, stifling a cry of relief. "Just...don't say anything."

With that, he turned and walked out the door. I flinched at the click of the lock, but the open window kept me from dissolving into a gibbering heap. I crossed to it, pressing my face into the opening as far as it would go. Outside, a calm ocean spread out beneath a peaceful blue sky. Fresh, salty air brushed my cheek, filled my lungs.

What the devil had Farnsworth found? And what in that devil's name did Rupert fucking Sudworth have to do with it?

A small voice inside whispered *Sudworth killed Goddard, and now he's after you.* Completely ludicrous, of course, the idea that Sudworth would pursue me all the way to America just because of my connection to Goddard. If Sudworth had killed Goddard, as I suspected, he'd had his revenge. He had nothing to gain by going after me. And I couldn't imagine that Sudworth had troubled to discover that I was the one who had warned Marcus away from him all those years ago. Even if he had, why wait until now to strike at me?

And then there was Marcus himself.

If Nicholas was asking about Sudworth, then his man had probably found documents with Sudworth's signature. Had Marcus somehow managed to slip one of these into my coat pocket while we'd been speaking? If he was looking for someone to pin the theft on, my appearance on the ship must have seemed fortuitous.

Of course that left the question of Miss Wood. She hadn't taken anything out of my pockets, but perhaps she'd put something in.

But *why*?

I pushed off from the wall and began to pace. As my footsteps fell into a steady rhythm, a thrum rose in the metal walls. How solid were those walls, I wondered. How solid was the door? I glanced at the painted steel bands studded with screws that took the place of molding. If I took a run at the wall, I could probably leave a dent, though I'd likely dent myself in the process. On the other hand, the door hinges didn't appear to be fortified in any particular way.

I stepped back toward the window to give myself room to pick up speed.

Just then I heard voices and footsteps in the corridor. The voices—men's voices, three of them—approached but stopped short. I heard Nicholas's office door open and close, and then the men were inside. Abandoning my earlier plan, I pressed my ear to the wall my cell shared with the office.

Nicholas was speaking in calm, firm tones. Then another man spoke—Marcus, I recognized. I strained to hear the words, but the layers of books and papers in his bookcase muffled the conversation. There was a third, weaker voice—the Colonel, I assumed. I pressed myself so hard into the metal that my head should have gone through it. But still, nothing concrete. Nicholas and the Colonel spoke for some time, with an occasional interjection from Marcus. Eventually the voices subsided and I heard the men take their leave. A few moments later his office door opened again.

"Nicholas!" I called, banging on my cell door with my fist.

I heard him pull his office door shut, unhurried. Then his footsteps paused. I tried to imagine the expression on his face. Wondered whether his conversation with the Colonel had changed his mind in any way. I called out again. Then I heard the sharp rap of his heels on the steel floor as he turned and walked away.

It was evening before anyone returned again. The sky beyond the little portal had gone dark, and I'd nearly worn a hole in the floor with my pacing. It had taken a continuous effort to convince myself he'd not left me to suffocate and rot. When someone knocked on the door, I stifled a burst of nervous laughter.

"It's me," Nicholas said.

"Come in." As if I had a choice in the matter.

The key rattled in the lock, and the door opened slowly.

"I won't rush the door," I said, though in truth, I'd been considering it. I'd turned on the gaslight as evening had fallen, and he could see me clearly enough standing on the other side of the room behind the chair.

"That's good, because I brought you some supper."

"A last meal for the prisoner?"

He stepped inside, holding a tray with a covered dish. Next to the dish was a napkin artfully folded around a set of cutlery. He held a bottle of wine under one arm and two glasses between the fingers of his other hand. He did not, I noticed, close the door.

"Actually, you're free to go. But I hope you'll have a drink with me before you do."

"Oh?"

He took an exaggerated step away from the door, as if to emphasize that I might leave at any time. After a moment, I stepped out from behind the chair and gently took the tray from his hand. While I set it onto the chair, he produced a corkscrew and addressed himself to the bottle. I lifted the cover of the dish and released an ambrosial cloud of vapor: steak, and vegetables roasted in butter. Looked like something from the first-class kitchen. Did I catch a hint of apology? I heard the soft pop of a cork behind me and the gurgle of wine being decanted into glass. When I turned, his expression wasn't exactly affable, but neither did he appear eager to harm me. He handed me the glass.

"So you've decided I'm innocent after all," I said.

"Eh, well, er…" He ran a hand through his sandy waves, looking away. "The Colonel refused to press charges."

"Well…that's a relief." And a mystery. But I'd take it.

"But not because I proved you weren't involved. The fact is, I'm still convinced you were. I just can't figure out how you managed it."

I took a long slug of wine. It was a nice one. The perfect balance of fruity and tart.

"But you know where my cock was at the time of the burglary," I said. "I think you'd have noticed if the rest of me had stepped out for a moment."

"Yes…" He huffed out a laugh, then shook his head, as if still in disbelief. "As long as we're speaking hypothetically, now, would you like to hear my theory? Just for a laugh?"

"Certainly."

He downed half his wine in one fortifying pull. As he spoke, I had the impression that, despite feeling a bit stung by what he perceived as my betrayal, he was more interested in solving the puzzle than in either revenge or justice. That, and he was ever so happy to have *someone* to listen to his ideas.

"Your Miss Wood, to begin with—"

"She's not *my* anything," I said.

"She's your confederate. Not that it matters anymore. In addition to stealing the Colonel's property, she stole the name of one of the other passengers. The real Miss Lila Wood is in her fifties: an upstanding and well-spoken lady who has not had her throat mangled in any way."

"What was the other one doing in the children's room, then?" I asked.

"Don't ask me. She's your confederate."

"She's not—"

"Not that it's of any significance now. Back to my theory. I think that while you were, er, distracting security—stroke of genius, by the way—your partner let herself into the Colonel's stateroom."

"But—"

"*Then*," he said, talking over me, "you decided to cut her out of the deal. Have her taken up for assault and make off with her share. Or perhaps you sensed she was about to betray you and attempted to discredit her before she could. We never did find her, by the way—not in third class or anywhere else.

"The one thing I don't understand is why the Colonel dropped the investigation like a hot coal the moment I mentioned your name. He had seemed very happy when I'd told him I had a suspect in custody. You must tell me how you're acquainted. Just for my own curiosity."

"We're not," I said. "I swear to you, I'd never heard of him before this week."

Nicholas wasn't convinced. He looked like he'd suddenly come to the last piece of a jigsaw puzzle and had nowhere to place it. He shrugged and poured us each a bit more wine. "At any rate, there's really nothing more I can do if he doesn't want to pursue it."

"The Colonel ordered you to drop it? Not his assistant?"

Marcus had to be the key here. Perhaps he felt guilty about the way he'd left things between us. Perhaps he was acting out of belated gratitude for my past kindnesses. Perhaps Marcus had done the job himself and was having second thoughts about pointing the finger at me.

Nicholas frowned. "Why would his assistant order me to do anything? You have a very good friend in the real Dr. Lazarus, by the way. He and his wife were prepared to take White Star to court to defend you."

That surprised me. Not that they would defend me—I'd do the same for them. But that their defense was so impassioned as to make such an impression.

"Really?" I asked.

"They were ready to call down all manner of solicitors and specialists. Unlike you, however, they clearly don't have the resources to take the case very far. But they would have spent all they had."

That left me speechless for a moment. He continued.

"That was the reason for my remaining sliver of doubt in the case. I've read about Dr. and Mrs. Lazarus and their work in the papers. If people like that are convinced of your innocence, then I have to admit the unlikely possibility."

"I shall have to thank them," I said. "By the way, what exactly did Mr. Farnsworth find in my bedroom?"

He drained his wine and cast a surreptitious glance at the dinner tray. "Two large-denomination bank notes issued by Midlands Bank and signed by Rupert Sudworth. Of course Dr. Lazarus explained that you'd recently received a bequest administered by Mr. Sudworth, and he invited us to contact Sudworth's office to verify the fact." He shook his head. "If you'd simply admitted this at the time, Mr. Adler, it would have saved us all a lot of trouble—and you an afternoon locked in a bare metal room."

"If you'd ever met Rupert Sudworth, your first instinct would be to deny any connection to the man."

"That's as may be. But like I said, none of it matters now. The only thing is, if my theory is correct, I can't figure out what you did with the rest of the money. We searched this entire ship down to the nails in the floorboards, and the only trace of Colonel Wright's property was the notes Farnsworth found in your pocket." He cocked his head. "Are you going to eat your steak? Because all this ratiocination has made me hungry."

"Share it with me." I laid the tray on the floor, and we sat on either side of it. The food had cooled a bit but was well cooked and flavorful.

We finished it quickly, and in silence. After the last bite was gone, I said, "I didn't do it, Nicholas."

He shrugged. "It's not my affair. Not anymore."

"And I didn't make a fool of you. Our time together was a bit of fun, that's all."

"No more than that?"

"And no less. My only motive was getting into your trousers. And if you'll remember, it was you who made the first move."

That shy smile returned, and for the first time since his return, he met my eyes. "That's true." He let out a dramatic sigh. "First time I've failed to definitively solve a case. It rather smarts. Egad," he said, frowning. "Perhaps I'm not as clever as I thought."

"Impossible," I said. "Thank you for supper. I do hope we can part as friends."

I held out my hand. He took it, but his expression turned serious.

"You may have bested me once, Mr. Adler. But if you ever find yourself aboard the *Teutonic* again, you'd do well to keep your nose clean and your head down."

CHAPTER SEVENTEEN

You do find yourself in the most preposterous situations," Lazarus said as we made our way down the deck toward the gangplank the next morning.

The passengers were leaving in two streams—emigrants to the left, where they would likely spend the day undergoing horrifying, drawn-out bureaucratic processes, and visitors like us, to the right. The emigrants' line appeared to comprise mainly steerage passengers—tired-looking people whose journey to a new life had only just begun. Nicholas was nowhere in sight. I hoped he was enjoying a well-deserved rest, though I suspected he was probably up to his neck in paperwork. I didn't see either the Colonel or Miss Wood, in either line, and I was glad.

Rain was pissing down from a sky of industrial gray and brown. Past the landing, New York City hunkered down, looking so much like London, it was difficult to contain my disappointment. Mr. Cuttle had sold me my wardrobe for the journey based on the assumption that America was blazing hot at all times, with sun so bright one never went outside without a pair of tinted glasses. I hadn't bought those, though. The only people I'd ever known to wear tinted glasses were syphilitics, and that wasn't the impression I wished to create.

"And I must thank the both of you for arguing in my defense," I said. "If it hadn't been for you, I'd still be sitting in that room, waiting for the police."

"Sounds like the Colonel had more to do with it than us," Bess replied. "But thank you for saying so."

"Do you think it was your friend Marcus who convinced the Colonel to drop the charges?" Tim asked.

I shrugged. "That was my first thought. Though in retrospect, it doesn't ring true somehow. On the other hand, having never met the

Colonel, I can't imagine what else might have inspired him to react so strongly to my being accused of the crime."

"Well, I think we should just count our blessings and be on our way," Bess said.

We tottered down the gangplank, a trio of porters bearing our luggage behind us, our legs wobbling from a week at sea, and proceeded through a surprisingly efficient admissions process, emerging an hour or so later beneath gray skies and steely sheets of rain.

"Tim," Bess said over a rumbling wave of thunder, "why don't you take Claire to buy our train tickets? I'd like to send a wire to my sister, informing her of our arrival. Ira, I believe you also wanted the telegraph office."

"Yes," I said, brightening at the prospect of sending a cheery little message to Lawrence. "Yes, I do."

The telegraph office was one of a small cluster of buildings that appeared to comprise an array of services for travelers. While Tim and Claire headed for the railway building, Bess and I hurried across the dock and ducked through the door.

Inside, the telegraph office was cramped and warm. The large French window that made up much of one wall was fogging over from the collective heat of the crowd of people escaping the rain. Bess and I pressed our way to the counter. I wrote my message on one of the forms provided—nothing too deep, or which could lead to trouble for either Lawrence or myself—just a pleasant little "hello" from America, and regrets that my return would be delayed—and handed the form, and the appropriate coins, to the clerk. We'd exchanged money aboard ship, and though it would take practice to become comfortable with American dollars and cents, I was able to complete the transaction with at least an appearance of competence.

"Adler," the elderly clerk asked, glancing from the telegraph form to me. "Mr. Ira Adler?"

"Yes, that's me."

"Lucky you stopped by. Two telegrams arrived for you yesterday—within minutes of each other, as a matter of fact."

"Two?"

The clerk had already turned around and started toward a cabinet filled with pigeonholes that covered the entire back wall. He licked his fingers and pulled two pieces of paper out of one of the holes, then brought them back to me. I thanked him, glanced at the one on the top, and smiled.

Hope the journey treated you well. Beware of rattlesnakes.
—L.

Hmm. Not bad news, but a bit disappointing. When I'd seen Lawrence's name in the sender's box, my heart had given a little jump. I supposed he was just being cautious, as I was. Still, given the unresolved depth of feeling to which we'd both admitted back at Victoria, the message seemed a bit perfunctory. Shrugging, I flipped to the next one. It was from St. Andrews.

Message received.
Messenger received. Delightful. Many thanks.
Regarding our problem: the conclusion is obvious. The
solution tricky.
Please advise.
Andrew

My cheeks burned, and not because of the fire crackling away in the stove of the telegraph office, or the hot press of bodies around me. Was it my imagination, or was St. Andrews hinting that he'd poached my playfellow? The clerk had said that the messages had arrived within a few moments of one another. Which meant that Lawrence and St. Andrews had likely gone to the telegraph office together. Had they been together this entire time?

Another flush of heat, but this time it was shame. Lawrence was free to keep company with whomever he pleased. To tell the truth, St. Andrews was a much better match for him in both background and personality. And hadn't I spent the last seven days gaining unlawful carnal knowledge of one Nicholas Flynn, Security Chief aboard the SS *Teutonic*?

Still, it stung a bit to think that the very same day he'd declared some measure of deeper sentiment, Lawrence might have ended up in St. Andrews's bed.

But that was another question for another time. The important part of St. Andrews's message concerned our investigation. Oh, how pleasant it had been, for those lost seven days, to put aside the vexed and painful question of Goddard's murder. But now, free of my freckle-nosed, well-endowed distraction, submerged once again in London-like filth and rain, it all came back to me: the explosion, Goddard's broken body, the bones of his house exposed to the elements, and all his fine things scattered for the taking. My smashed nose—now mostly healed—and the all-too-real menace of Sudworth's young associate back at Victoria Station.

Regarding our problem: the conclusion is obvious.

I'd left London convinced that Rupert Sudworth had arranged for the explosion that had killed Cain Goddard, and would have killed me as well. It seemed St. Andrews agreed. But where to go from there?

I elbowed my way back to the counter and took a second form from the stack. Addressing it to St. Andrews's Baker Street home, I wrote,

Re our problem: contact Henry Watkins, Dorset Street. Ginger beard, gold tooth. Also—Liverpool snoozer Lila Wood. Connected?

Fleetingly, I wondered whether St. Andrews would recognize the street word for thief. I also wondered whether I wasn't inventing connections where there were none. But of all the things she might have planted on me, banknotes bearing Rupert Sudworth's signature seemed too coincidental for comfort.

Finally, I had to ask myself whether it wasn't a mistake to send St. Andrews to see Watkins. Having been Goddard's right-hand man for as long as he had, Watkins would know about the longstanding enmity between Goddard and St. Andrews. On the other hand, in the years I'd known him, Watkins had always struck me as even-tempered and judicious. His main concern would be putting paid to Goddard's murderer, not exacting revenge for some long-ago offense against a dead man, regarding the nature of which Watkins was surely ignorant. Still, Watkins had said he had a suspect in mind. If his evidence lined up with ours, he might be in a position to do something about it. If his suspect were different, St. Andrews's interference might just save a life.

As an afterthought, I added, *My best to Lawrence.*

Let them interpret that as they would. We were all adults, and I had no control over what they did or did not do in my absence. And I would do best to keep telling myself as much, whenever thoughts arose to the contrary. Straightening my tie, and my dignity, I slid my form and the appropriate coins across the counter again. And turned to find Bess Lazarus as trembling and white as a blancmange.

"Bess?" I asked.

She turned to me, her eyes wide, a telegram clenched in her hand. Through the din and chaos of the crowded telegraph office, I heard her say, "It's from my sister Irene. The house caught fire last night. She and my mother escaped with their lives, but their home was burned to the ground."

CHAPTER EIGHTEEN

We didn't have the time, or the privacy, to explore the matter further before Tim and Claire arrived, having arranged for a complicated series of trains that would take us, and our luggage, to Sacramento. A few hours later, we found ourselves aboard a crowded, comfortably shabby wooden carriage, hurtling southwest through New Jersey, on course for the American plains.

"It's a little less than twenty-four hours to Chicago," Tim explained. "I didn't bother with a sleeper carriage. Better to save the money. Though if you—"

"It's fine, Tim," Bess said. She turned to him with a wan smile. "I grew up in tents and shacks all over Asia and spend my days working in East London, which, most of the time, isn't much better."

"Sorry, dear." Tim squeezed her shoulder. "I forgot to whom I was speaking."

He and I had taken the aisle seats on two facing benches, with Bess and their daughter on the inside. Though my friends seemed to have forgiven me for the incident with Sudworth's man at Victoria Station, I still felt that close brush with disaster keenly and found myself remaining a little more vigilant than the average doting uncle. I still wasn't convinced that Sudworth would pursue me once we'd left London. How much further could I pry into Goddard's murder from across the Atlantic? Nonetheless, danger had never seemed to be more than a breath away since I left my Aldersgate Street flat so long ago, and one could never go wrong by being too prepared for it.

As for Claire, she'd settled into her corner without her usual constant and trenchant commentary, pulling her legs up under her heavy dark skirts and gazing out the soot-smudged window, her wooden horse clutched in one hand. It had been a long morning of standing, waiting, and shuffling through crowds of fast-moving, fast-talking people.

It wasn't that New Yorkers looked so very different, aside from the occasional thin tie and flat-topped, wide-brimmed hat. The women's corsets were just as unreasonably tight, their hair was piled just as ridiculously high, their balloon-like dress sleeves as comical as any worn in London. But the crowd had a very different feeling. Everyone spoke in short, direct communicative bursts, and all in that strange, nasal accent. They rushed about as if they'd somewhere important to be and were not only already late, but were being personally impeded by *you.* And an astonishing number of men carried pistols.

Bess had been subdued since receiving her sister's telegram. Between her missionary childhood and her work on Raven Row, she'd seen some shocking things, I was sure, but I had the impression this was the first time events had ever touched her family. While Tim settled into his *New York Times*, she read the telegram over and over, as if she might have missed some key piece of information. Eventually she tired of it and folded it back into her handbag, replacing it with some sort of needlework.

"Did your sister say if she thought the fire was an accident?" I asked after a while. New Jersey was well behind us, now, and outside the windows, the Pennsylvania countryside rolled out in both directions in a palette of light and dark green.

"She didn't, though I can't imagine it was. California is hotter than blazes in the summer, so they wouldn't have had a fire in the hearth, and Ma would have put out the stove before she and Irene went to bed." She sighed. "Papa bought her that stove right before he died. She was so proud of it."

"Surely no one would do such a thing on purpose," Tim said.

Bess shrugged. "How else could it have happened?"

"Do you think it was an Indian attack?" I asked. I knew nothing of Indians, of course, save for the lurid stories in the penny papers written by people as ignorant as myself. But, as we rocketed through dense forests, emerging every now and then onto trimmed rolling hills dotted with farms, I couldn't help looking for painted faces in the trees.

Bess shook her head. "There haven't been any clashes in that part of California for years. Diseases the settlers and miners brought with them killed almost all of the people originally living in the area. Most of those who were left have been forced onto reservations. From what Irene writes, if violence ever did break out in Pyrite, a drunken ranch hand would be at the center of it, and he would well deserve his comeuppance."

"It sounds like a terribly wild place, Pyrite," Tim said jokingly. "The lawless West."

"Not really. It's small—only a few hundred people. Ranchers, mainly—cattle and horses, some sheep. Although from what Irene says, Samuel Curtis has been buying up every scrap of land he can get his hands on for his own herd—if you can call ten thousand head of cattle a herd."

"Doing quite well for himself, isn't he?" Tim asked.

"At the expense of the smaller ranches, which are being driven right out of existence. According to Irene, his goal is to be able to travel from Oregon to Mexico without ever leaving his own land, and he's well on his way."

"Blimey," I said. "Maybe Irene should have married him."

This earned me a very black look from Bess.

"I'm starved," Claire said, though she sounded more sleepy than hungry.

Bess pulled the toy satchel out from under the bench and produced the apples and sandwiches she'd purchased from one of the many vendors on the platform back in New York.

"Where are the chocolates?" Claire asked with an unreasonably delightful pout.

"What chocolates?"

"The ones you bought when you thought I wasn't looking."

Tim gave his wife a surprised look. Of the two of them, Bess had been the most firm about Dr. Browning's dietary edicts. For Bess's part, she did her best to look put out, but she was trying hard to suppress a smile.

"Proper food first," she said primly.

"Oh, all right." Claire held out her hand, and Bess pressed a paper-wrapped half-sandwich into it.

"Ira?"

"Yes, please," I said.

The sandwich was plain compared to the posh food aboard the *Teutonic*, but it was surprisingly satisfying. The bread was cut into thick slabs, and though it was probably at least a day old, it was flavorful and generously slathered with butter. Inside were thick chips of salty ham. The apples were different than any I'd tasted—juicier, though not quite as sweet. They were also rather rectangular in shape.

"And plain cheese for Daddy," Bess said, handing the last one to Tim.

A warm, grateful expression lit his face. Even if the world sneered at his budding culinary scruples, at least his wife took them seriously. "Thank you, dear."

The entire atmosphere seemed to lighten after we'd filled our bellies, and the gentle back-and-forth motion of the train, the rhythmic shushing of the pistons had everyone yawning. While Claire curled up on her half of the bench, leaning her head against the wall, I reached across to the opposite bench and teased out a section of Tim's *New York Times*. It was an interesting publication—significantly less conservative than the London *Times*, and quite a bit less sensational than the other papers I'd perused back in New York. A movement was building across America to ban alcoholic drink—imagine! Several states had already outlawed "the demon liquor," and the movement—an unholy alliance of God-botherers, trades-unionists and women's-rights advocates— appeared to be picking up steam. Meanwhile, a flood of new, cheaply made handguns into large Northern cities was causing a crime wave.

"Why is it, do you think, that Americans are so keen to ban the occasional medicinal whiskey, but seem to want to put a gun in the hand of every man, woman, and child?" I asked.

"I think that's really oversimplifying things, Ira," Bess replied.

"Is it? Did you see how many people in New York had pistols under their jackets?" I'd noticed the telltale lumps of pocket weapons and the occasional shoulder holster once we'd cleared customs. It had been a very unsettling feeling and left me wondering whether even Claire would be issued her own revolver once we left civilization for the wild American West.

"It's a problem in the cities, I'll grant. But most of the states west of the Mississippi have very strict gun laws. You can have a rifle for hunting and home defense, but if you go into town, you have to leave your firearm with the sheriff. It's illegal to carry a pistol at all most places in California." She frowned, picking up the sandwich paper Claire had dropped, folding it, and tucking it into her handbag. "You'd think it would be the other way around. New York has a large, organized police department, whereas in places like Pyrite, the sheriff might be in the next town, and the nearest U.S. Marshal might be a week away. Yet the crime rate is so much higher in the Northeast."

Well. Wouldn't St. Andrews be surprised to learn that his dreams of six-gun-toting cattle-wranglers and saloon shoot-outs were a figment of the fertile imaginations of penny-dreadful scribblers? I made a note to telegraph him the bad news the moment we arrived. He could share it with Lawrence over breakfast. In the meantime, I relaxed a bit, knowing that Lawrence's fear—and my own, quite frankly—that I'd find myself gunned down by outlaws was becoming less likely with every passing mile.

Eventually night fell, and, having exhausted both the available means of entertainment and our physical reserves, we fell into an uncomfortable sleep, sitting up on our poorly padded benches. Claire was dubious about this arrangement after the luxurious accommodations aboard the *Teutonic*. But, being her mother's daughter, she soon resolved to make the best of the situation and was snoring away with her feet in my lap as night fell over northeastern Indiana. We pulled into Chicago Union Station early the next morning.

"We should be in Council Bluffs by dinnertime," Tim said, as he helped his wife and daughter off the train and set their hand baggage down on the platform. "But first, we'll have breakfast—a proper one— at the station restaurant. Union Station isn't yet five years old, and the restaurant has already been mentioned in the London papers."

As we made our way across the crowded platform toward the passenger terminal—or the "head house," as Americans called it, crowds of people bustled around us, hems gliding over tile floors that hadn't existed long enough for the soot and grime to become a permanent part of the pattern. The people seemed just as rushed as they had in New York, though they spoke more slowly, and their pronunciation was decidedly more nasal. Chicagoans also seemed to favor more practical clothing in sober colors. I noted fewer concealed shoulder holsters and fewer towering, feather-and-flower adorned coiffures than I'd seen in either London or New York.

When we reached the terminal, Tim began to hold forth on the Corinthian columns supporting the high, painted ceilings. He and Bess had both developed an interest in building architecture and had spent many mornings walking the London streets, marking the sights. It was cheaper than a vacation, he often said. And, she would add, an excellent way to ensure that Claire would be ready for a long nap in the afternoon. While they each tried to outdo the other in spotting unique feats of art and engineering, I borrowed the ticket envelope, found a porter, and arranged for our larger luggage to be transferred to the Council Bluffs train. When I returned, Tim was finishing his briefing regarding the rest of the journey.

"And from there, we'll board the train to Sacramento."

"And after that, what? We'll walk to Pyrite? Or perhaps ride horses?" I asked.

"From Sacramento, it's just a short hop—one last train, no more than a couple of hours. Pyrite just received its own depot last year," Bess said proudly. "But I really can't think about any more travel right now—at least not on an empty stomach. Forward, gentlemen."

The train whistles and echoing voices and footsteps faded to almost nothing, as we stepped out of the bustling lobby into the restaurant. A fawning maître d' greeted us with characteristic American enthusiasm and warmth, then led us across a thick carpet to a table laid with crisp linen and shiny silver. A small fountain lapped in the background, while a pianist plinked out an unobtrusive tune on a polished parlor grand. It rather reminded me of the Savoy, and yet, unlike at the Savoy, the present staff was uncommonly tolerant of the bedraggled appearance and frayed nerves of their travel-weary diners. The waiter was especially kind to Claire and even brought her a fat pillow to set upon her chair, so that she could see over the table like everyone else.

The American breakfast appeared to be a very serious undertaking indeed. The menu was two full pages long and included four different kinds of fish; broiled, roasted, and grilled beef; numerous cuts of pork prepared in different ways; and, to Tim's relief, a startling array of porridges.

"What's the difference between a pancake and a johnnycake?" Tim asked. He buttered one of the thick pieces of toast that had appeared immediately with the coffee and handed it to Claire.

"A johnnycake is made out of corn—maize," Bess said, translating for the Englishmen at the table. "Pancakes are made out of wheat flour and served with fruit and syrup." She waggled her eyebrows at Claire when she said this.

"I want that!" Claire cried.

"And you shall have it," said Bess. "And so shall I."

"What's hominy?" Tim asked.

"Also corn. It's a sort of porridge, generally served savory."

"I'll have that," Tim told the waiter, who appeared to have materialized out of nowhere, a steaming silver coffee pot in his hand. "And the scrambled eggs and potatoes. *And* some more of that wonderful coffee. Americans certainly know their business when it comes to coffee," he said as the waiter refilled his cup.

While the Lazarus family chatted happily over their breakfast, I plowed through plates of sausage and potatoes, scrambled eggs with bacon, a stack of the aforementioned pancakes swimming in the unspeakably luxurious combination of butter and maple syrup—I'd be taking a few hundred bottles of *that* home with me; Lawrence would love it—and at least two pots of coffee, hot and black. By the time we were finished it was time to roll ourselves back to the platform and get on the train for Council Bluffs.

"I'm afraid it's not much to look at," Tim admitted when we found the train that would take us to the far end of Iowa. "But we'll be in Council Bluffs before nightfall, and then we'll pick up the Central Pacific and won't have to move again until we reach Sacramento. You'll love it, Bess," he said, his voice rising with the renewed optimism of one who has eaten much and well. "We'll have our own berths on the Pullman coach—"

"What's a Pullman coach?" Claire asked as we reached the platform.

As Tim described the train we would board later that evening—a long string of bright-green carriages with padded benches that folded down into beds at night, and curtains to pull across for privacy—I eyed the smaller Council Bluffs train with distaste. The benches would be as hard as the ones that had borne us from New York, I could tell. The windows would be jammed shut, and the curtains would stink of stale tobacco and forgotten apples.

"There will be a dining car, of course, but our coach will have a porter to look after us as well." He brushed a stray lock of hair back behind Bess's ear. "Because I dare say, some of us could use a little looking after."

Bess smiled thinly. "I'll just be glad to see my family and settle this whole business with the mine."

We climbed aboard the dusty little train and found our seats. The carriage was exactly as I'd expected, though twice as crowded. The other passengers appeared to be as happy about this as I was. But Tim and Bess looked relaxed and contented. Claire was cheerfully tying knots in her dolly's hair. As we pulled out of Chicago, I shook out the newspaper I'd purchased at the station and kept my remarks to myself.

Chapter Nineteen

The train to Sacramento chuffed on its track, vibrating with the excitement of a racehorse. The bright-red engineer's cabin gleamed in the light of the setting sun. The fires were stoked, and heat radiated from the tall, black smokestack in curling waves I could feel on my face. A long string of carriages stretched back from the engine toward the tiny town of Council Bluffs, Iowa, silhouetted against the darkening horizon. Just a few miles in the other direction, the flat, green fields of Nebraska rolled out toward the rapidly setting sun.

Nearest the engine were the first-class carriages, their gold and red paint so fresh it still looked wet. Inside, the cars would be divided into well-appointed private cabins—little havens of wood, velvet, and polished brass, like the one in which we had traveled from London to Liverpool. Two dining cars separated these from the long string of bright-green Pullman carriages. The Pullmans were communal cars, where second-class passengers like us could configure our benches into seating during the day and beds at night. Billed as affordable luxury, the Pullman cars made up the bulk of this particular train, though there were two third-class carriages at the very end, just before the observation car. Third class had served acceptably for the short trips to Chicago and Council Bluffs, but I doubted even Tim could have tolerated eating crushed sandwiches and sleeping upright on a hard wooden bench all the way to California.

A shrill whistle cut through the noise of the crowd. The conductor cried "All aboard." Gathering our hand baggage and herding Claire, we made our way toward one of the middle carriages.

Inside, the green sleeping car was even better than Tim had described. The benches were well padded and newly upholstered in a sturdy, dark fabric. The walls were comprised of varnished wood with brass flourishes. The ceiling, against which rows of folding beds were secured for daytime travel, was painted a cheery off-white, which made the carriage seem much larger than it actually was. The richly patterned damask curtains were spotless and fragrant with the smell of the lavender water Goddard's maid used to use for ironing. The floors were blessedly clean. We were probably too tired to appreciate it properly. I did, however, sink down onto the plump bench with great pleasure and extraordinary gratitude.

Our fellow passengers filtered into the carriage from both ends, gradually filling the benches around us. Most of them appeared to be of the same solid, sensible Midwestern stock we had observed in Chicago—scrubbed, earthy sorts in well-made, though plain suits; dresses in muted colors and patterns, and hair that was clean and styled, though by no means *fancy*. Bess Lazarus looked entirely at home. It was a tight fit, though. A lot of people were traveling to Sacramento that evening, and we witnessed quite a few accidental collisions and murmured apologies as we all put away our hand baggage and arranged our seats.

A smartly dressed Black man in uniform stood near the far end, ready to assist. He looked to be in his mid to late thirties, with a neatly trimmed mustache; smooth, very dark skin; and well-defined features that were simultaneously masculine and refined. His dark-blue trousers and jacket were tailored to his trim figure. The line of brass buttons down the front of the jacket gleamed in the lamplight, setting off the gold braid across the brim of his cap and the engraved brass badge on the front of the cap that read PULLMAN PORTER. The American slaves had been emancipated a mere thirty years before, and the porter would likely have been six or seven at the time. I wondered if he had spent those early years in slavery.

As if feeling my gaze, the porter met my eyes and gave a crisp nod. Embarrassed, I nodded back and pulled my eyes away.

Eventually the engine heaved a long sigh, and a cloud of steam obscured the crowded platform on the other side of the window. I sat down quickly as the train lurched forward, then eased into the push-pull rhythm that had settled into my bones over the last few days.

"I could get used to this," I said, bouncing experimentally on the bench next to Claire.

"Don't get too comfortable," Tim said, gesturing toward the bunk folded against the wall over the window. "You're sleeping up there."

"I see."

I stood, spreading my legs a bit and bending my knees to

accommodate the back-and-forth motion of the train. I glanced out the window. Council Bluffs was invisible now against the dark horizon. Outside the windows, flat land rolled out in all directions—green fields, I imagined, though in the gathering night it was difficult to tell.

Mindful of my friends' heads, I pulled the bed down from the wall and locked it into place. I was pleased to find the mattress as thick and firm as the bench cushion had been. Fresh sheets and a blanket lay on top of the mattress, and while Tim and Bess folded their benches flat, I made my bed. The curtain of night was falling fast around us. Outside, the darkness was nearly complete. It was a bit early for bed for anyone who hadn't already been traveling for days, and while we prepared for sleep, most of the other passengers were tucking into newspapers, books, and the occasional card game, their conversations providing a pleasant background hum.

"Ain't this great?" a man called from the other side of the aisle.

I turned, unsure if he was addressing us. But he met my eyes, and a crooked grin spread across his stubbly face. He looked to be in his mid-twenties, with pasty skin, lank dark hair in need of a cut, pointed features, and a creased suit that was fraying at the cuffs. A step down from the other passengers, I thought. Not just travel-grime. His suit was cheap, the toe of one shoe was pulling up from its sole, and his bowler had seen a lot of use. Something about him set my teeth on edge, and it wasn't just his sartorial shortcomings. A few of the passengers glanced up at the interruption, then went back to their entertainments.

"This here's the sleeping car," the man continued. He spoke loudly, and I could smell his tobacco from where I stood. "Observation car's down that end." He gestured with his head. "You want anything, you just ask that boy over there. My name's Floyd, by the way. Floyd Wilkes. Where you folks from?"

Tim pulled the curtains shut across his window with a snap and glanced over his shoulder. Bess had warned us that Americans tended to become overly familiar overly quickly. Leaving her husband to deal with the intrusion, she sat Claire on the bench and began to prepare her for bed.

"What boy?" Claire asked, kicking at the seat while her mother attempted to unlace her shoes. Bess gave her daughter's knee a light smack, and the kicking stopped.

"You know." Wilkes nodded toward the porter. "He'll do whatever you say. Bring you a drink, shine your shoes. Just like at home. Bet you got servants at home, little lady, don't you?"

"No," Claire said as if it were the most ridiculous thing she'd ever heard.

"Awww. Ain't that cute? Where you from, little darlin'?"

"That's quite enough," Tim said sharply.

If he hadn't said it, I would have. It might have been just friendly chat, but in East London, where we lived and where Claire was learning how to relate to the world, such unwarranted personal interest often signaled a hidden agenda. And considering the various unsavory characters we'd met since leaving Victoria Station, and their equally unsavory agendas, I had no interest in engaging another.

"Forgive me," Tim said, softening. "We've had a long journey and my wife and daughter are tired."

"No, I'm not," Claire said brightly. Then she launched into a fanciful story about trains and boats and mermaids. Bess glanced out of the corner of her eye from time to time. When the child turned the conversation to the future, though, she intercepted without mercy.

"Come, now, Claire. I'm certain Mr. Wilkes has no interest in where we're—"

"So you're headed to Sacramento?" Wilkes said.

"Granny lives in Pyrite," Claire chirped. "She has a gold mine."

"Really? And you ain't got no servants at home? What's your daddy do?"

"He's a doctor!" Claire squealed before anyone could stop her.

"That will do!" Tim stepped between them, and when he spoke again, his words were to Claire, but he was unambiguously addressing Wilkes. "I'm sure this man doesn't want to listen to your prattle all the way to…to wherever he's bound."

Wilkes's grin widened. "Just so happens I'm headed for Sacramento myself."

Tim grimaced. "What a wonderful coincidence. Come, Claire. It's time for bed."

Ignoring her protests, Tim reached up to the rail above my bed and yanked down a set of floor-length black curtains, marking a distinct boundary between Wilkes and his family.

"But what about Elizabeth?" Claire whined behind the curtain.

Elizabeth—Elizabeth Blackwell, to be precise—was Claire's most prized possession. The doll had been a gift from the *real* Elizabeth Blackwell, founder of the London School of Medicine for Women, and one of Tim and Bess's do-gooding acquaintances. Bess had been doing her best to encourage Claire to treat the porcelain-headed doll gently—

which Claire interpreted as dragging it everywhere unless physically stopped.

"She's in her bag where she should be," Tim said. When Claire started to whine, he added, "These floors are hard wood. You wouldn't want her to fall out of bed and break, would you?"

"Nice to meet you, Doctor," Wilkes called, seemingly oblivious to Lazarus's signal that the conversation was over. "As I said, my name's Floyd."

Tim scowled at the outstretched hand, but politeness gained the better of him. "Lazarus," he muttered.

And then he climbed into his berth next to Claire and Bess, and pulled the curtain shut around them.

"My name is Adler," I said, though Wilkes appeared to have no interest in me whatsoever.

"Dr. Lazarus." Wilkes turned the name over in his mouth as if tasting it. Then, as if catching himself, he said, "I can tell you folks is tired, and I didn't mean to disturb you. I do hope you'll let me make it up to you."

Behind the curtain Tim sighed. "That's really not—"

Wilkes whistled sharply through tobacco-yellowed teeth. "Hey, George! Bring the little lady some hot chocolate or something, and make it snappy." He turned back to me—the only person who hadn't put a curtain between Wilkes and themselves—grinning that crooked grin again. "They's all named George, you know. After George Pullman, the man who owns the company?"

There was a commotion behind the curtains, and Claire stuck out her head.

"They're *all* named George?" she demanded. Tim's hand appeared and made a futile attempt to retrieve her. She slapped it away. "All of them?"

Wilkes shrugged. "They probably got real names, but everyone calls 'em George. They don't mind. Hey, George, get over here!"

On the far end of the carriage, the porter glanced over. From the look in his eyes, his name was not George, and he *did* mind—though not enough to risk a complaint from a customer so early in the journey. The porter straightened his jacket, pausing just long enough to show that he was approaching of his own volition, then made his way down the aisle.

"Good evening, sir," he said, nodding to Wilkes, then to me. Tim emerged from behind the curtain. The porter tipped his hat to Bess when she, too, reluctantly appeared. "Ma'am. How can I help you fine folks this evening?"

"I'm so sorry," Tim said, rubbing a hand over his face. "We don't require anything at present. But thank you for—"

"George, get these good people something to drink. Is this how we treat foreign visitors, now? Go on, boy, chop-chop."

When Wilkes clapped his hands at the man, Tim and Bess looked ready to die of mortification. Clearly Wilkes wanted to impress us by ordering the staff about—I'd seen plenty of the Piccadilly set behave in a similar way. But there was nothing impressive about acting like an ass.

"No," Tim said firmly. "Thank you. And I'm sorry for—"

"We're not traveling with this man," I said. "If we require anything, we'll ask you ourselves. We're dreadfully sorry for having disturbed you for nothing."

The porter nodded to me, tipped his hat once more to Bess, and said, "It's never a bother, sir. That's what I'm here for. And my name is Calvin," he added with a conspiratorial wink to Claire. Claire grinned back.

"Well, even if they don't want nothin', I'll have a whiskey, thank you very much," Wilkes muttered.

"Yes, sir," Calvin said. His tone was indulgent, but the wry set of his lips made it clear he was humoring the man.

By now the other passengers had started to turn around to see what the fuss was about. Calvin, humming a little tune, let himself out the back of the carriage, presumably to find a drink for Wilkes. I busied myself with my bedding, hoping to avoid any further confrontation. In a little while Calvin returned with a tumbler of watered-down whiskey, which Wilkes grudgingly accepted. Seeming at last to have understood the meaning of the curtain Tim had pulled across the little alcove where his family were lying down to sleep, Wilkes settled down in his seat with his drink and stared out the window.

Having eased my own bed into place, I hoisted myself up. It was comfortable enough—infinitely more so than the upright bench upon which I'd spent the previous night—but sleep eluded me. Perhaps it was because I'd napped much of the way from Chicago. Or perhaps I just had a lot on my mind. After an hour or so of tossing and turning, I climbed back down and went for a walk.

The other Pullman cars appeared to be more or less identical to ours, from the salt-of-the-earth-looking passengers to the attentive porters—all well-turned-out Black men, I noticed, between the ages of twenty and fifty, watching over their domains with an air of calm authority. There was a dining car between the last Pullman and the third-class cars. It was bright and cheerful, with polished wood, white tablecloths, and muted gaslight. Travel-giddy passengers filled the tables. The air sang with the clink of glass and silver, and was warm with the smells of well-cooked pork and roasted potatoes. I thought to stop for a drink, but all the tables were occupied, and finding no room at the tiny bar, I hurried through the spare, uncomfortable confines of third class until I reached the observation car at the end of the train.

I spotted a few comfortable chairs in there, but it was clear the intent was for passengers to stand and enjoy the view of the passing countryside. Windows made up the upper half of each wall and arced up toward a glass-covered ceiling. The lamps were turned very low. Most people, I assumed, did their observing in the daytime. Outside, the sky was black, but from time to time, I glimpsed lighter sky through the wall of trees growing on each side of the tracks.

A door at the back of the carriage opened onto an uncovered deck enclosed by a railing. I stepped outside and stood for some time, watching the moonlight glint off the train tracks as they disappeared behind us. The rhythmic sound of the wheels, the clean, balmy air rushing by, and the gentle swaying of the carriage were almost hypnotic. If there had been a chair bolted to the deck, I might have happily slept there.

I lit a cigarette as we rocketed through the last of the trees and emerged onto a vast, moonlit expanse punctuated with distant farmhouses—vague shadow outlines with twinkling house lights. We were well into Nebraska at that point. Though darkness obscured the details of the landscape, this state appeared to be just as flat and just as verdant as Iowa had been. Seen from the tail end of a moving train, it was breathtaking, even obscured by darkness. So much space, and so clean. How very different from the cramped, teeming streets of London. I ground out my cigarette, suddenly ashamed to be polluting this pristine panorama. How different might my life have been, had I been raised in a land of clean air and endless vistas? Suddenly the Americans' openness, ambition, and relentless optimism made sense to me. A strong work ethic seems a natural outcome when one's days are filled with honest, physical labor. And when one is raised among a small number of people whom one has known his entire life, of course he develops a trusting nature—a nature, which, on the streets of East London, would be suicidally naive.

I drew long breaths of the moist, grassy air, enjoying the sensation of tension draining from my neck and shoulders—tension, I realized, that was always with me. As I stood there, watching the tracks disappear over the horizon, something awakened inside me, like a hatchling shaking off its shell and opening its wet, trembling wings. I was a man of means, now. I could live where I pleased. Would it please me to live in a quiet farmhouse with the nearest neighbor a half-hour's walk away? Would I enjoy waking every morning to bright sunshine, birdsong, and endless green?

Or would loneliness and boredom set in and make me more miserable than I had ever been?

I jumped at the sound of the observation car door snicking shut behind me. I whirled. Through the window, I could see the silhouette of a man retreating unhurriedly through the observation car. He opened the door to the passenger car beyond it, then disappeared inside. My hand reached instinctively for the door handle—only to find it firmly locked.

"Hey!" I cried, cursing the complacency of the past few years that had led me to leave my picklocks in a little jar on the mantel of my flat in London. "Out here!"

I pounded on the window, wondering if anyone could hear me. My first thought was that I'd missed some notice regarding the opening and closing times of the observation car. But the outdoor deck wasn't so large that anyone would have missed seeing me there.

"Open the door!"

The vast Nebraska night seemed to swallow my cries. I banged my fist against the glass as hard as I thought I could without breaking it. Eventually the noise must have made its way to the passenger car, for a face appeared in the window.

"Here! I'm back here!" I rapped on the window some more.

He was an older man, stout of build, wearing a dark suit. He shaded his eyes with his hands, as if trying to get a better look. After a moment, he let himself inside, made his way across the car, and unlocked the door.

"How'd you get out there, young man?" he asked. He must have been riding in the very last third-class carriage to have heard me, but he looked satisfied with his lot. His face was round, like his belly, and above his full, combed beard, his mouth was creased around what looked to be a habitual smile.

"Just went out for some air. Does the observation car close at a certain time?"

He frowned. "Not that I know of."

"Then did you see who locked the door?"

"Didn't see a thing until you woke me up with your caterwauling. Now why don't you come back inside and stop making all that noise?"

His friendly tone softened the words, and I began to feel a bit silly. I followed him back through the observation car, then into the third-class carriage from whence he'd emerged. A few of the other passengers looked up. Most ignored me. As I returned to my own carriage, I glanced around, looking for anyone who appeared out of place—anyone who looked as if he'd been running, or anyone I didn't remember seeing on my way through earlier. But to no avail.

Someone had deliberately locked me out. Who? And why?

Quite naturally, my thoughts turned to Wilkes. He'd shown an unnatural interest in our party and a hint of aggressiveness behind the chatty facade. But Wilkes had ignored me while peppering the Lazaruses with questions. I'd spoken sharply in his presence but had given him no reason to wish me ill. Why would he have followed me? It seemed ridiculous. Nonetheless, thinking of Tim, Bess, and Claire asleep in the Pullman car with nothing but the curtain to protect them, I walked faster.

Eventually I returned to our carriage to find the Lazaruses exactly where I'd left them. Wilkes was there, too, snoring away, empty whiskey cup in one hand, his head pressed up against the window. I narrowed my eyes, looking for any sign that he had recently made a mad dash through a string of railway carriages, but found none. He didn't appear to have broken a sweat recently, and though one could likely falsify a snore, I wasn't so certain about the drool.

"Tim," I whispered bending down through the curtain. Then I poked his shoulder. "Tim!"

After a pause, Lazarus said in a heavy, sleepy voice, "Yes?"

"Just checking to see if everything is as it should be."

"Yes," he said.

"Good night, then."

"Good night, Adler."

At that moment the door of the carriage opened and softly closed. I looked up to see the porter, Calvin, taking his place once again at the seat in the rear.

"Is everything all right, sir?" he asked, pleasantly enough. It had been a man's figure I'd seen retreating through the passenger car, though the lighting had prevented me from discerning more than a vague outline of his back. Would the porter have reason to lock me outside on the deck?

I shook my head. My imagination was gaining the better of me.

"Yes," I said. "Everything's fine."

Chapter Twenty

Everything was *not* fine when I woke the next morning.

"Someone's been through my handbag," Bess was saying as I blinked awake, trying to understand why the painted wood ceiling of the carriage was so close to my face. I pulled Goddard's battle-scarred watch out of the pocket of my waistcoat. Ten forty.

"Is anything missing?" Tim asked.

"No. But nothing's in the right place. Look, they put my prayer book in the zipper pocket. I never keep it there. And my pen is just rolling around at the bottom. Why couldn't they at least put it back in the case?"

Gingerly, I sat up and lowered myself to the floor, threading my arms back through the waistcoat I'd been using as a pillow. My billfold was still in the breast pocket and still fat with money. I wanted to keep it close. My shirt, however, I'd been wearing since we left New York. I was looking forward to changing it. From the thick, humid, gamey air in the cabin, I'd imagine most of the other passengers would be as grateful for the opportunity to change clothes as I would be. The Lazaruses had already folded their beds back and opened their window shades—as had most of the other passengers. Harsh sunlight streamed into the carriage. Outside the windows, the view was bleak and brown, rising toward a subtle ridge on the north side. Overnight the rolling pastures had transformed into a stark, arid landscape of grasses and brush. The sky was a shocking blue, and the sharply delineated clouds felt unnaturally heavy and low.

"Where are we?" I asked.

"Wyoming, I think," said Bess. "The porter said we'll be stopping in Cheyenne in an hour or so."

A child's wail cut through my thoughts.

"Elizabeth Blackwell! She's gone!" Claire cried. She was wearing a fresh dress, and Bess had gone to quite a bit of trouble to wash her face and comb her hair as best as one could on a train. The reddening cheeks, the twisting lips, the gathering tantrum ruined the effect.

"Did you look under the seat?" Tim asked.

"*You* made me put her in the bag, and she's not there now! She's *gone!*"

Tim checked beneath the bench again, while Bess poked at the neatly folded blanket sitting atop it. I took the opportunity to look through the satchel in which Elizabeth Blackwell usually resided when Claire was playing with something else. The doll was as long as my forearm. It would have been difficult to miss her.

"Somethin' the matter, little lady?" Wilkes asked, looking up from the hangnail he'd been picking. Tim's face clouded over at the sound of the man's voice. He opened his mouth to speak, but Claire was faster.

"Someone's stolen Elizabeth Blackwell!" she cried. Then she buried her face in her mother's skirts and sobbed.

"Aww, I'm sure she just stepped out for a minute. Maybe she's gone down to the observation car to get some air."

Claire paused her sobbing to give Wilkes a disdainful glare worthy of her father.

A prickle ran across the back of my neck, and I shot a sharp glance at Wilkes. He avoided looking at me. Had he been the one to lock me out the night before, the better to rifle through my friends' bags?

"Aww, she'll be back, darlin'. She couldn't have gone far. Say, maybe your granny can buy you a new dolly with the money from her gold mine."

"That's really not helpful," Tim said as he unfolded the benches again to search them. Finding nothing, he sighed and wrestled them back into place while Bess once more went through the hand baggage.

"I'm afraid Claire may be right," Bess said, frowning. "I can't see any sign of Miss Blackwell. Claire, are you certain—"

"I put her back in the satchel myself last night at bedtime," Tim said.

"She's been stolen!" Claire wailed. "She's been...been... *kidnapped!*"

"Excuse me, folks. May I be of assistance?"

At some point, the porter, Calvin, had appeared at Bess's side. His uniform looked freshly pressed, his shoes newly shined. He had looked just as polished at ten the night before. I wondered when he'd found the time to sleep.

"I'm terribly sorry, Mr..." Bess said.

"Sutter," he said. "But passengers typically address porters by name."

"Extraordinary," Tim muttered.

"Mr. Sutter," Bess continued. "Calvin, my daughter has misplaced her doll."

"I didn't misplace her!" Claire shrieked. Bess set a hand on her shoulder as the girl again dissolved in sobs.

"It was a very special doll," Bess said. "A gift from a family friend. She's about this long." She held her hands apart in approximate measure. "With light hair, a checked dress, and a little straw hat. She has a porcelain head, hands, and feet."

Sutter knelt down and looked Claire in the eye. He didn't touch her shoulder or cheek, as Lawrence might have. As Floyd Wilkes certainly would have, if he hadn't sensed that Tim would have taken his hand off. His manner was gentle, but he didn't patronize. And Claire responded to him—drying her eyes and stilling her trembling lip while he spoke.

"Ma'am," he said gravely. "This is my car, and you are my guests. Nobody steals from my guests. I will find your Miss Elizabeth Blackwell before we reach Cheyenne, or—"

His words were lost as a sudden boom jostled the moving train on its tracks and pitched us nearly off our feet. The brakes screeched. The train shuddered along the rails a few yards longer, then lurched to a halt.

"What's happening?" I asked as I steadied myself against one of the benches.

"This isn't Cheyenne," said Tim.

Sutter said, "No, sir, it is not."

We weren't anywhere that I could tell. Outside, the prairie stretched out in an endless field of faded gold and brown, with no sign of civilization, save for a dot on the horizon that might have been either a distant barn or a trick of the eye. Several hundred shaggy, brown, hansom-cab-sized animals grazed in the distance, pulling up the tough scrub with their powerful jaws and occasionally taking a swipe at one another with their massive horned heads.

"What the devil are those?" I asked.

"The great American bison," Sutter replied. "They can jump six feet in the air, run forty miles an hour, and have a reputation for being, shall we say, irritable. Have a good look, sir. They're all but extinct in most parts of the country."

I wasn't so certain that was a bad thing.

The passengers were beginning to grumble. Somewhere in the next carriage, someone cried out in alarm. Sutter raised his chin as if scenting the wind for trouble and squared back his shoulders.

"Ladies and gentlemen." Sutter turned to address the whole of the cabin. "Please do not panic. I'm certain there's nothing to be alarmed about. Probably a minor mechanical problem, which will be sorted out as quickly as possible. Please remain in your seats, while I ascertain the reason for our stopping. Union Pacific apologizes for the delay." Turning to Claire, he said, "Excuse me, ma'am. I won't be but a moment."

He turned on the sharp heel of his boot and marched purposefully down the aisle.

"Now, hold on just a minute, boy."

My heart stopped as Wilkes shot out of his seat, producing a pistol from under his jacket. The passengers drew a sharp, collective gasp.

Where had that come from? Briefly, I found myself wishing we'd still been traveling with gun-happy New Yorkers rather than the placid, moon-faced Midwesterners who'd boarded at Council Bluffs. Sutter slowly turned, his hand still on the handle of the door.

"You ain't going nowhere." Wilkes waved him away from the door. Never taking his eyes from Wilkes, Sutter took one measured step to the side. Wilkes turned his attention to Lazarus. "Now, everybody just stay calm, while the doctor gives me what's mine."

All heads swiveled toward Lazarus, who stammered, "I-I have no idea what you're talking about."

Wilkes smirked. "Very funny, Doctor. The key?"

Lazarus shrugged.

"Come on, now." He gestured expansively with the gun. "These good people want to be on their way, and you're the only thing holding them up. Just give me the key, and I'll hop off this train, and none of you will ever see me again."

"Give it to him!" someone cried.

"I swear I've never seen this man before in my life! The only key I have goes to the front door of my house in London!"

Sutter cleared his throat. "Sir," he said, addressing Wilkes. "This train arrives in Cheyenne every morning at eleven o'clock, without fail.

In all the time I've worked for Union Pacific, it has not been late once. It is now five minutes before eleven. They're probably organizing a search party as we speak. If the doctor has something that belongs to you, I suggest we all wait until we get to Cheyenne, where the sheriff can sort it out."

"I don't need no sheriff to sort out nothing." Wilkes cocked his pistol and leveled it at Lazarus's chest. "I don't know where you put that key, Doctor, but you've got five seconds to hand it over. Five."

Lazarus's jaw dropped. The color bled from his face. Next to him, Bess opened and shut her mouth, as if trying to form words that wouldn't come. Suddenly, Claire's voice cut through the silence.

"Elizabeth Blackwell!"

She'd seen it a split second before I had—the doll's porcelain hand, her checked sleeve, peeking out of an inner pocket of Wilkes's jacket, just below his shoulder holster.

"Claire, no!" Bess cried.

But it was too late. Claire wrenched out of her grip and shot past us. Tim and I both charged after her. We passed through the aisle at the same time, wedged tight between the rows of seats, and tumbled to the ground in a tangle of arms and legs.

"Blast it, Adler!"

"Blast it yourself!"

A shot rang out above our heads. Somewhere behind us, a window exploded. A woman screamed. Shards of glass tinkled to the floor as cool air rushed in from outside, stirring the acrid smell of gunpowder that hung in the air.

"Now everybody simmer down," Wilkes said. His rising voice suggested the man wasn't a habitual murderer, although that didn't mean he'd necessarily turn down the opportunity to practice that day.

Claire was clutching Elizabeth Blackwell to her chest. And Wilkes was holding Claire across the shoulders with one arm. His other hand was pointing his pistol at her temple. Still flattened against the polished wooden floor, I could feel my heartbeat reverberating through the floorboards.

"Anybody move and the little lady gets one between the eyes."

"Let the child go!" a man cried.

Wilkes casually moved the barrel of the gun away from Claire and trained it on him. "Sir, I ain't got no quarrel with you, but I will shoot you if you get in my way."

The man sat down so fast the carriage shook.

"That's better. Now, Dr. Lazarus, stand up, stop your blitherin', and give me the dadgum key."

Slowly Tim picked himself up and brushed his clothes clean. When Wilkes failed to shoot him dead, I did the same.

"What bloody key?" Tim asked, with a rare display of profanity.

"There another Dr. Lazarus on this train?"

"Possibly."

"Another one who come over from England aboard the SS *Teuton-ic* and is headed for Pyrite, California?" When Lazarus didn't respond, he nodded. "Then you best hand over that key right this minute." He ran his fingers through Claire's thick, dark curls. Her eyes were wide, and she was gripping Elizabeth Blackwell so tightly her knuckles were turning pale. "Such a clever little girl. I'd hate to see them brains splattered all over this here train car."

Would he do it, I wondered. He was young and impulsive and no stranger to violence—his broken nose and quick draw had testified to that. But his gun hand was trembling ever so slightly, and I couldn't help but wonder whether, if it came down to it, Floyd Wilkes would actually shoot a child. I took a cautious step forward. Wilkes's eyes flicked toward me, and he cocked the gun.

"Was that what you were looking for when you went through our bags?" Bess asked. "A key? It had to have been you. That's how you got hold of Elizabeth Blackwell. But surely if you thought Dr. Lazarus had your key, you'd have gone through his Gladstone rather than my purse and my daughter's toy bag." A split second of confusion flickered over Wilkes's face. Taking advantage of it, she continued. "I assure you, we have no key. I don't know who told you that, but they were mistaken."

Wilkes frowned. Doubt crossed his features, and something else. I wasn't willing to take the chance—not with the barrel of the gun still pointing at Claire's head—but something told me that Floyd Wilkes was considering the fact that he might be not just wrong, but in significantly over his head.

"Who told you that?" Bess asked. Gentle but firm. Just like when she was ferreting out misbehavior among the Turnbull House gang. She always got to the bottom of it in the end.

"She said Dr. Lazarus had the key. It were in his satchel-bag."

"She?" Bess probed for the truth.

But the moment was over. Wilkes had said too much, and he knew it. His expression hardened, and he pulled Claire tightly against him.

And suddenly I understood. I didn't know how Wilkes was connected, or what the key meant, but I realized now why Miss Wood had been so desperate to climb into my trousers with me.

And why she'd become entangled in Claire's toy satchel in the process.

And the true extent of the trouble I'd caused by swanning about for a week posing as my friend Dr. Lazarus.

The only thing was, Tim, Bess, Claire and I had all been through that toy satchel a hundred times since Miss Wood accosted me aboard the *Teutonic*, and no one had come across any damn key.

"Throw me the bag," Wilkes said. He gestured toward Bess with his gun. "Throw me the satchel-bag and I swear I'll let her go."

Bess glanced at Tim. Tim nodded. Never taking her eyes from Wilkes, Bess knelt to pick up the satchel. Setting her jaw, she very deliberately removed Claire's toy horse and her blanket. Then she slid the bag down the aisle toward Wilkes.

"Thank you kindly, ma'am," Wilkes said. Then to Claire, "Pick it up."

Claire did as instructed. Wilkes crumpled the satchel into his coat pocket with one hand, keeping the pistol pressed into Claire's curls with the other. Then he reached for the door, pushing Claire ahead of him toward it.

"Claire!" Bess cried.

"Sorry, ma'am. On second thought, I'm gonna need some insurance."

"Mama!"

"No, sir," Sutter said, stepping between Wilkes and the door.

Wilkes startled at the sight. I don't think he'd expected that kind of defiance from an unarmed railway employee. The sun emerged from behind a cloud and glinted off the brass buttons of Sutter's uniform, leaving Wilkes squinting in the glare.

"I'll be your hostage. The little girl stays here."

"I don't think so, boy. You said yourself, a posse's on its way. You think they're gonna care if I shoot some overdressed—"

"Exactly my point," Sutter said. "The penalty for accidentally shooting a thirty-eight-year-old sleeping-car porter would be a damn sight less than for kidnapping a little girl—a visitor from a foreign land, no less. Wouldn't want to think what'd happen if you caused *her* any harm, accidental or otherwise."

Tim tensed at this, his hand closing around the back of the bench.

Wilkes seemed to be considering the idea. After a moment, he took the gun off Claire and nudged the brim of his hat.

"There," Sutter said in a soothing voice. "Let the child go to her daddy, and then I'll go with you. There's a little town just over that ridge. It's a stop on the stagecoach line. You'll be long gone before anyone thinks to look for you."

Wilkes nodded slowly. Behind me, Bess held her breath.

"Well, go on, then," Wilkes said, giving Claire a little push.

The entire carriage exhaled in relief as Claire ran toward her parents and let them scoop her up in their arms. Then Wilkes turned his attention back to Sutter.

"Now you, George," he said, gesturing for Sutter to precede him. As they passed through the far door of the carriage, Sutter glanced back and met my eyes. It wasn't a plea for help. It wasn't a plea of any kind. It was more like he was saying that he'd done his bit, and now it was my turn to do mine.

CHAPTER TWENTY-ONE

We have to go after them," I said. It was a stupid decision—rash and dangerous and not at all thought out. But it was the right thing to do, and I knew it. I rolled up the rumpled silk sleeves of my shirt and straightened my sleep-wrinkled waistcoat.

"Are you out of your mind?" Bess asked, still clutching Claire to her in an iron grip.

At the same time, Tim said, "I'm coming with you."

"Now wait a minute, sir," a man said. He was the same man whom Wilkes had silenced with a jerk of the wrist, and I had a feeling he was more one for speech than for action.

"He just saved my daughter's life, and probably some of your lives as well," Tim said sharply. He glanced around the carriage, as if welcoming an argument. His face was flushed, and the fatigue had left his expression. His bright eyes flashed with something that, in a less rational man, I'd have described as the thrill of the chase. "Wish I'd brought my Webley," he muttered. "I'd give that bastard one between the eyes myself."

The hardness in his voice chilled me. They say never to come between a mother bear and her cubs, but at that moment, the father appeared to be the more dangerous of the two.

There was a crash—a muted thud that shook the carriage—then a cry. Then suddenly my fellow passengers were ducking, diving, and hurling themselves out of the range of the bullets they were clearly anticipating. When none came, a tense silence gradually descended, and, heart pounding, I slowly rose from the corner near the cabin door, where I'd crouched. Pressing myself against the front wall, I glanced through the window into the vestibule.

"It's empty," I said, relieved to see no Calvin-shaped corpse on the floor between the carriages. At the same time, where the hell had they gone—down the stairs, out onto the prairie with the bison? Or into the next carriage, to God knew what?

"Do you think Wilkes is working alone?" I asked. One gun-waving American I could handle. Maybe. With Tim's help. If there was more than one, the outlook was bleak.

Tim said, "There's always a group of them in the stories. They chase down the train on horseback and jump aboard."

"With all due respect to your pleasure reading, Tim, that really stretches the limits of plausibility," Bess said. "Do you know how fast this train was going? And besides, no horse that can run that fast is going to come that close to a moving train."

Tim looked embarrassed. "You're probably right. Still, we don't know what that boom was right before the train stopped. Sounded like it could have been an explosion. Maybe Wilkes went looking for his associates so they could escape together."

"And if the rest of them are armed?" Bess said. "I don't like the sound of those chances."

Neither did I. My hands were shaking, sweat-sticky against the cool wood of the cabin wall. One would think that for all that I hated these sorts of situations, I'd be better at avoiding them. Swallowing, I looked at the other passengers—the maize-fed farmers smoothing their hats and string ties, the pinch-faced clerks straightening their spectacles, the dour schoolmasters still frowning—our unsuspecting fellows, who had thought they were buying tickets for a week of rocketing across the Great American Plains in the lap of Pullman luxury. They looked as terrified as I felt, though not one of them seemed to have heard the call to action still ringing in my ears.

"Well," I said, forcing back an inappropriate laugh, "anyone have a pistol to lend?"

An elderly gentleman in an equally elderly tweed suit cleared his throat and said, "Son, you're not in New York anymore."

I sighed.

I glanced again through the window into the vestibule between the carriages, then opened the door and motioned for Tim to follow. The door to the outside was shut fast, and though I looked for the men on the horizon, all I saw was oppressively bright sun beating down on a sea of endless scrub.

"They must have gone through to the next car," Tim said, echoing my thoughts.

"Right. I'll go first. If it gets ugly, you run back and protect Bess and Claire."

He looked as if he couldn't decide whether to be offended or relieved. I reached for the door to the next carriage. Someone had pulled the blinds down over the window, and I couldn't hear either voices or movement. Holding up one hand, I silently counted down from three.

I eased the door open, surprised at how silently it moved on its hinges. Then I glanced back at Tim in confusion. The carriage—a Pullman like ours—was empty. Most of the beds had been folded back into benches, though a few of the dark curtains still hung down from the ceiling next to the upper beds, the bedclothes of the upper bunks still rumpled, as if their occupants had been interrupted while attempting to return them to their daytime positions. The air was still—unearthly still. The only movement was the dance of the dust motes floating gently down in the sunlight flooding through the windows. The silence was so complete, I was almost afraid to breathe. I took a step inside.

My eyes barely had time to register movement to my right, when a pair of hands pulled me inside and threw me to the polished floorboards. Tim cried out in surprise. Then a crash sounded as he joined me on the floor.

"These more of 'em, Marshal?" a voice asked.

"Marshal?" I gasped.

I twisted against the boot planted between my shoulder blades but saw nothing, save for a shiny flash of leather and the pressed hem of a pair of dark trousers. A rich laugh rumbled somewhere to my left.

"Well, Mr. Adler? Dr. Lazarus? *Are* you a pair of train robbers?" Whatever the expression on my face must have been, it made the man laugh again. "Let them go, Mr. Wallace. These men do have a role to play, but it's not the role of outlaw. At least not today."

The hands that had thrust me down helped me up and brushed the footprint from my back. I sputtered some dust from my lips, then turned to find a young porter—a Black man in his twenties, grinning sheepishly—and beside him, Calvin Sutter.

"No offense intended, sir, but we had to be sure," the young man—Wallace—said.

"None taken," I replied. Then I turned to Sutter. "Marshal?"

Sutter, looking inordinately pleased with himself, cocked an eyebrow. He was still dressed in the porter's uniform, but his demeanor had changed to the point that I doubt I'd have recognized him as the same man who had tolerated Wilkes's behavior with such aplomb. I would, however, have recognized him immediately as a cop. While I stretched the kinks out of my back, Sutter produced a silver badge from the pocket of his jacket: a star, its points buried in a surrounding circle, with his title engraved across the front.

"Calvin Sutter, U.S. Marshal, at your service. These are my associates, Mr. Jenkins and Mr. Wallace."

An unexpectedly robust police presence on a routine train journey, I thought. I wondered what sort of trouble they were expecting. "Are they marshals, too?" I asked.

"Mr. Jenkins and Mr. Wallace are actual Pullman porters, but they've been invaluable to me during this investigation."

"What investigation? What's happening?" Lazarus asked.

"Well, now, I was hoping you might be able to tell me. I understand it's something to do with a key, isn't that right, boy?"

It was only then that I noticed Floyd Wilkes sitting on a bench behind Sutter, glowering. A bruise was blossoming on the cheekbone beneath his right eye, blood was crusted beneath his nose, and his pasty skin looked even pastier. His hands were bound in front of him with metal cuffs. Wilkes worked his wrists in a nervous gesture, the cuffs clinking softly in the thick quiet of the train car. All the while he gazed at Sutter, his eyes simmering with murderous intent.

"That key again!" Lazarus sighed. "If I knew anything about it, I assure you I'd tell you, if only to be done with the whole ridiculous matter. But as I said earlier, the only key I have unlocks the front door of my home in London. I don't know what this man is talking about, nor do I wish to. Now, we've been traveling for almost two weeks. My wife's family is expecting us, so whatever your business, Marshal, I'd appreciate your concluding it as quickly as possible, so that this train can be on its way."

That vein in Tim's temple was pulsing again. Out of the corner of my eye, I thought I caught Sutter suppressing a smile.

"That's what I thought," Sutter said. "I've been watching you both since you left New York, and somehow I just can't see either of you involved in this mess."

"What mess?" I asked.

Sutter ignored me. Instead, he reached to the upper bunk, where he'd stashed the one-handled toy satchel Wilkes had taken from Bess.

"I believe this belongs to you, Doctor," Sutter said. Lazarus reached out to take it, but Sutter held it up. "Just a minute." He gave the satchel a shake, then rummaged around inside. After a moment, he pulled out a very small, very shiny brass key.

"What?" Lazarus sputtered. "How on earth…"

"There's a hole in the lining, near the corner," Sutter explained. "The key is small enough that I'm not surprised you didn't notice its weight. Here's your bag, but I'll hang onto this, if it's all the same to you."

Shaking his head, Lazarus said, "Good riddance to the blasted thing."

I said, "I knew that woman was up to something."

Sutter turned sharply toward me, narrowing his eyes.

"What woman?" Lazarus asked.

"Miss Wood, aboard the ship. That night, she acted like she wanted…well…er…" I was usually a lot more blasé about that sort of thing, but for some reason, the thought of being mauled by that woman made heat rise to my face.

"Like she wanted to get to know you better," Lazarus said delicately.

"Yes. But I couldn't imagine that any woman would want to… that is to say—"

"Why not?" Sutter asked. His words were casual, but his expression was intent.

"Because…"

"Because Mr. Adler had just suffered a great and personal loss," Tim said. "He's traveling with us because I suggested a change in surroundings might do him good."

"I see," Sutter said. And for a terrifying moment I wondered whether he actually did.

At any rate, I continued. "Miss Wood was outrageously aggressive with her intentions—or so I thought. When I finally managed to push her away, she was tangled in the satchel. She must have been putting the key inside. Planting it on me."

Sutter nodded. "She didn't want to be caught with it. Probably figured she'd find you later and get it back."

"Because she assumed we were stopping in New York," I said. "And she planted the money on me, probably to make me look even guiltier if I was caught with the key." I turned to Sutter. "Who is she? What's going on?"

"Miss Lila Wood, also known as Lisa West, Laura Wild, and Lizzie Ward. Her real name—as far as I know—is Liza DuBois. She's a Liverpool-based criminal. Started out as a pickpocket but ultimately found her calling as a hotel thief. She's been expanding her territory, working passenger ships between Liverpool and New York. Why don't you have a seat? It's a long story. Oh, and Mr. Jenkins, would you please go make sure our man in the luggage car has things under control? We thought ol' Floyd's partners might get greedy and try to crack the safe. Pulling the brake was my man's signal that they'd made their move and he'd responded," he said to me and Lazarus.

"Yes, Marshal," Jenkins said, walking swiftly toward the far door of the carriage.

"There are more of them, then?" I asked.

"Three in all. The Wilkes Brothers. Doubt you've heard of them. Floyd and his little gang are budding train robbers, aren't you, boy?" Sutter asked, grinning menacingly at Wilkes. "They've carried off one or two heists already. Nothing too impressive, but they might have gotten lucky in time. They like to board a train, wait until it gets out in the middle of nowhere, too far away to send for help, and then relieve the passengers of their belongings. Only this time, it looks like they bit off more than they could chew."

Lazarus sat down on one of the benches near the middle of the carriage. I fiddled a window open, then took the adjacent seat. Sutter lowered himself onto a bench across from us. Mr. Wallace was leaning up against the wall, beside the door where Lazarus and I had made our humiliating entrance. With one eye on Wilkes, he examined his fingernails. He'd heard the story before, it seemed. As for Wilkes, he was twitching his arms rhythmically now and staring straight ahead at the prairie that seemed to stretch out forever in all directions.

"I was working in New York—on the Liza Dubois case, incidentally—when the security officer aboard the passenger ship *Teutonic* contacted our office with a strange story," Sutter said.

"Nicholas," I said.

Sutter cocked his head and regarded me for a moment. "Yes. Mr. Nicholas Flynn told a strange tale of a theft aboard his ship. Someone had broken into the cabin of a Colonel Jeremiah Wright and had taken a quantity of money, some documents, and this key." He held it up and it glinted in the light of the harsh Wyoming sun.

"Colonel Wright again," Lazarus muttered.

"Do you know him?"

"No!" Lazarus cried, exasperated. "But he and his misfortunes seem to be following us. Please tell me he's not on this train."

"No, sir. From what I understand, the Colonel and his companion were on their way to California, where Colonel Wright has business interests, but the theft of the documents and the key upset their plans. They stayed behind in New York to try to settle the matter before going west."

"What does the key go to?" I asked.

Sutter frowned. "Couldn't tell you. Even if I could, I can't see how it's any of your business."

"That's fair enough."

"You're absolutely certain you've never met the man? Mr. Flynn seemed to think otherwise."

"I know the Colonel's companion," I admitted.

"Benjamin Spark?"

"Is that right?" Tim asked.

"That's the name he goes by now. Once upon a time, I knew him as Marcus Harrington."

Sutter stroked his jaw. His chin was clean shaven, though tightly curled black sideburns crept down the sides of his face in front of his ears. His thick mustache was neatly trimmed, with a few gray spirals working their way in around the edges. "Now that's interesting."

"Not really. Marcus and I come from the same part of London. He had something of a checkered past. Nothing too serious, but enough that he felt he had to reinvent himself to work for the Colonel."

Sutter frowned. "Mr. Flynn didn't seem to suspect Mr. Spark of any wrongdoing."

"No," I said quickly. "Marcus—that is, Mr. Spark—said he worked hard to attain his position, and to keep it. I believe him. He wouldn't do anything to jeopardize what appeared to be an extremely comfortable situation." The nature of the comfort, as well as just how I knew Marcus, I would keep to myself.

Sutter nodded. "If you and, more importantly, Mr. Flynn believe Mr. Spark is innocent, then I have no reason to question it. What I do question, though, is why Colonel Wright would drop the case like a hot potato once Mr. Flynn had told him he had you in custody, Mr. Adler."

I shook my head and shrugged. "I've been trying to figure that out myself since we left the ship."

"Do you think your friend Mr. Spark might have convinced the Colonel to let it go in order to protect you?"

"Possibly...but...We weren't that close, and Marcus really seemed attached to his position. Actually, I think if Marcus suspected

I'd stolen from the Colonel, he'd have done everything in his power to see me pay for the crime."

"I see," Sutter said. "Well, whatever the case may be, Mr. Flynn was so perplexed by the turn of events that he contacted our office when the ship reached New York. When he mentioned the woman, Miss Wood, and how she'd seemed to disappear into thin air, I knew it had to be Liza DuBois. I sent my men to comb the area around the docks, and they're still looking. As for me, I decided to follow up on the pair that Mr. Flynn believed with all his heart to be Miss DuBois's accomplices—Dr. Timothy Lazarus and Mr. Ira Adler."

"Now see here!" Lazarus cried. I opened my mouth to protest, but Sutter held up a calming hand.

"I followed you to Chicago and then to Council Bluffs."

"So you say," I said. "But I never—"

Sutter snorted. "Nobody notices the baggage handler, the dining-car attendant, the porter. Put a Black man in a uniform, and it's as good as making him invisible. Why, I've been close enough to snatch the hat off your head for almost a week now—"

My cheeks burned again. Glancing at Lazarus, I saw my own embarrassment reflected in his expression. It was the same kind of invisibility that made St. Andrews's Irregulars so effective—the human eye tends to overlook those whom it underestimates and dismisses. It didn't speak well of the beholder.

"Made my job a damn sight easier," Sutter said with a laugh.

"So?" Lazarus said. "Have you determined that we're master criminals?"

"Exactly the opposite. After observing you closely for several days, I concluded that you're a nice little family—you, the missus, and your little girl. As for you, Mr. Adler, I haven't quite figured you out yet, but you seem pretty harmless."

"Thanks, I think."

"Which is why I noticed with such interest when the Wilkes brothers boarded the train in Council Bluffs. I informed the other porters immediately and asked them to keep their eyes open. When Floyd himself took the seat across from y'all, I switched cars with Mr. Wallace, here, and waited to see what would happen. Your little girl was never in danger, Dr. Lazarus." Sutter opened his jacket to reveal an impressive pistol. "I just didn't want to start a gunfight in the middle of a crowded railroad car."

"But what does Wilkes's gang have to do with Miss Wood?" I asked.

"Ol' Floyd, here, hasn't been too forthcoming, but I expect we'll get the whole story out of him at some point. That is, if he wants keep his scrawny neck out of the noose. But what I think is that—"

With a sudden clatter of metal, Floyd Wilkes, somehow now free of his cuffs, sprang out of his seat and hurled the handcuffs at Mr. Wallace's head. When Wallace threw up his hands to protect himself, Floyd landed a brutal punch to the porter's solar plexus, pushed the gasping man to the ground, and burst out the door into the bright, blazing day.

CHAPTER TWENTY-TWO

S on of a bitch!" Sutter swore as he launched himself off his bench. He glanced at Wallace, who was still groaning on the floor, then at me, and said, "Well? Come on, then."

Why he expected me to follow, I couldn't say. Perhaps my ill-advised rescue attempt when I'd neither gun nor clue had impressed him somehow. More likely he just wanted an extra pair of hands. I glanced at Tim, but the good doctor had already dropped to his knees at Wallace's side. He gestured me on.

I eased past them and sprang after Sutter, through the vestibule and down the steps, emerging onto a vast, flat spread of green, gold, and brown. As my feet crunched through dried vegetation, I amended my impression. The ground wasn't flat at all. It was riddled with dry dirt mounds and grassy clumps and holes just waiting for a convenient ankle to break or a knee it could turn. The sky above was dizzyingly clear and a shade of blue I'd never seen before. It exhilarated and terrified me all at the same time. I tried not to look at it.

Wilkes had the advantages of youth and surprise. I watched the distance between him and Sutter grow. I watched the distance grow between Sutter and myself. I'd always thought myself reasonably fit, but damned if a man with nearly a decade on me wasn't making me look like a sluggard. There was no way I'd catch either of them before they reached the distant cluster of buildings on the horizon.

"Adler!" I stumbled to a stop at Lazarus's voice behind me. It sounded small and faint, as if the prairie were swallowing it up. He said something else, but it was lost in the *swoosh* of exhaust and a metallic screech.

"—back! The train! The train is starting to move!"

Up ahead, Wilkes was still sprinting toward the town, with Sutter closing the gap. Behind me, Lazarus looked like a spring-toy, waving frantically from the doorway of the vestibule. I watched helplessly as the wheels began to turn and the train picked up speed.

"I'll—I'll catch up with you!" I shouted to Lazarus, though I'd no idea when, or how—or even where. Somehow, at some point in the future, I'd have to make my way to Pyrite, California—wherever that was.

Hearing a cry up ahead, I whirled in time to watch Sutter pitch forward, face first into a clump of dry brush.

"I'm coming!" I shouted.

I lit out across the prairie as fast as I could, Floyd Wilkes's figure growing smaller on the horizon. When I caught up to Sutter, my muscles were burning, and I was gasping for breath.

"I'm fine," Sutter called as I approached, though his face looked pained and he was clutching at his knee. "Keep going!" he growled out between clenched teeth. "Don't let him get away!"

The buildings were coming into focus now. A very small settlement, possibly only a single street. My thighs were beginning to cramp. Wilkes must have been tiring as well, because if I squinted it looked like the distance between us was finally, infinitesimally, decreasing. My lungs hurt. The harsh, dry air was abrading my throat. But that tiny encouragement was enough to fuel one final burst of energy. Moments later, I could taste his dust. A few seconds after that, and I could almost reach out and touch him. Then luck intervened and he stumbled.

I leaped.

My arms around his thighs, we both went down, choking and spitting dust. We rolled across the hard, crumbling earth, crunching over the desiccated grass. Suddenly I heard a dry, ominous sound, like a broom through fallen leaves, and something shot out from a clump of weeds and slithered across our legs.

Wilkes screamed. I sprang away, stifling my own shriek, my heart nearly beating out of my chest as the snake disappeared back into the brush.

"Oh, Lord!" Wilkes moaned. He stripped off one shoe and pulled up his trouser leg. "It was a rattler! I know it was! Oh, Lord, I'm gonna die!"

"A what?" I asked. "Did it *bite* you?" I didn't know anything about snakes, but I'd heard that everything in the American West was either poisonous or covered in thorns. The snake had been as thick as my arm, longer than my leg, and striped cream and brown.

"A rattlesnake, you idiot! And yes, it bit me!"

Two red marks stood out from the pale skin just above his ankle. *Beware of rattlesnakes*, Lawrence had said. I hoped no more were about.

"What should I do?" I asked.

"Ain't your friend a doctor?"

"The train's gone! It left!"

I followed Wilkes's gaze to where the train, now, was just a dot in the west.

"Oh, Lord!"

"Come on. Stand up. We can make it to that town over there. They have to have a doctor."

I wrapped his arm around my neck and painfully, slowly we stood.

"There," I said, gesturing toward the buildings. "Just over the ridge a bit."

"What's that?" Wilkes asked suddenly.

The sound had started as a vibration—a low rumble I felt through the soles of my feet before I heard it. Wilkes looked at me, as the sound grew deeper and louder. Beside us, a dusty green shrub began to tremble.

"Is that an—"

"Stampede!" Wilkes croaked.

I'd been about to say earthquake—I'd heard they were common in these parts. But as I turned in the direction he was looking, I knew that the tremors were coming not from the bowels of the earth, but from the pounding of a thousand hooves upon it.

The bison Sutter had pointed out earlier—hundreds and hundreds of burly, bearded beasts—were thundering toward us, kicking up a cloud of dust all around them.

"The train musta spooked 'em," Wilkes gasped as I stared in horror at the enormous herd bearing down on us. Like a deer facing a wolf, I stood rooted, my muscles frozen.

Wilkes, apparently having better sense, lunged, jerking me back to reason. Seemingly forgetting his injury, he hopped forward, pulling me along with his arm around my neck. We staggered toward the distant buildings, but the herd was more like a bison ocean, spreading out along the eastern horizon, encompassing everything we could see.

There was no way we were going to outrun it.

"Oh, Lord," Wilkes moaned.

"Keep moving," I said, though by this time I could make out the faces of the animals. The dazzling sun illuminated the horns protruding from their massive, shaggy heads and turned the churning cloud around them to orange. I could see the malevolent glint in their eyes, taste the beginnings of the dust that preceded them.

"Keep moving," I gasped again. But I already knew it was no good.

Suddenly someone cried out behind us. I whipped my head around to see Sutter charging toward the herd, shouting like a madman. He was limping, but moving fast, waving his arms. As he came closer, he let off a couple of pistol shots into the air.

"Yah! Get away, you overgrown milk cows!"

Wilkes screwed his eyes shut, clearly thinking the same thing I was. But though I had no desire to see the marshal pounded into mincemeat before my very eyes, I couldn't look away.

"Yah!" Sutter shouted again. He fired another shot over their heads.

I lost sight of him then—and them, and everything else as a great cloud of dirt and grit engulfed us. For one very long moment, the world consisted of choking dust, the thunder of hooves, the trembling earth and air. Wilkes's arm was so tight around my neck I thought he might break it. The smell was overpowering. A pair of black, hoofed legs pushed through the dust a mere yard away. And then another and another.

And then, miraculously, the herd began to turn. The surging tide of lumbering, oafish beasts veered away as one—gracefully, almost beautifully—and kept running. A young bull barreled forward, so close I could see its breath push aside the particles of dust around its muzzle. Its hindquarters whipped around, slamming Wilkes into me and both of us onto the ground.

Where we watched the sea of bison race past us to the left, bound for some destination that only they knew.

"God*damn!*" Sutter called as a hot breeze dispersed the dust. He stepped out of the receding cloud like a wraith, grit streaking his face, sitting on the shoulders of his jacket, piled on top of his tightly coiled hair like snow. One leg of his trousers hung in shreds. He was favoring his right leg, holding his pistol loosely in one hand and staggering to the point I feared he might drop over. But a grin lit his features, and as he came closer, the horror he must have seen on my face made him burst into laughter. "Goddamn! If that doesn't make you glad to be alive, Mr.

Adler, nothing will! Now." He turned to Wilkes, still sniggering. "Are you going to come along quietly, boy, or should I whistle them back here?"

I have to admit, I was only partly convinced he was joking. My legs were shaking as he helped me to my feet, and not only because I'd be seeing devil-eyed bison in my nightmares for decades to come. In my thirty years, I'd looked into death's eyes more times than I cared to admit and had seen my share of adventure. But never, in all my time on the mean streets of East London, had I witnessed such a bold, brazen, selfless, and heroic act. Sutter's eyes met mine, and for an instant, I could swear he was about to tip his hat and call me "ma'am."

But of course his hat—his crisp, billed porter's cap—had been trampled into shreds and buried in the dust somewhere behind us.

By the time I shook my head clear, Sutter was looming over Wilkes, an exasperated look on his face. "You planning to sit there all day, boy?"

"It's his leg," I interjected. "A rattlesnake bite."

"You have *got* to be kidding me." Sutter rounded on Wilkes. "Is this your idea of a joke?"

"No, Marshal. I swear it! That rattler just shot out of the brush and bit me!"

"I saw it, too." I shuddered at the memory of the snake slithering across our legs. "It was about five feet long, as thick around as my wrist, with brown stripes."

"Light brown or dark brown?" Sutter asked.

"Light brown. Tan and cream."

"Did you see the head or tail?"

"I saw the tail. It thinned out and tapered to a point." It was amazing how much detail I could remember in retrospect. At the time, my only thought was getting as far away from the snake as possible. "And I definitely heard it rattle," I added.

"Hmm." Sutter crouched next to Wilkes. He brushed the dust away from the twin punctures. The skin was going pink around them. Wilkes cried out as Sutter gently palpated the flesh around the holes until watery, amber-colored drops of liquid emerged. Then Sutter checked his watch. "Give me your bandana," he said to Wilkes.

"Ain't got one!"

Rolling his eyes, Sutter pulled a knife from his boot and cut Wilkes's trouser leg off below the knee. He sliced the ring of fabric open and wrapped it around Wilkes's calf, right above the wound. Then he sighed and stood, brushing the dust from the knees of his trousers.

"Boy," he said, turning to Wilkes. "This is your lucky day. You see that cluster of buildings over there? That's the town of Snake Ridge, where I know for a fact they have a fine doctor. We're going to help you get there. Now, do I have your word as a gentleman that you're not going to put up a fight?"

"Yes!" Wilkes cried. "Yes, anything! Just don't leave me here!"

"What about his gun?" I asked.

Sutter patted his coat pocket. "Took care of that earlier. But that's good thinking, Mr. Adler." He turned back to Wilkes. "Now, before my friend and I take the word of a known felon, are you carrying any other weapons?"

Wilkes swallowed hard. "There's a knife…in my other shoe."

Sutter turned to me. "Mr. Adler, will you help him with that? And make sure that's all he's carrying."

The knife was where Wilkes had said it would be. I slipped it into my pocket. Then I patted Wilkes's legs and felt around his coat pockets and under his coat, just to be sure.

"Now, help me get him up," Sutter said. "And grab his other shoe. He's going to want that later, if he's still around."

Wilkes's eyes widened at the words. Sutter winked at me over Wilkes's head. I almost felt sorry for old Floyd but was strangely pleased to be in on whatever the joke was that was dancing in Sutter's eyes. Bending down, I looped Wilkes's arm around my neck and helped Sutter to help him up.

"Now, hold on, tight," Sutter said. "We're all going to head over to Snake Ridge together. It ain't going to be fun, but we'll get there if we keep moving. Just don't give me any trouble, boy, or I'll have no compunction about putting you down and leaving you to rot."

Wilkes swallowed hard, then nodded. "Yes, Marshal."

CHAPTER TWENTY-THREE

By the time we limped into Snake Ridge, the sun was high in the unnaturally blue sky, beating down onto the single-lane dirt road that made up the town. I fished Goddard's pocket watch out of my waistcoat pocket. The sun glanced off the cracked crystal, temporarily blinding me.

Sutter laughed. "That watch has seen better days."

"It has sentimental value," I said. "Though it seems to have stopped." I gave the knob a few turns. Slowly the second hand creaked back to life.

"You know how to tell time by the sun?"

"We don't see the sun very often in London."

He narrowed his eyes as if trying to decide whether to believe me. Then he shrugged. "When it's right on top of you like that, it's midday, give or take. Lunchtime. After we drop off this load with the sheriff, I could definitely use something to eat."

"Sheriff?" Wilkes squawked. "I need a doctor!"

"The doc can visit you in jail. *If* you don't drop dead before we get there." Sutter growled. Once again, he shot me a sly look behind Wilkes's back. "How are you feeling?"

"I ain't dead yet," Wilkes said peevishly.

"Thank goodness for small miracles. That leg swelling? Let's have a look."

We stopped, and Sutter crouched down to inspect the wound. It didn't look swollen, and Wilkes had been tentatively touching his foot to the ground now and then as we walked. The skin was turning pink around the punctures, but it didn't look nearly as grim as I'd expected it to. Sutter's expression told me he concurred.

"Boy, you just may live," he pronounced.

A wood-framed saloon dominated the street. Two stories high, it towered over the bank and nondescript office that flanked it. In the front window, a handwritten sign read ROOMS AVAILABLE. Two women leaned against the balcony railing above the saloon, shading their eyes from the sun. Their tight, garishly colored dresses suggested they wouldn't feel out of place in certain parts of Whitechapel. They looked bored and sun-wilted. A walk made of planks ran up and down the road in front of the buildings. The street felt deserted, though, more likely, the residents were inside somewhere, taking shelter from the heat. A few horses tied in front of the saloon strengthened that suspicion.

"Now, before we make our big entrance, we ought to take a moment to make ourselves presentable. Here," he said, leaning Wilkes against a railing like the one to which the horses were tied across the street. There was a trough of water beside it. The water was clear, but a sluggish green line of algae was forming around the edges. "Don't try anything stupid," Sutter said to Wilkes. "Mr. Adler, you look like you walked out of a dust storm."

I brushed the grit from my coat and splashed a bit of water on my face and neck. The water was hotter than any bath I'd ever had. I recalled countless bone-cold London days when I'd have paid an unreasonable sum to bathe in that very trough, algae be damned. Sutter was methodically picking the last remaining bits of dirt from his jacket. His face and hands were already clean. I watched him glance over his shoulder, then quickly dunk the top of his head in the water and shake off like a dog. He grinned when he caught me looking.

"Won't help us any if folks can't tell who's the law and who's the criminal." He looked down at his tattered trousers and sighed. "I suppose Union Pacific will send the bill to the Marshals Service."

Slowly we made our way down the walk, our boots making an uneven five-footed clump on the boards. Eventually, we came upon two old men sitting on either side of a barrel of pickles, in front of a little store. They watched us impassively, one of them spitting a stream of brown juice into a metal container near his feet.

"Afternoon, gentlemen," Sutter said. Their expressions turned wary until Sutter produced a pair of silver coins from his trouser pocket and flipped them to the men—a gesture that transformed them immediately from world-weary cowboys into eager children.

"Marshal Sutter!" one of the men cried, springing to his feet. He was in his seventies, I'd have wagered. He was reed-thin, his face tanned and weathered from the sun, and his torso was swimming in his shirt. "Where'd you come from?"

The other one—slightly younger, balder, and sporting a paunch above his silver belt buckle—followed, hastily removing his wide-brimmed hat. "It's an honor to meet you, Marshal!" he cried. Then he frowned. "But where *did* you come from? Where's your white horse? He always rides a white horse," he told his friend in an authoritative tone.

"Well, now, that's an interesting story. Maybe I can tell it to you on the way to the sheriff."

"Local sheriff's in Cheyenne, Marshal," the first man said. "But we've got a deputy. You capture an outlaw, Mr. Sutter?"

"And let me guess—he broke his leg trying to get away! Don't that beat all?" the other cried.

"Snakebite," Sutter replied. "I think our friend, here, met up with a rattler while running away from the train he was robbing. If your doc's around, have him meet us at the deputy's office. I'd hate to have a death on my conscience—even his."

"Ain't much you can do if it's a rattler," the first man said.

"Now, that much is true," Sutter said. "But at least we'd be able to say we tried."

"Deputy's right this way, Marshal. You go on ahead with Wilbur, while I fetch the doc."

The older man sprinted across the street, while the younger one, Wilbur, led us back the way we came. Eventually we arrived at a modest shop front with a large window that looked out onto the street. The door was open. As we entered, a tall, thin man swept his long legs off the desk and stood.

"Deputy?" Sutter asked.

"Marshal Sutter!" the deputy cried. Recognition sparked in his eyes, along with a good measure of the excitement we'd seen from the two old men. He hurried out from behind his desk to meet us.

"I've heard the name, but I never thought I'd meet the legend," the deputy bubbled. "It is a pleasure, let me tell you. The name's Clark. Deputy Matt Clark, at your service."

"Pleased to meet you, Deputy Clark. Would you mind giving me a hand with this man?"

Clark moved like he was made of wires and springs, from his long limbs to his tightly curled light-brown hair. As he helped us move Wilkes to a hard wooden chair, I adjusted my initial estimate of his age up a few years. His freckles and pale skin—now pink from the sun—made him look very young, but he was probably close to thirty.

"Cuffs," Sutter said, nodding to the set attached to Clark's belt.

Clark unlocked the cuffs so quickly he dropped them. Sheepishly, he handed them to Sutter, who shackled Wilkes's wrist to the ladder-back of his chair in one deft movement. He stepped back with a sigh of satisfaction.

"What brings you to Snake Ridge, Marshal?" Clark asked once the prisoner had been secured.

"I'm glad you asked that. In a bewildering series of coincidences, my friend Mr. Adler, here, and I found ourselves together aboard a train that Mr. Wilkes and his brothers were attempting to rob. My men apprehended the other brothers, who are likely being taken into custody in Cheyenne as we speak. But Floyd," he indicated Wilkes with a nod, "decided to try his luck on the prairie."

"If it weren't for Marshal Sutter, Wilkes and I would both have been trampled into dust by bison," I said.

Clark said, "I saw that. Had to have been three hundred head at least. Wonder what spooked 'em."

"Wish you'd left me there," Wilkes moaned. "Anything's better than dying of snakebite in a jail cell. Oh, my leg!"

I gaped at Wilkes, who had not an hour before been begging us not to leave him.

Sutter just laughed. "Aw, you're not dying of that or anything else, you big baby."

"But I saw it!" Wilkes cried. "So did he!"

"And I heard the rattle," I said.

Sutter nodded. "A bullsnake looks a lot like a rattler. Same size, similar markings—except a bullsnake is lighter in color. It's even taught itself to make a rattling sound by flicking its tail against the dried vegetation. Makes other animals leave it alone. But it's the tail that's the key, Mr. Adler. You said it was tapered to a point. A rattlesnake's tail is rounded—that's the rattle."

"But—" Wilkes protested.

"Not to mention that if it was a rattler, your leg would be swollen to twice its size by now," he said, turning to Wilkes. "The pain would be getting worse, not better. You'd probably also be having trouble breathing."

Wilkes looked relieved, but only for an instant. Seconds later, murder replaced relief in his eyes. "Why didn't you tell me? What'd you let me worry like that for?"

Sutter chuckled. "Didn't want you getting ideas about running off. You've got a nasty set of elbows, there, as Mr. Wallace will surely attest, and I wanted to keep them out of my ribs."

"Somebody call for a doctor?"

A kindly looking older gentleman stood in the doorway. He wore a carefully maintained black suit, a string tie held together by a silver medallion, and a wide-brimmed hat that had been recently brushed. The gladstone he carried reminded me of Tim's.

"Come on in, Doc," said Deputy Clark. "Your patient's cuffed to the chair, there."

Sutter said, "Allow me to introduce you to Floyd Wilkes, the youngest Wilkes brother."

"Now that does sound familiar." The deputy squinted at Wilkes. Then he crossed the room in a few long strides and began to riffle through the papers on his desk. Eventually he found what he was looking for: a poster bearing a reasonably accurate sketch of Floyd and men I assumed to be his brothers, along with a list of their crimes. The deputy whistled through his teeth. "Well, I'll be."

"Are they famous?" I asked.

Clark looked the poster over and snorted. "Maybe one day, if they keep trying. They're wanted for a couple of small heists on branch lines in Nebraska. Strictly small potatoes. All the same, Snake Ridge hasn't seen this kind of excitement in all the time I've been here—and I grew up in this town. I'm obliged, Marshal, if only for the stories I'll be able to tell my grandchildren."

"In that case, perhaps you could return the favor by directing us to the telegraph office, so I can wire the sheriff in Cheyenne and tell him the third brother is waiting in your fine jail."

"Right away, Marshal."

"I also need to send a wire to Union Pacific. If they can make a special stop for Mr. Adler tomorrow morning, it'll save him a week on a stagecoach."

"Not a problem, Mr. Sutter."

"You're not coming with?" I asked. On second thought, I wasn't sure why he would. He'd only been on the train to ascertain whether Tim and I were working as Miss Wood's accomplices. He'd already recovered Colonel Wright's key. All things considered, he should be heading back to New York.

Sutter nodded. "Floyd has to be charged with a crime. Then there's a prisoner transfer. I'd prefer to be here when the sheriff comes for him, but I doubt he'll come today." He laughed grimly. "And let's not get started on the paperwork."

"So you're staying the night?" Deputy Clark peered at us, something else in his face now. It wasn't hostile, exactly, but there was a distinct guardedness that hadn't been there before.

"One night for sure. Probably two or three."

The deputy cleared his throat. "Well, I suppose I could rustle up a couple of bedrolls, and you gents could lay them out right here in my office. And my wife could send our son over with some supper tonight—yours and the prisoner's. She's a mighty fine cook."

"Aren't there rooms available above the saloon?" I asked. I wanted a bed, not a blanket on the floor next to the jail. "I'm sure they have food there, as well."

Sutter flicked his eyes toward me but said nothing. Both he and the deputy pretended they hadn't heard.

"That sounds right nice, Deputy," Sutter said. "We'd be obliged."

The tension dispersed, and Clark's grin returned, albeit a bit diminished. "Good. That's good. And it really was an honor to meet you, Marshal. And you too, sir. Now if you'll just follow Wilbur, there, he can show you to the telegraph office."

We followed the portly cowboy back out onto the boardwalk. I slowed, allowing a comfortable distance to form between us, then turned to Sutter. "Is there something wrong with the rooms above the saloon?"

Sutter shook his head. "The rooms are fine. It's the marshal that's the problem."

"What?"

He raised his eyebrows sardonically. "These fine folks are happy for me to capture their outlaws, but they don't want the likes of me sleeping on their clean, white sheets or taking my meals from the soft, pink hands of their wives and daughters, if you know what I mean. You either. You've got a bit of a suntan yourself, you know. And you talk funny."

"But they said it was an honor to meet you," I said.

His expression turned resigned. "The slaves have been free for thirty-two years, but a lot of folks still think I should be picking cotton instead of picking on outlaws. They tolerate me because of the badge. They might even smile because of the silver. But at the end of the day, I'm still…" He smiled. "Let's go send a few telegrams, and then we'll go for a walk. I have a story to tell you."

CHAPTER TWENTY-FOUR

The telegraph operator was grinning by the time we left, no doubt planning the fancy new house he would build with what Sutter and I had paid for his services. Sutter had wired Union Pacific to arrange for the Sacramento train to stop for me the next morning. He'd sent a second wire to inform the sheriff in Cheyenne that the youngest Wilkes was waiting for him in the Snake Ridge jail. As for me, I wired Bess and Tim to explain what had happened and when to expect me. Then I sent one to St. Andrews to tell him I'd be in Pyrite in two days' time. I asked if he'd received any information from Watkins. I also informed him that I'd met both a cowboy and a marshal, and that the latter was infinitely more interesting.

And finally I wrote to Lawrence. It was surprisingly difficult, and not only because anything of substance would have to be heavily veiled. I wanted to say that my affection for him was undiminished, but it wasn't strictly true. Time and distance had diluted the sentiment that had seemed so compelling before I boarded that train to Liverpool. It was possible that everything would rush back the moment we saw each other again, but at present, it all seemed worlds away—the bustle of London, Goddard's murder, Turnbull House, my secretarial work…and Lawrence. And who knew when I'd be back? It was taking three times as long as I'd thought it would to simply arrive.

But I owed him something. A good story, at least, and I had that. I started with the train robbery, went on to the "rattlesnake," and finished with the bison stampede. No doubt the fact that they'd all occurred in the space of a morning would leave him breathless. I mentioned maple syrup—he had the sweet tooth of a seven-year-old—and promised to bring him some upon my return. I would not allow myself to dwell on the suspicion that he and St. Andrews had been frittering away sybaritic afternoons in St. Andrews's gilded Baker Street rooms—or in

Lawrence's Chelsea flat, for that matter. I'd done more than my share of philandering since leaving London, and his was really none of my business. Still, the whole thing left me with a lump in my stomach, and in the end, I wasn't sure I wouldn't have been better off trying my luck with a proper letter.

But then I would have had to really think.

Brushing lips with death does something to a person. I could still see the hooves reaching out for me from the dust and feel the grit in my throat. The sharp, gamey stink of the bison still hung in my nostrils. Rattlesnakes and stampedes might have been all in a day's work for Marshal Calvin Sutter, but I couldn't blink without envisioning the bloody details of my near demise. If I thought about it too hard, the very idea made me light-headed.

What's more, something inside me had been changing since I stepped onto the ship—growing, extending beyond the comfortable boundaries of the person I'd thought myself to be. I was now a man who thought nothing of washing his face in a horse's drinking trough. Who voluntarily pursued armed train robbers. Who saw the stark beauty of the endless prairie and felt its undeniable pull. It was as if something inside me were opening, unfolding in response to the vast, untamed acreage, the unblemished and limitless skies. Quite frankly, I was finding it difficult to imagine stuffing myself back into the cramped little box of my London existence—leaving behind the sun-drenched landscape for a single, squalid, coal-heated room, impenetrable clouds of sulfur and muck, and the interminable freezing rains.

"You look like someone shot your dog," Sutter said.

I was leaning against the wall outside the telegraph office, trying to fit myself into a narrowing patch of shade. Sutter was leaning next to me. He'd found someone to sell him a couple of wrinkled apples, and he handed me one. I polished it on my waistcoat and took a bite.

"I almost died this morning." I turned to face him. "And I never thanked you for saving us. Thank you. I'm truly in your debt."

He laid a hand over his heart. "Justice, integrity, service. It's what we do." His expression softened. "First time you ever looked your own mortality in the eye?"

"No." I gave a hollow laugh. "Not even the first time this month."

"Is that a fact?" He cracked a smile. "Yeah, I figured you for a roughneck. Knew you'd be good in a tight spot. Something around the eyes, in the way you set your shoulders. Or maybe it's just that someone broke your nose not that long ago. I don't think you go looking for fights, but if one found you, you'd be up to the task. The fact that you dress like a dandy and talk like the Queen of England herself—" I choked on my apple at this image, but Sutter continued, "makes people underestimate you. Now, don't take that the wrong way," he said as I opened my mouth to protest. "Most people object to being underestimated, but it's a powerful tool. Only thing I can't figure is what someone like you is doing with that nice little family."

"They're my friends," I said simply.

I didn't go into detail about how Lazarus and I had met. Our sordid past was so far in the past, it never came up anymore. Moreover, I wasn't sure what the laws were in this strange, new land, but I doubted folks here wasted their time with indecency trials. I did tell Sutter, in very broad strokes, about my upbringing on the streets of East London, my involvement with Tim's clinic, and the youth shelter we'd founded together. I'd mentioned a bit about a wealthy patron who had educated me, employed me as his secretary, then later passed away and left me a nice bit of money.

"Yeah." He laughed. "We've got that type here, too. Folks who feel bad for what they've got. Think they don't deserve it somehow, maybe. Or maybe they just like to meddle. Think they know best."

I nodded. Goddard did like to meddle. At times I'd felt like a puppet on his strings. He definitely thought he knew best. But I'd seen another side of the late Duke of Dorset Street. Someone who truly cared about bettering the lives of the young men he'd taken in. Wanted to educate them above their circumstances. Had he felt that he didn't deserve the riches he'd amassed? It appalled me how little I knew about Goddard's origins. Wherever he might have come from, it had been a long, arduous climb from there to Cambridge—that much I had deduced. Losing his position at the university hadn't made him a criminal—he'd already started down that path before the scandal that had resulted in his dismissal. But it had made him bitter, angry, and determined.

"The Lazaruses have been good friends to me. I was at a bit of a loose end when they asked me to come to California with them. I believe they thought a change in scenery would do me good. And I thought I could use some of my inheritance to ease their journey. Tim's almost pathologically tightfisted. If it hadn't been for me, his wife and daughter would have spent seven days in *steerage*."

"God forfend," Sutter said wryly. "So were they right? Has a long trip to an exotic land helped you to clear your mind?"

I glanced at him, unable to shake the feeling that he was making fun of me somehow. But his tone and his expression were kind. I shrugged.

"I suppose. We left London two weeks ago, and I'm already finding it hard to picture my life back home. It's almost as if it all happened to someone else. As if what I'm doing now *is* happening to someone else. It's a very strange sensation. Nothing here is like anything I could have imagined. Even the air tastes different. I'm a different person. Does that make sense? And it frightens me a bit, because I could very easily picture not going back."

"Would that be so bad?" he asked.

Would it? I had the resources to set up house anywhere I pleased. And if I became bored, I could always purchase a new typewriting machine and start looking for clients. Or, I could build a little cabin out in the Wyoming countryside and idle away the rest of my life soaking up sunshine.

"No, but…"

"But maybe there's someone you think you should go back to. I've never seen a wire as long as the one you sent just now."

"That was business," I said, quick to divert that line of speculation. "My business in London." I shook my head. "That doesn't seem real either, anymore."

Sutter nodded slowly. Took another bite of his apple. "I remember my first time away from home. It was exciting and frightening all at the same time. Both the smartest thing I'd ever done, and the most foolish."

"Exactly," I said. "That's it exactly."

"Only I was eight."

Calvin Sutter didn't strike me as particularly loose-tongued, especially with regard to his own life. But as we leaned against the wall, eating our apples and watching the shade disappear, I assembled a rough sketch of his past from what he did say. Sutter had been born on a plantation in Louisiana. When he was four or five, war broke out, and, amid rumors that Union troops were burning plantations and freeing slaves, the plantation owner had moved Calvin and a number of others to his land in West Texas. It was there where Sutter had learned to tell a rattler from a bullsnake and how to divert a stampede. Sutter had been six when the president had ordered emancipation, but it had taken nearly three years for Texas to enforce that order.

Under circumstances I could tell he was none too eager to discuss, eight-year-old Calvin Sutter had struck out on his own and had been a rolling stone ever since. He grew up moving westward among different Indian tribes. He learned their languages and ways, and became known for helping to settle disputes that arose between those tribes and white settlers. When he was just turned twenty, he was recruited as a deputy marshal, owing to his negotiating skills and knowledge of various tribal languages. He'd been promoted quickly and had served as a federal peace officer for the past decade. The last promotion had taken him to New York, where he'd been working for nearly two years.

"I didn't expect to find myself back West so soon," he said. "But it's nice to know my prairie skills haven't deserted me."

"Do you think you might ever move here?" I asked.

He shrugged. "Maybe one day. I like the excitement of the city, but how I have missed the sunshine, the peace, and the wide-open spaces."

I could certainly identify with the sentiment, though for me it was the other way around. The noise, crowds, and grime of London felt a decade in the past. As for the stark American West, it struck me as a pleasant and not entirely implausible future.

CHAPTER TWENTY-FIVE

At nine thirty the next morning I finished the bacon, eggs, and toast Deputy Clark's son had brought, shook Sutter's hand, and headed south across the dirt and scrub toward the railroad tracks. At a little past ten, the Union Pacific bound for Sacramento stopped in roughly the same place I'd jumped off nearly twenty-four hours before. The conductor welcomed me aboard, and I was off across the Wyoming prairie like a streak of lightning. The train arrived in Sacramento close to dinnertime. I treated myself to a meal at the station restaurant, then bought a ticket on the last train that would pass through Bess's town that evening.

I arrived in Pyrite at a quarter to eleven that night. The depot itself wasn't much more than a shaded wood-plank platform with a bench and a shingled ticket office, its gingham curtains drawn for the night. Through the darkness, I could discern the dim outline of low, widely spaced buildings spreading out on either side of the depot. Lamps lit a few of the windows, but it appeared that most of the town had already gone to bed. Mountains rose up sharply to the east, their jagged outline a darker shadow against the star-peppered sky. A cool wind rushed down through the valley, suffusing the town with the bracing and pungent scent of some kind of tree. Having never stepped outside of London, the natural world was a mystery to me, but not an unpleasant one. All around, I could hear the rushing of what a fellow passenger had told me was the Kaweah river, and peace descended—a profound, bone-deep serenity such as I'd never before experienced. I had to steady myself against a telegraph pole for a moment while the stars seemed to pulse above me.

"Mr. Adler?" A woman's voice startled me out of my thoughts.

I turned to see a young lady of about twenty standing near

the ticket office. The light from the lamp she was holding gave her features a warm, smooth cast and made her large eyes stand out like black marbles on snow. Her dark hair was piled atop her head in a style simultaneously fetching and practical. Her light-colored dress was sturdily made and cut for function rather than fashion. But, perhaps as a nod to that fashion, or to youthful high spirits, she had permitted herself a bit of matching lace around the collar and on her bonnet.

"Miss Campbell?" I replied.

Her hand fluttered to her chest. "How ever did you know?"

I wanted to say I'd have recognized anywhere the broad, strong cheekbones she shared with her sister. The wide, smiling mouth, intelligent expression, and eyes flashing with mischief. I wanted to say she looked just like Bess, but of course she didn't. Irene Campbell was younger, yes. But her features had a delicacy her sister's lacked. Where Bess was solid and strong, Irene was fine-boned and graceful—though by no means weak, I would imagine, considering her origins. She was, quite simply, breathtaking—a cleansing, fresh breath of cool mountain air—and I could see how any man would be smitten.

Well, any man with a taste for ladies, that is.

"There's a strong family resemblance," I eventually managed.

"Irene! So that's where you've gone!" Bess appeared in the entrance and crossed the platform to meet us. "I haven't seen you since you were knee-high, and the first thing you do is go running off! Hello, Ira," she said, her smile softening her chiding tone. "Nice of you to join us. Did you capture your train robber? I see you've met my little sister, but since you're English, we'll have to make it official. Ira Adler, please meet my sister, Miss Irene Campbell."

"Charmed," I said. Snapping my heels together, I executed a little bow and lifted the back of her hand to my lips. What possessed me to do such a thing, I cannot say. Simply that it seemed the most appropriate response to the circumstance. Judging from Bess's expression, she either thought I was mocking her sister or, more likely, suffering from some sort of hopefully temporary travel-induced insanity.

Withdrawing her hand, Irene giggled.

"Are all Englishmen as debonair as you, Mr. Adler?" she asked.

Bess snorted. "Thankfully, no."

"Well, your Tim certainly is. Mother's already mad about him, as she will be about you as well, I'm sure, Mr. Adler. Oh! The only thing better than one English voice in the house is two. I do love an exotic accent. Come on, then, let's not keep Mother waiting."

Irene extended her elbow toward me. In a clearly peremptory
gesture Bess hooked her own arm through it, placing herself between
Irene and me, and gave me a cautioning glare. I shrugged in reply. A
lively girl filled with spirit and joie de vivre, a blanket of stars, and a
meeting of new friends and old. What did she have to be so sour about?

"So did you really singlehandedly foil a gang of train robbers,
Mr. Adler?" Irene asked as we exited the station and began down
an unpaved street toward a lit window in the distance. Between the
shadow-line of the mountains and the peace of the little town, it was
like her voice was the only thing in the world. "Did you really leap off
a moving train in pursuit?"

"Well...er..." I thought of fumbling through the scrub with
Wilkes, nearly shrieking like a girl when the snake touched me, then
almost meeting my end beneath a thousand thundering bovine hooves.
"It wasn't as glamorous as you make it sound."

"But surely you're a hero of some kind, don't you think? What do
you think, Bess?"

"I think it's late and you both need to go to bed."

No lamps lit the windows of the long, one-story house where Bess
and her family had parked their bags. There was no sound, save for
our footsteps on the dirt path and the lapping of the Kaweah River
in the distance. Apparently Howard and Florence Adams, the friends
of Bess's mother who had taken her and Irene in after the fire, had
already retired for the night. We stepped up onto an unenclosed porch
covered by a shingled awning. I tripped over a heavy pottery flowerpot
but caught myself, more or less, on the wooden swing hanging from
the porch roof.

"Shh!" Bess cautioned me. "Everyone's gone to bed."

"Already?"

"It's after eleven," she said. "Besides, ranch chores start early—
before it gets too hot."

As Bess let herself inside, I took a quick look around. I'd never
seen a ranch before. The back garden appeared to be thick with
vegetation, but I didn't see any animals.

"Where are the cattle?" I asked.

Irene said, "You can't see them from here. It's not a herd, exactly.
Mr. Adams retired early—another small operation that couldn't

compete with Cattle King Samuel Curtis. But they still keep animals for their own use. You'll probably hear the rooster in the morning."

I followed Irene inside, where Bess had lit a lamp on a table beside the door. Its gentle light revealed a small, cozy front room. A colorful quilt hung over a brick fireplace on the opposite wall. Two chairs sat before the fireplace. They looked as if they'd been hacked from branches of the same trees whose trunks made up the walls. To the right, a doorway opened onto what might have been a dining room and, beyond that, I assumed, the kitchen. A long, dark hallway extended to the left. I guessed that's where the bedrooms lay.

Bess said, "They have just enough room for Ma and Irene, but they really aren't set up to host all of us as well. I hope this is all right with you."

She shone the lamp into a far corner, where someone had arranged my trunks like a wall around a military-style folding bed. A pillow lay on the bed, with fresh sheets and a blanket folded next to it. I could smell the lavender water that had been used to launder them.

"It looks very comfortable," I said. "I'll thank them in the morning."

"Good night, Ira," Bess said.

"Good night."

"Oh!" Bess stopped in the mouth of the hallway. "I almost forgot to tell you—a letter arrived from London. It was addressed to you in care of my mother, so the postmistress brought it here."

My heart gave an unexpected little leap. Perhaps it was from Lawrence—though chipper little telegrams were much more his style. Or perhaps St. Andrews was writing with more details about the explosion. Either way, I found myself unexpectedly nervous when Bess took the envelope from the pocket of her skirt and handed it to me.

"Thank you," I said. I glanced at the return address, and my spirits sank just a touch. It was from St. Andrews. I looked back at the women, who were regarding me expectantly. "Good night, ladies."

Bess nodded. "I'll just leave you the lamp, then, shall I?"

"Thanks."

She set the lamp down on one of my trunks, then turned and disappeared into the hallway. As I ran a finger beneath the flap of the envelope, I felt Irene's gaze upon me. I looked up.

"Good night, Irene. It was really lovely to meet you."

A smile flashed across her face. It was a smile that, for a split second, lit the entire room like daylight. And then just as quickly she was gone.

Shaking my head, I slid St. Andrews's missive out of the envelope. It was dated a week earlier—we'd been on the train coming west.

Dear Ira—

    A lot has happened since you left—a lot, which requires more discretion than the telegraph—as amusingly quick as it is—allows. I won't bore you with the usual small talk. Neither of us has much patience for it anyway.

    L related your encounter with Sudworth's associate at Victoria Station in vivid detail.

It was *L* now, I noticed, and not Mr. Grey!

    L is very excitable and had to recount the story several different times in order for me to separate the facts from enthusiastic embellishments. Still, L is even more delightful than I remembered, and I thank you!

Did he now. The very cheek. But I read on.

    L's tale alone was enough to implicate S in my mind, but I followed up with Scotland Yard and the fire brigade just to be sure. I was able to call in a favor with the police, which resulted in a few very uncomfortable moments for Mr. S, when he was forced to produce records of his dealings with G's interests—his legal interests, at any rate. I'm sure there's quite a bit of documentation that is kept off-premises, but it was the best I could do.

    Did you know G owned part of an oil field in California? Is Kern County near where you are, by any chance? Apparently they're using oil instead of coal to fuel locomotives in some parts of America, now. If that technology catches on, G's heirs, whoever they might be, stand to become unspeakably wealthy.

    I spoke to a Fireman B. Nice young chap, not long on the job, but as smart as you please, and quite loquacious when offered the right inducement. He agreed that the explosion was set deliberately. He reckons there was a time-delay device inside the clock in the vestibule. Very clever, actually—any surviving parts would look enough like clock parts that most people wouldn't look twice. Except someone who had apprenticed to a watchmaker before finding it intolerably dull and joining the fire brigade. Not that it will do any good, as higher-ups have made it very clear that the explosion was caused by a water heater and no one is to say otherwise.

I did conduct one reconnaissance mission at jolly old York Street. Someone appears to have been quite busy investigating G's sanctum sanctorum. The explosion didn't touch the office—but somebody's greedy—and careless—fingers certainly did. I might have learned more, had it not been for the hulking brute with a machete who was apparently guarding the place. You'll be pleased to know I was uninjured in this encounter; however there was an exciting chase through Regent's Park. Fortunately, my pursuer lacked either the ability or the volition to follow me over the wall into the zoo. A good thing, too, considering the lion I found waiting for me! And I shall save that story for your triumphant return! By the way, have you remembered my cowboy?

One final note: honor compels me to inform you that L and I have been more or less inseparable since the day you left. L worried that you might be upset, but I replied that you're a very good sport. Upon further reflection, L admitted that your friendship was not exclusive—though I think it's only fair to inform you that L and I have decided that our friendship is. Hope you don't mind, old chap. And if so, please blame me. L is a delicate soul and would be crushed to think you'd been hurt in any way. As would I, of course.

At any rate, hope this letter finds you alive and well, and enjoying the delights of Sunny California.

Yours sincerely,
Andrew

Indignation burned through my veins. I'd suspected as much, of course, what with Lawrence's and St. Andrews's telegrams arriving to New York within minutes of each other, and St. Andrews's cheeky references to having received both messenger and message. It was my own fault, of course. I'd said nothing to St. Andrews to indicate that Lawrence and I had anything more than a casual arrangement—because the last time I saw St. Andrews, that had indeed been the case. Moreover, the feelings that Lawrence and I had expressed at Victoria Station had been so new, we hadn't had time to discuss whether our arrangement would change upon my return.

It didn't help that this letter and the telegram I'd sent to Lawrence from Snake Ridge had crossed in transit. It was all my fault, one hundred percent. Nonetheless, the whole thing felt like a kick in the teeth.

I tore up the letter and tossed the pieces into the dustbin. It would do no one any good at all to find something like that lying about. Besides, the tearing felt good. Then I took off the jacket and laid it carefully over one of the trunks. I removed my shoes and waistcoat, then made up the little bed. It was like something Lazarus might have used to drag soldiers off some godforsaken Afghan battlefield—a length of canvas stretched between two poles and raised on folding legs—but it would do for the night.

I set the lamp beside my jacket and lay down on the cool sheet, then dropped my head onto the pillow, releasing the scent of lavender water and feathers. Goddard's burnt-out, disfigured pocket watch ticked away in my waistcoat pocket. So his enemies had caught up with him at last. Inevitable, in retrospect. Yet at some level, I'd thought he'd always find a way to make good his escape. I listened to the watch for a while, marveling at its steady beat, like an unconquerable heart in a battle-scarred carcass. And then I fell asleep.

CHAPTER TWENTY-SIX

It wasn't a cock that woke me the next morning—or even a rooster—but an argument.

"This is my final offer, Lillian," a man was saying in the next room. "My price is more than fair. Damn it, woman, why won't you see reason?"

"The more you insist your price is fair, Samuel Curtis, the less inclined I am to believe it." That had to be Bess's mother. The words, and the indignant tone, sounded very familiar.

"It's just a mined-out old scrap of land too far away from anything to build on!"

"Then why are you offering so much money for it?"

"Because I'm trying to be fair. We've been neighbors for years."

"And I've never trusted you for a minute of it, Samuel Curtis. I'm even less inclined to do so, now."

I sat up, stretched, and peeked through the doorway into the next room—the dining room, it looked like. Bess was sitting at a long table, stirring her coffee with great concentration. Next to her sat a woman of about sixty, who shared Bess's stout build, dark hair, fiery eyes, and apparently indefatigable thirst for truth and righteousness. On the other side of the corner sat the man I assumed to be Samuel Curtis—a tall man, perhaps in his mid-forties, with dusty-brown hair and a cattleman's weathered, tanned hide. They were glaring at one another across a battlefield of cold food scraps and abandoned post-breakfast dishes. The smell of strong coffee hung in the air. I was torn between a ravenous desire for a cup of it and the equally compelling need for a fresh set of clothing. I gave my shirt a quick sniff and decided the coffee could wait.

Sunlight was streaming in through the front window. Outside, the

Central California countryside rolled out in a carpet of bright greens, yellows, and whites, rising to meet waves of gently sloping mountains. Farther on I could make out two parallel lines of tall, thin trees— possibly along the banks of the Kaweah river, whose rushing song I could hear, though the river itself was too far away to see. Choosing one of my trunks, I upended it with a floor-shaking thud. The conversation in the next room stopped abruptly.

"Good morning," I called, giving a little wave.

Bess looked up and waved back. "Ira, good morning. You slept through breakfast, but there's some coffee left in the kitchen, if you want it. Tim and Irene took Claire out for a walk. They should be back soon."

I selected a new set of clothes and slipped into them as quickly as I could while crouching behind the trunk. Then I emerged into an atmosphere thick with the ghosts of breakfast past and conflict present.

"Don't be shy," Bess said, pressing a mug into my hand as a woman in her sixties bustled in from the kitchen. "Florence, this is our friend, Mr. Adler. He came in late last night."

"Florence Adams. Pleased to meet you." Mrs. Adams was in her sixties, with hard-working hands and a wiry build that suggested a person in constant motion. Her hair was a mixture of silver and ash-blond, and though her bone structure suggested she'd likely been on the plain side in her youth, age had given her an attractive strength and dignity.

"Pleased to meet you," I said.

"Howard's gone out to water the livestock before it gets too hot, and then he's going to help a neighbor mend a fence. We may see him around suppertime."

"This is my mother, Lillian Campbell," Bess said, indicating a woman who might have been a third sister. Unlike Florence, Lillian reached out her hand and gave mine a warm squeeze.

"And this," Bess said, plastering on the smile she reserved for placating objectionable yet generous donors, "as you might have guessed, is Samuel Curtis."

"Good morning," I said.

Curtis looked me up and down, grunted a response, then pushed back from the table. "Lillian, my offer is more than generous. You can ask anyone. But it won't be open forever. You don't need that land, you'll never be able to sell it for more than I'm offering, and you don't have the desire or the resources to do anything with it."

"Maybe I can build a new house there," she said. "As you might have observed, we no longer have one."

Curtis narrowed his eyes. "That's why I'm even more surprised you don't take my offer. You have nothing now. For what I'm prepared to give you, you should at least be able to repair some of the damage."

Lillian shot up from her seat. "Damage that's awfully convenient for you, Samuel Curtis!"

Curtis's eyes went wide. He inhaled sharply. "For the last time, I didn't set that fire! If you don't believe me, you can take a trip to Visalia and read the sheriff's report yourself!"

"Nobody else had any reason to do it," Lillian countered. "You've been as angry as a snake ever since Irene turned you down!"

"If she's anything like her mother, I'd say I dodged a bullet!" Curtis retorted. "And if you want to know what happened to your house, you might want to talk to Jed Walker. He found something very interesting out there the other day, I heard. Some kind of peace pipe or something. Maybe Indians burned your house down."

Lillian sputtered. "I'm not even going to dignify that hogwash with a response. But you know what I will do? I'm going to head into Porterville myself today and do some research. Find out what on earth could be so interesting about my little mined-out scrap of inconveniently located land."

"You do that, Lillian."

He slammed the door behind him.

I stood in the doorway, blinking.

"Well," Lillian said. She turned to me and smiled. "I'd say we have our work cut out for us today. Anyone fancy a trip into Porterville?"

"Porterville." Irene's voice sounded from the back door. She swept through the kitchen, Claire firmly in tow, and alighted in the doorway of the dining room. That morning she was wearing a light-colored dress with a subtle floral pattern, a straw bonnet, and flat-soled boots. A country girl's finery, I thought. Combined with her enthusiasm, the effect was very fetching and went far toward dispelling the foul mood that had been settling over me in the wake of St. Andrews's letter. "Why, I haven't been there for the longest time. May I go, too? Please, Mother?"

"I don't see why not," Lillian replied. She looked at me. "Why don't you come along, Mr. Adler? Irene's been singing your praises all morning, and I'm sure you'd like to see what passes for a city in these parts. We can make a day of it."

Irene blushed at this, but it wasn't an ugly blush. It made her look radiant.

"Make a day of what?" Tim asked, belatedly walking through the back door. "By God, it's beautiful out there. Bess, we should take a walk down by the river later. It's amazing. So clean and peaceful—"

"There are little baby fish," Claire cried. "And pollywogs and dragonflies and birds and—"

"It sounds lovely, Claire," Bess said. "I can't wait for you to show me." She turned to Tim. "Samuel Curtis was just here. That man won't take 'get lost' for an answer. Ma figures there must be something on that land worth all this fuss and thinks someone in Porterville might be able to tell us more."

"It's an old gold-rush town," Lillian said. "I reckon we'll have our pick of geologists there. Then we can have some lunch and do some shopping."

"Fantastic!" Irene cried. "Oh, Mr. Adler, it'll be such fun."

Her eyes flashed. My stomach leaped. Then it growled. My train-station supper was long in the past. I snatched the last bit of cold toast from a plate and an orphaned strip of bacon. Not the breakfast of fantasies, but beggars and choosers and all.

"And while you're gone, I'll try to have a talk with Jed Walker's parents," Florence said. She looked thoughtful. "He's a bit of an odd duck but real smart. Only twelve years old and already sort of an expert on local Indian lore."

"I thought you said there weren't any more Indians in this area," I said to Bess.

Florence answered, "Not like there were when I was a girl. But one or two families live on the outskirts of town. You see them from time to time."

"I wonder what that boy was doing poking around the ruins of the house," Lillian said. "What could he have found?"

Florence smiled. "That's what we're going to try to find out."

❖

The town of Porterville was hardly a great metropolis—at least not when matched against London or New York. But it was impressive compared to Irene Campbell's hometown. It was easy to understand how someone who spent her days in the sleepy cluster of ranches that was Pyrite might be excited by the noise and bustle inside Porterville

Station—which, though little more than a two-story version of the wooden depot in Pyrite, was alive with expensively dressed people hurrying toward far-flung destinations or emerging into the matrix of wide and busy streets that made up the town center. It was a new building, just seven years old, with still-gleaming glass in the ticket windows and paint that hadn't yet begun to fade and crack.

Irene was in high spirits, clutching my arm tightly and gazing longingly at the crowds, the departures board, and the train platforms. I watched her, feeling oddly protective—like an older brother, perhaps. It wasn't an unpleasant sensation, and, unlike Bess, who would have slapped down such a patronizing sentiment with her handbag, Irene didn't seem to mind.

I watched her study the women who passed by—their towering hairstyles decorated with rhinestones and feathers; their tight corsets and expensive, jewel-toned dresses. At one point she glanced down at her own staid calico frock, her boots that were made for walking the dusty, uneven paths between ranches, and her fine brow furrowed.

"You look beautiful," I whispered just above her ear.

She turned to me, a smile lighting up her face. "Oh, Mr. Adler, you know *exactly* what to say."

Bess, whom I'd thought to be engrossed with Tim in their usual game of architecture-spotting, stopped, turned, and gave me a warning look.

"*What?*" I mouthed.

Setting her jaw, she shook her head, chuffed with frustration, then turned her attention back to Tim.

Had I been another man, I might have understood immediately her concern—concern that would later turn out to be justified, though not for the reasons she was imagining. However, my upbringing had been very different from hers and Irene's, to say the least. Scratching out a living on the streets of East London hadn't left me sheltered, exactly. But neither had it given me an ounce of insight into the delicate workings of the female heart. At age thirty, I was only beginning to figure out my own heart's machinery—and making a stumbling mess of it most of the time.

Main Street Porterville, like Main Street Snake Ridge, was unpaved. But it was wide and carried a brisk traffic of horses and carriages. The dirt wasn't exactly moist, but at least it didn't rise up in dry, choking clouds to coat the nose and throat. The air was a little warmer than was tolerable and redolent with the smells of manure and sweat. The sunlight—direct, unrelenting, and powerful—made me grateful for the wide-brimmed American hat I'd purchased in London. If the unremitting glare continued, that hat would pay for itself by teatime.

On either side of Main Street, two- and three-story brick buildings rose like the walls of a low canyon. Shops of every description opened onto boardwalks crowded with pedestrians. Nearly every shop had unfurled a fabric awning over its portion of the boardwalk, providing an almost continuous shaded path. Side streets angled off from the main road at planned junctures, connecting to further streets to form a grid-like town center. Looking off into the distance, I could see a scattering of homes beyond the streets and over the tops of the buildings.

"It's not anything like London, I know," Irene said as we stepped, thankfully, into one of the long, shaded corridors. "I remember coming through London on the way home from Ningpo, and then New York, and the long boat ride between them. Arriving from rural China, both those cities seemed so big—too big, like they could swallow you up and you'd never be seen again."

"That's pretty close to the truth," I said.

"Too big," she repeated with a little shiver. "But I like Porterville. We don't get here often enough, but I always enjoy it when we do. I feel like I can breathe here, you know? Nobody's watching what I do, waiting to report back to Mother, and I can walk down the street and see people I haven't known half my life. There's always something to see—and people don't look all the same. In Pyrite it's all sunburned cattlemen, but here…"

Here, there were rough-handed men in dusty work shirts and boots, yes. There were women wearing simple dresses like Irene's and bonnets made for working under the hot sun. But there were also feathered coiffures, expensive suits, brightly colored dresses in fine fabrics, and gold-headed walking sticks. And I observed a variety of different skin tones—from the sun-shy shades of the European settlers, to Black men like Sutter, to the different hues of brown that represented the waves of Mexican, Spanish, and indigenous people who had populated the area before them. The different populations managed an intricate dance—each carving out a place for itself in the crowd, never crossing the unspoken lines, together but separate. I wondered whether Sutter would find it easier to avail himself of services in Porterville than he had in Snake Ridge. I wondered whether my own "suntan" would make a difference.

Gently taking Irene's elbow, I guided her to my left side to avoid a steaming, fly-clouded pile of manure just off the edge of the boardwalk. The gesture felt very natural—a feeling that she seemed to share, judging by the shy smile with which she responded.

We let the crowd carry us down the shady corridor, all the while pointing out things in the shop windows that we would buy, if we had the money. Or rather Irene pointed out, and I listened. For someone who had been brought up so practically, Irene had quite an eye for color and design, and I made note of several items that would make a lovely surprise gift, should the occasion present itself. There was something so pure about her, so unspoiled and honest, it made a person want to indulge her. What a lucky man it would be, who finally won her heart. Behind us, Claire and her granny strolled along in a world of their own. Claire was spinning some story about trains and bad men and unicorns, Miss Elizabeth Blackwell playing the central role of Claire. Lillian was listening intently. As we passed a store specializing in textiles, Tim stopped and turned.

"The man at the station said there was a geologists' office on this next street. Cassidy & Wells."

"I've heard of them," Lillian said as Claire suddenly slumped against her full skirts. The little girl's cheeks were red, and she was pulling at her bonnet strings. That was the real danger of the heat, I reckoned—not the temperature itself, but the way its effects could sneak up on a person. Lillian continued. "Cassidy evaluated some of the most famous gold claims in the area. Don't know anything about Wells, though."

Bess said, "Must be doing a good business if he's taken on a partner. Is there still gold in the area?"

Lillian shook her head. "No, but there is oil. People are getting real excited about it, too, if you believe the papers. Though what they're going to use it for, I can't fathom."

"I'd heard people were experimenting with using it to fuel locomotives," I said.

Lillian's eyes widened. "Hadn't heard that, but if so, then…" She gave a low whistle.

I wriggled against my suddenly too-tight waistcoat. My shirt had begun to stick to my back. "I'll just be glad to get out of this heat for a while."

"Amen," Irene added.

We followed Tim and Bess around a corner, onto a narrow, uncrowded lane. A breeze blew down the corridor between the buildings, temporarily lifting the hot air that seemed to suffuse the entire town. The geologists' office was several doors down, toward the middle of the block. A large window looked out onto the bleached buildings. Black lettering across the glass read CASSIDY & WELLS, GEOLOGISTS AND SURVEYORS.

"Good afternoon," Tim said as we stepped inside. Maps of California's Central Valley covered the walls: Kern County—where Goddard supposedly owned land—Kings County, Tulare County, Fresno. The young man behind the desk near the back of the room started upright and blinked at us through round, wire-rimmed spectacles.

"Good afternoon," he said after a moment. He stood and extended a hand toward Tim. "Gordon Wells, at your service."

He was probably in his mid- to late twenties, with a round face, pointed features, and light-brown hair that looked as if he might have been absently running his fingers through it before we arrived. He had the air of someone who often did things absently—dreamily, with his mind on higher things. He was a diminutive man, no taller than Irene, but seemed to have avoided the pugnacity that often characterized such men.

"I'm sorry, we only have the two chairs for visitors." Wells gestured toward two straight-backed wooden specimens parked off to one side. "Please, madam," he said to Lillian.

"Thank you." Pulling the chair before the desk, Lillian tucked her skirts beneath her and took her seat, lifting Claire onto her lap.

"Ma'am?" He gestured for Bess to take the other. He glanced at Irene, and a look of alarm passed over his face. Then, remembering his own chair behind the desk, he smiled and brought it around.

"If you please, miss." He set the chair in front of her with the air of a magician producing a rabbit from a battered topper.

"Thank you."

Irene sat daintily on the edge of the chair and took a sketchbook and pencil from her handbag, clearly prepared to entertain herself. I liked that. As she leafed through the sketches to find a blank page, I peeked at them over her shoulder. They were quite impressive— detailed and realistic with touches of shading, texture, and light that created distinct moods and even suggested weather. I recognized the rolling, brush-covered hills that surrounded Pyrite—plants that I had seen and quite a few that I hadn't. When I looked up, I saw that Wells, too, was watching with interest.

"Now," he said, giving me an abashed grin. "How can I help you?"

Wrapping an arm around Claire's waist—the child had already begun to squirm—Lillian reached down to the handbag she'd set on the floor. After a moment, she pulled out a fat envelope, which she laid on the desk.

"I've recently come into possession of a small piece of land. I was hoping you might be able to tell me more about it."

While Lillian launched into a story about cattle corridors and abandoned gold mines, I let my eyes wander around the office. To the right of the desk stood a system of wooden filing cabinets. A small staircase on the back wall led upward. Neat stacks of papers sat on one side of Wells's desk, beside a clean blotter and an inkwell. A very expensive keyboard typewriter graced the upper left corner. A Remington. Nice. Goddard had given me one just like it once. Cassidy & Wells must have been doing very well for themselves indeed.

Over on her grandmother's lap, Claire's squirming had turned to a determined escape attempt. She'd behaved well on the train, having become a seasoned traveler, but the combination of the heat and the fact that her mother was seated so nearby but ignoring her in favor of boring adult talk was proving to be too much. I watched her glance at her mother, then raise the precious, porcelain-headed Elizabeth Blackwell high into the air.

Without even turning her head, Bess caught the doll before Claire could dash it to the ground. "Don't even think about it," she murmured.

"Shall I take her out for some fresh air?" I asked softly.

Bess looked up at me. "Are you sure?"

"Why not?"

She glanced at the watch pinned to the front of her dress. "It's past lunchtime, and she won't be having a nap this afternoon."

"We should have left her with Mrs. Adams," Tim said under his breath.

Bess said, "Dr. Browning says, 'a child must sometimes conform to the adult environment, in order to become an adult.'"

"I doubt he was talking about three-year-olds."

"She'll be turning four in—"

"I'll tire her out," I said. "Come on, Bess. I'm just as bored as she is."

Bess looked from Claire to me, then glanced over at Irene, who was making a sketch of some mineral specimens in a glass case. That apparently cinched something in her mind, and she nodded reluctantly.

"Some fresh air, then, but no treats. We'll be having an early dinner, and I don't want to spoil her appetite."

I knew from experience that nothing could spoil that child's appetite, but I nodded. "Come on, Raisin Bun," I whispered, holding out my hand. Claire, the devil having temporarily fled from her eyes, carefully laid the doll on her grandmother's lap and took my arm. Out of the corner of my eye, I saw Bess smile.

As we stepped outside, another breeze swept down the narrow lane, turning my damp shirt, for one glorious instant, icy cold against my skin. I sighed.

"I don't know about you, but if I had to sit in that room another minute, I'd have chewed off my own arm," I said.

Claire glanced up at me, as if not quite sure that I was joking. Then she giggled. I gave her a wink and led her back toward the bustle of Main Street.

"Where are we going?" she asked.

"I'd like to buy a newspaper, and then I want to buy a present for your Auntie Irene." There was a brooch I'd seen one or two streets back. A metal dragonfly with cut glass in bright colors. It was completely impractical but probably not too expensive. Irene would love it.

Claire frowned up at me. "Is she your sweetheart?"

"No!" I laughed. Nervously. Was that how it appeared? I was developing a very strong affection for Irene, it was true. She was bright and carefree. She sparkled. When we were together, I had the impression that one never knew what she'd say next. And, unlike any woman—or any person, to be honest—with whom I'd ever spent any time at all, Irene seemed completely untouched by the ugliness of the world and unburdened by its cares. I could quite happily have spent every moment in her company.

But, unlike Tim, I couldn't imagine summoning any sort of physical attraction for any woman, no matter how different and delightful she was.

"She's just...a very nice young lady, and I want to buy her a present," I said lamely.

"Do you want to buy me a present?"

Sweeping her up in my arms, I laughed, grateful the child was happy to accept my response without further interrogation. "Yes, Raisin Bun. I should like that very much."

We stepped into the thick crowd and shuffled down the shaded boardwalk for a while until we found a little store selling newspapers, tobacco, and other bits and bobs. I chose a pouch of Virginia tobacco, matches, a clay pipe with a bowl shaped like a horse's hoof, and a copy of the *Sacramento Daily Record-Union*. With any luck, we would find some place nearby where I could sit down to enjoy them while Claire ran about a bit.

We wandered along to where the next street bisected the boardwalk and continued on until the end. No benches, not even a patch of grass. Disappointed, we turned around and started back. The pink had returned to Claire's cheeks by this point, and I was feeling more than a little wilted myself. I did like the dry air and sunshine, but the heat was becoming oppressive. We walked slowly back down the street, stopping to rest and look in the windows. We eventually came back to the intersection where we'd turned to find Mr. Wells's office.

"Why don't we see how they're coming along?" I said.

"But I thought you were going to buy me a present!" She stamped her solid little foot, the storm that had threatened back in the geologists' office returning to her features in a rush.

"Steady on," I said.

"I want a present, now!"

I looked around, shocked and not a little bit mortified at the glares we were receiving from passersby. I was also puzzled. No one would have described Claire as a placid child, but she was generally reasonable. What had Bess said about missing both lunch and a nap? Could it really be making that much of a difference? I knelt down to her eye level, as I'd seen Bess and Tim do. "If you reason with a child," Tim was always saying, "the child will respond with reason."

"Claire, please," I said.

"Now! I want my present *now,* Ira! You *promised*!"

Her little face was quite red by this point, and sweat was running down from beneath her dark bonnet. Dark bonnet, dark coat over a dark dress and layers and layers of stiff undergarments. No luncheon, no nap. What had Bess been thinking? *A child must sometimes conform to an adult's schedule, in order to become an adult.* Never mind how wretched it made things for the rest of us. What had I been doing, agreeing to—no, *suggesting*—this godforsaken outing?

"That child needs a spanking," a man said as he passed.

"Why don't you mind your own business?" I snapped.

He stopped. "She's a nuisance. I'll take her over my knee myself."

I sprang to my feet. "Lay a hand on her, you mewling quim, and you'll pull back a stump!"

The man shrank back as he took in my fighter's stance and my long-lost East London accent that had decided, at that moment, to reassert itself. He stared a few daggers at me, then, as if thinking better of it, slunk away into the crowd, muttering something about the confounded Irish and their confounded brats. I glared at the people who had stopped to watch, who had formed a half circle around us, perhaps hoping for a bit of afternoon entertainment. Slowly, they, too, dispersed, leaving me tight-chested and shaking. Embarrassed, I glanced around, straightening my jacket. What on earth had possessed me, I wondered, as the thick, hot air leached the fight out of my bones. I tipped my hat back and wiped a sleeve across my brow. I hadn't courted a fistfight in years. I really had to get a handle on us both. Claire was staring at me, her mouth a tight, petulant little pout. I knelt again, clamping a hand over her shoulder—a bit too tightly, I must admit—and growled into her ear.

"You will come with me this instant, with no more of this infantile bolloc...er...nonsense. Do you understand?"

Her eyes went wide and, to my surprise, the defiance left her face—along with any trace of color. "Yes, Mr. Adler," she whispered.

"Good." I rose. As the red haze cleared from my view, I picked her up and settled her on my hip—consciously gentle, though my blood was still racing with the urge to bash something into slush. How did Bess do this, day after day? How did anyone? There was a delicate choking noise as Claire took a few hitching breaths. Her eyes suddenly filled and her lower lip began to quiver.

"No. Oh, no, no, no." What an utter bastard I was! Not just a bastard, but a bastard who threatened strangers in the street and made little girls cry. "Oh, now, it's all right," I said, my voice bouncy with false cheer. "It's all over now, no harm done." I jostled her up and down like an infant. She drew a few more tortured gasps, her shoulders starting to shake. "I didn't mean it," I said desperately. God, Bess would have my sodding head on a pike. "It's me, remember? Your old pal Ira. Listen, Raisin Bun." I gently took her thumb out of her mouth and met her eyes. "Can we start over? Just pretend none of this ever happened?"

She swallowed hard, drew in a long, tremulous breath. And then, blessed be God, she nodded.

"Good." I let out a long breath and smiled from sheer relief. The sun passed behind a cloud. A not-exactly-cool breeze stirred up swirls of dust and flies around the manure piles that dotted Main Street. Pedestrian traffic now flowed obliviously and non-judgmentally around us. She laid her head on my shoulder, and at long last, my legs stopped shaking enough to consider moving again.

We walked on for a bit, both stinging from the shock of first reproach. How long did almost-four-year-olds remember things like this? Would she tell her mother? I was entertaining a number of terrifying outcomes, when suddenly I felt Claire stiffen in my arms. I stopped and found myself in front of a large window with a staggeringly colorful display of sweets.

Sugar mice frolicked along a path of lemon drops that led through a forest of licorice trees. Peppermint pinwheels hung above like stars. In the background, a multicolored spiral lolly as big as a dinner plate loomed above a taffy-ribbon horizon like the fullest full moon. Gold lettering at the top of the window read KATIE'S CANDIES. Claire was staring, quivering like a hunting dog, at the universe of forbidden treats.

"Please, Ira," she said with fiercest desire, yet in a voice soft enough that if I were to say "no," she could pretend it had never happened.

"No treats," Bess had said. But sod that for a laugh. Claire and I had achieved a fragile truce, and I was loath to shatter it.

"Yes," I said. "Absolutely. Anything you like."

Inside, a pretty, round woman in her twenties, wearing a red-and-white pinstriped dress with enormous puffed sleeves, greeted us. Her full cheeks were flushed with the heat, and she wore her light hair in a complicated arrangement held in place by striped ribbons that matched her dress. She introduced herself as Katie and helped Claire select a toothache-inducing assortment of brightly colored sugary treats, which they packed together into a paper sack the size of my head.

"Now, don't eat it all at once," Katie cautioned us, as I handed over the appropriate coins. "In this heat, it'll give you a tummy ache."

I assured her we would do no such thing. Claire, her eyes glazed with disbelief at her luck, nodded solemnly and took my hand. I considered swearing the child to secrecy about the entire incident, but then figured it would probably give her an undesirable instrument of leverage—or at least cause her to commit to memory something best forgotten.

"Thank you, Mr. Adler," I prompted her as we emerged back into the afternoon crowd.

"Mgmfmmf," Claire replied through a mouthful of taffy.

"Good enough, I suppose."

As luck would have it, the jeweler's shop was just two doors down. Irene's brooch sat on a velvet cushion in the window, amid a display no less colorful than that of Katie's Candies, but designed to appeal to an older sort of girl. In truth, I wasn't feeling much like shopping anymore. And I was pretty full up with female company, besides. But we were there, we'd nothing better to do, and frankly, I wasn't sure that Claire wouldn't rat me out to Irene if I tried to get out of buying *her* present as well.

We opened the door and stepped into a quiet world of polished glass and precious metals. As a floorboard creaked under my weight, an elfin-looking elderly man looked up, his thin hair a white cloud around his head, one of his blue eyes magnified to ridiculous proportions by a head-mounted loupe.

"Good afternoon. Would you be so good as to show me the brooch in the window? The dragonfly."

A smile lit his creased face, and he set down the delicate tools he'd been using to work on a watch. "Oh, that one! Is it for a lady-friend? She must be very special."

"Yes," I said. I smiled back, but it was a nervous smile. I knew at that moment that I should absolutely, positively, *not* give that brooch to Irene. And yet now that I'd disturbed the little man—and now that Claire was watching, no doubt eager to report any wrongdoing to her mother and aunt—I couldn't find it within myself to back out of the transaction. The jeweler carefully drew back the rear door of the display, plucked the dragonfly off its perch, and crept back toward his post. As he spread out a piece of black velvet and laid the brooch upon it, I approached.

"Some of my finest work," he said. "Made it some years ago, for a man who wanted to surprise his fiancée. Didn't work out in the end." He tutted and shook his head sadly. "She left him for a schoolteacher. But you don't want to hear that." He looked up at me. He had to look quite far. "It's real silver, solid through and through. Garnet and topaz on the wings, and the eyes are peridots."

That sounded a lot more expensive than the cut-glass trinket I'd meant to buy for Bess's little sister.

Claire, suddenly at my elbow, gasped. "Auntie Irene would love that! May I give it to her? Please?"

"No, and you mustn't mention it, either. It's a surprise."

The jeweler grinned. "I'll just wrap it up for you, then. Seven dollars, please, young man."

I blinked. I had to stop myself from mentally converting the price to pounds, lest I realize how much I was spending on a young lady I'd met less than a day before, who was not and would never be my *sweetheart*. Claire had danced away and was now, quite deliberately, pressing sugary fingerprints into the glass walls of the display cases.

While the man wrapped the dragonfly in paper, I grudgingly laid the appropriate money on the counter. I was just beginning to think about how I was going to entice Claire away from the displays when she let out a little yelp and dashed out the door.

"Claire!" I cried. Stuffing the little package into my jacket pocket, I ran after her. She darted through the wall of pedestrians, intent on something she saw ahead. I tried to keep up, but somehow, people are much more forgiving of a small child shoving them aside than a grown man doing it. "Claire," I shouted again.

She screeched something I didn't quite hear. Pushing past a plump woman with a very tall coiffure—and dodging the subsequent swipe of her parasol—I finally came close enough to hear what the child was on about.

"Marcus Blooming," Claire was shouting. She was pointing straight ahead with one sugar-sticky hand, clutching her nearly empty sack of candy in the other. "It's Marcus Blooming!"

By God!

Five or six doors down, Marcus blooming Harrington—Marcus *sodding* Harrington, more like—had stopped in the middle of the boardwalk. Not having lived long enough as Benjamin Spark, he had turned at the sound of his actual name and now stood facing us, looking for all the world like a straw-boater-and-seersucker-clad rabbit facing a three-foot-tall lion. The Colonel was beside him, balancing himself between Marcus's arm and a dark wood cane, while the foot traffic diverted around them in two fast-moving streams. The old man was still facing the other direction and appeared to be attempting the laborious process of turning around. The wheelchair was nowhere in evidence.

"Marcus," Claire squealed. "What have you done with his chair?"

"Claire, no!" I shouted as she barreled toward him, arms outstretched.

Pedestrians scattered as I raced to retrieve her. Marcus looked horrified at the prospect of the child's sticky, dirt-smudged hands and face landing on his immaculate suit, and I didn't blame him. Not to mention what might happen if she bowled the Colonel over in her enthusiasm.

"Stop, Claire!" I cried.

And Claire did stop, to my relief, pulling up just short of Marcus's pressed blue-and-white striped suit. She stopped and swayed like a miniature drunken sailor in a dark-blue dress and bonnet, as the Colonel—clad in cream-colored linen that likely cost more than my passage from Liverpool—was finally finishing the tortured act of turning around.

"Ira," Claire said in a weak, shaky voice. "I feel..."

At which point she decided it was better to demonstrate, which she did, by vomiting a stream of crushed lemon drops, masticated jelly bird eggs, and half-digested taffy onto the Colonel's handmade Italian kidskin shoes.

CHAPTER TWENTY-SEVEN

The shoes were brogues—pointy-toed, tan leather brogues hand-stitched by some hundred-ten-year-old master Italian cobbler from no less than six pieces of exquisitely expensive leather and dotted with pinhole detailing that would never, ever, *ever* be fully clean again.

"Oh!" I cried, too horrified to find actual words. "Oh!"

"What…have…you…*done*?" Marcus demanded through clenched teeth. He was staring, his light-blue eyes bulging, an alarming shade of purple rising along his neck. For a moment I feared he might explode. I reached out a conciliatory hand toward him. At the same moment, Claire let out a strangled cry and dissolved into a quivering heap of sobs.

"Oh!" I cried again. I gave her shoulder an ineffectual pat, and the child began to wail in earnest. I hugged her to me with one arm, but I couldn't tear my eyes away from the Colonel's ruined brogues. Dear God, the *leather*! Out of the corner of my eye I saw Marcus begin to shake.

Then someone let out a long-suffering sigh. A trembling hand—the Colonel's hand—held out a silk handkerchief that had probably cost more than the shoes.

"Take it…Ira."

I looked up at the sound of my name.

Up into the scar-riddled, heat-rippled face of Cain Goddard.

"Oh!" I fell backward. My arse hit the boardwalk with a resounding thud. Claire plunked down heavily in my lap. "Oh, God! You…you're…"

"Take the handkerchief."

I gasped for breath. *Alive!* The man was alive! He'd seen better days, to be sure, but…oh, God, and *here*! In Porterville!

"How…?"

My chest clenched while my heart tried to beat its way out through my throat. I tipped back my hat and wiped my sleeve across my forehead. It had to be a hallucination brought on by the heat. But when I looked again, he was still as solid as the boardwalk and the shops and the little girl softly sobbing in my arms. My own hand trembled as I reached toward the handkerchief and, with a quickness borne of superstition, snatched it from his fingers. Then, giving Claire a squeeze, I rose to my knees.

I mopped her face clean, grateful for the opportunity to look away and not think, for just a few seconds, about what I'd just seen. Cain Goddard. Not dead. Not dead, but alive and standing in front of me, covered in my charge's vomit. My chest seized again, and while images of the explosion and his battered body flashed through my mind's eye, I prayed to be saved by a quick and merciful heart attack. My chest clenched painfully, but there was, ultimately, no such reprieve.

"Thank you," I managed, when I was finished. Standing, I held the soiled silk out to him.

He sighed. "Keep it."

At that point, I realized he'd probably meant for me to use the handkerchief to mop off his shoes. I let my hand drop.

"You're…you're not dead."

"Not yet, anyway."

Beside him, Marcus was breathing in long, noisy pulls, as if trying to tamp down his temper. He had a foul one, if I remembered correctly. And this entire incident was unambiguously my fault.

"Marcus…I mean…oh, God, I'm sorry…Mr. Spark…"

"You've ruined *everything!*"

No sooner had the words left his mouth than Marcus pushed Claire aside—straight into the mob coalescing around us—and launched himself at me.

"Not the nose!" I cried, my hands flying to my face.

He stopped suddenly and looked around, as if he'd suddenly forgotten where he was and what he was doing. And in that moment, in his face, I saw simultaneously the lighthearted young man who had once been a friend of mine and a slightly older, slightly wiser man who was terrified of losing the new life he'd worked so hard to build and maintain. I didn't want to make trouble for him. Why couldn't he see that? What had Goddard *said* to him to make him think otherwise? Marcus's mouth quirked—halfway between tears and a nervous smile. He opened it, but no words came out.

Then he turned and ran.

Claire had stopped crying by then—out of shock, I imagined. Not taking my eyes from Goddard, I pulled her back toward me. Bess was going to draw and quarter me. I wanted to run, but my feet felt rooted to the spot.

"I'd go after Mr. Spark myself," Goddard said in an eerily calm, soft voice. "But though my physician is impressed with the speed of my recovery so far, running down city streets is still temporarily beyond me." He bent forward a bit anyway, grimacing, and I noticed that he held his torso stiffly, as if wearing a brace or a full-body bandage of some sort. "As is bending down to clean my shoes, unfortunately."

"Do you want me to bring him back?" I asked.

A faint smile twitched across Goddard's scarred face. Hundreds of tiny scars, as if from hundreds of shards of window glass. "He'll be back. He just needs to calm himself. When he does, he'll come find me, and he'll be dreadfully embarrassed. But right now I really must clean this…" He shuddered. "*Matter* from my shoes, and then I must sit down." He grimaced again. "In my impatience to heal, I've overtaxed myself once more." He sighed. "I do wish dear Benjamin had insisted on bringing the chair. Sometimes he listens too well."

He held out his arm. After a moment I realized he was asking for my help. Though I'd rather have done almost anything than what he was asking, I couldn't just leave him there, covered in *that*. Spotting one of the ubiquitous horse troughs just off the edge of the boardwalk, I helped him lean up against the post beside it. I wet the handkerchief in the water, then knelt and cleaned the leather as best as I could. Then I cast the handkerchief aside and washed my hands in the trough.

"Thank you, Ira." He was deliberately restraining his voice, taking shallow breaths. Broken ribs, I surmised. Probably quite a few of them. "I wouldn't have asked it of you, except…"

"It's all right. I should have known better than to fill a child with sugar after we'd spent the afternoon walking around in this heat. Eh, Claire?" I gave the girl's shoulder an apologetic squeeze.

His lip curled in a familiar sneer that left me feeling simultaneously nostalgic and insulted. "Good God, it's not yours, is it?"

"This is Tim Lazarus's daughter." Protective rage burned in my chest, and I wrapped an arm around Claire's shoulders. "You sent flowers to her mother once."

"Ah, yes," he said absently. "Good afternoon, young lady."

Claire gave a little yelp, then darted behind my legs. After a moment she peered out from behind me, her dark eyes wide.

"Sorry," I said to Goddard. "She's usually very outgoing."

"No, no. The child has good instincts."

The singular outlandishness of this situation hadn't escaped me. I was introducing my best friends' young daughter to a murdering, pandering, diamorphine-slinging prince of the London underworld, as if he were a kindly gentleman acquaintance. Never mind I'd thought him dead before Claire had emptied her gullet onto his shoes. His beautiful, beautiful shoes. A week and a half ago, I'd have given my left arm to see Cain Goddard again, but at that moment, I wanted to be anywhere but there, exposing Claire to his withering scrutiny. And yet I couldn't very well leave him there, hardly able to hobble about on his own—especially when his companion's departure was more than a tad my fault.

"There's a tea shop three or four doors down. Shall we sit and wait for Benjamin to find me again?" Goddard asked.

The absurdity made me laugh. "Tea. Sure. Why not?"

He took a step forward with his right foot, then placed the cane on the boardwalk about sixteen inches in front of his left. Then, with excruciating deliberation, he swung his left leg painfully forward and set it down behind the cane. I could see the sign for the tea shop, but if we kept going at this pace, Claire would be my age before we got there. Gritting my teeth, I put out my left arm for Goddard to lean on. He took it, gratefully. Claire clung to my right, still keeping her distance. Fortunately, the task of assisting the both of them across the thick flow of pedestrians provided a few blessed moments of distraction from the horror of my situation.

After a few more steps, Goddard stopped to catch his breath.

"Dislocated hip," he explained. "Four crushed ribs on the same side. Burns and lacerations. Those things will heal, if I allow them the time to do so. Still, all things considered, it could have been much worse."

"I saw you when they brought you out. They said you were dead. You looked really, really dead."

"Dead." He gave a derisive laugh. "I wouldn't give them the satisfaction."

He took my arm and we began again. The tea shop was just a few yards away, now. I steeled myself for one final push. We tottered across the boards, Goddard hanging onto one of my arms and Claire clutching the other. After what seemed like a week, we finally limped through the white-painted frame into an alien world of cushions and lace. A pleasant, pink-cheeked young woman seated us immediately at a table by the window. As she brought an extra cushion for Claire, she gave me a knowing smile. Daddy, daughter, and grandpa out for a stroll. If she only knew the truth. While I ordered tea, Claire settled herself near the window and stared out, watching the people go by. I waited for Goddard to continue, but he seemed content to watch the people as well.

"You said 'them,'" I prompted him. "So you know who set the explosion at York Street?"

He turned sharply back toward me, as if I'd shaken him awake. Blinked. "Watkins is still investigating, but I'm not holding my breath for his answer. He has better things to do than pursue this. Besides, it doesn't really matter, since I've no intention of returning to London."

"You don't?"

"Mine's a rough business, as you know. There's always some enterprising upstart trying to gain the better of you, take your territory, knock you off your pedestal. You can keep them at bay for a while, but eventually some young pup will bring the old wolf down. That explosion was a gift. Made me realize those young pups weren't snapping at my heels anymore, but at my throat, and that the next time I wouldn't be so lucky."

It was a lot of words at once, I thought uncharitably, for the usually laconic Duke of Dorset Street. Perhaps he was hurting for intelligent conversation. But his loquacious spell seemed to have passed, and he was looking out the window again. For Marcus, I realized. For *Benjamin*.

"So the entire thing was a ruse?" The anger in my voice surprised me. I took a deep breath, glancing around at the crowded tea room. Shouting at him would have been so very satisfying, but Claire didn't need to see me acting like a bully. "The reading of the will, the *burial*?" I demanded in a fierce whisper.

"Yes and no. The explosion was real enough, but it set a plan in motion that I'd drawn up a long time ago. My confederates in the fire department took me to a secret location and summoned my personal physician. When I regained consciousness and it was determined I'd live, I had a decision to make—to stay and fight, or to activate my contingency plan. I chose the more graceful exit."

"Your confederates in the…so I have you to thank for my broken nose?"

He winced. "Yes, probably. Sorry about that, but it does rather suit you. At any rate, Watkins carried out the orders I'd given in case of my death—the burial—a coffin filled with dirt, in this case—the monetary disbursements to you, my household staff, and a few select others—and his own ascension to my former role. I stepped into my false identity, took the emergency cash and documents I had waiting for this instance, and Benjamin and I came here to start over."

"Start over?"

He smiled—a painful shadow of that old Goddard smile—the one that said he'd been waiting for me to apprehend the great plan that had been there all along. The fire had done the left half of his face noticeable damage. Beneath his hat, I could see patches where his neat dark hair—now mostly frosted over—might never grow back. But intelligence still animated his eyes, and now that he'd caught his breath, I could see that his strength, confidence, and determination still drove him. The unutterable power that had drawn me to him was still there.

Goddard cleared his throat. "Yes. A new life in a new place. With Benjamin."

A new life. With Benjamin. What sort of a bastard was I that the thought caused jealousy to flicker somewhere in my heart's recesses? I didn't want Goddard back, and in many ways, he and Marcus were made for each other. But though my initial anger at his deception was receding, I had to admit that the thought of Goddard wasting himself on Marcus was threatening to make my blood boil.

When I forced my thoughts away from that dark place, Goddard was still speaking. "This country is growing rapidly. I've been investing in various enterprises here for years."

"Like oil," I said.

The surprise in his face was inordinately gratifying. It wasn't every day, or even every week, that a person managed to sneak up on the Duke of Dorset Street.

"Yes," he said, stumbling to a recovery.

"In Kern County."

He inhaled sharply. I saw in his face how badly he wanted to ask me how I knew that. At the same time, I could see he wasn't certain that he'd be satisfied, ultimately, with the answer. Fatigue was also creeping back in, deepening the lines around his eyes and mouth.

"Yes, Kern County, not far from here. In fact, that's why we're in Porterville. We were on our way to the bank to sort a few things out and then to talk to a geologist to try to obtain copies of the documents pertaining to…the oil." He shook his head. "The robbery aboard the ship threw a good-sized spanner into the works, I'm afraid."

The waitress brought a pot of tea. I distracted myself by fixing us a cup—milk, no sugar for me, neither for him. It wasn't bad. On the other side of the table, Claire had laid her head down in her arms and was either sleeping or close to it.

"Well, thank you, at any rate, for insisting Mr. Flynn drop his case against me. It must have only added to your inconvenience," I said.

"Indeed. We were in New York for two days attempting to set our paperwork in order. Fortunately authorities here are as amenable to monetary persuasion as they are in the rest of the world. But I knew you hadn't done it, and there would be no profit in seeing you charged with the crime."

I thought to ask whether Sutter had managed to get his key to him. Then I figured if he thought it was any of my business, he'd tell me.

"So you're starting again…in Porterville," I said.

"Porterville is a convenient center for my business interests, but we haven't yet decided where we'll live. Anything more will depend on the good graces of Cassidy and Wells, I suppose. What is it, Ira? You look like you've seen a ghost."

What I had seen had been much more frightening than that. The image in my mind was what might have happened had Goddard and Marcus walked into the geologists' office while Tim, Bess, and the rest of them were still there.

"It's nothing," I said.

"There must be something."

He was looking at me, now, meeting my eyes. His brown gaze was still firm but somehow not quite as commanding. He had new lines around his eyes—or perhaps that fine network of ruts was the result of broken glass and inadequate stitching. I felt the strangest combination of pity, sorrow, anger, and jealousy. At the center of it all was a single question.

"Why did you call me back to the house that day—the day of the explosion?" I asked.

Goddard cocked his head. "Why do you think I did?"

"Truth?"

"Always."

"I thought you'd set the explosives. I thought you wanted to take me with you."

He frowned. Then he gave a weak laugh. It was upsetting to see him weak. "You always did have a flair for the dramatic, Ira."

"Then why?" I asked.

He sighed. Smiled sadly. "I missed you. I realized what we had once was lost and that it was my fault in every way. And Benjamin and I...well, we'd been together for more than a year. He'd done well for himself since parting company with you. Managing that bookstore, as a matter of fact. That's where we met—officially, anyway. I was going to invite him to come live at York Street, but I wanted to say good-bye to you properly before that happened."

I sat for a moment, searching for the right words. Or for any words. I wasn't prepared to behold the soft underbelly of the steel-hard Duke of Dorset Street. Why was he showing it to me now? Because his "death" had destroyed any possibility of reconciliation? Because now, after everything that had passed over, under, through, and between us, it didn't actually matter anymore? I couldn't decide whether I wanted to take his hand or slug his smug face across the table.

"He's very threatened by you, you know," Goddard said. "Thinks I'd throw him over in a minute if you came back."

My first thought, of course, was *would he?* Then I realized I didn't actually want to know.

Goddard smiled self-mockingly, as if reading my mind. "But you haven't told me what divine coincidence has landed you not only here, but at almost every stop along my journey." He glanced at Claire, who was softly snoring now. "I assume the good doctor and his wife are involved somehow."

I made a dismissive gesture. "Some business with her family. A dispute over a land claim. They're speaking with Cassidy and Wells right now, as a matter of fact."

Goddard's lips tightened in a mild smirk. "That would have been awkward."

"To say the least. At any rate, they were tired of seeing me moping around in the wake of your supposed death and thought a trip to America might cheer me up."

He cocked an eyebrow. "So the idea of my death saddened you?"

I nodded, a bit embarrassed.

"And your inheritance didn't ease the sting?"

"The money…" I shook my head. I was grateful for it, of course. In part terrified he might want it back. But at some level, the deception of it all—the unnecessary grief I'd suffered—it really annoyed me. "What possessed you to leave me that kind of money, Cain? I almost had a heart attack when I read that letter."

"The second most pleasant way to meet one's end, I should think."

I barked a cynical laugh and shook my head.

Goddard's head swiveled sharply toward the door. I followed his gaze to the gangly, seersucker-clad figure filling the doorway. Marcus searched the room. When his eyes fell on Goddard—and me at the same table—the increase in tension was enough to make other customers look up.

"Benjamin!" Goddard's eyes lit up as he waved the young man over. Years seemed to drop from his face. He really did care for Marcus, quite a bit, it seemed. The realization stung, but I forced myself to at least pretend I was happy for them.

Marcus wasn't happy to see me there, but I watched him compose himself, then stride purposefully toward us.

"Please forgive me, Jeremiah," he said contritely. "It was inexcusable to leave you like that."

"Don't be silly, dear boy. This beastly heat brings out the worst in all of us. But I do believe you owe someone else an apology."

Marcus scowled but took a deep breath and fortified himself for the inevitable. Then, as if maintaining his former level of rage had proved too much for him, he heaved a great sigh.

"Sorry, Ira," he said sheepishly. "And I'm sorry, Jeremiah, for not telling you sooner that we were acquainted."

Goddard smiled indulgently and held out his hand. Marcus took it gratefully.

"There," Goddard said. "No harm done. Isn't that right, Ira?"

I wondered what Goddard must have said about me that would leave Marcus so consumed with worry after more than a year. Then I realized that, aside from Marcus's brief stint in the brothel where he and I had met all those years ago, his relationship with Goddard was the only stable situation he'd ever known. Of course he would defend it with everything in him. It struck me then, how few decisions stood between my own life and one much like his. I suddenly found an untapped reserve of compassion for my one-time friend.

"Think nothing of it, Mr. Spark. It was all quite understandable

under the circumstances." Rising from my chair, I offered it to him.
"Please," I said.

Marcus—Benjamin—took the chair, relief relaxing his features a
fraction as he glanced from one of us to the other and apparently failed
to apprehend any nascent plot to abandon him on the dusty streets of
Porterville. I placed a hand on Claire's shoulder and shook her gently.
It was time to leave.

"Don't go, Ira," Marcus said. Rising, he pulled another chair from
an empty table and offered it to me. "At least finish your tea."

"Thank you," I said.

Marcus gave me a shy smile, then pulled his own chair closer to
Goddard. Lowering his voice, he said, "I took the liberty of visiting the
bank, Jeremiah."

"Thank you, dear boy." Goddard's tone was indulgent, conciliatory.
He seemed to want Marcus to know that all was forgiven. He seemed
to want to put him at ease. It was touching and left me feeling strangely
jealous again. "What did they say?"

"They said that they'd received a telegram from a U.S. Marshal,
saying he'd recovered your key. He meant to deliver it personally as
soon as possible, but business has kept him away." Spark shrugged.
"Without our documents, there's nothing the bank can do until the
marshal delivers it—probably in a few days' time."

Marcus glanced over his shoulder at me. I wondered if he thought
I was as engrossed in the paper as I was pretending to be. I wondered
if he noticed that I'd been reading the same headline over and over
without comprehension: PASSENGER SHIP PILFERER EVADES POLICE.

By God!

*The burglar, identified by U.S. Marshals as Miss Liza DuBois
of Liverpool, England, was spotted by police in the railway
station in Council Bluffs, Iowa. Police tried to apprehend her,
but she disappeared into the crowd. Miss DuBois is believed
to have victimized passengers aboard ships traveling
between Liverpool and New York City. The Marshals Service
speculates she may be making her way west, though to what
end, they wouldn't say.*

"I see." Goddard sighed. "Well, at least we have the resources to
wait comfortably until that happens."

My mind raced. Obviously the key was for a safe or a strongbox maintained by the bank. I wondered whether Sutter was on his way to Porterville. I wondered how long it would take him to get here.

I wondered whether, once Goddard had put his affairs in order, I would ever see him again.

❖

I left not long after that. I claimed Claire's welfare as an excuse, but the truth was, Goddard and Marcus needed their privacy, and they shouldn't have had to deal with me at that point—a thought that left me strangely sad. Knowing I was being irrational somehow made it worse. What kind of man became upset when the lover he'd been rejecting for more than six years picked himself up and moved on? I felt that same familiar pang—that void left when I'd believed Goddard dead. Not so much the absence of the man himself, but more the absence of possibility. It was ridiculous. Yet I knew I wasn't imagining it.

My mind was still preoccupied when I carried Claire back through the door of Cassidy & Wells. Bess, Irene, and Lillian were standing near the front of the desk. Wells stood to the side. Half of his desk was covered in maps and schematics, which had been pushed aside to make room for a tin percolator and five modest cups. By the time we arrived, the coffee had been drunk, and the air was filled with a current of bored expectation. When Bess caught sight of me, she smiled sleepily and crossed toward us.

"Well, you look like you've been having fun," she said, moving to take Claire from my arms. Then her nose crinkled and she pulled back. I'd done my best to clean Claire's face, but the faint smell of vomit still hung in the air.

"Perhaps a bit too much fun," I said.

Grimacing, Bess pried the sleepy child off me. "Well, no matter. We're finished here, and Tim's gone down to the station to buy our tickets back to Pyrite."

"Was Mr. Wells able to help?"

"In a manner of speaking." Lillian crossed to join us. The lazy afternoon light pouring in through the window softened the wrinkles around her eyes and mouth, making her look more like one of her daughters than ever. "Mr. Wells says that our land is sandwiched between a piece belonging to Curtis and another parcel, where oil was discovered a few years ago. He's not sure if the oil extends to our property, but if it does, that would make the land a lot more valuable than anyone thought it was."

"Does Samuel Curtis know about the oil?" I asked.

Wells replied, "We have no record of dealings with him, and according to my maps, there's no oil on his land. But that doesn't mean he hasn't had someone else out there to evaluate."

"If there is oil under there," Lillian said, "then Samuel's original offer was a downright insult. At any rate, we're going out to have a look tomorrow morning. Why don't you come with us, Mr. Adler? We're leaving from here at nine o'clock."

Just then Tim walked back through the door.

"Success?" Bess asked.

He patted the breast of his jacket. "Six fares to Pyrite—well, five and a half, counting Claire—leaving in half an hour. Come on, then."

"I'm...er...staying here," I said.

"Staying?" Tim frowned.

The words surprised me as much as anyone, but it didn't make them any less right. I needed time to think, time to digest everything that had happened that afternoon. The unreal experience of spending the last hour in Goddard's company had only put off, for that hour, the shock of seeing him again. The realization that Cain Goddard was alive—it changed things. I wasn't certain how just yet, but it did. And there were other things as well: the fact that Miss Wood was apparently following us to California, my own ambivalence about returning to London, and my unresolved feelings—despite my best efforts to put it out of my mind—regarding Lawrence and St. Andrews.

"It's not fair to Mr. and Mrs. Adams," I said. "Their house isn't made to hold that many people, and they shouldn't have to feed me on top of everything else."

"But—" Irene was obviously protesting.

"I should hate to inconvenience you, more than anyone, Irene." Because I recognized that my affection for her—and her apparent affection for me—was another part of my confusion. The silver brooch suddenly felt unaccountably heavy in my pocket. It was right that I stay, that I figure things out and not complicate these good people's lives with my own problems. "I'll find a hotel for tonight and meet you back here tomorrow morning. But let me pay you for my ticket," I said to Tim.

"I can sell it back at the station." He narrowed his eyes, and something changed in his expression. Grasping me by the elbow, he guided us back onto the street. "Adler, what the devil's going on?"

I glanced back into the building to make certain no one else was listening. "Cain Goddard is alive."

Tim's face screwed up as if he were smelling something unpleasant. "Goddard? Are you sure?"

"I spent the last hour having tea with the man. Of course I'm sure. And in case you're curious, he and the Colonel—one and the same."

"By God!" He stalked a few steps down the deserted street, stopped, turned, then stalked back. Then he took off his hat and used it to fan his face. He kept opening his mouth to speak, then shutting it again, as if realizing it wasn't what he wanted to say at all. Finally he said, "In the wheelchair?"

"Yes."

"Does he actually need it, or is it part of some clever disguise? No, don't tell me. I don't care. God, Ira, he really *has* been following us!"

"Actually…"

While the late-afternoon sun beat down on the dusty street around us, I gave him an abbreviated account of everything that had happened since we'd boarded the ship in Liverpool. His expression alternated between disbelief, outrage, and other emotions that passed too quickly for me to recognize. When I came to this afternoon's vomit-spewing episode, though, he choked back a laugh.

"Good old Claire. I knew we should have left her in Pyrite, where she could have a nap. Still," he said, entertaining an uncharacteristically nasty little snigger, "as disgusting as it must have been, I can't say the man didn't have it coming. So, you're going to stay here to be with him, I suppose?"

"No." It astonished me to think that was even a question. The idea made me feel guilty somehow. "It's over. It's been over for years. I just hadn't realized it." I sighed. "I'm sorry, Tim. It's complicated. I just need to be alone for a bit. I'll come by at some point to gather my things, but for the time being, I think I'll stay here."

"I understand." He patted my shoulder. "Come. Tell the ladies good-bye, and then be off. I know Irene would be crushed if you didn't at least give her that."

I glanced back through the doorway. Irene and Wells were standing quite close. She was showing him her sketchbook. I felt a sting of completely inappropriate possessiveness.

"Ira?"

"I forgot to mention—it appears Marshal Sutter may be joining us soon. Apparently that key that was hidden in Claire's toy satchel belongs to a bank here in Porterville. Sutter's on his way to deliver it."

"The Colonel's key?" Tim asked. Then, in a muted tone, "Goddard's key?"

I nodded, adding, "And I thought we might ask Sutter to look into the fire at Lillian's home if he has time."

"I don't see why, if the sheriff in Visalia has already investigated."

"Well, it couldn't hurt for someone to have a second look, could it?" Lillian said, suddenly appearing in the doorway, Irene close behind. How long had they been listening?

"Oh, would you do that, Mr. Adler?" Irene asked. She was smiling brightly, her face aglow with excitement—a fact that seemed to be causing Mr. Wells no small dismay. "Oh, thank you! You do think of everything!"

CHAPTER TWENTY-EIGHT

Y ou're lucky, sir. It's our last room."
The man behind the reception desk of the Arlington Hotel slid
a key toward me as I signed the hotel register. He was a thin man in his
early thirties, with a thick brown mustache that turned up at the ends.
It was a nice hotel—clean and well maintained, with fresh paint on the
walls and polished woodwork—but not so nice that my host didn't feel
at home rolling up the sleeves of his crisp shirt in deference to the heat.

"That is lucky," I said. "Is it always this busy?"

"It is on the few days leading up to the Fourth."

"The Fourth?"

"The Fourth of July. Independence Day? The big festival?" A slow
smile crept across his face. "But then you're not from around here."

"No, I'm one of the oppressors, I'm afraid."

A brief frown flitted across his brow, and then he let out a laugh
that lit up his long, friendly face.

"Well, as long as you're not planning any surprise attacks, you're
welcome here, Mr. Adler."

After my experience in Snake Ridge, I'd wondered whether the
first two hotels had, indeed, turned me down because of my complexion.
But the manager of the Arlington—a very respectable two-story hotel
looking out over Oak Street—had no apparent qualms about letting me
a room.

Outside, the sun was dropping behind the low, rolling mountains.
The orange glow of sunset was receding across the horizon. My
stomach growled, and I realized that the last meal I'd had had been a
scrap of bread and half a strip of bacon snatched from the Adamses'
breakfast table.

"Anything else I can help you with, sir?"

The clock on the wall read seven thirty. Much too early for a civilized supper, but civilization could wait. I was ravenous.

"Could you recommend a place for an early supper?" I asked.

"Well, now, there are a number of places nearby, but you could do worse than Scottie's Chop House on Main Street. Early, late, it never closes. And there's a saloon attached, if you're of a mind."

"That sounds excellent, thank you."

I returned the key and walked back toward Main Street. The temperature was dropping rapidly. The first cool hints of evening were a blessed relief. Night was transforming the boardwalk. The shop doors were latched for the night, but other doors—saloons, restaurants, a place I suspected was a bordello—were just opening. Gone were the sun-beaten shop-goers, the delicately perspiring tea-room ladies, and the trail-dust-covered cowboys that had taken cover beneath the awnings. A different sort of folk was emerging now—some in their evening finery, others in slick suits and polished boots—and all apparently looking for excitement.

I found the chophouse quickly enough. The hotel manager's instinct had been exactly right. The place was perfect—dark wood and brass fittings, a clean floor, cloths on the tables, and air suffused with the smells of well-cooked beef and fresh bread. At the same time, the atmosphere was down-to-earth and welcoming—like so many parts of this country, it seemed. Unfortunately, what looked like half of Porterville seemed to be finding the place as appealing as I was. There wouldn't be a table available for at least half an hour, I was told before being kindly directed through a side door into the adjacent tavern.

The John Zalud Saloon was also busy, but I found an empty stool at the long, curving bar. The atmosphere there wasn't quite as friendly, but it did promise to be entertaining. The air around me buzzed with alcohol-fueled conversation, while a young man banged out a jolly tune on a piano on the other side of the room. Through a gathering tobacco haze, I observed card games at two tables. As I squinted to read one man's hand over his shoulder, someone else said behind me, "Evening, friend. What'll it be?"

The bartender was a middle-aged man with a broad chest and forearms like hairy bowling pins. He was smiling, though, beneath his mustache and thick sideburns. In the mirror that took up a good part of the wall behind him, I saw that he kept a hunting rifle on a shelf below the bar with the cleaning rags.

"What would you recommend?" I asked.

He cocked his head and narrowed his eyes. I could see him trying to figure me out: young man, expensive clothes, foreign accent, recently broken nose.

"For you? I have a nice cabernet sauvignon from the Sonoma Valley northwest of here. A little pricey—the valley's still recovering from the grape blight a few years ago—but it's worth it, I think. If you're looking for something a mite stronger, I have a very smooth Kentucky bourbon."

I thought for a moment, then opted for the wine. The cool of the evening had refreshed me, but I was still feeling drained from the heat—not to mention from hunger. Anything stronger than wine would likely do more harm than good. After a moment the bartender returned with a glass and a bottle, which he proceeded to uncork.

"Couldn't help noticing your accent," he said as he decanted the deep, dark wine into the glass. "Mind my asking where you're from?"

"London," I replied.

He looked impressed. "That's a long way to come." He wiped a drip from the neck of the bottle and set it beside the glass.

"You don't know the half of it."

"What brings you here?"

"I'm traveling with friends."

"Wouldn't be Colonel Wright and Mr. Spark, by any chance? An old man with a walking stick and his…nephew, maybe? They're from London. Why, they came in here for a drink before supper just the other night."

I wondered if he heard my stomach flip when he mentioned the Colonel. A quick glance in the mirror behind the bar showed that I'd managed to keep the panic from my expression, but the words had set my pulse and my thoughts racing again.

"No," I said.

Taking the hint, he smiled and changed the subject. "How long are you planning on staying?"

Now that was a good question. "I haven't decided."

"Well, welcome to Porterville. Hope you enjoy yourself. My name's Dan. And if you go next door for supper, I recommend the prime rib. Comes with a baked potato as big as a melon and drowning in butter."

My stomach made a ferocious noise, which I hoped had been lost in the din. "Thanks. That does sound good."

The bartender gave a little nod, then left me with my glass and bottle. The wine was excellent, and the atmosphere was perfect—not rough enough to make me keep a hand on my billfold, but not so polished that I couldn't relax. The wine was spicy and bold. I finished my glass and poured myself another, and then another.

As alcohol blurred the raucous bar sounds together into a pleasant wall of noise, the tension drained from my shoulders and neck. I tipped the last drops out of the bottle, leaned onto my elbows, and raised my glass to my reflection in the mirror. The face that looked back was surprisingly handsome despite a shadow of bruises across the cheeks and nose, the unkempt tilt of the hat, and the fact that the chin could have used a shave. Still, I wasn't looking to impress anyone that night. And with the help of the grape, everything had slowed pleasantly, my thoughts included—and that was an improvement.

Goddard was alive. In the warm glow of the cabernet sauvignon, I was able to examine the fact free of my initial shock. And when I thought about it, it wasn't actually that much of a shock. Part of me was ashamed I hadn't figured it out earlier. The man had survived assassination attempts before, and with the rigorous way he prepared for every eventuality, it would have come as a surprise had he *not* had some sort of escape plan in place. The real shock had come from seeing him again—from the resurgence of emotions I'd thought dead and buried long before the explosion.

What kept drawing us back together? It had seemed simple in the beginning—a business transaction—an extension of our relationship as client and whore. He'd been generous with his money, and with his affection. He'd offered me an education—something I hadn't realized I'd wanted. He'd taken my improvement seriously—tried to mold me into someone he'd be proud of. Before that, no one had ever considered me beyond what I could do for them. I'd thought I preferred it that way.

At the same time, Goddard had been controlling and exacting. Part of it was understandable. Running a criminal empire is a life-and-death endeavor with little room for mistakes. I'd seen his allies betray him over matters of very small gain. I'd seen him turn on people I'd thought were his friends, when they stood in the way of business. It was exciting at first, but in the final analysis, I didn't possess either the ambition or the ruthlessness to play a part in his organization—or to turn a blind eye to its operations forever.

When circumstances had reunited us four years ago, I'd spent a delicious week in his company, deceiving myself that we could regain the good parts of what we had, without the bad. Goddard himself showed me how wrong I was. And now he seemed content with someone else. I should just leave it alone. Why couldn't I leave it alone?

Because it seemed as if life had bent itself into a pretzel trying to bring us back together. Business interests in California! In *this part* of California! It couldn't be coincidence. But what did it mean?

I shook my head in disgust. It meant I'd drunk too much wine, that's what it meant. On an empty stomach, no less. And probably that, as much as I'd tried to convince myself that it was none of my business what and whom Lawrence was doing while I was gone, St. Andrews's letter had crept under my skin. Not to mention the fact that before that night, I hadn't had a moment's rest from my friends, and their friends, and their family, and their family's friends, and yet, when I thought about it, I was still somehow so goddamned lonely.

Was the bottle empty already? How in hell had that happened?

But I didn't object when Bartender Dan quietly took it away and set a second, unopened one down in its place, with a corkscrew.

I was fumbling with the cork when a hand landed on my shoulder. I'd drunk enough that I didn't quite jump out of my suit, but my expression must have said that I wanted to, because when I turned, Marshal Calvin Sutter let out a rich laugh. He'd shed the porter's uniform and was wearing an exquisitely tailored dark suit, his shiny badge prominent on the lapel. The white shirt beneath it was silk—like his thin black tie—and it was new. A gold chain hung outside his waistcoat pocket, connecting, one assumed, to an equally expensive watch within. My mind went immediately to the watch in my own waistcoat pocket—Goddard's watch. I resisted the urge to touch it, like a talisman, through the fabric.

"Sorry if I startled you, Mr. Adler. Thought you'd seen me in the mirror. You must have been thinking deep thoughts."

"Deep thoughts give you wrinkles," I said. Weakly. Sutter had a nice smile. He'd been to a barber. He cleaned up well, I thought. Much better than I'd have expected.

I set the unopened bottle back on the table.

"Mind if I join you?" Sutter asked.

"Of course not." I gestured with the corkscrew to the stool next to me. "Where are my manners?"

I signaled Dan for another glass. He brought it and then, without commenting on the mangled cork, proceeded to open the bottle himself and pour for two.

"Marshal," he said with a friendly nod, which Sutter returned.

"Bigger town, they're used to different kinds of folks," Sutter said, answering my unasked question as Bartender Dan withdrew.

"In London, too."

"That so?"

"Depends where you go, but in the part where I grew up, there are all sorts of people: Africans, Chinese, Hindus, Russians, Poles. That's not to say that everyone gets along all the time, but it's not so... monochromatic as, say, Snake Ridge or Council Bluffs."

"Monochromatic." He laughed. "Yeah, that's one way of putting it."

While I rambled, he scrutinized me with astute cop eyes. Eyes that were always looking for trouble. Not unfriendly, just...alert.

"'Course the badge helps. Men of my hue usually drink their"— he held up the bottle and examined the label—"*cabernet sauvignon* down the street."

He set the bottle down and raised his glass in a salute. I returned it, and we drank. I didn't argue when he filled our glasses again. By that time, my mouth was becoming numb, and when I moved, I could feel the acidy slosh of nearly one and a half bottles of rather expensive wine inside me.

"I'm surprised to see you here," he said. "Thought you were staying in Pyrite."

"I am, officially. I mean, my things are there, and my friends."

"But you're here?" Sutter asked.

"Dr. and Mrs. Lazarus are staying with friends of her mother. There isn't a lot of room, and I didn't think it was fair for them to have to feed me as well."

"Weren't they expecting you?"

Briefly I told him about the fire that had taken Lillian's and Irene's house while we had been traveling aboard the *Teutonic*. Then I confessed that I'd intended to send him a telegram in the morning requesting his assistance in the matter.

"I'm no arson investigator," he said, frowning.

"Yes, but you are an officer of the law. They said the sheriff in Visalia had already taken a look and found no evidence that the fire was set deliberately, but Mrs. Campbell doesn't agree. I've known her daughter, Mrs. Lazarus, for a long time, now, and if Mrs. Campbell is as much like Bess as she seems, I can't imagine she'd be either lying or letting her imagination run amok."

He seemed to consider this point for a moment. Then he shrugged. "I could probably take a day or two before anyone would miss me in New York. Does Pyrite have a stop on the railroad?"

I nodded.

"Let's meet at the station around nine. Take the first train."

"Actually, they're coming here in the morning. We're going to meet the geologist, and then we're all riding out to see Mrs. Campbell's land, which seems to be at the center of all the trouble. If you tell me where you're staying, I could drop by when we're done, and we could head down to Pyrite then."

He shrugged again. "I could always come to the site with you, talk to the people involved. Not like I have anything better to do."

"I don't think anyone would object to that," I said.

"Then it's a deal. Should I meet you at the geologists' office?"

"Yes. Cassidy and Wells, right off Main Street. Thank you, Marshal," I said.

"Calvin." He held out a hand.

"Ira," I said, taking it. The flesh was warm and dry, his grip sure and strong. I let my fingers linger in his just a touch longer than necessary.

When I let go, Sutter took a long, slow sip of his wine. Something in his gaze made me squirm. It wasn't entirely unpleasant. I felt as if he were looking through me, as if he was trying to place me among the types of people he'd encountered over the course of his life. He had very lovely chocolate-brown eyes, and the lamplight set off the almost blue tones in his dark, dark skin. Handsome, in a rugged sort of way.

Entirely too much wine on an empty stomach. I should have stopped after the first bottle.

I pushed my glass toward the far side of the bar. It reached the edge, tottered there for just a second, then crashed to the floor on the other side.

"Tarnation!" Bartender Dan cried from the other side of the bar. His voice sounded farther away than that, as if he were calling out from beneath a sea of Sonoma Valley cabernet. "Are you gents going to start tearing up the place, now?"

There was a smile in his voice, though, and within seconds he was placing a new glass before me.

"Ah, that's not really—"

"Thank you, bartender," Sutter said. He slipped a few coins across the bar. "Sorry about the mess."

While Bartender Dan made busy with a broom and dustpan, I laid a hand over the top of the new glass to make my meaning unambiguous. Sutter suppressed a grin.

"I didn't expect to see you in town," I said, attempting to regain a bit of dignity. "At least not so soon."

"Well, lucky for both of us, the sheriff came up from Cheyenne to fetch Wilkes just after you left Snake Ridge. By evening I was on the night train to Sacramento. Arrived in Porterville this afternoon, just in time to deliver that key I took off the doctor to the Bank of California before it closed."

"The Colonel will be relieved," I said.

"Is he here?"

I laughed. Miserably. Where to begin? "He certainly is. We took afternoon tea together."

His good humor dissolved. Something switched on behind his eyes, and I could tell he was considering me in a different—and not entirely innocent—light. I'd seen that expression on Nicholas's face—right before he all but arrested me for burglary. "Did you, now?"

"It's a long story. We were...acquainted once, in London."

"I see."

He took a long pull on his wine, then held the glass up to the light. The wine glowed an inky purple, nearly as opaque as Sutter's expression. I could almost see his mind trying to find a place for this new information, putting the pieces together. Nicholas had accused me of stealing the Colonel's key. The Colonel had told him to drop the case. The key had been found on a member of my party—when the youngest member of a band of aspiring train robbers had taken Claire hostage in order to get it. And then there was Miss Wood, whom Sutter had been chasing for quite some time before that. And who, as he had yet to discover, was not only involved but possibly on her way here.

"Well," Sutter said. "The Colonel has his property back, whatever's in the bank box is safe, and no one's complaining. All's well that ends well, I suppose." His tone was jocular, but the light in his eyes told me he wasn't quite ready to let the matter drop. "And this is an excellent cabernet—if one must drink a domestic wine."

Again that feeling that he was mocking me somehow. But my mind was racing too fast to dwell there.

"I read in the newspaper that Miss Wood—Liza DuBois—is still at large," I said, hoping to distract him from whatever conclusions he might be drawing about Goddard and me.

He glanced at me out of the corner of his eye, put his glass down on the bar, and sighed. "Yes. That was embarrassing. We were so close this time."

"The article said she was spotted in Council Bluffs and thought to be heading west."

He looked at me. Frowned. "Now, why would she do that, I wonder."

"Did you get anything else out of Wilkes, like why he wanted the key?"

His frown deepened. Behind his calm features, he was wrestling with some idea. *Why is this of such great interest to you, Mr. Adler?* I was feeling a bit nauseated, now. A bit as if I were the one under a sea of cabernet. It was probably a good time for me to shut my gob, but of course I did not.

"Wilkes and his brothers had to be working with Miss Wood, don't you think?" I said. "She stole the key and planted it on us. She thought we were stopping in New York. I *told* her we were stopping in New York. She probably thought she'd take it back from us later that day."

"And when she saw you getting onto a westbound train, she set Wilkes and his brothers on the case." His expression was thoughtful, now. The idea excited him. He either hadn't made this connection before, or he'd thought it but had dismissed it. He nodded, perhaps out of renewed respect for Miss Wood's criminal acumen. "Crafty lady. Means she's better connected on this side of the ocean than we'd previously suspected. And she's headed in this direction, you say?"

"Read it in the Sacramento paper this afternoon," I said.

"Well, I'll be."

He crossed his arms over his chest and swiveled on the stool to gaze out into the hazy, noisy, crowded barroom. The man whose cards I'd been eyeing earlier teased an ace out of his sleeve and worked it into his hand. No one at the table seemed to notice. I was suddenly very, very aware of Sutter's proximity. I could feel the heat of his body, smell the lime and bergamot cologne beneath the clean scent of shaving powder. It was an expensive cologne. And bergamot was one of Goddard's favorite scents.

I shook my head clear. If I didn't get my thoughts under control, the evening would not end well.

"The key goes to a safe-deposit box," Sutter was saying when I finally refocused on the conversation. He tossed back the rest of his wine and set his glass aside. "How would she know that? She'd have to know the Colonel very well, or know someone else who did. And Liza DuBois is based in Liverpool. That's a long way from London."

Now that was a conclusion I hadn't anticipated. I didn't like it. And I didn't like the conversation turning back to Goddard.

Of course she might not have known him. She might have known someone who knew him, though. Cain Goddard, by his own admission, wasn't the only master criminal in London. I'd no idea if his connections stretched all the way to Liverpool, but it was entirely possible that, at some point, his organization overlapped with one to which she might have belonged. Did she know who had tried to kill Goddard? Could she have been working, God forbid, for Rupert Sudworth? Was it possible that she'd heard, through some grapevine, that Goddard had escaped— and that he was headed to America to start a new life? What was in the safe-deposit box that was so important that she'd follow that key across the country?

And what would she do when she got here? If she knew who Goddard was, she could make a world of trouble for him and Marcus. Goddard had said his false documents were in order—he could deny everything. But what if she had some evidence that could prove who he was? What if she could tie him to some of the crimes in Britain of which he was really and truly guilty?

If she could convince the American authorities that the Colonel was Cain Goddard, the Duke of Dorset Street, she could have him sent back to England, where he would surely hang.

I had to warn him. I had to let him know. But where in this teeming, dust-covered city was he?

Suddenly everything was hot. My heart was pounding, and for the first time I noticed how chokingly smoke-saturated the air had become. A drop of sweat ran down my back. I tugged at my cravat. My stomach gurgled unpleasantly.

"Something the matter?" Sutter asked.

I stood. Swayed. Caught myself on the bar. "I need some air."

I slapped down a few coins and hoped it was enough. The dimly lit scene swam before my eyes—the gamblers, the piano player, the ladies of the evening. The music sounded distorted and unnaturally loud. As I stumbled toward the door, Sutter grabbed the bottle and followed me.

The air was cooler outside, and clean. My stomach slid slowly back into its place. The noise of the crowd was a lot easier to take when one wasn't cooped up in the same room with it. I stumbled around the side of the building, down a narrow alley, away from the festive din of

Main Street. Above, the star-filled sky angled dangerously. So many stars. Briefly I thought of Nicholas.

"Ira?"

Sutter was still there, walking a few paces behind me. He was carrying the wine bottle in one hand and had the thumb of the other hand looped into his belt. An amused smile played about his lips. I was happy *someone* was amused. We were standing at the intersection of two alleys. I leaned up against the back of the saloon, feeling the vibrations from the energetic piano through the wood.

"Forget what I just said about Godd—about the Colonel—about that woman. I'm drunk. Making connections that aren't there."

"Whatever you say." He chuckled, and I had the feeling he would not forget—that he was probably making every effort to recall my blather in detail and commit it to memory.

The situation felt all too familiar. I hoped when I left the United States, it wouldn't be with two officers pursuing me for being in the wrong place at the wrong time. It might have been pure paranoia to think that he was trying to fit me into the puzzle as more than an accidental participant. I might have been imagining the suspicion in his eyes.

I didn't think I was imagining it when he leaned up against the back of the saloon, facing me and standing just a bit too close.

I gulped. "What happens when Miss Wood arrives in Porterville to collect the key?"

Sutter snorted. "*If* she comes here. Makes me the luckiest lawman in these United States. I'd be able to write my own ticket from here on out. If I caught her, that is."

"Would you send her back to England?" I asked hopefully. Preferably before she had the chance to implicate Goddard.

He frowned. "Why do you care?"

"Would you?"

The noise from the saloon and from the traffic on Main Street gave the illusion of being in the middle of a crowd. But the truth was, we were completely alone. Calvin Sutter was a deeply attractive man. Beneath the well-cut suit, his shoulders were broad, and his trim figure hinted at a well-proportioned musculature. He was still facing me, so I turned and leaned on my left shoulder. From this angle, I was close enough to feel his warm, wine-tinged breath on the bridge of my nose.

After a while, he said, "Not if I could help it. I've been chasing that woman so long, I'd want to see her tried here. And if it's true what you say—and if Wilkes will testify that she hired them to get that key—then I could put her away for a very, very long time."

"But what if…" How to phrase it without giving it all away in a stumbling torrent of ill-chosen words? "What if, during the investigation, or the trial, she revealed something about…someone? Someone who had come to this country to make a new life? Something that could get him into a lot of trouble back in England if he was sent back because of what she said—and he would surely be sent back. Nobody wants that kind of person settling in their country." I was babbling, but I couldn't stop. As many times as I'd wished ill on Goddard, I just couldn't let the worst happen without trying to do something about it.

"What are you getting at, Mr. Adler?" He'd gone back to "Mr." That couldn't be good.

"Please. I can't say. I've said too much already."

He cocked his head and narrowed his eyes. He really was standing very close. And beneath his expensive cologne, his scent was so masculine it was making my eyes cross. He smiled. Knowingly? Sympathetically? God forbid, *pityingly*? I could count the isolated gray spirals in his wide, well-groomed mustache. The curve of his mouth was surprisingly sensual.

"I think I know what you're worried about, Ira." His voice was soft. Smoky. It felt like a velvet hand closing around my very core.

"You do?"

Licking his lips, he nodded. "It's a crime here, too."

"It is?" I frowned. At some point he'd leaped to a very different conclusion about my worries. I wondered if it weren't worse somehow.

"Shouldn't be, in my opinion. What a man does in the privacy of his own bedroom—and with whom—it's nobody's business."

Good God. A cold sweat broke across my back.

"Two of the tribes I lived with even considered a bond between men to be a sacred thing. Don't worry," he said. "I'll keep your secret."

I did mention that I was very drunk. I did mention that my tongue was loose—my inhibitions, it appeared, even looser.

Sutter licked his lips again, cleared his throat. "In fact…"

He didn't have a chance to finish. As he began to speak, I leaned forward, clamped a hand around the back of his head, and swallowed the rest of his words with a long, deep kiss.

His lips were firm, slightly chapped, and tasted like sage dust. His mouth yielded just enough for me to snatch a taste of teeth, of tongue—to pull him closer—close enough to feel his pulse pounding beneath my fingers, to hear his breath turn ragged as I pressed my body against his. I might have been full of wine and empty of good sense, but I wasn't imagining his strong arms pulling me close, or the hard evidence between us that he wanted this as much as I did.

Which is why it came as such a surprise when he put his hands on my chest and shoved. He didn't shove hard, but I stumbled back— mostly out of surprise. My fancy American hat tumbled to the ground behind me.

"I said I'd keep your unnatural inclinations to myself, Mr. Adler," he said breathlessly. "I didn't say I shared them."

"What? You must be joking!"

And yet the subsequent doubt that assailed me was crippling. Clearly I'd misjudged the situation. Though I couldn't imagine how I'd misinterpreted his reaction. Words lie, but the body never does.

"It's no joke." He straightened his shirt, his cuffs. "I won't hold it against you, but don't do it again."

Alcohol only goes so far as an excuse. Combined with the insult of St. Andrews's letter, the catastrophic horror of witnessing the resurrection of the Duke of sodding Dorset Street, and a loneliness so new, wretched, deep, and unexplored—the excuse could, perhaps, stretch a bit further. But not that far. I hadn't lived this long, plied the trade that I had for as long as I had, without having *some* sense of which men were likely to give me a shilling and which would give me a beating. Even with the stars spinning above me, and the ground tilting below, I did possess that much discernment. I also possessed the discernment to recognize the point at which one might turn to the other.

"I apologize," I said. "I should leave now."

I took a step, but the ground lurched beneath me. I flung myself back against the rear door of the saloon. Shaking his head, Sutter walked over, picked up my hat, and took me by the arm.

"Where are you staying? I'll walk you there. Shape you're in, you'll wind up in a ditch with your pockets turned out and your throat slit."

The last thing I wanted was to endure Sutter's presence for one second more, no less to rely on his assistance. Actually, dead in a ditch sounded preferable to the dread and embarrassment I was feeling just then. But then I remembered—I'd caused a child to vomit on Cain Goddard's shoes and lived to tell the tale. Surely I could survive this.

It was a long, shameful trudge back to the Arlington. I'd stopped apologizing but couldn't think of anything to say that wouldn't sound forced and desperate. Sutter seemed happy I'd finally shut my mouth.

"Nine o'clock sharp at Cassidy and Wells," he reminded me as he handed me off to the long-suffering desk clerk. Egad. I'd completely forgotten. That should be fun. "Are you going to be all right...Ira?"

"Fine, fine," I muttered. Though after everything that had happened that day, I doubted very much that I would ever be completely all right again.

"Then I'll just be on my way."

CHAPTER TWENTY-NINE

When the morning clerk—a barefaced little blond chap who couldn't have been more than seventeen—rapped at my door the next morning, he did not come bearing a bright, shiny new day washed clean of the embarrassments of the night before. He did, however, come apologetically, and with coffee.

"There was a note from the marshal," he began, handing me a china cup and saucer. The coffee inside it smelled strong and was thick with cream.

"Nine o'clock at Cassidy and Wells," I mumbled. My mouth felt like a carpet in an outhouse. Someone had taken a rusty ax to my skull and left it there. The gentle light in the hallway burned and pulsed like a malevolent sun. Gratefully, I took a long draught of the coffee, sighing as the constriction in my scalp relaxed. "What time is it now?"

"Eight fifty. I let you sleep." He winced. "Looks like you needed it."

"A plague upon the entire wretched Sonoma Valley."

"I also brought water for the basin." He handed me a porcelain pitcher decorated with little blue flowers.

"My gratitude knows no bounds," I said, slipping him a coin.

He nodded acknowledgment and pocketed it. "There's more coffee downstairs, but I wouldn't keep the marshal waiting, if I were you."

I shut the door, finished the coffee, and had a quick wash in the basin. Then I took a razor to my chin. I wasn't shaving for Sutter, I told myself, though I did, for a moment, consider leaving the mustache area to grow. When one is feeling obliterated, basic hygiene can mean the difference between meeting one's obligations and giving in to a day of well-deserved self-pity and sloth. I gazed longingly at the bed. Outside on the street below, the citizens of Porterville were going about their daytime business as if they hadn't made asses of themselves in the most egregious and reckless way possible the night before. As if they hadn't seen dead lovers return to life before their very eyes, hadn't been torn between the poles of desperate nostalgia and righteous repulsion. As if they were not marching inexorably toward a day of certain discomfort and humiliation.

They weren't, of course. That was just me.

But I wasn't about to march there looking a wreck.

I emerged fresher-smelling and slightly less disreputable-looking, though I'd have given my left testicle for a new shirt and my right for a pair of the dark-lensed syphilitic's spectacles I'd sneered at back in London.

"Have a good day, Mr. Adler," the clerk said as I passed the front desk on my way to the door.

I mumbled something about not telling me what kind of day to have, then went to meet my fate.

❖

The Lazarus party hadn't yet arrived when I poked my head through the door of the offices of Cassidy & Wells. Someone had turned the sun to its highest setting, and at a little after nine, I was already in danger of sweating through my shirt. Wells was sitting at his desk, a humble spread of food arrayed before him. When he heard the door open, he stood.

"Ah, good morning, Mr..."

"Adler," I supplied. "And I've clearly interrupted your breakfast, Mr. Wells. My apologies."

He glanced at the apple he'd been polishing on his brown-and-black plaid waistcoat and gave me a guilty look. "I wanted to get here early, so I brought it with me. No wife to care if I eat properly, you see."

My stomach issued a loud demand.

"You either?" Wells suppressed a smile and held the apple out toward me. I snatched it greedily, then, stopping, muttered an abashed thank you. "Sounded like you could use it more."

"You don't know the half of it," I said, biting off a clean third of the apple in one go. It was bruised. It was mealy. I'd never eaten anything so delicious in all my life. My stomach immediately began to settle.

"Coffee?" Wells asked.

"Yes, please."

He poured a second cup from his dented tin percolator, then split his bread and cheese into two portions, gesturing for me to help myself. He was a pleasant-looking young man. Vigorous and earthy, but with clean fingernails and the underlying refinement that comes with education. The round spectacles were a nice touch. And he had good taste in cheese.

"Mr. Wells, you've saved me," I said. I was beyond embarrassment by this point, and I tucked in with a ferocity that might have appalled me under other circumstances.

Wells waved off my thanks and said, "It's good to see you again. Will you be joining us this morning?"

"I promised Miss Campbell I'd come."

His smile faltered. Perhaps I hadn't imagined the interest that had flickered to life in his eyes the other day when he'd met Irene. As if hearing my thoughts, he cleared his throat. "Ah, yes. Well. The first train should be arriving from Pyrite any minute now. I expect they'll be walking through the door soon." He glanced up as a shadow passed by the window. "Perhaps they're already here."

As if on cue, the door opened—a searing blast of sunlight and hot air that stirred up the dust motes and sent the shadows scurrying. Sutter's lanky silhouette filled the doorway—a stunning black hat that day, of the cowboy variety; a charcoal-colored pinstripe suit with a long jacket that clung to his shoulders and flared slightly just below his hips. A breeze lifted one side of the jacket, revealing a shiny pistol in a leather holster at his waist. Well-cut trousers tapered down to a pair of polished black brogues that looked almost as expensive as the ones Goddard had been wearing. His badge glinted in the bright morning sun.

"Can I help you? Oh! You're a marshal! Come in, Marshal!"

Sutter stepped forward. "Good morning. Mr. Cassidy, I presume?"

"I'm Wells." He stuck out his hand. "Gordon Wells. My partner, Mr. Cassidy, doesn't come in until later. How can I help you, sir?"

"Actually, Mr. Adler, here, asked me to come." He nodded in my general direction, and I politely returned the motion. "I have business with the Campbell family, and Mr. Adler thought to save me a trip by meeting them here, rather than going all the way to Pyrite. If you have no objections, I'd like to join your party this morning."

"You're welcome, of course," Wells said. "Would you like to sit down?"

"Thank you, I'll stand."

Of course. All the better to impress us with his expensive clothing and exquisite physique. Or perhaps he simply didn't want to approach the desk, where I had seated myself. He wasn't radiating hostility, as I'd half expected, but neither would he meet my eye. While Wells popped the last bit of cheese into his mouth and tidied his desk, I watched Sutter casually scan the room, taking in the maps, the geological samples in their glass cases, and the brass instruments on display. A thick, uncomfortable moment passed when Wells disappeared up the stairs. A moment Sutter broke, by asking, "Sleep well?"

"Like a dead dog. You?"

"Like a well-fed babe. How's your head?"

"Splitting, if you must know. May the Sonoma Valley be swallowed up in an earthquake."

Sutter surprised me by laughing out loud.

Wells returned then, forestalling any further uncomfortable exchange. "We've a bit of a journey ahead of us. Mrs. Campbell's land is just across the line in Kern County."

I blinked. But before I could say anything, Sutter had joined Wells before a map of Central California that hung on one wall. Wells was gesturing, indicating the area where Lillian's claim lay.

"How large is Kern County?" I asked, determined not to look either foolish or cowed.

Wells said, "A little more than eight thousand square miles, but where we're headed is just on the other side of the county line. All the same, it's a good two hours over rough road. I've hired a cart—it was the only vehicle that could accommodate both the passenger load and the terrain." He eyed Sutter's clothing dubiously. "It's bound to get very dusty," he said apologetically.

Sutter shrugged. "A little dust never hurt anyone."

I suddenly had an image of him running across the Wyoming prairie toward a stampeding herd of bison. I could see his shredded trousers as he emerged from the cloud of dirt and grit, the grin on his face as he dunked his head in the horse trough before going to meet the deputy. He was rough when rough was called for but equally at home in cologne and an expensive suit. He hadn't mentioned any formal education, but he appeared to read and write fluently, and easily matched Goddard for brains. He was brave and kind and brimming with a vitality that neither slavery nor danger nor everyday grinding rudeness had managed to erode. I'd never known anyone like him.

And after last night, what little I knew of him would have to suffice, because I doubted he'd let himself be caught alone with me again. And that made me sad—and more than a little bit unnerved that this one-sided affection hadn't evaporated from my system with the alcohol.

"I'm sure Mr. Adler can handle it," Sutter said with a hint of his easy smile.

"I'm sure I can," I said primly. Though I'd handle it much better if I knew there was no chance of our party encountering Goddard's by some divinely contrived coincidence. Eight thousand square miles was a lot of land, though.

We all looked up as the door opened again, and the room suddenly filled with Lazaruses and Campbells—Lillian, Bess, Tim…and Irene.

"Ah, Adler," Tim said, catching sight of me. He'd set himself up for disappointment, with his clean, pressed linen suit. He'd have to wash all over again once we returned. But why ruin his good mood by telling him as much? "Good to see you're on time for once. Marshal." He turned to shake hands with Sutter. "Will you be joining us?"

"With your family's permission," Sutter said. "Mr. Adler believes I might be of some assistance regarding the matter of the fire at Mrs. Campbell's home."

"And so you well may be. I'm sure my mother-in-law would welcome a second opinion. Let me introduce you."

He led Sutter across the room, where Lillian, Bess, and Irene were gathered around the map with Wells. Greetings and introductions ensued. While Lillian and Sutter spoke, Tim crossed back to me. "Did you manage to sort things out last night?" he asked.

I glanced at Sutter. "Actually, I think I made them worse." Before he could ask, I said, "No Claire today?"

"Claire had quite enough excitement yesterday, thank you very much. She'll be having a quiet day at the ranch with Mrs. Adams, who is delighted to have a little one to look after again. I trust the Colonel has no plans to visit Pyrite."

"None that I know of. I didn't plan to run into him, you know. I'd thought him as dead as you had."

"I know." His expression softened. "I know, Adler. It's just the thought of that man anywhere near my little girl…"

"Believe me, I understand."

I might have said more, but a quiet conversation near the mineral samples caught my attention. Wells and Irene had broken away from the group and were examining something in one of the glass cases. He was holding forth about some subject, and she was listening intently, nodding, and gesturing to the sketchbook she held in her hand. I felt the slightest twinge of jealousy—and then shame, as she looked up, noticed me watching, and cut Wells off in mid-sentence to come over.

"Mr. Adler! Good morning!"

"Good morning, Miss Campbell."

She looked fresh and pretty that morning in a tan calico dress with lavender and green flowers, and a jaunty straw hat, face scrubbed and glowing, her hair neatly coiffed. She looked ready for adventure and kept glancing between Wells and myself, as if wondering who would step up to provide it. I caught Wells watching us from the other side of the room, and as she took a step toward me, I took a conscious step back.

"Are you ready for a trip out into the wilderness?" she asked.

"I suppose. Have you been there?"

She shook her head. "Up until now, it's just been a piece of paper. Isn't it exciting?"

"Oh, yes, quite."

There was a loud rumbling noise, and a heavy wooden cart pulled up in front of the office. The cart bed was shaded by a light-colored canvas canopy stretched over a series of round hoops, and two stocky bay horses stood ready in their harness.

"A prairie schooner," Tim said, as if he'd never seen anything so marvelous. I was just hoping for a bench under there.

Wells gestured toward the door. "Ladies and gentlemen, our chariot has arrived."

The journey across the sunbaked California countryside was bumpy, dusty, never-ending, and hot, though the benches that ran along the inside of the cart kept it from being intolerable, and the canopy likely saved our lives. The sun was searing, and without the canvas between it and us, we would have had no respite for the entire two and a half hours. By the time we reached our destination, I was stiff and choking grit. My skull throbbed from the previous night's excesses. The unremitting sunlight scalded my eyes, and my arse was bruised to hell. At least I wasn't burnt crispy on top of it. Bess and Tim looked about the same as I felt, and I was glad they'd left Claire behind. Lillian and Irene, by contrast, were glistening with sweat but appeared as fresh and eager for adventure as they'd been when we'd boarded the cart in front of Wells's office.

Calvin Sutter was more at ease than a person had a right to be, though it was gratifying to see that he hadn't any supernatural dirt-repelling powers, as I'd previously suspected. He'd spent the entire journey chatting amiably with Wells, with only the occasional glance in my direction. I'd caught bits and snatches of their conversation—geology, land features, mineral wealth, and politics—though the heat, which was moistened and concentrated by the canopy, kept me from giving it too much thought.

I was of two minds about his apparent equanimity. On one hand, I was grateful things weren't as uncomfortable as they might have been. On the other hand, his lack of overt hostility, combined with the initial enthusiasm with which he'd responded to my advance, chased around in my mind like a dog after its tail. He hadn't shrunk from my touch. His physical response made me certain he'd have happily followed my advance to its conclusion. But at the last moment he'd pushed me away—why? Not because he was repulsed by the idea of a man's embrace, whatever he might have said to the contrary, and not because he found me, in particular, repulsive. I could have accepted either of those. There was some other reason behind his rejection. What was it?

Wells lifted his pocket watch for perhaps the fortieth time and finally, *finally* made his slow, unstable way across the swaying cart to tap the driver on the shoulder. When the cart rocked to a stop, I rose on shaky legs and peered out the back aperture. The sun was high overhead, not a protective cloud to be seen in any direction. The sky was that same dizzying shade of blue that had so dazzled me in Wyoming. Low mountains rose in the distance, barren brown with scattered splotches of green. The land underfoot was mostly flat, with occasional gentle hills, like waves on a lazy sea. Knee-high clumps of vegetation sprung up here and there along the hard, crumbly ground, and I saw quite a few tree-like structures with thick branches covered in tongues of bark and spiky green balls at the end that were as large as a man's head.

"Joshua trees," Wells said, noticing the direction of my gaze. He patted me on the shoulder and sprang nimbly out of the cart. "Will you hand me the ladder, please, Miss Campbell? You'll find it beneath one of the benches."

She found the ladder and brought it to the rear of the vehicle. I moved aside so she could hand it to Wells through the back aperture.

"Here you go, Mr. Wells."

"And my pack, if you please."

Wells had brought a rucksack large enough that Claire might have ridden quite comfortably inside, and I wondered why he'd asked Irene to help, rather than one of the several able-bodied men. She seemed very chuffed to be asked, however, so I said nothing.

"Allow me," Tim said, rising to help her.

"Oh, no, Doctor," Irene said. "I have it."

She hefted the pack with ease, handing it carefully out the back, as if it were filled with eggs. Then she accepted Wells's assistance down the ladder.

"Thank you, Miss Campbell." He stuck an arm through one of the straps and heaved the pack onto his own back. "You'd make a fine assistant, you know."

"I'm sure anyone could hand you a ladder, Mr. Wells." Her flirtatious tone softened the words. Even with his face shaded by the wide brim of his brown felt hat, I could swear I saw Gordon Wells's cheeks turn a shade pinker. He cleared his throat.

Tim climbed out next, assisting first Lillian, and then Bess. I followed. Behind me, Sutter stretched and made his own leisurely way to the ground.

"Now, then, ladies and gentlemen, here we are." Wells gestured to the surrounding landscape. "Most of the land you see around you belongs to Mrs. Campbell."

It wasn't much to look at, eccentric vegetation aside. The heat would have killed any seedling before it reached the surface. The sun would have evaporated any water before it could penetrate the hard, thirsty ground. Lillian's claim was a moonscape sparsely populated by spiny plants Jules Verne might have imagined and scrabbling, venomous creatures that disappeared into the ground the minute one turned to look at them properly.

"For this they burned my house down," Lillian said under her breath.

"Where's the mine, Mr. Wells?" Bess asked.

Wells looked out across the barren land, then pointed toward a low hill rolling up a bit west of us. On one side, a frame of cracked and splintering wood held open a yawning hole. A curtain of spiderwebs hung from it, swaying in the languid breeze. "That would be your mine, Mrs. Campbell. Shall we examine it first? Someone once found something of value there. Perhaps we'll be lucky."

Without waiting for us, he struck off toward the little hill. Irene darted ahead to join him, then stopped, glancing guiltily back at me. I was flattered, really. I had to admit I enjoyed having her on my arm. But it would have been cruel to encourage her nascent affection simply to bolster my own vanity. The little package containing the dragonfly brooch sat like a lump in my pocket. Touching it through the fabric of the jacket, I smiled and gestured for her to go on ahead. Returning my smile, she scrambled to catch up with Wells. As we walked toward the mine, my head pounding with each step, their conversation drifted back toward us.

"I meant what I said before," Wells said once she came up beside him. "And I wasn't just talking about fetching and carrying. You have a fine mind, Miss Campbell, if you don't mind my saying so. I noticed the way you were examining the maps yesterday while I was discussing your mother's claim. You asked some very intelligent questions about the land. And your sketches of the mineral samples in my case were simply exceptional."

"My parents have always believed a woman should be capable of taking care of herself—and that includes reading maps and carrying things. As for the sketches, it's a way to pass the time when the chores are done."

"Do you have others?"

"Oh, hundreds. I must have reproduced every inch of land in a ten-mile radius around our house."

"So you don't mind a trudge over rough country? Oh, yes, I can see from your boots that you're quite accustomed to walking." His tone was definitely admiring.

"There's not a whole lot to do in Pyrite, I'm afraid. Long walks and drawing, and sometimes a trip to the library in the next town to read about the plants I've sketched."

"That is impressive," Wells said. "I would very much like to see your other drawings one day. That is, if you'd care to show me."

She tilted her head coquettishly, and even through the shade cast by her hat, I could see the impish curl of her lips. "You've been watching me quite closely, it seems, Mr. Wells."

"If something beautiful catches a person's eye, will that person not look as closely as he can?" He cleared his throat, then, as if noticing for the first time that five other people were present, he said, "Now then, ladies and gentlemen, step up. We've arrived."

The entrance to the tunnel stood a little less than the height of a man. The wooden frame was more cobweb than wood and appeared to be held open by sheer force of will. The floor sloped downward and disappeared rather quickly into darkness. Cool air wafted out like a graveyard breath.

Wells slipped his pack off and leaned it against the slope of the hill. He unbuckled the strap holding a lantern to the side and brought out a pickaxe and a little shovel, which he tucked into the loops on his belt. "Now, normally I'd ask the landowner to accompany me. But this mine has been abandoned for some time, and, quite frankly, it looks hazardous. I cannot in good conscience ask a lady to step inside."

"Very sensible," Lillian said. "Though I couldn't expect my son-in-law to put himself at risk like that."

"It's no trouble at all," Tim replied.

"Oh, thank you, Timothy. Didn't you choose well, Bess?"

"I'll go, too," I said. Part of me didn't want Lazarus to show me up. A larger part—the part suffering from alcohol poisoning—wanted to remove itself from the retina-searing sunlight.

"But Mr. Adler!" Irene cried. "Isn't it quite dangerous?"

"Probably," I replied. "But someone needs to protect the good doctor." Irene tittered, and I felt a flush of pleasure. Then I turned to Sutter. "Marshal? What about you?"

Sutter was squinting off into the distance, his expression intent. I followed his gaze—rolling hills of crumbling earth, Joshua trees, a glimmer of movement over a distant rise, but nothing that seemed to require such careful attention.

"What is it, Marshal?" I asked.

He stared a moment longer, then turned back toward me—still not meeting my eyes. "Thought I saw someone out there, but it was probably just a trick of the light."

"Are you coming?" I repeated.

"No." He gazed back out toward the horizon. "I'll stay here. Protect the ladies from rattlesnakes."

"Suit yourself," I said, feeling suddenly peevish.

"Right, then," Wells said. "Into the breach. Miss Campbell." He tipped his hat to Irene and gave a little dip of his head.

Irene looked from Wells to me, her face flushed with youthful thrill cleverly disguised as worry. I imagined she was trying to decide which of us was more deserving of her concern.

"Come on, then, Adler," Tim said into my ear. "There'll be plenty of time for flirting when the work is done."

"I'm not flirting," I said. Though I couldn't shake the feeling that at some level I was. Which would have been disturbing enough, had I, like Tim, harbored any sort of attraction for women in general. The fact that I did not simply added to my consternation. I hoped Irene hadn't discussed the matter with Bess, as I imagined sisters were wont to do. Even worse than Bess warning me off would be if she thought Irene could somehow reform me—as Bess herself seemed to have reformed Tim.

By the time I'd worked through these troubling thoughts, Tim and Wells were disappearing into the mouth of the mine.

"From what I read, this mine was never a big producer," Wells was explaining when I caught up with them. The cool and darkness provided a blessed relief for my poor, burning eyes. As we followed the bobbing light of Wells's lantern, the rocky walls and ceiling of the tunnel came into focus. The floor angled downward, and gradually the light from the outside grew smaller and dimmer behind us. The ceiling was low, and though Wells passed through it with ease, Tim and I had to duck our heads.

Wells continued. "There aren't any cart tracks, so possibly a pony or a mule brought out whatever gold there was. Now, please be careful. These old mines are often unstable and filled with unexpected dangers."

"When was the last time anyone was down here?" I asked, sputtering as a thick swath of spiderweb settled onto my face.

"Hard to tell, but I'd guess it was abandoned sometime in the late fifties after the Fort Tejon earthquake. There aren't many quakes in the Central Valley, but that one was huge. Ruptured two hundred twenty-five miles of the San Andreas Fault. It was centered in Bakersfield, quite a distance south of here, but all of California would have felt it. The owner probably thought the small amount of gold left down here wasn't worth the risk."

As if on cue, I heard a crack overhead, and a bit of grit sprinkled down on us.

Wells paused for a moment, listened, then sallied forth, swinging his pickax jauntily while explaining a bit about the geology of the area and nearby mineral resources. Tim made interested noises—no doubt quite genuine, while I strained my eyes to avoid the low beams and jutting rocks that were becoming more frequent as the tunnel went on. It was cooler down here, and, though it was not exactly damp, an almost imperceptible hint of moisture hung in the air. My neck and shoulders relaxed. The smell of dust and sage was long behind us, having been replaced by a distinctly mineral odor and something else I couldn't quite set a finger on.

Wells stopped, his nose twitching as if he, too, smelled something out of the ordinary. The flame in his lamp flickered.

"Do you smell that, gentlemen?"

"What is it?" I asked.

In the dim light of the lamp, I saw his face pucker into a frown. He turned his head left, then right, like a dog on a scent. Then he bent down, quickly, taking the light with him. I followed it to a dark patch on the ground, near where the wall met the floor. The patch was the size of a small tabletop—darkened earth around the edges, then a ring of mud that, in the center, deepened to a puddle of black liquid. It smelled of earth and decay, and the light played a dirty rainbow across the surface.

"That's…is that oil?" Tim asked.

Wells stirred at the puddle with one end of his pickax, then held it up in the lantern light. "That's called a petroleum seep. Instead of gushing up like a geyser, a seep percolates up slowly through the rock."

"So there's an oil field under Mrs. Campbell's land?"

"There's part of an oil field on the adjacent parcel. Hard to tell how much of it, if any, is under this land, without proper excavation. This seep is recent—after the mine was abandoned. Otherwise, I'm certain someone would have made an effort to explore it further."

"What caused it?" I asked, circling around the far side of the puddle. The path continued for several yards before disappearing into the yawning darkness.

"A seep can be caused by movement of the surrounding rock," Wells said.

"Like from an earthquake?"

"Precisely, Mr. Adler. I would guess the earthquake moved the rock around enough to relieve a small amount of the pressure caused by the oil below—enough to allow it to start creeping toward the surface, but not enough for a sudden release."

As I stepped deeper into the mine, the ground seemed to change beneath my boots. It was firmer somehow. I tapped it tentatively with the toe of my boot and was rewarded with an almost hollow sound. Frowning, I shifted my weight from one foot to the other.

"Is it worth anything?" Tim asked.

"Quite possibly. The owner of the adjacent parcel has been

drawing a very respectable income from his well for years. Now this is interesting. It turns out the land on this side of Mrs. Campbell's claim is owned by another Englishman. Colonel Jeremiah Wright is his name. I understand he's just arrived in Porterville. Perhaps you know each other."

Even in the darkness, I could hear Tim's teeth grind. Taking another step backward, I heard something groan beneath my feet. I stopped and scraped at the floor with my boot. Was it wood? Why would someone have laid down floorboards in a mine?

Wells continued. "The land on the other side, as it happens, is owned by Samuel Curtis."

"Good God. Curtis must have been poking around here and found the seep," Tim said. "No wonder he's been so insistent about buying Mrs. Campbell's claim."

"What did he offer her for it, do you know?" Wells asked.

"Two hundred fifty dollars."

"That's not bad, if you're talking about a piece of shrub land with nothing on it."

"Robbery, if he did know," I said. There were definitely wooden planks.

"Strong language," Wells cautioned him, "but I'd have to agree with you. If he knew."

"Would it be worth burning down someone's house for?" Tim asked.

"Excuse me?"

"Mr. Wells," I said. "Why would someone lay a wooden floor in a mine?"

The geologists' words were swallowed up as the wood suddenly gave way beneath my feet. I heard a sickening roar of timber and rock as the floor opened up and I plunged into darkness.

"Ira!" Tim cried.

"Mr. Adler!"

I tumbled against rock and dirt—God knew how far. The hole wasn't much wider than a sewer opening, but I fell freely through dark and damp—until some atavistic impulse caused me to lash out with arms and legs, wedging myself into a narrow bit, balanced on my elbows and heels.

"He's fallen down the winze!" Wells cried. "Mr. Adler, can you hear me?"

"What's a winze?" I cried. A scattering of pebbles clattered down over me. I listened for their landing, but they just seemed to vanish into the darkness.

Up above, I heard Wells tell Tim, "It's a shaft between levels. It could be a hundred feet deep, for all I know. Are you all right, Mr. Adler?"

"As long as my arms and legs hold out."

I could see their faces above, in the light of the lamp. I tried not to think about the chasm beneath me, how deep it went and what might have been waiting for me down there. I watched them confer, tried to hear their words. For form's sake, Tim stretched his arm down toward me. Then he reached down with Wells's ax, but it was no use. Even the tip of the ax had to have been twenty feet above me, at least. My shoulders quivered.

"Don't you have a rope?" I called.

"In my pack," Wells said, clambering to his feet.

"I'll stay here," Tim said.

"I'll leave the lamp," Wells replied.

I listened as his footsteps disappeared back toward the entrance.

"Are you injured?" Tim called.

"No, but I'm holding on with my elbows and heels. I'm not sure how long I can keep it up."

"Just be still. Wells will be back soon. Try some deep breathing."

You try some deep breathing, I wanted to retort. But the words brought an image to my mind—Cain Goddard, in the one or two times I had ever witnessed him under true duress, using that exact technique to fortify his already steely will. Closing my eyes, I forced away the thought that I was trapped in a deep hole, hanging on by two knobbly elbows and the heels of a pair of city boots. Instead, I concentrated on the cool of the rocks at my back, the mineral scent that pervaded the air, and the darkness that was such a welcome respite for my burning eyes and pounding head. I made myself draw long, deep breaths. Amazingly, I grew simultaneously stronger and more relaxed.

"So," Tim said, affecting a light tone that it was clear he didn't feel. "When I asked you earlier if you'd sorted things out with Goddard, and you said you'd actually made them worse—what did you mean, exactly?"

The question surprised me so much, I temporarily forgot my predicament. "Why the devil are you asking me this now?"

He had moved the lamp to the edge of the hole, and in its light, I could see the traces of a wry smile. "Because I might not get another chance."

"Bastard!" I marveled.

His smile widened to a grin—and then his face lit up with relief as the tunnel rang with returning footsteps. There seemed to be too many of them for just one man. "Oh, thank God. He's brought the marshal with him."

I let out a long breath and slumped out of my own relief—only to have to scramble back into position as my shoulders and heels slipped.

"Mr. Adler!" Sutter called. "Mr. Adler, are you all right?"

"I'll be fine if you send down a rope down before my elbows break."

"Carefully," Tim said. "He's balanced rather precariously."

I heard Sutter say, "Hand me that rope, Mr. Wells. Can you see me, Ira?" he called.

The lamplight outlined his face and Tim's, looking out over the rim of the hole. One of my knees suddenly buckled, and I listened to the grit tinkle down, then disappear.

"I—I can see you," I said, my pulse beginning to race.

"I'm lowering the rope now. Just keep your eyes up here, on me. We'll have you out of there in two shakes."

"Two shakes of what?" I cried.

"Very quickly," Sutter explained. The smile in his voice gave me courage. He wouldn't be making jokes, surely, if the situation were truly dire. "Here it comes."

I watched the end of the rope descend into the hole. Slowly—too slowly. My shoulders felt ready to pull out of their sockets. I closed my eyes and forced down a few more deep breaths. After several lifetimes, I felt a tap on my chest.

"There it is," Sutter said. "Can you grab it?"

The lifeline sat on my abdomen—rescue so close, and yet the way my elbows were quivering, I wasn't at all certain that, once I moved them, I could grasp the rope in time before I plunged into the void. My legs shook. My eyes suddenly burned, and my entire body was buzzing with fear. My right heel twitched, sending another shower of pebbles clattering down the wall before falling silent in the darkness.

"I—I don't know. I don't think I can let go of the wall and grab the rope before I fall."

"For God's sake, try!" Tim said.

I took a deep breath. *What would Goddard do?* I thought. And then, strangely, *What would Sutter do?* For I realized that, for all their opposite qualities, both men shared a certain decisiveness under pressure—a distinct certainty in their own abilities, from which I had, at different times, drawn courage. If I didn't act, there would be only one outcome. If I made a move—as Goddard would have, as Sutter would surely have—at least I had a chance. I opened my eyes. The muscles of my back were burning. The tendons of my legs screamed in pain. I wrenched my elbows free and grabbed for the rope.

And fell.

"Ira!" Tim's cry was almost drowned out by my own.

"I'm all right!" The words came before my mind realized it was true. Moving my arms had dislodged me—and an enormous amount of grit and gravel—but by some miracle of instinct, my fingers had grasped the rope before I'd fallen to my death. I was now swinging, my feet kicking out over oblivion, the hemp digging into the flesh of my palms, wrists most certainly pulled out of joint, but I was alive. I wanted to sob with relief, but I was too terrified to move. "I—I have the rope," I managed to say.

But I'd no idea how to proceed from there. Overhead, the three men exchanged murmurs. Then Sutter called down.

"Wind the rope around one arm, and hold on with both hands. Use your legs to climb the wall while we pull you up."

"That sounds…possible," I said.

"Possible!" Sutter said in that warm tone that fortified me from inside. "When this is over, you're going to wonder what all the fuss was about."

All right. I could do this. I wound the rope twice around my left arm, swung my legs toward the wall, braced the soles of my boots against it, and signaled for the men to pull me up. Slowly, carefully, I began to rise.

"Just keep your eyes on me," Sutter said. He was standing at the edge of the hole, holding the rope and directing Tim and Wells, who, I assumed, were pulling from behind. The lamp illuminated his face, giving his features a golden glow. "Just put one foot in front of the other, and don't even think about anything else. It'll be over quicker than you think."

My heart was thundering, my arms and legs were jelly, but I did as he said. Between my own efforts, and the three grown men pulling the rope, I ascended quickly. When I reached the rim, Sutter gripped my right forearm in one hand. Our eyes locked. He lifted me the rest of the way. Tim and Wells were still pulling, of course, but all I could see was Sutter, lifting me, holding me, keeping me from the drop. Something softened in his expression as he brought me onto firm ground. I'd be hard pressed to find words for it—and for a moment, it seemed he, too, was having trouble finding exactly the right thing to say.

"There," he finally managed. His voice was soft, almost breathless. "You're safe now…Ira."

"Thank you," I gasped.

"That was close," Tim said. His voice sounded far away. Sutter was wearing a struck-by-lightning expression, and at that moment, it was all I could see.

Sutter glanced down and noticed we were still gripping each other's forearms tightly. A nervous laugh, and then he pulled me roughly away from the lip of the hole and disentangled his arm. I stumbled toward the tunnel, caught myself against one of the cool walls, and laid my face against it.

"You saved his life, Marshal," Tim said as I gulped the cool, mineral-scented air.

Sutter shook his head. "Wouldn't have happened if Mr. Wells hadn't brought his rope."

"Should have taken it with us in the first place," Wells said. "Mr. Adler, I can't help but feel this was my fault, somehow. I should have—"

"Never mind," I said. I turned back toward Sutter. My heart was racing—only in part from my near brush with eternity. Something had jolted through us—or at least through me—when he'd brought me up. Something had changed in me and would never be the same. I had to know if he'd felt it as well. But his attention was on the rope. He was winding it carefully around one arm, his expression detached and businesslike.

"All's well that ends well, I suppose," I said. The disappointment in my tone could, perhaps, be interpreted as lingering upset from my ordeal. "Now we know why Curtis was so anxious to relieve Mrs. Campbell of her useless land and exhausted mine."

"Yes, indeed," Sutter said. "That we do."

❖

Half an hour later, we stumbled, shaken and shaking, out of the tunnel, into the bright afternoon sun. I was floating between giddiness over my narrow escape and my unexpected frustration with Sutter. Lightning had struck us both. I'd seen it in his face. Of course he wouldn't draw attention to it in front of Tim and Wells, but I at least expected a surreptitious wink or some other tiny acknowledgment so I wouldn't be driving myself out of my mind, wondering if I'd imagined it all. The brash sunlight hit my eyes with murderous force, but its warmth was such a contrast to the cold death at the bottom of the hole, I nearly moaned with pleasure. Before my eyes had a chance to adjust, Irene flung herself into my arms, all warm, glowing skin and lilac perfume.

"Mr. Adler, thank God!"

It was more an exhibit of youthful exuberance than anything else, I was certain. And though her enthusiasm was difficult to resist, her soft lips on my cheek, the ardent embrace of her thin, delicate arms just seemed…wrong.

"I'm all right, Miss Campbell," I said, gently untangling myself. I glanced at Wells, who looked distinctly unamused. "I'm fine," I told everyone. "Thanks to these men's quick action."

Bess had caught Tim in a similar embrace, though Tim looked quite at home in it. Sutter was regarding me with an unreadable expression, while Wells seemed to be attempting to tamp down a spot of jealousy. Much too complex a situation for the likes of me.

Stepping pointedly away from Irene, I turned to Lillian. "There's oil in there."

"Oil?" she repeated.

"Quite a bit of it, too, it looks like," Wells added. He pulled his tie tight and smoothed his features back into their professional mask. "I wouldn't presume to put a value on it just yet, but if I were you, I certainly wouldn't take less than five thousand for the land."

"Five thousand!" Lillian cried.

"Of course it'll cost quite a bit to excavate."

"Oh, my!"

This pleasant speculation was cut short as a high-pitched feral cry cut through the air. Sutter's head whipped to the west. I followed his gaze to a low hill some thirty yards away.

A lone figure on horseback appeared atop the rise. Extending the brim of my hat with my hand, I could make out a stocky horse with patches of brown and white. The rider was shirtless. An exquisite feathered headdress wrapped around his forehead like a crown, then plunged down his bare back in twin rows of brown and white feathers—all the way to an American-style saddle. His trousers were tanned hides, and his cheeks were emblazoned with colorful stripes. The man gave another ululating cry and brandished some sort of ax above his head.

"Is that an…" I said.

"Indian!" Irene cried.

"What the…" Sutter seemed more annoyed than concerned. He shouted something in a foreign tongue, but if the man on the horse had heard, he gave no indication. Cursing under his breath, Sutter took off running toward the figure. It seemed a brash and foolhardy thing to do. Exchanging a glance with Tim, I perceived that Tim agreed. I looked from the rider, now staring imperiously down at Sutter, to the cart waiting just a bit too far away to serve as a refuge. Tim must have been making the same calculations, for he said, "Bess, take your mother and Irene just inside the mine until it's safe."

"Tim," I said.

Sutter was quickly closing the gap, slowing as the rider made no move to bolt. The rider's gaze still fixed on Sutter, he calmly raised his ax over his head and threw.

"No!" I cried.

The ax whistled through the air. The rider's aim was wide, though, and the ax sailed past Sutter, several yards to the right, before bouncing to the ground. With a high-pitched scream of rage, the rider gave his horse a vicious kick and tore off down the hill, disappearing in a cloud of dust.

"Marshal!" I cried. He was unhurt—the ax hadn't landed anywhere near him—but my legs propelled me across the crumbling ground as if they'd had a mind of their own. Sutter and I reached the ax at the same time. Acknowledging me with a flick of his eyes, he bent over and picked it up.

"Calvin," I gasped. "Indians! My God!"

Sutter straightened, hefting the ax in one hand. It was a beautiful thing up close, with a polished, though dull-looking head and a handle encased in a tube made from thousands of tiny, multicolored beads. Sutter frowned at the ax, then turned his frown to me. When he spoke, he sounded almost offended.

"That was no Indian," he said.

Chapter Thirty

How can you be so sure?" Bess asked, after Sutter had stalked back across the dusty expanse of earth, with me stumbling along in his wake. He'd reiterated his suspicions with an expression somewhere between outrage and amusement.

"We all saw him," Wells said.

"You saw someone on a horse, wearing a war bonnet and brandishing a tomahawk," Sutter said.

"And that wasn't an Indian?" Tim asked, obviously confused.

"War bonnets come from the Plains, not California. On top of that, they're ceremonial objects, not something one wears to harass unsuspecting landowners. As for the tomahawk—do you see the beadwork on this thing?" Sutter held up the ax so we could examine the intricate patterns of mustard-seed-sized beads that decorated the shaft between the ax-head and the handle. "Definitely from one of the Plains tribes, and definitely not something just anyone should be tossing around—especially someone with such pathetic aim." Shaking his head, he regarded the weapon. "This probably came from someone's collection. Worth quite a bit of money, I would imagine, if that knucklehead didn't knock half the value off it with that miserable throw."

"But he was shirtless and wearing war paint," Irene said.

"War paint." Sutter scoffed. "The sun was behind him, so we couldn't even see the color of his skin properly, not to mention how he'd done up his face. And that saddle looked like something you'd buy in town. I could swear I saw those boots of his in a shop window on Main Street."

"Didn't Mr. Curtis say a young man had found some sort of artifact around the site of your house fire?" I asked Lillian.

"Jed Walker," she said, nodding. "A peace pipe, he said."

"That didn't look like an act of peace," Tim said.

"But," I said, "you did mention the boy was something of an expert on the Indians who live around here."

"That wasn't Jed on that horse," Lillian said. "That was a grown man."

"But maybe he knows something."

Sutter nodded. "This whole thing stinks like an outhouse in summer." He turned to Lillian. "Mrs. Campbell, I agree that someone's trying to scare you off your land, and I'd put money on the house fire being part of it. I'd like to go back to Pyrite with you, talk to that young man."

Lillian nodded. "I'd be much obliged, Marshal."

He turned to me. "And I'd like you to accompany me, if you would, Mr. Adler."

"Me?" Though it had hurt to feel as if he were avoiding me, his sudden attention made me nervous.

"You had some interesting ideas about the Liza DuBois case the other night. Put a few things in perspective for me. You're observant—and quick on your feet. I could use someone like you if the situation turns tricky." He addressed the rest of the group. "And then when I return to Porterville, I'll ask around, see if any museums or private collections are missing a war bonnet and a tomahawk. In the meantime, I suggest you stay away from Samuel Curtis. Something tells me it won't be long before he knows that you know what's under that land."

We arrived back in Pyrite as the sun was hanging low in the sky, imbuing the air with a last blast of furnace-like heat. After briefly recounting the day's adventures to Mr. and Mrs. Adams, and asking directions to Jed Walker's home, Sutter and I set out to interview the young man who had found an Indian pipe in the ruins of Lillian's house. It felt a little unreal, accompanying Sutter like this. I appreciated the trust he placed in my abilities, though given everything that had transpired between us in the past twenty-four hours, I couldn't decide if I wanted to flee his company or stay close to see what might develop.

Walker Ranch was a fifteen-minute walk from the Adams home, at the end of a winding dirt track bordered with short, scraggly trees. The property comprised a series of fields penned in by weathered wood fences. In one of the fields, half a dozen horses wandered about in the sun, nibbling on limp grass. Other fields had dirt tracks—for exercise, I surmised. A new barn stood in the distance. As we came to the end of the road, we happened upon a circular corral, where a middle-aged man, his pale face darkened from days spent beneath the harsh sun, was running a gray colt around at the end of a long lead. A thin, bespectacled boy of around twelve sat on one of the fence posts, looking up from his book every so often, as if to prove that he was paying attention. Nearby, men were hauling, raking, hammering, and shoveling. They glanced over when we approached.

"Mr. Walker?" Sutter called.

The man in the middle of the ring looked up.

"U.S. Marshal." Sutter held up his badge.

"I'm Abram Walker." He brought the colt to a slow stop, untied the lead, and exited the ring to meet us. He looked us both up and down, his eyes fixing on the badge that Sutter had reattached to his lapel. "A Black marshal. There's something you don't see every day." His tone was friendly enough—curiosity rather than hostility. I imagined we must have made a curious pair.

Sutter said, "Makes it easier to get close to a criminal if you don't look like what he's expecting."

"Well, now, that makes sense, I suppose. And what are you," Walker said, glancing at the beaded ax beneath my arm, "some kind of Indian?"

"Mr. Adler is my assistant."

Walker wound the lead into a neat series of loops, hung it on a fencepost, and tucked his hands under his arms. "How can I help you gentlemen?"

"Actually, we came to speak to your son, Jed," Sutter said.

At the sound of his name, the boy looked up from his book, eyes going wide behind his spectacles.

"My boy in some kind of trouble?"

"No, sir. The truth is, we're hoping he might be of some assistance. I'm investigating the fire at Mrs. Campbell's home."

Walker frowned. "Oh yeah. Florence Adams stopped by the other day to talk about that. I thought the sheriff closed the case. Accident, he said, or at least no crime worth pursuing."

"Mrs. Campbell disagrees," Sutter replied. "I was in Porterville on some other business, when the family approached me and asked me to have a second look, see if I could come up with any reason to re-open the investigation. They said Jed had found some sort of a pipe at the site, after the fire. I was hoping he might show it to me."

"Sure, I'll show you, Marshal!" The boy hopped down from his post and bounded over, his book still under his arm. "It was a red stone pipe—a calumet—they use it to smoke tobacco in ceremonies. Only I don't know what it was doing in Pyrite, seeing as we don't have that kind of stone around here."

"Did you show that pipe to Samuel Curtis?" I asked.

"No, sir, he showed me."

"Everyone knows, you got a question about Indians, you ask Jed," Walker said proudly. Then, in a resigned tone, he added, "He'd rather read about artifacts and legends than learn his family's business. Anyway, when Curtis found that thing, he knew Jed'd be interested."

Jed piped up. "Mr. Curtis said someone must have been smoking near the house and set it on fire, only I don't know how that could be. The bowl was clean, and there weren't no residue around the edges or nothing. It's in my desk drawer. You want me to go get it?" His eyes fell on the ax I was carrying and he grinned. "Wow, is that a tomahawk, Mister?"

Walker said, "Why don't you take them inside, son? Ask your ma to make up some lemonade for us all. I'll join you after I put Smokey away and feed and water the others."

"Sure, Pa." Jed flashed us a grin that said this was the most exciting thing that had happened in his entire life. "Come on, Marshal!"

Jed sprinted toward a low house made of tired-looking wood. Up ahead, a spotted dog dozed on the house's sagging porch. A hanging swing creaked back and forth in the dry air. Wind swept across the land, rattling the desiccated leaves on the spindly trees and raising spirals of dust along the path in front of us.

"So Curtis brought the pipe to Jed's attention," I said as we followed the boy up the path. "When he was at the Adamses' house the other day, I overheard him tell Mrs. Campbell that Jed had found it."

Sutter narrowed his eyes. "Do you know which tribes live around here?"

"Mrs. Campbell said there aren't any specific groups—the government forced the tribes onto reservations some time ago, but one or two families are living on the outskirts of Pyrite."

"Sounds like Curtis wants to put the blame for the fire on them. You met this Curtis, you said? What does he look like?"

"He wasn't the man on the horse, if that's what you're asking.

Curtis is older, heavier, paler. But it does seem like quite a coincidence that Curtis seems to have planted a ceremonial pipe in the wreckage of the fire—a pipe made from stone not found in this area—and that a mock Indian turns up when we're visiting the mine."

"Dressed like a chief from the Plains," Sutter said.

A ruddy-faced woman met us at the door. She looked to be in her late thirties, with work-roughened skin, her blond hair pulled up into a practical knot on top of her head. Jed's mother, I assumed. Wiping her hands on her apron, she said, "Afternoon, Marshal. Jed told me you were coming. Come on in out of the heat. Would you like some lemonade?"

"Much obliged, ma'am," Sutter said, tipping his hat.

She showed us to a spare but comfortable front room. A rag rug lay over a newly swept wood floor. Two rough-hewn chairs flanked a sofa with thin cushions and a colorful quilt draped over the back. I took one of the armchairs, while Sutter lowered himself onto the one facing it. I laid the beaded ax on the table that sat at knee level between us. After a few moments, Jed emerged from one of the rooms at the end of the hallway.

"Here it is, Marshal." The pipe he handed to Sutter was carved from a reddish stone. No longer than a man's hand, it was artfully done, with a sculpture of an owl sitting just behind the bowl.

"You're right," Sutter said, turning the pipe over in his fingers. "This pipe has never been used."

"I tried to tell Mr. Curtis that, but he didn't want to listen. It's a pretty little thing. Never seen anything like it. Near as I can tell, it's made from a stone called argillite, only we don't have none of that around here." He sighed. "That sure is a swell tomahawk. Can I take a look?"

"Help yourself," I said.

Jed picked up the ax, reverently stroking the beaded handle. He ran a finger over the blade and frowned. "Ain't too sharp, is it?" He looked at Sutter. "This ain't from around here, no, sir. Around here, they wrap the handles in leather, and you don't get this fancy beadwork."

"That's what I thought," said Sutter. "But that leaves the question of where it did come from. Don't suppose you've heard of any burglaries at museums in the area or private collections."

The young man looked thoughtful. "Actually, I read something like that in the papers some months ago. I saved the article. Let me go get it."

He excused himself and disappeared back down the hallway. A few moments later, he returned with a carefully torn slip of newsprint, which he handed to Sutter. "Right here, in the *Tulare Times*. May fourteenth," he said, while Sutter read. "A bunch of things were stolen from a private collection up in Visalia. Don't say nothing about a calumet, but—"

"But the items were all from the Midwest and included a war bonnet and a beaded tomahawk," Sutter said, handing the article back.

Jed said, "That's the strange thing. The *Times* always follows up on local crimes. Not a lot happens in these parts. Usually they mention if a crime has been solved, but so far, nothing, and I've been watching."

"Visalia?" I said. "That's where the local sheriff is, right?"

"That's right, sir," Jed replied.

"The sheriff who investigated the fire at Mrs. Campbell's house."

"Sheriff Daniels. That was him."

Sutter and I exchanged a glance over the table. The war bonnet the mock-Indian had been wearing and the tomahawk sitting on the Walkers' parlor table had to be the ones stolen in Visalia. The pipe Curtis had given to Jed had likely come from the same collection. But had Sheriff Daniels simply failed to solve the robbery and then botched the fire investigation, or was he in on both?

"Thing is," Jed said, "Mr. Curtis keeps going around telling everyone about the pipe. That some Indian was smoking it when the house caught fire. I keep trying to explain, but nobody's listening. I even wrote to the sheriff in Visalia, but he never wrote back." He suddenly looked worried. "I hope this won't make trouble for Old Tom and his family."

"Old Tom?" Sutter asked.

"He's the leader of a small group of Indians—one or two families—living right outside of Pyrite. Never been any trouble between us, but like I told Mr. Curtis, if folks get to thinking Indians had anything to do with burning down Mrs. Campbell's house, there's no telling what they might do."

At that moment, Mrs. Walker emerged from the kitchen with a pitcher and several glasses. At the same time, the dog on the porch let out a surprised bark. Thunderous knocking on the door followed. With an irritated frown, Mrs. Walker set the tray on the table near my knees.

"I'm coming," she said as the knocking started again. She opened the door to a pale, thin-featured man. Dressed in a work shirt with rolled sleeves and worn trousers, he looked to be about her same age and wore a determined expression. "Albert Draper," she said, narrowing her eyes at the rifle in his hands.

"Jenny."

Several others stood behind Draper—lean, hard, sunburnt men. There was one more rifle in the group, as well as two shovels and a pickax. Beside me, Sutter slowly rose to his feet.

"What in Heaven's name do you mean by—"

"No time to talk, Jenny," Draper said, stepping past her. "Where's Jed?"

"Now, you see here!"

The other men began to file in past her, spreading out along the wall before the door. They weren't threatening us, at least not yet, but tension sizzled in the air.

"It's all right, Ma." Jed stood and faced the men. "What's the trouble, Mr. Draper?"

"We just heard Indians attacked Mrs. Campbell out on her land— this after they burned down her house. There's only one group we know of, and you know where they live. We're going to teach them a lesson, and you're going to take us there."

"But they didn't do anything!" Jed cried.

"It's true," I said. "We were with Mrs. Campbell this morning. There was no attack. Someone showed up waving an ax, but he wasn't an Indian."

Draper turned to me with a sneer. "Who are you?"

"Mr. Adler is my assistant," Sutter said. "Calvin Sutter, U.S. Marshal. I'm investigating both the fire and this morning's incident."

"Marshal?" Draper said, as if he'd never heard the word. He shook his head. "Well, *Marshal*, are you gonna stand by while someone attacks an innocent widow and burns down her home?"

"It wasn't them!" Jed tried to explain again. "The pipe—"

"That's not what Samuel Curtis is saying," Draper said.

"The boy's right," Sutter said, picking up the ax. "This is the tomahawk the man threw—at my head, by the way—out on Mrs. Campbell's land. It didn't come from anywhere around here."

"You can tell by the handle," Jed said.

"Someone robbed a private collection in Visalia," Sutter said. "We're pretty sure these things came from there and that someone—"

"What about the pipe, then? The one that burned down Mrs. Campbell's house?"

Jed cried, "Like I told Mr. Curtis, that pipe didn't burn down the house. It's never even been used! Someone put it there!"

"I'll tell you who put it there," one of the other men said. "Someone who wanted to burn Lillian Campbell's house down!"

"And we're going to show 'em nobody burns down a house in our town!" another cried. The men murmured their agreement.

"I don't like this," Sutter said under his breath.

While Sutter tried to reason with the men, Mrs. Walker, who'd been watching the proceedings with a wary eye, motioned her son over to the kitchen door, not far away from where I was standing. He was nearly as tall as she was, so she didn't have to bend too far to speak into his ear.

"Can you get to the settlement without being seen?" she asked, her words just above a whisper. Jed nodded. "Go on out the kitchen door, warn them to prepare for trouble. If you see your pa, tell him to get his gun and go with you."

Jed nodded again, then silently slipped past her into the kitchen. Meanwhile, Draper and his group were working themselves into a lather. Shooting me an exasperated look, Sutter crossed back toward where I was standing.

"Do you see Samuel Curtis in this group of numbskulls?"

"No," I said. "He's not here."

"But he started this mess. I'd stake my badge on it. Typical." Sutter shook his head, disgusted, and turned back toward the men. "All right, gentlemen, you've had your say. It's time to leave."

"This ain't your house," Draper said.

"It's my house," Mrs. Walker said, coming to stand beside Sutter. She folded her arms across her chest, and in her posture and expression, I could see where Jed had come by his unexpected resolve. "This is my house, and I'm asking you to leave, Albert Draper."

Draper looked taken aback. He glanced from her to Sutter, then nodded. "We'll just wait for the boy outside, then," he said.

"You're going to be waiting a long time," she retorted.

Draper fixed her with a hard look, then, glancing from her to Sutter, he tipped his hat and said, "Ma'am."

The men filed out, grumbling oaths and spitting their derision— and their tobacco—onto the porch.

"This is going nowhere good," Sutter said. He handed the ax to Mrs. Walker. "And it's going there fast. One thing's for sure, there's no way your boy's going out into that."

Mrs. Walker smiled tightly. "No indeed, Marshal. He's halfway to Old Tom's by now."

Sutter gave an appreciative nod. "Quick thinking, ma'am. Quick thinking, indeed." He sighed. "Well, someone's got to go out there and clean up this mess. Ira, you're with me."

"Errr," I said.

Sutter shot me a look that brooked no disagreement. Then he turned back to Mrs. Walker. "Bar the door behind us, ma'am, and stay inside until I tell you it's safe."

"Yes, Marshal."

I followed Sutter out onto the porch, flinching as I heard the front door lock behind us. Several men seemed to have joined the group, and more were jogging up the path. I felt a moment of relief as I recognized a few of the laborers we'd seen earlier. But a dangerous, unpredictable energy was radiating from Draper's group, and I was reminded of that instant of silent tension before Goddard's front room had exploded in a shower of splinters and glass. I wondered whether Mr. Walker's men would arrive in time to stop the violence, which, at that moment, seemed so inevitable.

"Gentlemen," Sutter said, raising his voice above the din. The group fell silent—a silence that simmered and seethed and filled me with dread. "I'm declaring this assembly unlawful. Please, go back to your homes."

"You can't do that!" one of the men cried.

"I can and I have."

Sutter stepped down onto the stairs, angling away from the house. If things turned ugly, I realized, he didn't want the group charging back into Mrs. Walker's home. As noble as that intention was, I thought it was a mistake for him to give up the safety of the porch. My stomach knotted as I watched the group turn with him, the hard-faced men fingering their weapons as if in anticipation. The ranch workers were arriving by then, though with the tension in the air, I now wondered if their presence wouldn't cause more problems than it would solve.

"You're assembling with intent to cause harm," Sutter said. "The law defines that as a riot. If you refuse to disperse immediately, I will arrest you. Do you understand?"

"Move out of the way, Marshal," Draper said. "This don't concern you."

"I'm afraid it does. You're—"

His words were cut off as someone lunged forward, swinging a pickax. Sutter ducked back, and the ax whistled past his face. Something came over me at that moment—anger and fear and a protective urge so primal and fierce it took my breath away. I surged forward with a cry and plowed into the man, knocking us both the ground. All hell broke loose, then, and, as the man and I struggled for control of the pickax, Walker's laborers threw themselves into the fray. For several terrible moments, there was nothing but shouts and cries and the occasional sickly squelch of flesh against flesh. The dog danced around on the porch, barking, but not quite brave enough to leave his roost.

At some point, Sutter managed to break free of the struggle and find his way back to the stairs. "You're all under arrest!" he shouted.

"That's what you think, boy." I heard a click and saw someone toward the back of the crowd raise his rifle.

"No!" I shouted. I threw off my opponent and ran toward the man with the gun. He whipped his head toward me, then fired a shot over my head. I threw myself to the ground, tasting dust, my face just inches from his boot.

"You leave him be," Sutter growled as the man stood over me. I glanced over my shoulder. Sutter's expression was murderous, and though it was completely inappropriate, I have to admit I'd never seen anything so magnificent. "Your beef is with me. Unless you're not man enough to deal with someone still standing on both feet."

I tried to roll up to a sit but soon found myself staring down a long double-barrel.

Not the nose, I prayed silently.

The other men were circling around us. The air was still tense with violence, but the fighting had stopped. A new spark of uncertainty was in the air, as if the gunshot had crossed some sort of line no one had intended to cross.

Sutter exhaled slowly, drawing himself up. He felt it, too. "Don't make it worse for yourselves," he said in a calmer tone. "Just lay down your weapons, and we can work this all out."

"You heard the man." A woman's voice sounded behind us, strong and true and unwavering. Mrs. Walker stood at the door, wielding a short-barreled shotgun like an expert.

"Now, we don't have no quarrel with you, Jenny," Draper said. He was still clutching his gun, but he was pointing the barrel carefully away from her. Perhaps the gunshot had reminded him of the reality of the situation. Or perhaps he was as intimidated by the sight of Jenny Walker as any intelligent person should have been.

"Then get off my property." She leveled the gun at him, then, one by one, at the men who'd come with him. "Benjamin Calhoun. Clay Everett, your wife know you're here making a damn fool of yourself? What do you think you're going to do with those guns, anyway? Ain't none of you ever shot more than a rabbit, and you, Albert Draper, cried like a baby when your shot went bad and you had to finish that poor bunny off with your bare hands."

"I was only ten," Draper mumbled.

"All the same, you ought to be ashamed, all of you."

Slowly I scrambled backward until I hit the stairs, at which point I stood. The ranch hands had surrounded the little group, and the men were slowly lowering their weapons. With a satisfied nod toward Sutter, Mrs. Walker stepped back.

Sutter glanced at her, amazement dancing across his face for just an instant, before he said, "Now lay your weapons on the ground."

One by one, the men set their weapons down, and one by one, Walker's laborers snatched them up.

"You all right, Ira?" Sutter asked, not taking his eyes from the proceedings.

"Fine," I said.

Sutter whistled two of the ranch hands over, instructing one to hold Draper and his associates, while he sent the other to the train station to send a telegraph to the deputy in Porterville. Then he turned to Mrs. Walker, who was still standing in the doorway.

"Thank you kindly, ma'am. I'm sorry I underestimated you."

"Sometimes it takes a lady to defuse a situation," she replied, tucking her shotgun under her arm.

Sutter chuckled. "Yes, ma'am, sometimes it does."

CHAPTER THIRTY-ONE

Despite our entreaties to stay for supper, Sutter went back to Porterville that evening with the deputy, his assistants, and the six unfortunate men, who would be charged with failing to disperse. Any other charges would be up to the deputy, though from his expression when he met us at Walker's ranch, he'd likely think of something good. Sutter didn't like leaving Samuel Curtis running free, but there wasn't much anyone could do about it. He hadn't taken a direct role in the scuffle, and any connection to either the fire or the incident at Lillian's mine came down to suspicion alone. Part of me was sorry to see Sutter leave, but combined with the disappointment was a fair amount of relief. Two brushes with death in one day had left me exhausted—too exhausted to even think about romantic complications that would have tested me sorely on a good day. All I wanted, at that point, was a few moments alone on Florence Adams's front porch with my new pipe.

It was surprisingly cool once the sun went down. For such a small, isolated place, Pyrite had an amazing variety of nighttime sounds. Rodents rustled through the desiccated brush. Wind rattled the dry leaves and scrub. Somewhere in the distance, coyotes called to each other in mournful tones. As the dark cover of night pulled across the sky, the heat receded. The sage-scented air wasn't exactly cool, but it was pleasant. Heaving a sigh, I filled my pipe with the lush Virginia tobacco I'd purchased from the little shop in Porterville, and soon a fragrant cloud surrounded me. The taste was light and sweet—much more so than the Egyptian cigarettes to which I'd become accustomed back in London. One might have called it a dessert tobacco and not been far wrong. I took a deep pull from the pipe and relaxed against the back of the porch swing, letting my thoughts unwind. A moment later, the front door opened, and two small feet stepped tentatively onto the doorstep.

"Mr. Adler?" Irene asked.

My initial irritation dissolved the moment I saw her standing in doorway, lit from behind by the house lights. She'd donned a fresh dress—a light, loose gown of ethereal fabric and slightly more frivolous design than her usual daytime wear. The trail dirt was gone, the grit brushed from her hair. Her black curls were artfully arranged, and a mist of perfume surrounded her. She was a lovely young woman— flawless, in every way. I shifted to face her, and the dragonfly brooch, still in my jacket pocket, nudged against my hip.

"After all we've been through, Miss Campbell, I think you might call me Ira."

A smile lit her face—pure, innocent joy. "Ira. Please call me Irene."

"Would you care to sit?" I moved to one end of the bench.

She took her seat at the opposite end and folded her hands in her lap. She cleared her throat—a soft, feminine sound that discreetly managed to convey expectation. The swing rocked slowly under this new weight, the creaking of the chains, the rustle of her skirts blending in with the shushing grasses and the soft, distant lapping of the Kaweah River.

"What you did today was very heroic, Ira."

I laughed nervously. "Which part? Falling down a mine shaft or throwing myself to the ground when some farmer pointed his rifle in my general direction?"

She giggled. "And so modest, too. The way you rushed to the marshal's rescue when that man threw that ax at him."

Was that how she'd seen it? I certainly hadn't felt heroic. It had felt reckless and clumsy and ill conceived, but I wouldn't correct her.

"And then at Walker Ranch. Oh, when the marshal told us how you charged the man with the pickax! Why, you could have been killed!"

"I'm sure if I'd been thinking clearly, I'd have been hiding under the chair with the dog."

"Oh, Ira!" She laughed again—a sound like little tinkling bells.

"Jed Walker is the real hero. Running to the settlement with his father to warn Old Tom and his family. And Mrs. Walker! Californian women are a different breed, I must say. I can't imagine a London lady facing down a group of armed men with a sharp tongue and a shotgun."

Irene smiled. "We're not all that tough."

"I'm pretty sure you're stronger than you think, Irene."

Her expression suddenly went shy, and she ducked her head,

glancing back at me from beneath her eyelashes. "Do you like your women tough, Ira?"

"Excuse me?" I swallowed. My collar had suddenly gone tight. I tugged at my cravat.

"Well," she said. "It's just…we've been seeing a lot of each other, haven't we? And I do enjoy your company, ever so much. It seems that you enjoy mine as well."

"Of course," I said. Apprehension crept over my shoulders, up my neck, and across my skull. I'd been hoping to avoid this particular conversational turn, but, though Irene tended to be less direct than her sister, it was clear that she was just as adept at arriving at the point.

"Oh, Ira, I'm so glad you think so, too! I do miss you so much when we're apart. And you're going to be going back to London one day soon. When that day comes, I'm afraid I shall die!"

I snorted, creating a brief but welcome break in the tension. Melodrama didn't become the Campbell women, and she knew it.

"Or at least miss you so, so much," she amended with a self-conscious smirk. "Forgive me, Ira. It's just that nearly losing you in the mine, and then in the riot this afternoon, made me realize—"

"It was hardly a riot," I said, tugging again at my cravat. The sun had retreated, but the air suddenly felt very, very hot.

She edged closer to me, her expression now like that of a parent giving a serious but gentle correction. She patted my forearm, letting her hand linger there. "Like Mother, I believe in taking the bull by the horns, which is why I hope you'll forgive me for being so forward, but I was wondering if there was anything you'd been planning to ask me before you left?"

She blinked at me, her dark eyes glittering in the light from the house. My stomach sank. Good God, this was all my fault.

"Actually," I said carefully, "I haven't made any departure plans."

"Then you're going to stay?" she asked, clapping her hands together.

"Not exactly. I…er…just haven't given any of it much thought, really."

She looked crestfallen. "You haven't made *any* sort of plans?"

"Beyond finishing this pipe? No."

I took a long drag on the pipe to illustrate. The words sounded callous, and I immediately regretted them. But I was terrified of giving her any more encouragement than I already had. I should never have gushed about her beauty within five minutes of our first meeting. Or let her parade about on my arm through the streets of Porterville. The clasp on the dragonfly brooch had come undone, and the pin was poking my side. I would return it to the jeweler at the very first opportunity.

"Oh." She set her hands in her lap and looked away. "Because I thought...we've been spending so much time together...and we get along so well...and the things you say to me...and...well...I thought there might be something you were planning to ask me, that's all."

And there it was. And there it had to stay.

"I'm sorry, Irene."

"No?"

"No."

Though mere inches separated her skirts and my leg, a bottomless chasm opened up between us. When she spoke again, facing straight forward, shining eyes looking out into the deepening gloom, her voice sounded very faint and far away.

"It had such a nice ring to it. 'Irene Adler.'"

"Arthur Conan Doyle thought so, too," I said.

"Who?"

"Never mind. Listen, Irene—"

"It's just that we have so much affection for one another. At least I have. Don't you?"

"Yes, yes, of course," I said. "I'm filled with affection for you." I took a deep breath, then leaned forward pointedly, staring at the side of her face until she met my eyes. She was young, but she was Bess's sister. She could handle the truth. She deserved the truth. "Brotherly affection," I said.

Her mortification was palpable. I wanted to take it all back, to apologize, to place the dragonfly in her hand and make her happy once again. But as much as I wanted to spare her this pain, I knew that prolonging the illusion would only make things worse.

"I see," she whispered, looking away again. Her eyes filled, and I felt like an unspeakable shit.

"I'm sorry, Irene. I never meant to lead you on."

"No, no, it was I who misunderstood your intentions." Her voice broke, and my own eyes suddenly burned. "What an idiot I am!"

She pressed her fingers to her eyelids, desperately trying to push the tears back before I saw them. I wished I were anywhere else. Back in the refuse-cluttered alley having my nose broken by a corrupt fireman would have been pleasant by comparison. Good God, Bess was going to flay me alive.

"You're no idiot. I do have the deepest admiration for you," I said honestly. "You're good company. You're bright and witty and fun and interesting—"

"But not beautiful," she said.

"Yes, beautiful, too!"

"Not beautiful enough, though. And too outspoken, probably. As much as my parents told me that doesn't matter, I can see it does. And no doubt you're used to women in fancy dresses who don't tramp all around the countryside in *boots*, making useless sketches and thinking about…well about *anything*!"

"Are you joking, Irene?" I took her hands in mine. She pulled away as if burned. "Listen, if I were looking for a…a sweetheart, you would be just my sort. But I'm not."

Her brow furrowed. She took a few deep breaths, as if considering this. "Why not?" she asked after a moment.

"It's a very long story." And one that I would keep to myself. As forward-thinking as all the Campbell women might have been, I couldn't imagine she'd think far enough forward to embrace that particular truth.

She thought about it for several moments, and then understanding lit her features, along with a bit of relief. "Is there someone else? Someone back in London?" Her voice became sober, and she slid away from me, toward the opposite end of the bench. "Of course. How could there not be? That's it, isn't it?"

"Well, yes…no…not exactly. There was somebody, but h…she's gone now. That's why your sister and brother-in-law invited me to accompany them to California. To take my mind off it."

"Oh, Ira." She slid back toward the middle of the bench again and took my hands in hers. This time her grip was sure and strong. Comforting, rather than seeking comfort. "I'm so sorry. I didn't know."

The pain she no doubt saw in my expression was real, but it wasn't for Goddard. Perhaps a bit of it was for what might have been with him, under other circumstances. There was a bit for Lawrence, who already seemed to be fading into the past. A bit more for my continuing embarrassment over what had happened with Sutter.

But some of it was for Irene, who really would have been exactly what I'd want in a woman. And part was for myself, for the first time wishing my tastes ran to women—if only for the fact that it wouldn't be so dreadfully difficult to find someone and make it work.

"What was her name?" Irene asked.

"Who?"

"Your sweetheart, in London. The one who's...gone."

"Oh. Cain...ella."

"Cainella? That's an odd name. I suppose it's quite common in Britain. I'm ever so sorry for your loss, Ira. And I feel terrible for embarrassing you like this."

I wrapped both of my hands around hers and gave them a brotherly squeeze. "Think nothing of it, please. I'm just grateful to have made such a charming friend."

She gave a pained smile. "Yes." She sighed and withdrew her hands. "A friend."

"And I do hope you'll invite me to your wedding, when the time comes."

She frowned. "Of course, I will. But to be frank, it's pretty slim pickings around here. I can't imagine marrying, well, *anyone* I know in Pyrite. And besides, if I had to stay on this miserable little patch of dirt for the rest of my life...Ugh, it's hopeless!"

I laughed. "It most certainly is not."

Her embarrassment seemed to evaporate like the aftermath of a sudden desert shower, and she turned to me with the same shrewd eye that all of the Campbell women seemed to have.

"Don't tell me you haven't noticed the way Gordon Wells keeps buzzing around you," I said. I did my best impression of the geologist's nasal American accent. *"You have a fine mind, if you don't mind my saying so, Miss Campbell. I'd love to see your sketches."*

Irene giggled. "Mr. Wells is very sweet," she admitted. "And handsome. And I do enjoy his company."

"He respects you. You'd never be just an ornament to him. Plus, he lives in the bustling metropolis of Porterville," I added.

She cocked her head thoughtfully. "That's true."

"And even if it doesn't ultimately work out between you, I'm pretty sure he'd give you a job—a job that would allow you to lead a very interesting and fulfilling life in the big city."

"Also true."

This thought brought the light back to her eyes. I could see her weighing this new set of options. They seemed to please her, and I was glad. Perhaps none of the Campbell women were destined for an ordinary life. And perhaps Irene would one day come to embrace this fact.

"No one can tell what the future might bring, Irene, but you have a long, happy life ahead of you. Make the most of it. And don't rely on other people to define it for you."

As I had for too, too long.

Irene sighed. She wasn't exactly happy, but at least she no longer appeared to be on the verge of tears. She had a lot to think about, now—not the least of which was the uncomfortable new tension between us that only time would dissipate.

"Thanks, Ira. Listen." She gave my shoulder a pat and stood up. "Could we say good night now and pretend this conversation never happened?"

"I'd like nothing better."

"Good. Then, if you'll excuse me, I'm going inside to put a dab of liniment on my pride before heading to bed. Good night."

❖

After a respectful amount of time had passed, I went inside, discreetly gathered some fresh clothes and a few toiletries into one of my suitcases, and then left on the last train to Porterville. I'd had enough of romantic misunderstandings and their awkward aftermaths. I needed to be away from crying women and their vengeful sisters, and I needed a drink. I also needed to find Gordon Wells. Anyone with eyes could see that he was mad about Irene, but he needed a bit of a push to move forward. I might have broken Irene's heart that night, but something better was just around the corner for her. It might not ultimately involve Gordon Wells, but it very well might. If I could help it along, I had to try.

After leaving my suitcase in my room at the Arlington, I headed down Main Street to John Zalud's saloon. Wells might have chosen half a dozen places to while away the evening, but from what I'd seen, Zalud's was the most popular saloon in town—and if I didn't find Wells there, my friend Dan, the bartender, might have a better idea where the man could be found.

The saloon was full to bursting when I arrived. Everyone who had come into town for tomorrow night's festival seemed to have convened there, and I had to elbow my way to a place at the bar and shout my order three times before one of the beleaguered bartenders nodded his acknowledgment. A single Kentucky bourbon with water. Lots of water. I wasn't planning to repeat earlier mistakes. Three men were tending bar that night, each of them run off his feet. I watched mine pour two fingers of bourbon into a tumbler and fill a large glass with water. At the same time, I caught sight of Dan. He flashed me an exhausted smile, then took the glasses from the other man and brought them over.

"Glad to see you, Mr. Adler." He set the glasses on the bar before me. "Heard there was some trouble down in Pyrite today." He mopped his brow with a muscular forearm. His sleeves were rolled above his elbows, and rings of sweat darkened the armholes of his waistcoat.

"Wouldn't know anything about it," I lied. I didn't want to think about it, and he was too busy to press. "Have you seen Gordon Wells this evening?"

"The geologist? Isn't that him?" He gestured toward a point in the crowd. After a moment I spied Wells pushing his way through a clot of patrons, an empty beer mug in one hand, his other hand trying to keep his brown bowler in place.

"Thanks." I pushed a few coins across the table, turned around, and waved. "Mr. Wells!"

I had to shout a few times before he heard me, but eventually he looked up, his expression like that of a startled deer—as if he'd never expected someone might be interested in his company. Then he grinned and hurried over.

"Mr. Adler. Glad to see you survived this afternoon," he said, making a spot for himself at the long, polished counter. He set down his mug and gestured for another. He'd given himself a good scrub in the hours since I'd seen him. A dash of cologne and a fresh suit. "I still feel bad about that."

"No harm done. Besides, it was only a prelude to what happened once we returned to Pyrite."

He listened breathlessly while I recounted—in short, shouted sentences—the riot and the arrests. He seemed appropriately impressed by my theories regarding the fire and the stolen artifacts—or perhaps the smiling and nodding were covering the fact that we could hardly hear each other over the music and conversation that made the air throb around us.

"Well," he said at last. "No one can say you lead a boring life, Mr. Adler."

"There are times I'd give my eyeteeth for a few days of boring," I replied.

It wasn't the ideal setting for broaching the sensitive subject of Miss Irene Campbell. I doubted anyone was listening, and if they were, I couldn't imagine that they'd care. All the same, it seemed disrespectful, somehow, to discuss intimate matters of the heart in raised voices. I threw back my bourbon and chased it down with the water.

"Do you mind if we step outside for a moment?"

Wells frowned and cupped a hand around his ear.

"Outside!" I bellowed. "We need to talk!"

"Oh, sure. Let's go."

The night was far from cool, but compared to the sweaty air inside the saloon, it almost felt chill. I drew a few long, delicious breaths as we walked down the boardwalk. Eventually we found a place that was both sparsely occupied and far enough away from the front door of Zalud's that we could hear one another. I leaned against the waist-high railing that separated the boardwalk from the street.

"I'm so glad I ran into you, Mr. Adler," Wells said before I had a chance to even think about how to put my thoughts into words. "I have something to ask you." He was still carrying his mug, and before he spoke again, he took a long slug. "It's about Miss Campbell. You see, I've never met anyone like her."

I choked on a laugh. Was it really going to be this easy? Or had fate not yet finished making an ass of me that day?

"I don't meet a lot of ladies in my profession—or outside of it, for that matter," Wells said. "And I'm not the most charming man in the world…"

I gestured at the line of beer foam now sitting atop his upper lip. With an abashed smile, he dabbed it away. "You see what I mean."

"Yes, but I think Miss Campbell would disagree," I said. "She seems to find you quite charming."

He looked at me, his expression like that of a terrified rabbit. A smile quivered at the edges of his mouth. "Really? Has she…has she said something?"

"A few things. Small things. But those things have led me to believe that she does hold you at some level of esteem." Good God, he seemed to be sincere.

He opened and closed his mouth, as if finding words, then discarding them just as quickly. "Really?" he finally managed to say.

"I can't speak for Miss Campbell," I warned him.

"Oh, no, of course not. I wouldn't ask you to. It's just that the two of you seem so close. Frankly, I was certain she was already spoken for. Is that the case? Because if it is, I'll back right off…"

I clapped his tweed-covered shoulder, biting back another laugh.

The last thing anyone needed was for him to think I was taking the piss out of *him*.

"There's nothing between Miss Campbell and myself," I said. "Nothing except a most chaste and brotherly affection."

The words seemed to work a miraculous transformation on the man. His nervousness receded. He seemed to grow taller, somehow, though the brim of his hat was still level with my earlobe. His cautiously friendly face was lit with excitement. "So you wouldn't mind if I paid her a call one day?" he asked.

"One day?" I really did laugh then. "I should think sooner rather than later. Young ladies of her caliber don't grow on trees, you know."

"Oh, I know that." His face grew serious. "I have only the utmost respect for Miss Campbell. She is quite pretty, but I've always believed these things should be more than that. Pretty only goes so far. After that, a man needs someone he can talk to. Someone he can rely on."

"Someone who's ready to tramp across rough country and carry her own equipment?"

"Why yes, that's it exactly." He frowned. "Do you find something funny, Mr. Adler?"

I'd started to chuckle out of sheer relief, truth be told, that I hadn't completely fouled up one, small thing during this entire disastrous voyage. For once, my instincts seemed to be true. For once, my trying to do something right hadn't made the situation one hundred percent worse.

"I'm just happy for you," I said. "Happy for Irene. Happy to think that two kindred souls might actually find each other in this chaotic mess of a world."

Smiling, I reached into my coat pocket and took out the little package from the jeweler. The paper had come unwound, and I gingerly tucked the brooch's pointy bit back inside before laying the package between us on the wooden railing.

"I've known Miss Campbell for less than a week," I said. "But I've known her sister for almost eight years. If they're anything alike, I'd say she's pretty much exactly what you're looking for. Here. I bought this the other day when I saw her admiring it in a shop window." I nodded toward the package. "Go ahead, open it."

He carefully unwrapped the paper. The dragonfly slipped out into his palm, its silver and gemstones twinkling in the moonlight. Wells gasped.

"I've seen this. It's beautiful work. It must have cost a mint. Oh,

Mr. Adler, I couldn't possibly." He tried to hand it back to me, but I pushed it toward him.

"I bought it because Miss Campbell loved it so. As you can imagine, it would be difficult not to want to give her her heart's desire. But after considering it, I realized the gift would send the wrong message, coming from me. Coming from you, later, once your feelings have had time to develop and grow, I think it'd be exactly the right message."

He was doing that stammering thing again, as if his thoughts were coming too quickly for his mouth to keep up. With nervous hands, he finally pulled out his billfold.

"How much was it?" he asked.

"For you, nothing. Just…be good to her. She's special."

His stared for a moment, as if disbelieving. Then he let out a joyous laugh. "Oh, thank you, Mr. Adler!" He wound the brooch once more in its paper, then tucked the package into the breast pocket of his coat. "Thank you very much indeed! And I will treat her well. I surely will."

Chapter Thirty-two

It was nearly midnight by the time I made it back to the Arlington. The night clerk was dozing in a chair behind the counter, the gas lamp turned low. I hated to wake him, but I wanted my bed, and the sooner I retrieved my key, the sooner we could both have our rest.

"Psst," I hissed.

The young man jerked awake, glanced around for a moment, and then his gaze settled on me and he relaxed.

"My key, if you please. I promise I won't be going out again tonight."

"That's good," he said around a yawn. He rose to his feet, stretched, and began to fumble through the pigeonholes along the wall behind him. "Because you have a visitor."

My heart stopped. "Where?"

The clerk gestured with his head toward the doorway of the hotel's parlor. "Came in around suppertime. Told him you'd been gone all day, didn't know when you'd be back, but he insisted he'd wait. Don't know if he's still there, but I didn't hear him leave." He finally found the right key, extracted it, and handed it to me over the counter.

Sutter had been there since suppertime? Part of me was happy the marshal wanted to see me. The entire way back from Pyrite, images from the afternoon kept flipping through my mind's eye: the undeniable charge that shot through both of us when he took my wrist and pulled me over the rim of the mine shaft to safety; his quick and accurate analysis of the mock-Indian incident; the selflessness and boldness with which he confronted Albert Draper's angry bunch. His fearlessness, intelligence, and burning pursuit of righteousness made me tremble.

They also made it easy to lose sight of the fact that he'd stated outright that he had no interest in pursuing anything with me beyond the boundaries of professional courtesy.

I sighed. "Thank you."

"Thank me by stepping lightly when you go upstairs. My replacement comes in at six."

❖

The hotel parlor was elegantly but sparsely furnished with a few quality pieces made from sumptuous fabrics and dark, heavy wood. A small bookshelf was built into one wall, to the left of a cold fireplace. The week's newspapers sat neatly in a rack beside a velvet armchair that wouldn't have been out of place in Cain Goddard's study. The understated aroma of expensive tobacco spiced the air. It was a very masculine space, dimly lit by a single lamp on a table between another armchair and a sofa.

Perhaps because my mind's eye could so easily picture Goddard there, the actual sight of him failed to startle me. His dark suit blended into the shadowy contours of the velvet armchair. The muted light mellowed the pallor of his skin. His black lacquered walking stick was invisible against the black linen of his trouser leg.

"You weren't expecting me?" Goddard asked, smirking slightly when his movement caused me to jump. He folded the magazine he'd been perusing and replaced it on the table beside him.

"Should I have been?"

"I suppose not. Sit with me, please. I've been waiting a long time."

It would have been rude to take one of the chairs on the other side of the room, as much as I'd have preferred it. So much was unresolved between us—so much that I'd thought over and done with. I was angry at him for having deceived me, and to some degree I blamed him for having stirred up the past. It was ridiculous, of course. Had either of us foreseen our paths crossing, we'd have both endeavored, I'm certain, to avoid it. At the same time, I couldn't deny being happy he hadn't perished in that explosion. Relieved. But it did reopen a lot of questions I'd thought closed for good.

"Where's Marcus?"

"Nearby. He knows I'm here." He sighed. "And that I'll need his assistance returning to our lodgings. His name is Benjamin, now. You know that."

"And you're Jeremiah Wright," I said. I didn't roll my eyes, but the sentiment was in my tone.

He shrugged. "Names are for other people's convenience. I know who I am."

"Who's that? A hero of the second Afghan war? An oil magnate? Or a crime lord, looking for new territory?"

"A philanthropist, if all goes as planned. Cigarette?"

He took one from his gold cigarette case, then held the case out to me. I took one as well, then leaned forward while he lit it. He leaned back and took a long pull from his own, closing his eyes as he released the smoke toward the ceiling. It occurred to me that expensive Egyptian tobacco was likely one of the few old pleasures he had left—at least until he fully recovered from his injuries and established himself in California. He seemed to be deriving inordinate satisfaction from it.

"So, a philanthropist," I prompted him.

As long as I'd known Goddard, he'd maintained a coldly logical outlook. To him, everything—and everyone—was a balance sheet of risks, benefits, costs, and gains. He'd contributed generously to causes that had profited him in some way but considered pure philanthropy a waste of time. In our last significant conversation before the explosion, though, he admitted he'd been experimenting with the latter—a shameless and transparent attempt to win back my favor. He'd sent the pregnant Bess Lazarus a flood of anonymous flowers and reported no resultant injury to himself. But neither had he reported any sort of benefit.

"Forgive me if I can't quite see it," I said.

Instead of irritation, he regarded me with a thoughtful expression. "No, perhaps not. But tell me, have you heard of Stanford University?"

"No. Is it American?"

He nodded. "It's located some distance north of here. A man named Leland Stanford founded it a mere ten years ago, with oil money."

Oil money—like the wealth upon which Goddard was ostensibly building his American empire. Dear God, was he actually suggesting—? As a young man, Cain Goddard had scrabbled his way up from murky origins to a coveted academic position, then lost everything following a scandal of a very personal nature. Despite his success in the criminal world, he'd always wanted to return. But could a person just *do* that? Was it possible, having been ejected from the brotherhood of scholars, to simply...

"You're not thinking of starting a university, surely," I said.

"Stanford has the best faculty money can buy. As well as a very progressive vision. 'Stanford is hallowed by no traditions; it is hampered by none. Its finger posts all point forward.' So said the president at the opening-day speech. Astounding, isn't it? A businessman and his wife founding a university. And it's taken quite seriously."

Well, it was good to see that whatever his physical condition, the old Goddard nerve was still intact.

"So, Cain Goddard University?" I said.

"Jeremiah Wright College. Or perhaps something more neutral."

"Can you do that?"

"There's no law against it—nor any tradition, as far as I'm aware. My resources are sufficient. And it would certainly be one in the eye for those bastards at Cambridge."

A slight smile curled at the edges of his lips. I found myself mirroring it.

"That would be impressive if it worked."

"Of course it will work. You don't believe me now, but just wait."

I found myself wondering why he was telling me this—why he'd come. We were chatting like old pals, but a tension lurked beneath the conversation. We weren't exactly friends, Goddard and I, and neither of us was much for chat. His tone and expression contained a certain defiance. Was he trying to prove something to me? He'd never needed my approval—or anyone's—before. I couldn't imagine he needed it now.

"I believe your intentions," I said. "I believe in your resources. It's just that the idea is contrary to everything I'd ever thought a university to be, that's all."

His smile broadened. And though he still cut a weak, thin, pale figure—though he would likely always bear the marks of his injury, the vitality of purpose shone in his eyes.

"Exactly. Which is why it can't help but succeed."

I hoped so. I really did. So much had passed between Goddard and me, both good and bad. I'd loved him. I'd wished him dead. When it had appeared he'd died, I'd mourned. He'd put our life behind him, as had I. Yet I couldn't find it within me to wish him ill.

"Have you chosen a location?" I asked.

"Fresno, perhaps. Or Bakersfield. That should keep me out of trouble for a while, don't you think?"

I didn't know what to think.

Did Cain Goddard, the dread Duke of Dorset Street, really intend to abandon his criminal activities? After all this time, would he even be capable of doing so? Four years ago, when we'd parted for the second time, he'd told me he was trying to understand the altruistic impulse. He'd intimated that he was changing, transforming himself. Since then I'd wondered from time to time what degree of transformation would be necessary for us to come together again—to begin anew, free of the old moral conflicts and dynamics of power. Was this what he was trying to tell me—that he was ready to put our past behind us and try once more? Or was it more basic than that? Was it a simple need to declare his transformation—regardless of what I might think about it?

"Do you want to stay out of trouble?" I asked.

He thought about it for a moment, the flickering shadows of the kerosene lamp deepening the lines of his face. "Trouble isn't necessary anymore," he said eventually. "Quite a bit of the business that made me rich in London is perfectly legal here—which means that it isn't as profitable. Oil is profitable."

"But also legal," I said.

He shrugged. "Everything has disadvantages." He laid a hand over mine. I felt his fingers, warm and dry on the back of my hand, the wooden arm of the chair smooth and cool against my palm. "What do you think, Ira? Could you love an oil baron?"

So that was the real reason for his visit. Could I love him, he wanted to know, in this new land, unbound by traditions—either society's or our own? Could the man I had become embrace the one he was becoming? I'd imagined this very moment so many times. How I would throw myself into his arms and never let go. How I would utter something sharp and unforgivable. How I would turn and walk away without a word. If I said yes, it would mean a new beginning. But it would also put an end to the myriad possibilities that had opened to me since coming to this country. The room seemed to shrink, and everything came into sharp focus—the heat of his fingers on top of mine, the too-bright flicker of the lamp's flame, the ticking of the mantel clock, which seemed to ring through the wooden walls of the parlor.

Yes, I thought with the fevered desire of a convert. The wood became moist beneath my palm. My pulse pounded, and I was certain he could feel it through the skin of my hand. *Yes, Cain, I could love you. Once more and always.*

At the same time, the thought made something deep inside me twist and cry out. Would it be a new beginning or a cage door slamming shut? A return to the domination and control that had walked hand in hand with his generosity—that had been the framework of all of our interactions from the very beginning? *No*—some elemental part of me cried—*No, and never again!*

How could a person want two opposite things, equally, and with every particle of his being?

My cigarette had burned down to nearly nothing. I gasped as the smoldering end bit my finger and dropped the burning stub into the ashtray.

Goddard searched my face, the depths of his own dark eyes unreadable. I had to admire the risk he was taking. He'd already lost so much. And what of Marcus? If I said yes, would Goddard fulfill Marcus's most desperate fears by putting him unceremoniously back on a train to New York? Somehow the idea seemed unspeakably sad.

"Benjamin..." Goddard said, bringing me back from my thoughts. For a moment I thought he'd read my mind. But then I realized he'd interpreted my silence as a response. Or perhaps he was unwilling to accept a "yes," if I had to think about it. I opened my mouth to explain but saw in his eyes that he'd made his decision. When he spoke again, I could hear him marshaling his conviction behind it. "Benjamin has been very good to me. Very loyal."

I nodded, even though I felt as if I'd been slapped. "As long as I've known him, he's only ever wanted to be useful," I said.

I couldn't believe I was arguing for someone who'd very recently wanted to punch out my lights, but it seemed fitting somehow. If I wished Goddard well, I would honor his choice, even if part of me wanted exactly the opposite.

"He's much more than that." Goddard looked away, but his fingers curled around mine. "I care for him, and I flatter myself to think that he cares for me."

"He does. I've seen it." Marcus understandably guarded his hard-earned position, but the tenderness and devotion I'd witnessed between him and Goddard went well beyond professional duty.

"And it's not every young sharp who would tie himself down to a crippled old man."

"You're not—"

"Not forever." He turned his gaze back toward me. "But for a while yet. I daresay I even love him." He smiled sadly. "And he'll make an excellent secretary one day." He set his cigarette end in the ashtray and crushed it out, as if for emphasis.

The words felt like a punch to the gut. I'd been Goddard's secretary. I never would be again. And it was right. I knew it was right, even if I wished it could be otherwise. Goddard's hand tightened around mine, and I smiled though it felt like I was splitting apart inside. We sat there for quite some time, the ticking of the clock reverberating through the wood-paneled room. Muted footsteps passed by on the street outside, followed by a screech of drunken laughter that faded away into the night as quickly as it had come. Goddard patted my hand, then pulled away.

"If I come across any like-minded oil barons in the near future, shall I send them your way?" he asked.

I laughed, discreetly pressing my fingers against the corners of my eyes. "Don't you dare."

He laughed as well. And for the first time, I felt like the muddy, bloody, trampled ground between us was finally washed clean. It was right. It was as it should be, and one day my heart would recognize what my mind had already known for some time. He patted my hand again, then removed his quickly. The time for that had passed.

"And you, dear boy," he said gently. "What's in your future?"

Sighing, I shook my head. "I wish I knew, Cain. I'd be satisfied to settle the matter of Bess's mother's land claim and go home."

Home. What did that even mean anymore? To London? It seemed absurd. London was so far away, in time as well as space, and I'd done my damnedest to burn every last bridge before I'd stepped onto that boat. But what was there for me here? Bison and tumbleweeds and romantic mishaps? At this point, it was a matter of which *home* contained fewer embarrassments and failures. I might as well flip a coin.

"Where is Mrs. Campbell's land?" Goddard asked.

"Out in Kern County—adjacent to your parcel, as a matter of fact. God, is that a mess."

"The good doctor hasn't convinced the buyer to back off?"

"No." I leaned back into my chair and crossed my legs. It was a relief to be speaking of someone else's conflict for once. "In fact, our being here only seems to have made things worse." Briefly, I told him about the house fire and the incident with the mock-Indian at the mine. I left out my mortifying tumble down the mine shaft and the undeniable current that had passed between Sutter and me when he'd pulled me out. I'd invited enough embarrassment that evening already.

"Astounding," he said when I finished. Then he frowned. "Why wouldn't she sell, again?"

"Curtis's offer is insulting, especially considering the oil seep we discovered there the other day. Also, I have a feeling that, once crossed, Lillian Campbell holds a grudge like a champion. Reminds me a bit of you, in that respect."

He chuckled. "Is that so?" A thoughtful look crossed his face. Then he said, "Ira, will you allow me to take care of this?"

"How?" I asked suspiciously.

A smile twitched at the edges of his lips. "Nothing illegal, though in this country that gives me quite a bit of latitude. Why don't we say, nothing that would offend your delicate moral sensibilities. Please." He reached out his hand, then, as if in deference to the new boundaries he'd set, settled for brushing a bit of imaginary lint from my shoulder. "Let me do this one last thing for you—without expectation or agenda."

The Duke of Dorset Street acting without agenda—was it possible? If so, I'd have paid to see it.

"All right," I said warily. "And in return, I have a bit of information that might interest you."

"Oh?"

"I'm pretty sure it was Rupert Sudworth who blew up your house."

Several seconds ticked by on the clock while he considered my statement. I'm quite sure that whatever he'd expected me to say, the idea that I'd meddled in his attempted murder hadn't occurred to him. He took out his cigarette case, glanced at the few that remained, then put the case back in his pocket.

"I wondered about that. What makes you think it was him?"

"After it happened, the papers were all printing this rubbish about the water heater. I knew that couldn't be right, because the only water heater in your house was in the upstairs bathroom, and it was quite intact." I paused. "I enlisted the help of Andrew St. Andrews to confirm my suspicions."

Goddard sucked in his breath. I tensed, but he simply let it back out again and shook his head.

"I figured that, being dead and all, you wouldn't mind," I said. "And St. Andrews has built up a very successful and well-respected consulting detective business."

"I had heard that."

"It became evident very quickly that someone had planted the water-heater story with the fire brigade. Sudworth even referenced it when I went to collect the money you'd left me. He was so smug. Couldn't help himself, I suppose. You've already admitted that the fireman broke my nose indirectly on your orders, but Sudworth didn't want me poking around either."

I told him about the incident with Claire at Victoria Station and about St. Andrews's subsequent use of the police to harass Sudworth—an idea that seemed to please Goddard quite a bit. When I was finished, he said, "That scheming prick."

"Any idea why he might have done it?" I asked.

"No. None at all."

I didn't quite believe him, but I figured he had his own reasons for keeping the information to himself. Besides, it really couldn't matter that much now.

"And then there's the matter of Liza Du Bois," I said.

"Who?"

"She was the one who broke into your cabin on the *Teutonic* and stole your key. Small-time thief out of Liverpool. She's been robbing ships between there and New York for some time, and now it appears she's building a network in the United States. You've never heard of her?"

He shook his head. "Never."

"Think she might be involved with Sudworth?"

"How would I know? I can't imagine it, though. Sudworth prefers to do his thieving on the right side of the law. Anything's possible, though, I suppose."

"Well, according to the papers, she's on her way here, if you want to meet her. She's a dainty little thing, blond, with a scar across her neck like someone tried to cut her throat. Difficult to miss. Why would she want that key?"

"It's a safe-deposit-box key," he said.

"Yes, I know."

"You do?"

"She planted the key on me, along with a few bank notes from Midlands Bank, bearing Sudworth's signature. That's why the *Teutonic*'s security officer was so certain I was the thief. He found the notes and assumed my guilt. Anyway, she thought she'd take the key back from me in New York. When that failed, she sent some of her functionaries after me to do the job. A U.S. Marshal recovered the key and brought it back to the bank."

"Yes, but how do *you* know what the key is for?"

"The marshal and I became…friends of a sort."

Goddard's mouth twitched. "Oh, really?"

"No." The shame and horror of the other night returned in a rush, and the tobacco-infused air suddenly felt too thick to breathe. "Nothing like that. He helped me, I helped him, and that's the end of it. Strictly professional. But he did tell me it was a safe-deposit-box key."

"I see."

"There's nothing between us," I said.

He smiled knowingly.

"Really," I said.

"Well, it's none of my affair anyway," he said airily. "The key does indeed go to a safe-deposit box at the Bank of California. I've been keeping important documents there. Also a significant amount of cash."

"How did Miss DuBois know to take the key?" I asked.

He exhaled a long, thoughtful breath. His fingers hovered over the pocket containing his cigarettes. A muscle near the corner of his left eye began to twitch. Finally, he said, "I don't know. But your marshal returned the key. It's safe now, and it doesn't matter."

"He's not my marshal."

He cocked an eyebrow. "Time will tell."

Infuriating man. I changed the subject. "So that's that, then? You're going to be an oil baron and a philanthropist. No more brothels, no more rackets, no more Duke of Dorset Street?"

He smiled, as if at a cherished memory, then shrugged. "London spat me out. I'm finished there. I have enough money, and the promise of so much more that if I chose, I could do absolutely nothing, ever again, for the rest of my life."

I shook my head. "You'd hate that."

"I would. So why not do something I've always dreamed of? It was only sheer obstinacy that kept me from trying it sooner. The first thing, though, will be to build a house for Benjamin and me. Somewhere close enough to a city to take advantage of the amenities, but far enough away that no one will ask questions about two unrelated men living together under the same roof." He smiled. "I think that should keep us busy enough for a while."

I swallowed the sudden lump that had formed in my throat—a bit because I knew, even then, that this would be the last intimate chat I would have with my old friend. Yes, having come to this resolution, I believed I could consider him my friend—but the larger part of my sadness was because I didn't belong anywhere now. I'd no idea where

I'd go, what I'd do with myself, or who, if anyone, would be waiting for me in the future.

But that was no longer Cain Goddard's concern.

"Indeed," I said, rising to my feet. I held out my hand in what I hoped was a sporting manner. "I wish you both every happiness."

Goddard took my hand and leveraged himself up painfully between it and his cane. Then, before I could draw back, he cupped my face in his hands and kissed me. It was a kiss full of tenderness, full of apology, full of memories of every good thing that had passed between us, and everything we had wanted to say, but hadn't. I kissed him back with all my heart and soul.

I kissed him good-bye.

"Good-bye, Ira," he whispered, as I turned, hurrying for the door before I embarrassed myself.

As I reached into my jacket pocket for my key, my arm brushed against a hard lump beneath my waistcoat. Goddard's watch—his scorched and dented pocket watch, still faithfully, steadily ticking, despite its disfigured case.

I turned, holding it out toward him. "I found this—or rather Mr. Watkins found it—at the…the site. It still works. Would you like…"

He smiled. "Keep it, Ira. Keep it well."

The trudge up the short, single flight of stairs seemed to last forever. When I finally reached my room, I didn't even bother with the lamp. I undressed in the dim light the moon cast through the curtains, laid my clothes across the chair, and flopped down onto the coverlet. A better room in a better hotel might have provided a bed with mattress springs, but at that point, I didn't care. All I wanted was oblivion.

A muffled thump on the carpet woke me a short time later—followed by a whispered curse and the cloying sweetness of rose-scented lamp oil. I jerked upright in my bed, only to feel the cold steel muzzle of a pistol against my temple.

"Don't move, Doctor."

"Miss Wood?"

She was the only one who still thought I was Lazarus. And the only woman whom I could imagine bringing a gun into my bedroom—except, perhaps, for Bess Lazarus after learning I'd broken her little sister's heart. Without shifting my head, I ventured a look out of the corner of my eye. It was her, Miss Wood, in the flesh—or, rather, in a gray plaid dress wrinkled from a week of sleeping upright in the cheap section of a train.

"Perhaps I should say, Miss DuBois," I added.

"Where is it? Where's the key?"

"I don't have it."

"Bollocks, you don't. I put it in your bag myself."

I should have been more frightened. Miss Wood's hand was trembling slightly, and her voice was tense as if she were at the end of her tether. If Rupert Sudworth had sent her to harass Goddard beyond the grave and across the ocean, and she'd failed him, she ought to be nervous. If she knew she was trying to rob the Duke of sodding Dorset Street, and she had any brains at all, she'd be more nervous still. And yet after everything that had happened over the last forty-eight hours, I was more irritated than anything else and would have considered just giving her the key if it would have meant she'd leave me alone. Slowly but deliberately, I eased myself up onto my elbows. I was still naked—a fact that she noticed at approximately the same time I did.

"Don't even think about it," she said through clenched teeth.

A thousand rejoinders danced on my lips, but her hands were shaking, now, and she was pressing the gun harder into the side of my head. For once, good sense prevailed.

"The marshal recovered the key from that genius you hired, Wilkes. He returned it to the bank the other day. Listen, shall I pick up the lamp before all the oil leaks out? I don't want to have to pay for this carpet."

"I don't care what you don't want to pay for."

"At least let me put some clothes on."

She thought about it for a moment, then eased the barrel away and stepped back.

"I'll get your clothes." Keeping the gun trained on me, she reached for the pile of clothing on the chair behind her. When she ventured a backward glance, I rolled off the mattress, snatched up the lamp by its neck, and lunged forward, swinging. The glass globe flew off the lamp and crashed to the floor as the base smacked into her gun-hand. The pistol discharged with an explosion of light and sulfurous smoke. Somewhere above us, someone screamed.

"Rape!" Miss Wood shrieked as I tossed the lamp aside and launched myself at her. We both went down, rolling through broken glass and sickly sweet lamp oil. "Rape! Murder! Fire!"

Lots of people were rousing themselves now. Running footsteps thundered in the staircase, raised voices all around us. I had her by the wrists, but her two-handed death-grip on the pistol seemed impossible to break. Over and over we rolled, until we crashed into the chair. My clothing tumbled down over us both. I clambered on top of her, pinning her wrists to the ground, the gun pointed over her head, toward the door.

"Let me go," she snarled.

"I never asked you to break into my room!"

Someone pounded on the door. "What's going on in there?"

"Rape!" she shouted.

"Stop that!" I cried. "No rape! Just—just—send the police!"

The knocking continued. "Mr. Adler!"

In the dim light of the moon, I saw a gleam come into Miss Wood's eye. "Adler? *You're* Ira Adler?"

"What do you mean by that?"

She laughed. Then she spat up into my face. "*The Colonel* left you quite a pile, didn't he? Should have gone after you instead. Maybe saved meself some trouble."

"How do you know—"

"Went through his papers after Suddy blew the house up, didn't I? Learned a lot of things, too. That's a right load for someone who was only a *secretary*."

My muscles suddenly went weak. She knew who Goddard was. She'd guessed who Goddard and I had been to each other. She was in a position to scuttle everything he had planned and everything I might conceivably plan in the future. Fear coursed through me, tightening my grip, taking away my breath. Her mouth twisted into a cruel grin. Good God, was I going to have to kill her?

At that moment, the door crashed inward so hard it left a dent in the wall.

"U.S. Marshal! Put your hands in the air!"

The sound of his voice made me nearly cry out with relief.

"She has a gun," I called instead. "Mr. Sutter, she has a gun!"

Seizing her advantage, Miss DuBois wrenched her arms from mine, pushed me off, and rolled onto her stomach—coming face-to-face with the barrel of Sutter's pistol. He didn't need to say a word. She dropped her weapon at his feet.

"Sit up," Sutter said, gesturing with his weapon. Never taking his eyes from her, he pocketed her pistol and tossed me my trousers. "You, too, Mr. Adler."

I was practically gibbering with relief at seeing him. But he was studiously avoiding my eyes. People were crowding into the doorway, pushing, trying to get a look at the situation. The light streaming in from the hall gave the entire mess an almost apocalyptic look. Bits of glass fell from my skin with a *plink*, and as panic drained away, various scrapes and lacerations began to sting to life across my bare back and shoulders.

"Looks like you bring trouble with you, Marshal," someone said. I recognized the deputy who had come to Pyrite to help transport the rioters.

Slowly I stood, spittle dripping from my face, and put my trousers on. Sutter secured Miss DuBois's hands behind her with a pair of shackles, then, glancing at the deputy, nodded toward me.

"What?" I protested as the deputy advanced toward me. "I didn't do anything! She—"

Sutter fixed me with a long stare. Admittedly, it didn't look good for me. A hallway full of witnesses had heard a gunshot, a woman screaming rape, then arrived to find us struggling together—and me without a stitch of clothing. I shut my mouth and let the deputy shackle my wrists. When he was done, he handed Sutter the keys.

"Thank you, Deputy," Sutter said. "I have the situation under control. Please escort these people back to their rooms. There'll be nothing more to see tonight." Slowly and unhappily the crowd began to filter away until only the night clerk remained. "You can return to your post, sir," Sutter told the clerk. "There won't be any more disturbances. But I'd appreciate it if you left your lamp."

The clerk nodded, setting the lamp on the chair. He hung in the doorway a moment more, then slipped away.

After the clerk had left, Sutter kicked the door shut behind him. Miss Wood, still sitting on the floor, swallowed hard, then tried to pull her face together into the imperious scowl of a woman wronged. My legs trembling, I sat down on the edge of the bed.

"Marshal, this man tried to—"

"Liza DuBois." Sutter shook his head. A slow grin spread over his face. "Do you have any idea how long I've been chasing you?"

Her self-righteous expression wavered for a moment, then evaporated, and the hardened Liverpool street rat returned. "I didn't know you cared."

"Oh, I care a lot when foreign criminals decide to set up shop in my country. You might say I take it personally."

"I don't know what you're talking about. This man—"

"This man," Sutter said, nodding toward me, "has put up with quite a bit from you. You set him up to take the blame for your shipboard crime—rather well, I might add. Then you sicced the Wilkes Brothers on him and his companions. Tonight, you broke into his hotel room, and when he asked you to leave—no doubt very politely—you threatened him with a gun and screamed bloody murder."

I cleared my throat. "Then why am I in handcuffs?"

"I'll get to you, Mr. Adler. The point is, Miss DuBois, I've been looking forward to this for a long time."

He'd *get to me*? What the devil did that mean? A cold sweat broke out along my back, and I forced myself to take a few long breaths. I'd done nothing wrong, here. A few stupid things, a few embarrassing ones, to be sure, but nothing *wrong*. A glance at Miss Wood showed she, too, was beginning to realize the enormity of the trouble she was in. The color had drained from her face, but she lifted her chin defiantly.

"Suppose you're going to send me back to England, then," she said.

Sutter laughed. "They want you back, they're going to have to send an army. Until then, you're mine."

She threw me a sidelong glance. "I have information. You let me go, and I can give you the case of a lifetime."

My heart stopped. She was talking about Goddard. She wanted to hand him Goddard.

Sutter said, "There'll be plenty of time for you to give a statement once you're safe in a cell, but I've been looking for you too long to just let you slip away."

"Are you working for Sudworth?" I asked. Surely one crime lord acting on American soil was as good as another. "Or did you just take advantage of the explosion?"

"What explosion?" Sutter demanded. "And who's Sudworth?"

Miss DuBois shrugged. "Done a few jobs for him, but I ain't his."

"But you knew he set the explosion."

"He set it all right, but it were my connections what found the man to make the bomb. That's why I figured I could have my pick of what were left over after."

A series of images flashed through my mind—the thick-browed man guarding the ruins of Goddard's home with his big knife; Miss Wood rifling through what remained of Goddard's office; the little stub of an article in St. Andrews's collection, about a woman attacked in the middle of the night, near the Baker Street entrance of Regent's Park; one of Goddard's men chasing St. Andrews through that very same park; the jagged scar that marked a gruesome border between Miss Wood's head and her shoulders...

"What are you talking about? What bomb?" Sutter asked. I bit back the overwhelming desire to tell him I'd *get to him.*

"Why did he do it?" I wanted to know. "I thought Goddard and Sudworth were friends."

She scoffed. "Them kind don't have *friends.* Besides, Suddy don't like people poaching his property."

"What?"

She sneered. "You can't say you haven't noticed *the Colonel's* striking new assistant."

Good God! Four years earlier, on the worst night of my life, Goddard had helped me spirit Marcus away from Sudworth. Goddard had said he'd taken up with Marcus about a year ago, but could it have actually started earlier than that? From what Marcus had said, he'd seen Sudworth only a few times before that night at the Wellington. Could Sudworth really have been holding that much of a grudge, and for so long?

"Mr. Sudworth thinks what revenge is a dish best served cold. But that ain't here or there neither. Now you tell the constable, here, to let me go, or I'm prepared to tell a little story about our Colonel, his assistant, and Mr. Ira Adler."

The breath left my body. I felt faint. I glanced from her to Sutter, who pinned me with a hard stare. After a long, tense moment, he gave a chuff of disgust.

"You can tell it to the judge." He'd heard enough from her, but in the subsequent look he gave me, it was clear we'd be revisiting the subject soon. There was something else in his expression—a combination of emotions so strong and intertwined it was difficult to pick just one. I wondered if I actually would be getting out of those handcuffs. "Liza DuBois, I'm arresting you for theft and breaking and entering—for a start."

He opened the door and shouted for the deputy. When the deputy arrived, Sutter instructed him to take Miss DuBois into custody. After they left, Sutter shut the door and turned to me with an expectant look. I stood.

"I can explain," I said, though I'd no idea how I would. Goddard, Sudworth, Marcus, me—what was there to say that wouldn't end things badly for everyone? As Sutter crossed the room, I began to shake. "Marshal, please, I..."

He was standing before me, his expression unreadable. Then he leaned forward, slipping his arms around my waist. I held my breath, too frightened to speculate what he intended to do—or worse, what he might say.

"You're going to tell me everything," he said softly, his lips grazing my ear as his gravely voice sent a shiver up my spine.

I didn't trust myself to speak. Twenty-four hours ago, I'd have given anything to be in his arms, but at that moment, it terrified me. What did he want? Shackled, I was utterly at his mercy.

"No convenient omissions, and no bull."

I nodded—a bit too eagerly. "No. I mean yes. No bull."

I meant every word, but good God, how was I going to do it? How would I tell him what he needed to know without doing Miss Wood's work for her? Hot breath caressed my ear. My pulse pounded as Sutter's chin burned a slow path across my cheek. There was a metallic *clink* and the handcuffs dropped to the carpet.

"Marshal." I gasped.

He laughed softly, grasping my arse and pulling me into him. "I thought I told you to call me Calvin."

CHAPTER THIRTY-THREE

His breath was ragged, his mustache tickled, and his skin was hot. I wanted to touch it. I wanted to touch it all over. My heart raced as his hands traveled up and down my bare back, kneading my arse through my trousers, holding me close. I was so happy he was there—there, and not arresting me, let's be honest—and thrilled at the vindication. I'd been right. I'd been *right*, sod it all—about him, and about him and me. But what was behind this change of heart?

"Stop thinking," he whispered, pressing me so hard against the door, I feared we'd go straight back through it. His whisper was tense, desperate, wanting. His fingers fumbled as he locked the door over my shoulder. "Stop speaking. Where's the bed?"

"Behind you."

He pulled back just enough to turn out the lamp and to allow me to breathe again. Moonlight shone through the curtains. He undressed quickly and efficiently, folding his trousers and laying them across the seat of the chair. Then the jacket—draped over the back—and the waistcoat. He started to fold his shirt as well, but by that point, his cock was straining toward the ceiling and his hands were shaking.

"Oh, hell," he said, and threw it onto the floor. When he looked at me, his expression was wild, a bit fearful. He took several long steps toward the bed. "Is the mattress quiet?"

I smirked. "No springs."

"Then come here. Don't make me beg."

I laughed nervously. I couldn't imagine him begging—not for me—not for anyone.

"Something funny, Mr. Adler?"

I laughed again. "No, sir, Marshal. Nothing at all."

I crossed the room in three giant steps. He folded me into his arms and kissed me so long and deep I could swear I lost consciousness for a second. I struggled out of my trousers, stomping them into a linen puddle. God, I wanted him so badly it hurt. I pressed against his hip impatiently, eliciting a nervous half-smile.

"I've wanted to do this since you boarded my car in Council Bluffs," he breathed.

"Really? You could have fooled me. You did fool me. As a matter of fact—"

"Shh. There are other things you can do with that mouth besides talking."

He laid me back down onto the cool sheets, covering my body with his, gently, rhythmically grinding his hip into my groin. Electricity crackled as he ran his fingertips ever so gently across my flank. He was so warm—iron and silk. He covered my mouth with his—which was fortunate, as when he shifted to bring our cocks together, I nearly cried out.

"Marshal," I gasped, when he pulled back for a breath.

"You know my name."

"Calvin. Marshal Calvin. Mmm…"

He silenced my chatter with another searing kiss. "Now stop talking. I mean it."

My mouth often leads me into trouble, especially when I'm nervous—and was I ever nervous. It wasn't enough that he was there—with me—doing *that*. I wanted to please him more than I'd wanted anything in a very long time. At the same time, he was an officer of the law, and a very intelligent man. If I pleased him too well, he'd wonder how I'd come by my skills. And as reluctant as he'd been to admit his desire, if he knew how I'd once earned my living, *disgust* wouldn't be a strong enough word to describe his reaction.

He made an impatient noise and pulled back. "Ira, I thought you wanted this."

"I do, more than—"

"Then, whatever you're worried about, put it out of your mind. Do you have any idea how hard this is for me?" *Something* was hard for him, that was certain. I nudged my hips up against his in what I hoped was a playful gesture. Chuckling under his breath, he lowered his head until his lips were barely brushing mine and brought our foreheads together. "I know you're nervous. I'm nervous, too. But we both want to be here. Don't we?"

"More than anything."

"Then more than anything, let's relax and pretend like we're enjoying ourselves."

Whatever he had to be nervous about, it wasn't his bedside manner, or so to speak. He was no virgin, whatever he might have protested. He took his time, touching, tasting, probing, claiming—expertly drawing pleasure from my body while taking his own. I felt like an exotic specimen—like a delicious treat. And he, too, was delicious, and powerful, and more beautiful than I'd ever imagined.

"Is this all right?" he whispered, as he gently stroked my opening.

"More than all right." I gasped.

His breathy laugh tickled my ear, and his fingers pressed gentle circles, dipping inside, teasing—then not so gentle—preparing, possessing. I spread my legs, opening to him, losing myself in sensation. For a while I forgot how to think, not to mention how to speak. When he pulled away unexpectedly, I nearly screamed with frustration.

"Don't worry," he said. "I'll be back."

I thought I would die when he rolled off me, stood, and crept back across the room. He returned with a small glass bottle, which he uncorked, releasing an unexpectedly floral smell.

"Ladies' beauty oil," he explained. He gave the bottle a little shake. "Many uses. See? It says so on the label."

"I'm no lady," I said.

"That much is obvious."

He tapped a generous amount of the oil into his hand, warmed it between his palms, then stroked it onto my cock, over my testicles, and down into my most intimate crevice. Despite the cloying fragrance, the slick pressure of his hands—so strong and assured and *expert*—almost brought the experiment to an embarrassingly quick end. As if sensing this, he released me and turned his attention to his own preparations.

"Do you always carry beauty oil in your pocket?" I asked.

He stopped, cock in hand, and gave me a wry grin. "I bought it yesterday after bringing those rioters back to Porterville."

"You don't say."

"I like to be prepared for any eventuality."

"An eventuality, was it?"

"The oil did come in useful, *eventually*."

The moon was setting—it set ever so late that time of year—but its receding glow poured over his trim body, softly defining the curves and recesses of his muscles and chest. A triangle of thin, dark hair curled across his sternum, a single tendril snaking down over his abdomen, toward the dark thatch surrounding his cock. He watched me watching him, stroking himself as I pondered the smooth, dark skin—perfection made human by a scattered handful of scars. I would ask him about those one day—but not that day.

"It was in the mine," he said. "You were almost at the top of that hole, my hand the only thing between you and death, and the knowledge that if I messed up, I'd never see you again. That thought was what changed my mind."

I knew I'd felt something then. I knew I hadn't been the only one. Sutter swallowed as if the memory were painful somehow.

"I've never done this before," he said.

"Bollocks," I said softly.

"What I mean is, I've never done this with someone I wanted to see again."

He didn't say anything more, and neither did I. It was easier for both of us to let our bodies speak. Filling and being filled. Consuming and being consumed. Rising and wrestling and switching places, trying out new agreements, new ways of saying those things words were inadequate to describe. I came without warning—a feeling so new, fresh, and intense, I had to muffle my surprise with a pillow. Seconds later, his arms tightened around me and I felt his shuddering release. He held onto me tightly for a moment, as if afraid I might slip away. And then he sighed deeply and set me free, gently, reverently, rolling to one side.

"I wanted you so bad the other night," he said. "But I just couldn't."

"It was a public place."

"It wasn't only that. I have to be so careful. I know you understand. The world isn't kind to men like us. But…I'm the first Black marshal. The only one that I know of. A lot of people hate that. Hate me because of it. All it would take would be a whisper of something like this, and—" He drew in a sharp breath and shook his head.

"You took a big chance being here."

His fingers found mine, tentatively wrapped around them, then decisively closed. "It shook me up, that business at the mine. Made me think. I like you, Ira. And you wanted me as much as I wanted you. I've never had that before. It scared me—not just the possibilities, but thinking how close I came to losing them. Does it make sense?"

I squeezed his fingers. "Perfect sense."

The kind of mutuality he'd described—I'd never had it either, at least not to the same degree. My years with Goddard had come close, but that had never been a relationship of equals. What Lawrence and I had shared might have eventually arrived there, but the time for that had passed.

"I've never been with anyone like you," I said. "Someone I could consider a friend as well as a lover." I snorted. "Never thought that person would turn out to be an officer of the law." To his raised eyebrows, I replied, "I have a bit of a history."

He cracked a smile. "You don't say."

"Nothing serious. Nothing violent. And all of it years and years in the past."

"Anything to do with the explosion and that Sudworth person?"

I knew he hadn't forgotten my exchange with Miss Wood, knew I'd have to explain. I just hadn't expected to have to do it right then. I took a deep breath and began, hoping I could provide the truth he demanded without incriminating either myself or Goddard.

"The Colonel's house was destroyed in an explosion just before we both left for America—that's where he sustained his injuries. The explosion was ruled an accident, though Miss Wood claims to have put Rupert Sudworth—one of the Colonel's business rivals—into contact with the person who built the bomb. She said she was picking over the Colonel's papers after the explosion, discovered that he had money and business interests in America. How she figured out he was alive, I can't even begin to speculate. But when she did, she decided to follow him and rob him."

Sutter was watching me. Behind his neutral mask, I could see his fearsome intellect connecting what I'd just told him with the facts he already knew.

"What was the nature of their business?" he asked.

I didn't answer. I couldn't begin to describe Goddard's endeavors. Couldn't and wouldn't. After a long, excruciating silence, I said, "I had nothing to do with the explosion. The Colonel and I were acquainted once, but I hadn't seen him for several years before we ran into one another a few days ago on Main Street."

"When you had tea together."

"Yes."

Nodding, he pulled himself up and leaned against the headboard. The moonlight was nearly gone, but I could still make out the outline of his naked form—dark on dark. The heat of our passion had cooled and was settling over us like a mist. I wanted to lean against him, to feel his arms around me, but there was something between us now. My refusing to answer his question had reignited his suspicion.

"And the Colonel's assistant?" he asked.

"Was on intimate terms with Sudworth, until the Colonel intervened."

"I see."

"As you said, the world isn't kind to men like us. Sometimes we're not kind to each other, either."

He blew out a long breath. I sensed he was evaluating, trying to figure out how much of what I said he could trust. He liked me. It was clear that our intimacy had touched him—as it had me. It was also obvious that he was wondering just how badly this case could make him regret it, if he took the wrong action.

"Do you mind telling me how you happened to find yourself in the middle of all of this?" he asked.

I shrugged. "I don't know what to say. Miss Wood—Miss DuBois—saw me on the ship and thought I'd make an unsuspecting mark—someone she could plant the key on and retrieve it from later. The fact that she chose me, specifically—I honestly think that was coincidence."

He considered that for a moment. Maybe he believed me, maybe not. But I felt him relax—perhaps deciding to put the matter aside for the moment. He took my hand and lifted my fingers to his lips. "I'll take your word for it now, Ira, but if it comes back to bite me, I'll come looking for you."

"That's fair enough, I suppose," I said, though the sentiment was becoming unsettlingly familiar.

We sat there quietly for a long time, watching the moonlight fade, listening to each other breathe—a period of near-perfect tranquility that I wished could have stretched out forever. It couldn't, of course, so I quietly broke the spell by asking, "So, what now?"

Sutter looked down at me. Smiling sleepily, he ran a hand through my hair, letting his hand rest on my cheek. "I don't know. This is all new to me. I want to see you again. Only problem is, at some point you're going back to London."

Was I? I supposed I was, though I couldn't imagine it.

"Or are you?"

"You're going back to New York."

He pursed his lips. "I have a hell of a mess to clean up here, first. Several of them. The rioters, Miss DuBois, Samuel Curtis—and if I have time, I'm damn well going to look into that artifacts theft. But when I'm done, there's no reason you couldn't come to New York with me."

"That's true."

Seen through driving rain and travel fatigue, New York hadn't impressed me, but it might be completely different when seen with someone I cared about. I tried to imagine walking the streets at his side, seeing the famous sights, exploring the shops during the day while he worked, then meeting him in the evenings for a drink and...

"You'd have to go back there anyway to get your boat home," Sutter said. "Is anyone waiting for you back in London?"

"Not anymore."

"Some amazing career, perhaps?"

I snorted. Goddard's words sounded in my mind. *London spat me out.* Me, too, apparently. If I thought about it, it'd been doing so for some time. "To tell the truth, I was becoming bored of London when I left. I've been ready for a change for quite a while."

"Then why not stay for a bit? You already know people in Pyrite, and I'm sure you have money. Bottles of cabernet cost a good day's wages for some folks. We can take the train up to Sacramento, San Francisco, maybe, then back to New York. Give you plenty of time to see the country and make up your mind. It'll be fine."

"How can you be certain?" I asked.

He looked at me. In his eyes, I saw the little boy who'd fled slavery into the vast, empty plain. I saw the young man negotiating between settlers and Indians—one group, which would have enslaved him, and another, which probably hadn't known what to make of him. I saw the grown man who'd run shouting into a herd of stampeding bison. My chest swelled with emotion, and I clutched his hand.

"I've spent every minute of my life jumping into the unknown." He smiled down at our interlaced fingers. "It's worked out so far."

I laughed. "I'll give it some thought."

"I'm glad. Listen." He swung his legs over the side of the bed, and I felt a sharp pang of disappointment. "I'd love to stay, but after all the excitement tonight, I'm sure nobody in this entire damn hotel is sleeping. The best thing for everyone would be for me to pretend the interrogation is over, release you on your own recognizance, then get back to my own bed down the road." He cupped my chin in his hand and kissed me—hard, long, and tenderly. "See you tomorrow, all right?

Meet me for breakfast at the chophouse—no, make that lunch. After the day we had, we deserve to sleep late."

"Yes sir, Marshal."

I watched him dress, watched him slide on his trousers, carefully button his shirt and tuck it in. Waistcoat, jacket, socks, shoes, hat. He was fading away from me, piece by piece. The promise of the new day seemed impossibly far away. I was already missing him before he walked out the door and pulled it shut behind him.

CHAPTER THIRTY-FOUR

July 4, 1895

When I'd first walked down Main Street with Irene on my arm, the boardwalk had been crowded with shop-goers. Their fine boots had made a jolly clatter along the planks, and their conversation had been a pleasant hum in the thick summer air. That day, as I made my way toward Scottie's Chop House, I found myself elbowing through clots of tourists standing in the middle of the path looking at maps, gawking at the goods in shop windows, or simply blocking the boardwalk for no apparent reason. Red-faced ranchers pulled at uncomfortable city clothes, their wives stumbling along unaccustomed to their new heeled boots, their children rebelling against starched clothing and pinching shoes. Despite the heat, though, an air of festivity animated the city. Half of California seemed to have descended on Porterville for the Fourth of July celebration. I hoped they wouldn't be disappointed.

I arrived at the restaurant at the height of an absolutely chaotic luncheon service. The room was groaning with diners sitting elbow-to-elbow at extra tables that appeared to have been scrounged up at the last moment to serve the hungry masses. As I looked out across the sea of red, sweaty tourist faces, a harried-looking man in a black suit cut through the crowd.

"I'm sorry, sir," he said, putting a hand on my elbow and turning me back toward the door. "You've come at a very busy time—"

"Mr. Adler!"

We both turned to see Sutter wave from his table—small, but in the relative privacy of a distant corner. Somehow he'd managed to hold on to an empty chair. He was dressed in brown linen that day, with a plaid waistcoat and a matching tie. His badge gleamed from his lapel.

"It's all right," I told the host, not even trying to suppress the happiness welling up inside my chest. "I've found my party."

I slipped my arm free, then wove through a maze of packed tables toward Sutter's little pocket of relative isolation. It was well into the noon hour, but he had a cup of coffee in front of him and an empty cup waiting for me. He looked well rested. His scrubbed skin glowed, and he appeared to be filled with an unseemly energy, considering everything that had transpired over the last few days.

"The coffee's excellent," he said. "I ordered you some."

"Somehow 'thank you' doesn't seem enough."

He laughed. "Rough night?"

"Tiring, though you seemed to have survived just fine."

"This old man is tougher than he looks."

A waiter arrived, then, to fill my cup. The two menus he laid down before us nearly covered the wobbly little table, which I suspected might have been a bar stool with the legs cut down. I glanced over the menu several times before realizing I hadn't actually absorbed any of the information.

"Is this awkward?" Sutter asked.

A smile was twitching at the corners of his mouth. Mirroring his half-smile, I looked out across the sea of diners, feeling the back of my neck go hot. I was so happy to see him, but I was having the damnedest time meeting his eye.

"A little," I admitted. "I'm relieved you turned up."

"Yeah." He forced his own features back into a more businesslike cast. "I hope you'll still feel that way when we're finished."

"Oh?"

My giddy bliss evaporated, and dread began to stir at the pit of my stomach. Before he'd left my hotel room, he'd given me the benefit of the doubt regarding my involvement in the DuBois case. I wondered if she'd given him reason to retract that benefit since then.

Sutter scanned the tables around us, as if looking for potential eavesdroppers. We were close enough to see a pat of butter melting on a baked potato at the next table—to count the pearls around a woman's neck. But we were almost shouting at one another over the roar of the other diners' conversation. I doubted that anyone would be able to pick up the thread of ours, even if they had the interest. All the same, before he spoke again, Sutter set his elbows on the table and leaned over toward me.

"Miss DuBois, currently a guest of the Tulare County jail, told me quite a few things last night. Quite a few things about you."

Sweat broke out across my back. My mind raced, trying to figure out what sort of information she might have gleaned from picking over the remains of Goddard's documents. I couldn't imagine Goddard would keep overtly incriminating evidence in his home, but one never knew. Sentiment combined with a sense of invulnerability could make anyone slip—even the Duke of Dorset Street.

"What did she say, exactly?"

"Nothing I hadn't already figured out from things you'd told me. Your past, your past with the Colonel."

So she hadn't told him Goddard's true identity. Perhaps she was saving it in case things became more desperate. Things would surely become more desperate. She was a smart woman, not divulging all of her knowledge at once. Normally, I admire smart women, but this one seemed determined to be the death of me.

"I have a feeling she's going to have a whole lot more to say before this is done. I just wanted to warn you."

"Thanks," I said unenthusiastically.

"Do you have anything you'd care to confess, Ira?"

I wondered if, while rifling through Goddard's office, Miss DuBois had learned how Goddard and I had met. How I'd spent several years peddling my arse up and down Dorset Street. I wondered if she'd said as much to Sutter. If so, he was doing an excellent job of hiding any opinion he might have had on the subject.

"Not at this time," I said. Then, "You said…" I made a vague gesture between us. "It's a crime, here. Should I be worried?"

He looked thoughtful. "I don't know. That kind of accusation could go any number of ways. If someone could prove you or the Colonel were part of her ring of thieves, personal accusations could certainly prejudice a jury—possibly even convince a judge to give a harsher sentence, if you were convicted. But the Colonel is the victim, not an accomplice, and you're not involved in the case in any significant way. I'm fairly certain of that."

That was a relief. But there still remained the question of whether Miss DuBois could use Goddard's crimes to broker a better deal for herself. Did American justice work that way? Sutter seemed so determined to put her behind bars, I doubted he'd take the bait. But what if someone above him saw things otherwise? I was unreasonably relieved when the waiter interrupted to take our order. Sutter asked for enough beef to start his own ranch. I suddenly found myself in the unusual position of having no appetite at all. After the waiter left, Sutter leaned back in his chair and folded his arms over his flat belly. He was frowning—not in a distraught manner, but in the manner of someone applying a formidable intellect to a challenging problem.

"The truth is, Ira, I don't know what's going to happen. I have a lot of evidence, a lot of material. I've built a very good case against Miss DuBois. But trials are complicated, and this is my first international case. It's my instinct and my opinion that the law will have no interest in the unrelated past offenses of persons not accused of the crime in question. Anything she might have to say about your character, or about the Colonel's, will likely be regarded as irrelevant."

"What if one of us has a significant criminal past in Britain?"

"You're not talking about yourself," he said.

"No," I replied.

He furrowed his brow. I could almost see the wheels turning behind his impassive face. I could sense him trying to click the tumblers into place. *What was the nature of their business?* Sutter had asked. It didn't take much intelligence—or even much effort—to realize I was talking about the Colonel. But I wouldn't betray Goddard that way—especially when, as Sutter said, Goddard was the victim of Miss Wood's crime—and when Goddard himself had argued so convincingly that he'd left his crimes behind him in London.

Finally, Sutter said, "There's a chance that if that person's crimes are of a certain magnitude, American authorities will alert the British government of his presence here. On the other hand, by the time anyone decides to do anything about it, that person could be long gone from California. Moreover, I don't believe Britain has an extradition treaty with the United States. Do you have any indication that this person intends to commit a crime here?"

That was a difficult question. Goddard's plans for starting a college had sounded too well thought-out to be a sham. I did know that he'd always wanted the academic life, and that if he hadn't been dismissed all those years ago, that's where he'd still be. He had plenty of money, and, if what he'd said about his oil claim was true, he'd soon have more than he'd ever know what to do with. Was crime in the blood, as current theories held? Was Goddard a crooked tree, warped from birth and without hope of redemption? Or would he, having been given everything he ever wanted—money, love, and not just an appointment at a college, but the opportunity to found one—would he make a new life in this new land of second chances?

I couldn't know. Probably Goddard couldn't even predict. But I had to hope.

"I don't believe he intends to," I said.

Sutter gave a sharp nod. "Then I would guess that neither you nor the Colonel has anything to fear—provided you stay out of trouble. And provided any prior trouble stays out of my case. I can't promise more than that. I hope it's good enough."

I'd wanted him to say he wouldn't let anything happen to us. I'd wanted some grand gesture of chivalry, but I was adult enough to recognize how unrealistic that was. And I was wise enough to know that sometimes good enough is as good as it gets.

"Thank you," I said.

The waiter brought the food then—a platter piled high with beef, fresh buttered vegetables, and, as the bartender had predicted the other night, a baked potato the size of a baby's head. I plucked my cup and saucer out of the way as Sutter's meal took over the puny table. Clouds of steam billowed up, filling the air between us with the aromas of corn, broccoli, and a beautifully cooked steak. I gazed at the spread, my mind filling with indecent thoughts.

"Hungry, now, are you?" Sutter asked, that half-smile dancing on his lips.

I glanced sheepishly up at the waiter and asked him to bring me something that wouldn't take too long. After the waiter had left, Sutter, demonstrating unspeakable restraint, laid down his knife and fork, and folded his hands across his lap.

"Please," I said, "enjoy your lunch while it's hot."

Ignoring my entreaty, he caught my gaze. Heart pounding, I forced myself to look into his deep-brown eyes.

"I meant what I said last night," he said. "Every word. Some opportunities don't come but once in a lifetime, if at all. I don't want to waste this one."

"Neither do I."

"It's not going to be easy, and I have to warn you, we'll have some tense times before this business with Miss DuBois is finished. My instinct is to trust you, but this is the biggest case of my life. I can't afford to let a lesser part of my anatomy do the thinking."

"I understand."

"So you'll stay in California for a while?"

"Are you ordering me not to leave the country?" I asked, venturing a wry smile.

"I could do that, but I won't…for now."

I nodded. I did my own sweep of the restaurant, lest some unfortunately overheard comment be misconstrued, amplified, and used against him. But the world seemed to be turning without us, borne on a fast-moving wave of conversation and food.

"I'll stay for a bit," I said.

"I'm glad."

The waiter arrived then, with a plate of sautéed vegetables, two fried eggs, and a basket of bread. I balanced the bread on my lap, as Sutter pushed his plate to one side. There was a long stretch of blessed silence as we tucked into our respective meals. Few things are quite so restorative as a good feed, and by the time it was over, I was feeling almost normal again.

"So, any plans for the day?" Sutter asked as I used my last crust of bread to mop up a bit of yolk.

"I should check on my friends in Pyrite. Start the long process of saying good-bye. You?"

"I'm headed up to Visalia. Going to pay a visit to the sheriff, return that tomahawk so he can get it back to its rightful owner. See you at the festival tonight? Nothing in the world like fireworks on the Fourth of July."

"I wouldn't miss it."

CHAPTER THIRTY-FIVE

Red, white, and blue bunting draped from the eaves of the Porterville depot, hung over the doorways, and wafted in the warm, lazy breeze. As I approached, the front doors opened, disgorging a wave of fresh-faced visitors dressed in gingham and linen. How fortunate that I'd already secured my room at the Arlington—though once I'd retrieved my trunks from Pyrite, I'd have to start looking for a more permanent place to hang my many hats. It was a lovely hotel, but the walls were thin, and now that I'd be having a regular visitor, privacy would be a top consideration. I moved to the side of the doorway to let the last of the stragglers pass, and then I stepped inside.

Only to very nearly collide with one Timothy Lazarus.

"Ira," he exclaimed. He'd shaved that morning and was wearing a green-and-white seersucker jacket with a jaunty straw hat.

"I was just coming to see you. Or, rather, to see my suitcases. What are you doing here?"

I turned to walk with him as he emerged from the depot and began to follow the groups of people making their way toward Main Street. A new optimism seemed to energize his steps, and his face held the look of someone trying to come to terms with a stroke of unimaginable luck.

"I'm glad you asked. Lillian received a telegram from Mr. Wells early this morning. Apparently someone has made a very decent offer on her land."

"Not Samuel Curtis, surely."

"I doubt it. Lillian actually seemed to be considering the idea. She and Bess left immediately for Porterville. I had an early lunch with Claire and Irene, then came up to join them." His tone grew serious. "I really hope this offer is legitimate. It would make everything so much easier. We're leaving in a week, and I want to see this matter settled before we do."

"A week?" I asked. That didn't seem very long. Not nearly long enough.

Tim frowned. "Didn't you have a look at your return tickets?"

I shrugged. "Probably. I just haven't given the matter much thought lately. A lot has been happening, if you haven't noticed."

"Oh, I've noticed." He shook his head and let out a long breath. "I'm ready to go back to London. It's been an adventure, but I want to sleep in my own bed again. I want to get back to work. Don't you?"

I didn't answer. A curious feeling settled over us, then—almost as if he'd been expecting I wouldn't share his enthusiasm. I'd told Sutter that I'd stay on for a while, but somehow the reality of my decision hadn't struck me until that moment. Yes, I wanted to see how things might progress with Sutter. Yes, the idea of trying to make a life in this land of second chances thrilled me as much as the idea of returning to London made me want to slit my wrists. But declaring my intentions to Tim somehow made everything real. Was I ready for that? We turned onto Main Street and made our way up onto the crowded boardwalk. Excitement crackled in the air, but it was making me irritable.

"You never did tell me how much my tickets cost you," I said as we passed Katie's Candies. It seemed like a lifetime ago, when he'd put the proposition to me over luncheon at the Criterion. He'd said that the tickets had been quite expensive—and not eligible for refund—but he hadn't given me a number.

"Don't worry about it," he said. "I'm sure between meals and moving us up to second class on the ship, we're nearly even."

"But you said the tickets couldn't be sold back."

He gave me a long look—surprise, concern, a touch of betrayal. Could he know what I was thinking? It was possible, I supposed. We'd been friends a long time, and he was a very perspicacious man.

"I'd like to pay you for them," I said.

He opened his mouth to speak, but before he could, we found ourselves in the doorway of Cassidy & Wells.

"Dr. Lazarus, Mr. Adler," Wells called. "I'm happy to see you. We were just about to head down the street for a celebratory lemonade."

Wells looked none the worse for our adventures, and the ladies were absolutely beaming. Bess and Lillian were seated in front of the desk. As one, they turned to smile at us. Lillian was still holding her pen.

Tim's face lit up. "So you've accepted the offer?" he asked Lillian.

"Eight thousand five hundred dollars!" Lillian set the pen down, gathered her lilac-colored skirts around her, and stood. The lace-collared shirtwaist and straw hat set about with dried flowers comprised an unusually decorative outfit for a practical Campbell woman. She must have sensed, before coming to Porterville, that she'd have reason to celebrate. "How could I refuse? Plus, I'll be receiving…what was that term you used, Mr. Wells?"

"Royalties," Wells said. "A small percentage of the profits from the oil drawn from the land, for as long as the oil lasts."

"Eight thousand five hundred dollars plus royalties!" Lillian beamed.

"So did Samuel Curtis finally do the right thing?" I asked.

"No!" Bess exclaimed. "That's the amazing part. It was Colonel Wright! As it turns out, he owns the adjacent parcel."

"Yes," Tim said darkly. "Mr. Wells mentioned that the other day."

"What's that scowl for, Tim?" Bess scolded. "The Colonel's doing us a favor. Apparently he brought a lawyer to Mr. Wells's office first thing this morning, and they drafted an offer right there and then. Mr. Wells telegraphed us the moment they left." A thoughtful look crossed her face. "Pity the Colonel wouldn't meet with us in person. As many times as our paths have crossed this past month, I almost feel like I know him."

"I thought you weren't willing to sell at all," I said to Lillian, before Tim could comment.

"I wasn't willing to sell to Samuel Curtis—though I might have been, if he'd gone about it honestly. I knew from the start he was trying to get away with something. I just didn't know to what degree he was trying to cheat me. Two hundred fifty dollars, indeed!"

So this was how Goddard had taken care of things. I couldn't suppress a smile. Quite frankly, I'd been expecting Samuel Curtis to meet his death by misadventure. And the offer was generous, at least in light of the value Wells had estimated when we'd visited the mine—generous, but not extravagant. Still, I couldn't quite believe it was an act of unfettered altruism.

"Did you read the papers thoroughly?" I asked.

"It was a pretty straightforward offer," Wells said. "But I had my own lawyer explain the terms to Mrs. Campbell once she'd had a chance to read it."

"Well, I'll be," I said. "I wonder how Curtis is going to take this."

"He's not going to have any choice but to take it." Lillian was gloating. "He must be as mad as a yellow jacket after the telegram I sent him. Told him he'd be lucky if the marshal didn't get after him, all the trouble he's caused. And if the marshal did come for him, it'd serve him right."

I felt my smile dissolve. It wasn't just that someone as persistent as Curtis wouldn't give up so easily. Lillian's jab about the marshal concerned me. An idea that had been stewing in the back of my mind since our meeting with Jed Walker suddenly came into focus. We all knew that Lillian's land was worth a lot of money. It was rather evident that between the fire and the incident at the mine, someone had been trying to frighten Lillian into selling.

As far as I knew, Curtis's had been the only offer. The sheriff in Visalia—Sheriff Daniels—had called off the investigation of the fire. He also seemed to be taking his time pursuing the artifacts' theft—if he was investigating it at all. And not only had someone attempted to frighten us off Lillian's land using what had to be the same missing artifacts, but Samuel Curtis had been running around trying to convince the people of Pyrite that Indians had been behind the fire.

And Sutter had gone up to Visalia some time ago to return the tomahawk to Sheriff Daniels.

"I have to go," I said.

"But we're going to go celebrate," Lillian cried.

I turned to Wells, trying to keep the panic out of my voice. "Mr. Wells, how long to Visalia by train?"

Wells cocked his head. "An hour, maybe a little more. Why?"

"What on earth are you up to, Adler?" Tim demanded.

"I think the marshal's in trouble."

He frowned. I could see him trying to follow my chain of thought and failing.

"There's no time to explain. I have to help him, Tim."

Bess started to speak. Tim made a quelling gesture, then, pursing his lips, gave me a tight nod. "Then I'm coming with you."

We managed to buy our tickets and dash to the platform just as the train to Visalia was pulling out of the station.

"Damn it!" I cried as the wheels screeched to life. The train disgorged a great cloud of steam, and for a split second, nothing but filthy heat and a wet and deafening hiss surrounded us.

"Damn nothing!" Tim shouted from somewhere in front of me. As the smoke cleared and the train began to pick up speed, I watched him break into a jog. At the very last moment he grasped one of the vertical handles beside the door and leveraged himself up. I scrambled after him, reaching for the bar. Just as the metal slipped through my steam-slick fingers, Tim's hand clamped down over my wrist. I grabbed the bar with my other hand and pulled myself up as the train left the station.

"Thanks," I said.

Tim grinned. For all his love of the comforts of home, for all his pursuit of security for himself and his family, he really did enjoy a good adventure. Would he seek out his own, once he no longer had me to drag him along on mine? Smoothing our jackets back into place, and rubbing the steamy residue from our faces, we climbed the stairs and found our way into a third-class car. The benches were hard, the window curtains limp and frayed, and grit crunched beneath our boots. For an hour's trip, though, it wouldn't matter. Tim forced open a window near the rear of the car and sat down beside it. I lit on the edge of the seat, then sprang back up. My worry for Sutter had filled me with restless energy, and I felt like I might jump out of my skin.

"Sit down, Adler," Tim said. "We need to discuss this."

Only two other people were in the carriage—an old woman near the front, absorbed in her newspaper, and a harried-looking mother, trying to comfort a colicky infant while her twin toddlers swarmed over the seats. But I could see his point. Discretion, discretion. I forced myself to perch on the seat next to him.

"So let me try to understand this," Tim said. "You think the sheriff and Curtis are in this together?"

"Two things were stolen from a private collection in Visalia: a tomahawk—that's a kind of decorated ax—and a ceremonial headdress. The items originally came from the Plains—just like the ones the false Indian had at the mine. I think the sheriff and Curtis colluded in the theft and used the artifacts to try to scare Lillian into a settlement, then to blame the fire on Old Tom and his family."

"Are you saying the ax the man threw at Sutter, and the headdress he was wearing, are the same ones stolen in Visalia?"

"It'd be some coincidence if they weren't," I said.

"And the pipe?"

"The newspaper article didn't mention a stolen pipe, but Jed Walker has done a lot of research and doesn't think the pipe originated in this area. Sutter agreed. Jed did say, though, that Curtis was spreading the rumor that the pipe—which had never been used, by the way—had caused the fire."

"And how are you connecting Curtis and the sheriff?" He frowned.

"The sheriff investigated the fire and ruled it not suspicious enough to investigate further. Also, Jed has been following the theft in the newspaper. The Visalia paper has a page devoted to crime, and they're diligent about following up on cases reported there. The first article appeared in May, right after the theft, but no articles have appeared since."

"It might just be that the sheriff hasn't solved the case," Lazarus said.

"Maybe."

"Tell me again how Sutter fits into this."

"I ran into Sutter this morning at the chophouse. He said he was heading up to Visalia with the tomahawk. If it was the one from the newspaper article, he intended to return it. I'm worried that when Curtis received Lillian's telegram—where she told him he'd be lucky if the marshal didn't come after him—he took it to mean that Sutter had figured out their plan. I'm worried that Curtis panicked and sent a wire to the sheriff, telling him just that."

"So Sutter conveniently walks through the door of the sheriff's office."

"And into a very dangerous situation."

Tim shook his head. "I don't know, Adler."

"I do."

"Or at least you're concerned enough about it to put yourself into the same situation. Don't you think the marshal can look after himself?"

"I'm sure he can, as long as he knows he's walking into an ambush. But I have information he doesn't."

"I guess I don't understand. Marshal Sutter has helped us quite a bit, and I'm grateful, but that's his job. I'm pretty certain he can handle any problems that might arise better than we can. The problem we came to solve is finished. It'd be nice to see justice done regarding Lillian's house, if a crime was committed, but you said the official conclusion was that there was no crime. If you ask me, we should be back in Porterville trying to find some way to celebrate the end of all this nonsense."

"Then why did you bother to come?"

He looked at me as if the answer were obvious. "You're my best friend, Adler. Whether you're walking into hellfire or humiliation, I'm going with you."

I smiled. I hadn't expected that. "Thanks."

"But if you don't mind my saying, you seem to be taking a personal interest in this."

"Calvin Sutter saved my life twice. He's gone to a lot of trouble to help—"

"Yes, but, Adler..." His expression became thoughtful, and I watched him carefully weigh his words. "Forgive me if I'm wrong, but I couldn't help noticing a certain tension between Marshal Sutter and you the other day. I'm not saying that...I mean, it seems absurd... and yet at the same time, that tension was palpable. I know I wasn't imagining it."

He knew. At some level he knew, without my having said a word. I shifted on the hard little bench. Ran the pad of my thumb over the corner of wood poking out from the worn fabric. Normally, bedding the local constable would have been something to smirk about, but this was more than that. I didn't want to reduce what was building between us to a dirty little joke. Part of me wanted to shout it from a mountaintop. Another part wondered whether it wouldn't be best to just keep my mouth shut.

But this was Tim, my closest friend, and he knew already.

I let out a long breath. "Yes," I said finally.

Tim's eyes went wide. "Yes?"

Good God, he'd been guessing.

I looked to the front of the carriage, where the old woman was still immersed in her *Tulare Times*, then glanced at the young mother now crouching on the floor, babe in the crook of her arm, peering under the seats for something while the twins wailed. I leaned closer to Tim and dropped my voice.

"Yes. Sutter and I. Yes, all right?"

He blinked. Then he ran his hand through his hair, shook his head, and said, very softly, "Is it possible, Adler, for you to get through a week without some man jumping into your bed?"

"That's really not how it happened."

"How did it happen?"

I gave him the highlights, omitting, of course, the moments of most abject humiliation. When I was finished, he stared at me for a long time. A few times he opened his mouth, then closed it again, as if the words he'd chosen simply weren't adequate for what he wanted to say.

"So yes, this is personal for me." I continued in a series of terse whispers. "It's too early to say where it might lead, but there's more to it than simply jumping into bed. For the first time in as long as I can remember, I'm thinking about more than just a bit of fun, and so is he."

Lazarus continued to stare for a moment. "So you're staying in California, then."

"I think so, yes. At least for a while. I need to explore this, Tim. Nothing's left for me in London."

"Don't be dramatic." He sounded almost hurt. "There's...you have your work."

"I don't need to work."

"You have friends."

I gazed at him for a long time. All that we had gone through together, Tim and I—love, hate, explosions, expulsions, the births and deaths of friends—it had bound us like brothers. Pulling each other out of one scrape after another, each buoying the other up when he was down, or tethering him to the earth when needed. And yet life was leading us inexorably in different directions. Tim had two charities to run and a family that was first in his heart. I was quickly outgrowing the carefree life of easy work and meaningless liaisons that had allowed me to be such a frequent interloper in his endeavors. I was ready for something new. This was my opportunity, and I had to grab it with both hands.

"I shall miss you, Tim, with all my heart, and every single day."

After a moment he smiled—sadly, I thought. "I'll miss you as well."

With a squeal of brakes, the train gradually slowed. Somewhere in one of the cars ahead of us, the conductor's voice announced Visalia Station. The train pulled to an eventual stop. The old woman folded her newspaper and stood, while the younger one gathered up her charges. Tim and I waited until they'd cleared the train. Then we, too, made our way to the stairs. As we stepped out of the carriage onto the platform, Tim muttered under his breath. "Though this isn't the first time I wish I'd brought my Webley."

CHAPTER THIRTY-SIX

S o tell me again how this is meant to work," Tim said as we walked as quickly as was decorous toward where the man at the station had told us the sheriff's offices lay. Under other circumstances I'd have liked to take my time exploring Visalia. It was a lively looking town with enough saloons to hint at a promising selection of entertainment, come nightfall. But I would enjoy no entertainment until I was certain Sutter was safe.

"We'll start by telling the sheriff we think we've found the missing artifacts," I said as we turned onto Main Street. "See if he reacts suspiciously."

"What do you mean by 'suspiciously'?"

"*Suspiciously.*" I scoffed. "Shifty eyes, mustache twirling, an evil laugh. Tim, please."

Tim rolled his eyes.

"If he says the marshal has already turned in the tomahawk, that's a good sign. I mean, if he's done anything to Sutter, he'll probably avoid any mention of the man."

"He could say Sutter was there, dropped off the tomahawk, and left, regardless of what actually happened. Then what?"

"Then we can say we were doing our civic duty, leave, and decide what to do next."

Tim gave me a long, hard look. I had to admit, it all sounded pretty thin when I put it into words, but by the time the train had pulled into Visalia, I was convinced that my theory about Curtis and the sheriff was correct—a fact that had left me stupid with worry.

"I'm sorry, Tim. I know it's a rubbish plan, but I'm not wrong about this. Something's happened to Sutter, I can feel it, and I'd rather look foolish than risk—"

"All right, all right, Adler." He let out a long-suffering sigh. "I did say 'hellfire or humiliation.' The sooner we get this over with, the sooner we can get back to Porterville and pretend it never happened."

The sun beat down on the unpaved thoroughfare that was Main Street. The patriotic bunting that appeared to have been hung with optimism now sagged over the doors of the long, two-story buildings that flanked the wide road, and drooped over their windows. The air was thick with dust and the smell of horse piss. I was well on my way to sweating through my shirt.

Somewhere in the distance a clock struck four.

"There it is," Tim said pointing toward a distant wood-framed building. "Just like the man at the station said."

The Tulare County Sheriff's Office was smaller than I expected, given the size of the county on the map on Wells's office wall. The curtains had been drawn across the windows—out of deference to the heat, I imagined. It would have been much more efficient to open the windows on either wall to encourage the hot air to circulate, but we weren't there to make suggestions about improving ventilation.

"Help you?" asked a rangy man with a droopy blond mustache as we walked in. He was leaning back in his chair, feet resting against the Remington typewriter that sat on one corner of the desk. Behind him, pen-sketches of "wanted" criminals glowered down from a series of advisories tacked to the wall.

"Good afternoon. Sheriff Daniels, I presume." I said.

He pulled his thick eyebrows together as he examined us. Sweat had gathered along his forehead, and he mopped it away with the sleeve of his well-worn shirt. Unhurriedly lifting his feet from his desk, he said, "Sheriff Daniels stepped out for a minute. I'm the deputy. Name's Lennox."

I approached the desk and offered my hand. "Deputy Lennox, I'm Mr. Adler, and this is Dr. Lazarus."

He rose to his feet, and we exchanged businesslike handshakes across the desk.

"What can I do for you gentlemen?"

"We have some information that might interest you," I said.

"Oh?"

"We read about a theft of some Plains Indian artifacts a few months back—a tomahawk and a feathered headdress. Recently, we saw items very similar to the ones described in the article, down in Pyrite. We thought you might like to know."

Lennox paused. He didn't exactly start twirling his mustache, but in that split second, I surmised that the artifacts had been on his mind recently. Moreover, he certainly hadn't expected a stranger to walk in and start prattling about them.

"The headdress was made from large white feathers with brown tips—sort of like a crown, with two tails coming all the way down the back," I said. "The tomahawk had a wooden handle decorated with small, colored beads. They certainly looked like the items described in the article. Can't be that many about in this part of the country."

This time the deputy did reach for his mustache—to smooth it—a nervous gesture. I'd originally taken him to be about my age, but up close, he appeared younger—rather young to be deputy for an entire county, I thought. He glanced toward the empty desk on the other side of the room—the sheriff's desk—as if he might find some sort of guidance there. Then he let out a long breath.

"I'm sorry. You gentlemen have wasted a visit." He took a ring of keys from a hook near the entrance to a long hallway and walked over to the other desk. He rattled around in one of the drawers, then produced an ax—the ax—the very one Sutter had left that afternoon to return. I inhaled sharply.

"That's the one," I told Tim under my breath.

"Are you sure?"

"On my life."

Never would I forget the sight of that ax hurtling toward Sutter. Never would I forget the intricate beaded design or the not-quite-sharp blade. The very thought sent a rush of anger through me, bubbling up, threatening to spill over and ruin our not-so-carefully laid plan.

"We recovered this a few days ago up in Fresno from someone trying to make a quick sale," the deputy said.

"But—"

I couldn't have heard correctly. Sutter had handed the ax over—that afternoon, not a few days ago. The deputy was lying. I'd anticipated his lying, but somehow I'd thought—I'd hoped—I'd been certain—that at the last moment he'd tell the truth, and Tim would be right—it would all prove a great misunderstanding.

"Something the matter, Mr. Adler?" Lennox asked.

"No, no," I said, my voice wavering disconcertingly. "We must have been mistaken. Sorry to have wasted—"

"What do we have here, deputy?" a voice asked behind us.

Tim and I turned to see a wall of a man standing in the doorway. Even lit from behind by the glare of the day, he was apparently in his mid-forties, with broad, meaty shoulders, pasty skin, and small, dark eyes that sat a bit too close together. The harsh sunlight gleamed off the handle of a pistol strapped to his wide hips.

"Oh, Sheriff," Lennox said nervously. He slapped the head of the ax against his hand and stepped gingerly away from the sheriff's desk. "These men have come up from Pyrite. Said they seen them missing artifacts. You know, the ones we recovered the other day up in Fresno."

"Is that so?" The sheriff's voice was even, but his eyes were hard and his expression calculating. He took a thoughtful breath and adjusted his belt. "As you can see, we recovered the artifacts, but thanks for making the trip."

"You have the ax," I said. "But what about the headdress?"

"Adler." Tim was trying to warn me.

But I couldn't stop myself. The deputy's lie had left me in utter shock. I felt like I'd been slapped—or possibly like I could have used a slap. Meanwhile my mouth kept moving despite the protests of my better judgment.

"That headdress was exquisite and probably worth quite a bit. And we saw it over the line in Kern County just the other day."

"Thought you said it was in Pyrite," the deputy said.

The sheriff cocked an eyebrow but held up a hand toward the deputy. "What makes you so sure it's the same headdress?"

"I can't imagine that two Plains-area ceremonial headdresses might appear between here and Mrs. Campbell's land."

"Adler!" Tim cried.

He was right. But I couldn't keep the triumph out of my voice. I felt like a stage magician pulling back the curtain. *And the vanished lady has now reappeared...*

"And the ax the deputy is holding is the same one the man wearing that headdress threw at the marshal out on that very tract of land. I was there, and I'd recognize it anywhere."

"Adler, for God's sake!"

Tim's words echoed in the sudden deathly silence. Sheriff Daniels turned and gave the door a push. It closed with a shudder.

"Well," Daniels said quietly.

Tension crackled in the air as we faced each other. The clock on the wall ticked seconds slowly past. The deputy shuffled his feet.

"Sir," Tim said. "My friend and I were clearly mistaken. Forgive us for wasting your time. Come along, Adler."

"No, Tim. They didn't find that ax in Fresno. The marshal brought it in this afternoon." I turned to the sheriff. "Where is he?"

The deputy said, "Now, I don't know about any—"

"He was here," I insisted.

Tim put a hand on my elbow. "Adler, let's go."

He pulled me toward the door, but Daniels stepped in front of us—a brick wall, or perhaps an angry bison.

"We're leaving now," Tim said.

"No," Daniels replied. "You're not."

The sheriff was my height but probably outweighed me by fifty pounds. And he had a gun. The deputy's gun hung from a belt draped over the back of his desk chair. As quick as I was, I doubted I could get to it in time to do anything more than get one of us shot.

"Gentlemen," Daniels said. "We need to talk."

"Sheriff," Lennox said. His tone was nervous again.

"Shut your trap, Deputy. You've said too much already. I'll deal with you later." His fingers danced on the handle of his pistol. He nodded back toward the hallway. "That way."

"Now-now-now, Sheriff—"

"I told you to shut your mouth, unless you want to join them. I've had about all I can take of your waffling this morning."

Lennox swallowed. He was afraid of the sheriff—a fact that could work in our favor if we approached the situation from the right angle. More likely it would work against us.

"That's what I thought," Daniels said. He gestured again toward the hallway. "Now move."

"No, sir," Tim said.

The sheriff's heavy brow furrowed. Clearly the man wasn't used to being defied. Sweat ran down my back, and I had the same sensation of time standing still that I recognized from that day some weeks ago, when I'd paused at Cain Goddard's doorstep half a breath before his York Street house had exploded. The sheriff licked his chapped lips.

"Deputy, I believe this man is resisting an officer of the law."

The deputy swallowed. He was definitely scared of Daniels. Or scared of what he'd do—or what he'd already done. Good God, what had he already done? I tried to catch the deputy's eye, but he pointedly looked away.

"Sorry, gentlemen." Lennox picked up the keys from the sheriff's desk. I heard a metallic jingle as he took a set of handcuffs from the hook in the doorway. Unlocking them, he stepped toward us.

Tim glanced at me. There's something to be said for long, intimate acquaintance. He didn't have to say a word. He'd told me once how his military training had taught him to rush an attacker—the attacker rarely expected it, and the resultant surprise was often enough to allow a person to escape. Besides, even if Daniels managed to draw his gun before we collided, he couldn't shoot both of us.

Daniels reached for his pistol. At the same time, Tim charged into him, tackling him and grabbing his wrist just as the sheriff drew his gun. The sheriff stumbled back, but Tim's weight wasn't enough to knock him off his feet. While the two men grappled for the pistol, I leaped onto Daniels's back.

I'm no tiny thing, but it was like riding an angry rhinoceros. I wound one arm around the sheriff's neck, my legs around his waist, pulling at him while trying to remember some neck lock Goddard had taught me.

A pair of arms wrapped around my waist. The deputy was trying to pull me off.

"You're only making it worse for yourself," Lennox said through clenched teeth. "Nobody can reason with the sheriff when he's like this."

"Get off!" I cried.

I flailed out with one arm, trying to dislodge the deputy. Daniels shook himself like a wet dog. Lennox and I tumbled backward into the sheriff's desk. It tipped onto two legs, then fell over with a bang. The chair skittered across the floor and toppled. Suddenly papers were everywhere. The ax clattered to the ground. I rolled off the desk, lunging for it. Lennox threw himself on top of me.

As we wrestled on the ground, I glanced over to see that Tim had pulled an arm free. The sheriff let out a strangled cry of surprise as Tim jammed a knee into his crotch. Tim struggled out of Daniels's grip and stepped back just as the big man toppled to the ground.

"Sheriff?" Lennox asked, looking up.

In that split-second of distraction, I coshed him across the side of the head with the ax handle. While he blinked, dazed, I pushed him off and ran for the gun belt draped over the back of his chair.

"Everybody just stop where you are," I said, pulling the gun out of its holster.

Lennox, still blinking stupidly, put up his hands. Tim was crouching over the sheriff, breathing hard, his eyes glazed with disbelief and triumph. Gingerly he pried the sheriff's gun away and tucked it into his own pocket. Daniels, insensible to anything but his own pain, moaned and curled into a ball on the floor.

"Get the deputy's cuffs and fasten him to the desk." I trained the gun on Lennox. "And don't even think about moving."

Powerful emotions surged through me like lightning. Was this what it was like to be a hero? I didn't feel heroic. My hands were trembling, and I was very close to being sick. I wanted this to be over. I wanted to know that Sutter was all right, and I wanted to go home. Of course at that point, it wasn't at all clear how, or even if, that was going to happen.

I watched Tim glance down at the sheriff, who was breathing in quick, painful gasps, then cross to the deputy and secure his hands behind his back and around the leg of the desk.

"Enough of this nonsense. Where's the marshal?" I demanded.

Lennox opened his mouth to answer. At the same time, a violent pounding sounded from the end of the corridor—someone throwing himself against a door.

Sutter!

"I'm coming!" I cried.

Sparing one last glance at Tim—who, having secured the deputy, was now diligently examining the damage he'd inflicted on the sheriff—I ran down the corridor, past three empty jail cells, to a wooden door.

"Calvin! It's me!" I cried.

A man's voice shouted something unintelligible, and then the door shuddered again under another assault.

"Tim!" I shouted. "Keys!"

Pausing in his examination, Tim took the keys from the sheriff's belt and slid them down the hall to me. My fingers shook as I fumbled first one, then another into the lock. Finally the tumblers made a definitive click. I shouldered the door open with a cry.

Sutter stood to the side, his hands bound in front of him. Shafts of sunlight angled in through cracks between the boards nailed over the windows, onto an overturned chair. Near the chair was a length of rope, which I assumed had bound Sutter's ankles.

"Did they hurt you?" I asked, working quickly to untie the red bandana that had been wrapped around his head for a gag. He shook his head. The bandana loosened and fell to the floor, and I went to work on his hands. Sutter spat, then licked his lips.

"They didn't know what to do when I walked in with that ax. The sheriff would probably have put a bullet in me right away, but the deputy thankfully had more sense. Are they still out there?"

"They're not going anywhere, and Tim has a gun in case they try."

The ropes came loose at last, and Sutter shook his wrists free. He sighed deeply, looking around as if to reassure himself it was all over. I watched his shoulders relax.

"What happened?" I asked.

He rubbed at his wrists, stretched his arms. "I came up on the two o'clock to return the tomahawk, like I told you. Lennox and Daniels were both there, and they were surprised, to say the least. Somehow they got the better of me. They knocked me cold and put me in that back room." He rubbed at the back of his head and winced. "I think they were going to find a way to dispose of me once they'd figured out that nobody knew I was here. I was just starting to come to when I heard your voice." He met my eyes, and a little shiver went through me. "God, it was good to hear your voice."

"I'm so glad you're safe," I said, unable to hide the tightening of my throat.

He frowned, then smiled shyly. He made a little gesture with his finger. "Come here." He cupped my chin in his hand and kissed me with a tenderness that made me gasp. "There'll be plenty of time for that later, but first we need to clean up this almighty mess."

"Of course. Oh, God," I said, remembering the pistol. My hands were trembling, and the very thought of that thing in my jacket pocket terrified me. "Here." I pressed the gun into his hand.

"What's this?"

"I went a little crazy when I thought they'd hurt you." I'd been ready to pull the trigger. I'd been looking for an excuse. The thought of how much I'd have enjoyed that made me slightly queasy now, as I followed him back up the corridor to where Tim had the situation well in hand.

Sutter smirked. "You kill anyone?"

"No, but not for lack of trying."

He laughed. "Then I wouldn't worry about it. How did you even think to come up here after me?"

I told him how, after he'd left Pyrite following the talk with Jed

Walker, my mind had connected the fire at Lillian Campbell's house with the artifacts' theft. "The sheriff was the common link," I said. Then I told him about Lillian's gloating telegram to Curtis.

"That's quite a leap of logic," he said. "I'm impressed…and very grateful."

Tim looked up when we emerged in the sheriff's office. Sutter cocked an eyebrow as he took in the damage. The sheriff's desk lay on its side. The chair was overturned in the corner. The blade of the tomahawk glinted from beneath a pile of papers. More papers littered the floor.

"Cyclone?" Sutter asked.

"Hurricane Adler," Tim said, looking up from his patient. Daniels was lying on his side, still moaning, but at least he seemed to be breathing a little better. "Hello, Marshal."

"Hello yourself, Doctor. Looks like you've been busy."

"I'm not the only one." Tim stood, brushing off his trousers. Then he picked a piece of paper from one of the piles on the floor. "Have a look," he said, handing it to me.

"What's that?" Sutter asked as I took the folded yellow sheet with the words WESTERN UNION across the top.

Tim said, "It's a telegram from Samuel Curtis, sent this morning, warning the sheriff that the game was up and the marshal was coming for them. Of all the improbable events, Adler—you were exactly right!"

CHAPTER THIRTY-SEVEN

It was nearly eight in the evening by the time Tim, Sutter, and I had secured Daniels and Lennox in their respective jail cells, contacted the appropriate authorities in Porterville and in the Marshals Service, put out a warrant for the arrest of Samuel Curtis, and written our statements regarding our understanding of the day's events. The latter task was made considerably quicker thanks to the typewriter that had been gathering dust on the deputy's desk and my proficiency with it—something that both Tim and Sutter had watched with fascination.

"And done," I said. I pulled the last page from the machine and slipped it to the bottom of the stack. "That should make someone some interesting reading."

"You're a man of many talents, Mr. Adler," Sutter said with admiration. "And it could make you a very nice career, if you were so inclined. My office in New York is always looking out for sharp folks who can handle a typewriting machine. Plus," he added, leaning in and dropping his voice, "it'd let me keep an eye on you, make sure you stayed out of trouble."

"Trouble finds Ira, wherever he is," Tim said, turning back from the window, from which he'd been watching for the man the Porterville deputy had promised to send. "But I must say, it'd probably be for the best if, the next time it happened, he was surrounded by armed officers of the law."

The sun's last rays were pushing an orange glow through the curtains pulled across the front window. Shadows passed by—people making their way toward Main Street for their evening's entertainment, or perhaps toward whatever Independence Day festivities the city of Visalia had planned. Tim had said that Bess and Claire were looking forward to the fireworks in Porterville. They must have been wondering what was keeping us. Wells would look after them, no doubt, but I felt a pang of disappointment at the thought that we might not be there to enjoy the celebration with them. A sharp rap on the door interrupted my thoughts.

"Mr. Travis," I said as I opened the door to a thin, dark-haired man. Frank Travis, an assistant deputy from Porterville, had responded to the riot back in Pyrite. It was a pleasant surprise to see him again.

"Mr. Adler." Travis stepped forward to shake my hand, an easy smile resting on his features. "Can't say I was expecting to see you here."

"I can't take him anywhere," Tim said, as Travis walked over to shake his hand and then Sutter's.

"Thank you for coming, Mr. Travis," Sutter said. "We've got a real disaster here. Probably take us weeks to sort it out. But we've done all we can for today. Right now, we just need someone here tonight to keep an eye on those two knuckleheads back there."

"Be happy to, Marshal," Travis said.

"And we'd be much obliged if you could set this office in order while you're at it," Sutter said, shaking his head at the wreckage. "I'll be back first thing in the morning, but right now I have to get some supper and clear my head."

"Yes, sir." Travis rubbed his hands together, clearly happy for this second spot of excitement in as many days.

We left Travis amid the chaos of the sheriff's office and made our way back to the train station. My mind was crowded with thoughts, but the idea of opening my mouth to express them just made me tired. At the station, we filed into the line at the ticket counter and wordlessly waited to purchase our passage back to Porterville. At the last moment, Sutter stepped off to the side.

"Aren't you coming?" I asked, breaking the silence that had surrounded us like a cocoon.

"I should probably stay here, just in case Mr. Travis needs me."

The intensity of my disappointment shocked me. Of course it would be the logical thing for him to do, but after all we'd been through, I suppose I'd been looking forward to a bit of fun together.

"But what about the fireworks?"

Sutter blinked. Then he laughed. "You sound like a disappointed six-year-old."

I couldn't help it. I felt like a disappointed six-year-old. Perhaps the excitement from the fight—now rapidly draining away and leaving me feeling like an empty shell—had sapped my reason. Or maybe exhaustion was playing tricks on my mind. All sorts of emotions were churning inside me. It was hard to pick just one—but disappointment was the loudest at that point, and the most clear.

"Surely Mr. Travis can sit on two men locked in two different jail cells," Tim said, coming to my rescue. "You've earned some recreation, Marshal. Please come with us."

"Please," I said.

Sutter paused, but only for a moment. "Well, all right, then. You did say 'please.'"

It was a little after nine thirty when the train pulled into Porterville. The sun was settling behind the low mountains, and a wave of dark blue was chasing the rusty traces of the day westward across the sky. As we walked down Main Street—Tim, Sutter and I—a warm, dry breeze kissed my cheek. The only thing that would have made me more content, I realized, as we followed the slow, thick flow of pedestrians toward the celebration, would have been to loop my arm through Sutter's while we did so. A glance from him told me that he was thinking much the same thing, and though our own private celebration would have to wait, it would come, and it would be well worth the delay.

Porterville was marking the Fourth of July in a field just outside of town. The smell of hot buttered corn filled the air, as well as roasted peanuts and spun sugar. Hawkers' cries and the distant whistles of trains punctuated the hum of excited chatter. A series of lanterns hung around the perimeter of the field, while darkness quickly gathered. Over in a corner, a band was playing. It was a kind of music I'd not heard before—fiddles, a mandolin, and a big bass violin—but it sounded energetic and optimistic.

"There are Bess and Claire!" Tim said, indicating the unmistakable forms of his wife and daughter over near the roast-corn seller. He looked from them to me—and reflected in this one simple gesture, I saw the twisting path we'd walked together since the day I stumbled into his clinic all those years ago. I saw the fork in the road before us. He glanced at Bess again—it was almost as if he was worried that his choice might offend me.

"Go on then," I said, shooing him off with my hands. I smiled as I watched him stride over to join them. I'd miss him, by God, but we would have plenty of time for proper good-byes in the morning.

"Should I get us something to eat?" Sutter asked.

"Not yet. Let's find somewhere to stand and enjoy the music."

We found a secluded spot along the fence near the stage. The wood pulsed against my back with the steady rhythm of the bass. The violin's music soared around us—bright and daring and free. Stars were winking into existence overhead—a thousand dazzling pinpricks against a blackening sky. I felt the warmth of Sutter's arm against mine, smelled his exhilarating scent of lime, sage dust, and sweat. My future felt as open as the endless western sky, and for the first time in all my life, I felt as if I was exactly where I was meant to be.

"Mr. Adler!" Irene's voice cut through the music. The crowd seemed to part as she walked toward us—a vision of flashing dark eyes and wide, bright smile. "Did you take care of your business in Visalia? Oh, good evening, Marshal."

"Ma'am." Sutter tipped his hat.

She was absolutely glowing that evening, her dark hair swept up into some complicated arrangement, lilac-scented perfume surrounding her like a cloud. Her dress was surprisingly sophisticated—a dark, daring burgundy with lace cuffs and a tight corset, though she still wore her boots. Every man who passed by slowed to stare, but she only seemed to have eyes for one.

I followed her gaze to Gordon Wells, who, clad in a jaunty plaid sack coat and matching trousers, was approaching with two mugs of a fizzy substance. Nodding to us, he handed one of the glasses to Irene. "Sarsaparilla," he told her. "Good for everything that ails you."

"Nothing can possibly ail me now that you're here," she said.

Even in the dim lantern light, I could see his face darken a shade. He cleared his throat.

"Hello, Mr. Adler. Marshal. Good to see you again. Hasn't it just been quite a week?"

"Indeed it has," I said.

Just then the violin let out a screech, and the band struck up a new tune with a vaguely Scottish feel.

"Oh! The Virginia reel!" Irene cried. She took a belt of her drink, wiped the foam from her lips with her sleeve, then thrust the glass at me. "Ira, would you hold this for me while Mr. Wells asks me to dance?"

Wells's eyes flew wide. "Oh...I...well...I don't mind if I do." Grinning, he handed his drink to Sutter. "Please enjoy it, Marshal, with my compliments. Shall we, Miss Campbell?"

Sutter and I watched as they clasped hands and ran to take their places facing each other at the end of two parallel lines of dancers. The mandolin player called out some preliminary instructions, and the dancers began to move.

"Do you dance the Virginia reel, Ira?" Sutter asked as the couple at the heads of the lines bowed and took a few steps forward. His tone was wry, and I had the feeling, once more, that he was somehow making fun of me.

I laughed. "Not even if my life depended on it. You?"

He shook his head. "I like to do my dancing in private. With a single partner."

The back of my neck went hot, and the image that his words brought to mind made my knees go weak. The light from the lanterns played off his blue-black skin, and it struck me, once more, how unutterably beautiful he was. I felt the flush rise along my neck to my face, and I was grateful for the darkness. "That's how I like it, too."

Sutter nodded. "A single partner for the entire dance."

Somewhere in the distance, a child squealed. I glanced over to see Claire race past the stage, her little hand clutching a stick that was shooting off sparks. Now deep in the throes of the Virginia reel, Irene whirled by, her head thrown back in laughter, while overhead, the first of the fireworks screamed toward the sky.

"Of course some folks get bored dancing with the same partner every time," Sutter said. He was looking away, as if steeling himself in case I should agree with the sentiment.

"I have a feeling things are never boring when you're around," I replied. "Even when boring is the better part of valor."

A smile twitched at the edges of his lips. I wanted to capture that smile in my mouth, hold it on my tongue forever.

"And I have a feeling, Mr. Adler, you wouldn't have it any other way."

HISTORICAL NOTES

The character of Marshal Calvin Sutter was inspired by legendary lawman Bass Reeves (1838–1910), who was also the inspiration for the Lone Ranger.

Born a slave on the plantation of an Arkansas state legislator, Reeves escaped during the American Civil War and made his way to Indian Territory (now Oklahoma), where he lived among the Creek, Seminole, and Cherokee peoples until the end of the war.

In 1875, Reeves was hired as a Deputy U.S. Marshal, owing to his knowledge of Indian Territory and his fluency in three Native American languages. A master of disguise and an expert marksman with superior detective skills, Reeves served as a peace officer for thirty-two years. By the time he retired, he had personally brought some 3,000 felons to justice.

Like the Lone Ranger, Reeves always rode a white or light-gray horse and was said to have handed out silver coins as tokens of goodwill. He often rode with a Native American companion, an expert tracker, who was instrumental in collaring outlaws.

You can read more about Bass Reeves in the book *Black Gun, Silver Star: The Life and Legend of Frontier Marshal Bass Reeves* by R. T. Burton.

The porters of the Pullman Cars played a number of important roles in American history. After emancipation, the Pullman company hired large numbers of Black men, many of them former slaves, to serve as porters in their sleeper cars. It was hard work and poorly compensated, and attempts at unionization were ruthlessly put down. At the same time, the steady nature of the work helped to provide the stability that played a large part in the development of a Black middle class. Later, the organization of the Brotherhood of Pullman Car Porters would be integral to the AFL's eventual inclusion of Black workers. The Brotherhood also had a significant role in the Civil Rights movement in the 1940s and 1950s.

The character of Samuel Curtis was inspired by cattleman and land-developer Henry Miller who, by the end of the nineteenth century, was one of the largest landowners in the United States. It was said that he could travel from one end of California to the other without ever leaving his own land. He built his fortune raising cattle, and his conglomeration of cattle interests and land holdings was largely responsible for the death of the individual ranch in California. He was also instrumental in the development of the San Joaquin Valley in Central California.

The Tulare County Sheriff in 1895 was not Abner Daniels but Al P. Merritt, who was, by all accounts, a good sheriff and an upstanding citizen.

About the Author

Jess Faraday is the author of several novels, including the Lambda finalist *The Affair of the Porcelain Dog* and the steampunk thriller *The Left Hand of Justice*. She lives and writes in the American west.

Books Available From Bold Strokes Books

Fool's Gold by Jess Faraday. 1895. Overworked secretary Ira Adler thinks a trip to America will be relaxing. But rattlesnakes, train robbers, and the U.S. Marshals Service have other ideas. (978-1-62639-340-0)

The Indivisible Heart by Patrick Roscoe. An investigation into a gruesome psycho-sexual murder and an account of the victim's final days are interwoven in this dark detective story of the human heart. (978-1-62639-341-7)

Big Hair and a Little Honey by Russ Gregory. Boyfriend troubles abound as Willa and Grandmother land new ones and Greg tries to hold on to Matt while chasing down a shipment of stolen hair extensions. (978-1-62639-331-8)

Death by Sin by Lyle Blake Smythers. Two supernatural private detectives in Washington, D.C., battle a psychotic supervillain spreading a new sex drug that only works on gay men, increasing the male orgasm and killing them. (978-1-62639-332-5)

Buddha's Bad Boys by Alan Chin. Six stories, six gay men trudging down the road to enlightenment. What they each find is the last thing in the world they expected. (978-1-62639-244-1)

Play It Forward by Frederick Smith. When the worlds of a community activist and a pro basketball player collide, little do they know that their dirty little secrets can lead to a public scandal…and an unexpected love affair. (978-1-62639-235-9)

GingerDead Man by Logan Zachary. Paavo Wolfe sells horror but isn't prepared for what he finds in the oven or the bathhouse; he's in hot water again, and the killer is turning up the heat. (978-1-62639-236-6)

Myth and Magic: Queer Fairy Tales, edited by Radclyffe and Stacia Seaman. Myth, magic, and monsters—the stuff of childhood dreams (or nightmares) and adult fantasies. (978-1-62639-225-0)

Balls & Chain by Eric Andrews-Katz. In protest of the marriage equality bill, the son of Florida's governor has been kidnapped. Agent Buck 98 is back, and the alligators aren't the only things biting. (978-1-62639-218-2)

Blackthorn by Simon Hawk. Rian Blackthorn, Master of the Hall of Swords, vowed he would not give in to the advances of Prince Corin, but he finds himself dueling with more than swords as Corin pursues him with determined passion. (978-1-62639-226-7)

Café Eisenhower by Richard Natale. A grieving young man who travels to Eastern Europe to claim an inheritance finds friendship, romance, and betrayal, as well as a moving document relating a secret lifelong love affair. (978-1-62639-217-5)

Murder in the Arts District by Greg Herren. An investigation into a new and possibly shady art gallery in New Orleans' fabled Arts District soon leads Chanse into a dangerous world of forgery, theft...and murder. A Chanse MacLeod mystery. (978-1-62639-206-9)

Rise of the Thing Down Below by Daniel W. Kelly. Nothing kills sex on the beach like a fishman out of water...Third in the Comfort Cove Series. (978-1-62639-207-6)

Calvin's Head by David Swatling. Jason Dekker and his dog, Calvin, are homeless in Amsterdam when they stumble on the victim of a grisly murder—and become targets for the calculating killer, Gadget. (978-1-62639-193-2)